I AM NOT Starfire

I AM NOT Starfire

written by
Mariko Tamaki

art by
Yoshi Yoshitani

letters by
Aditya Bidikar

Starfire created by
Marv Wolfman & George Pérez.

Diego Lopez Editor

Steve Cook Design Director – Books

Amie Brockway-Metcalf Publication Design

Tiffany Huang Publication Production

Marie Javins Editor-in-Chief, DC Comics

Daniel Cherry III Senior VP – General Manager

Jim Lee Publisher & Chief Creative Officer

Joen Choe VP – Global Brand & Creative Services

Don Falletti VP – Manufacturing Operations & Workflow Management

Lawrence Ganem VP – Talent Services

Alison Gill Senior VP – Manufacturing & Operations

Nick J. Napolitano VP – Manufacturing Administration & Design

Nancy Spears VP – Revenue

I AM NOT STARFIRE

Published by DC Comics. Copyright ©
2021 DC Comics. All Rights Reserved.
All characters, their distinctive likenesses,
and related elements featured in this
publication are trademarks of DC Comics.
The stories, characters, and incidents
featured in this publication are entirely
fictional. DC Comics does not read or
accept unsolicited submissions of ideas,
stories, or artwork.
DC – a WarnerMedia Company.

DC Comics, 2900 West Alameda Ave.,
Burbank, CA 91505
Printed by Worzalla, Stevens Point, WI,
USA. 6/18/21.
First Printing.
ISBN: 978-1-77950-126-4

Library of Congress Cataloging-in-Publication Data

Names: Tamaki, Mariko, writer. | Yoshitani, Yoshi, artist. | Bidikar,
    Aditya, letterer.
Title: I am not Starfire / written by Mariko Tamaki ; art by Yoshi
    Yoshitani ; letters by Aditya Bidikar.
Description: Burbank, CA : DC Comics, [2021] | Audience: Ages 13+ |
    Audience: Grades 10-12 | Summary: Seventeen-year-old Mandy, who dyes her
    hair black and hates almost everyone, is not like her mother, the tall,
    sparkly alien superheo Starfire, so when someone from Starfire's past
    arrives, Mandy must make a choice about who she is and if she should
    risk everything to save her mom.
Identifiers: LCCN 2021014286 (print) | LCCN 2021014287 (ebook) | ISBN
    9781779501264 (trade paperback) | ISBN 9781779511201 (ebook)
Subjects: LCSH: Graphic novels. | CYAC: Graphic novels. |
    Identity--Fiction. | Ability--Fiction. | Mothers and daughters--Fiction.
Classification: LCC PZ7.7.T355 I25 2021 (print) | LCC PZ7.7.T355 (ebook)
    | DDC 741.5/973--dc23
LC record available at https://lccn.loc.gov/2021014286
LC ebook record available at https://lccn.loc.gov/2021014287

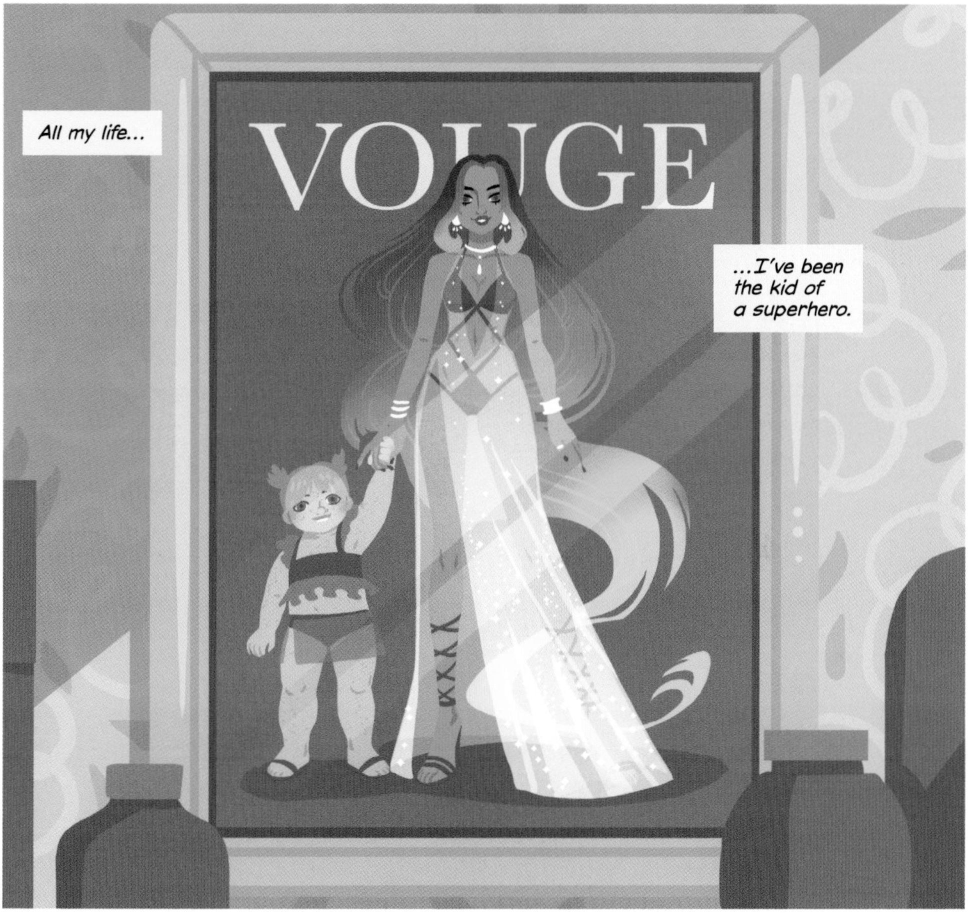
All my life...
VOUGE
...I've been the kid of a superhero.

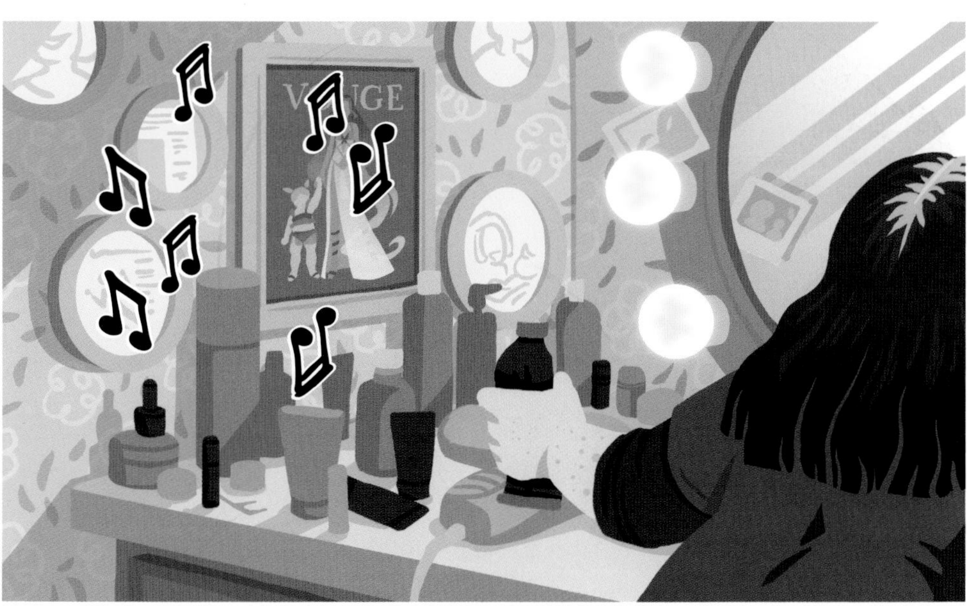
VOUGE

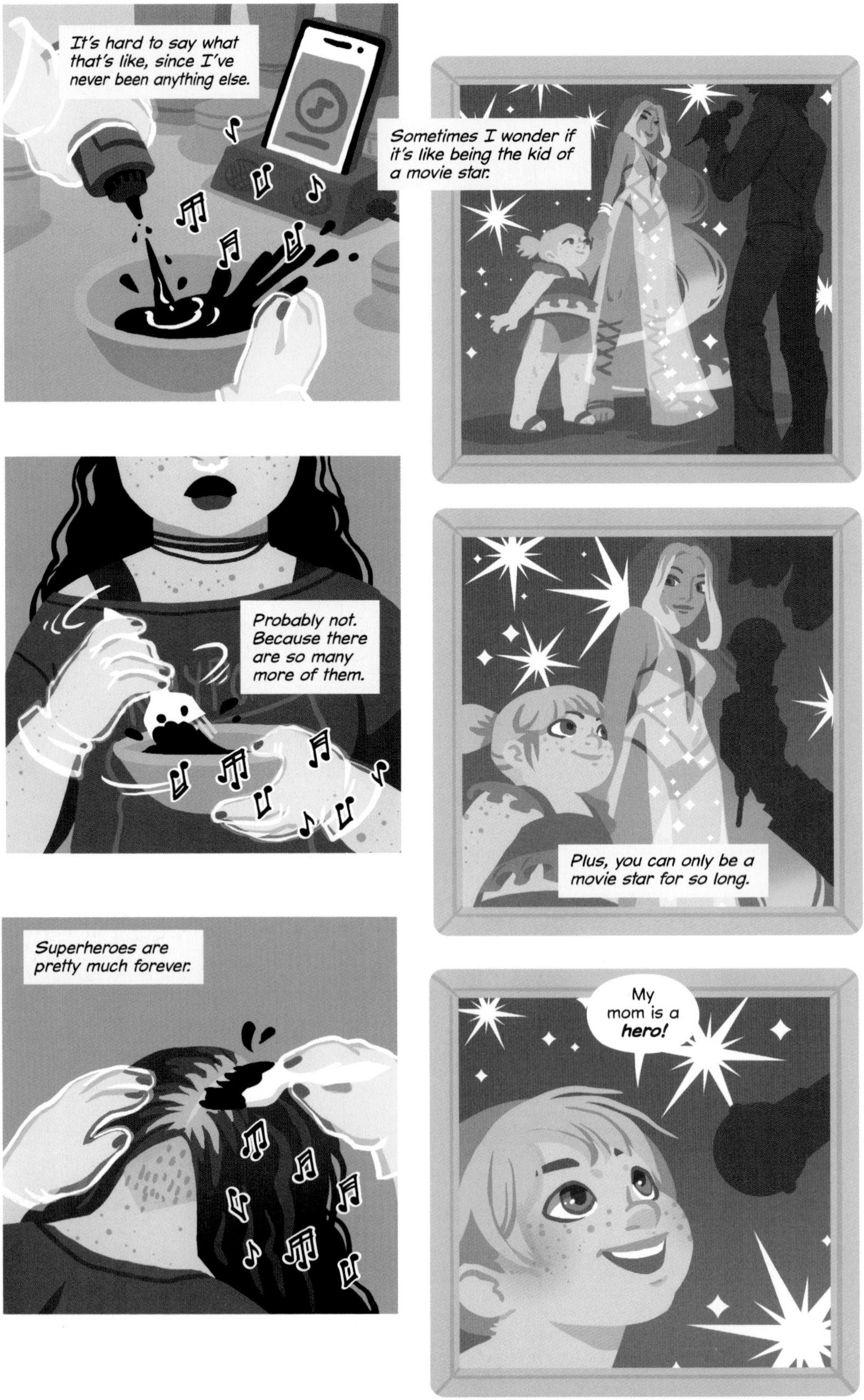
It's hard to say what that's like, since I've never been anything else.
Sometimes I wonder if it's like being the kid of a movie star.
Probably not. Because there are so many more of them.
Plus, you can only be a movie star for so long.
Superheroes are pretty much forever.
My mom is a **hero!**

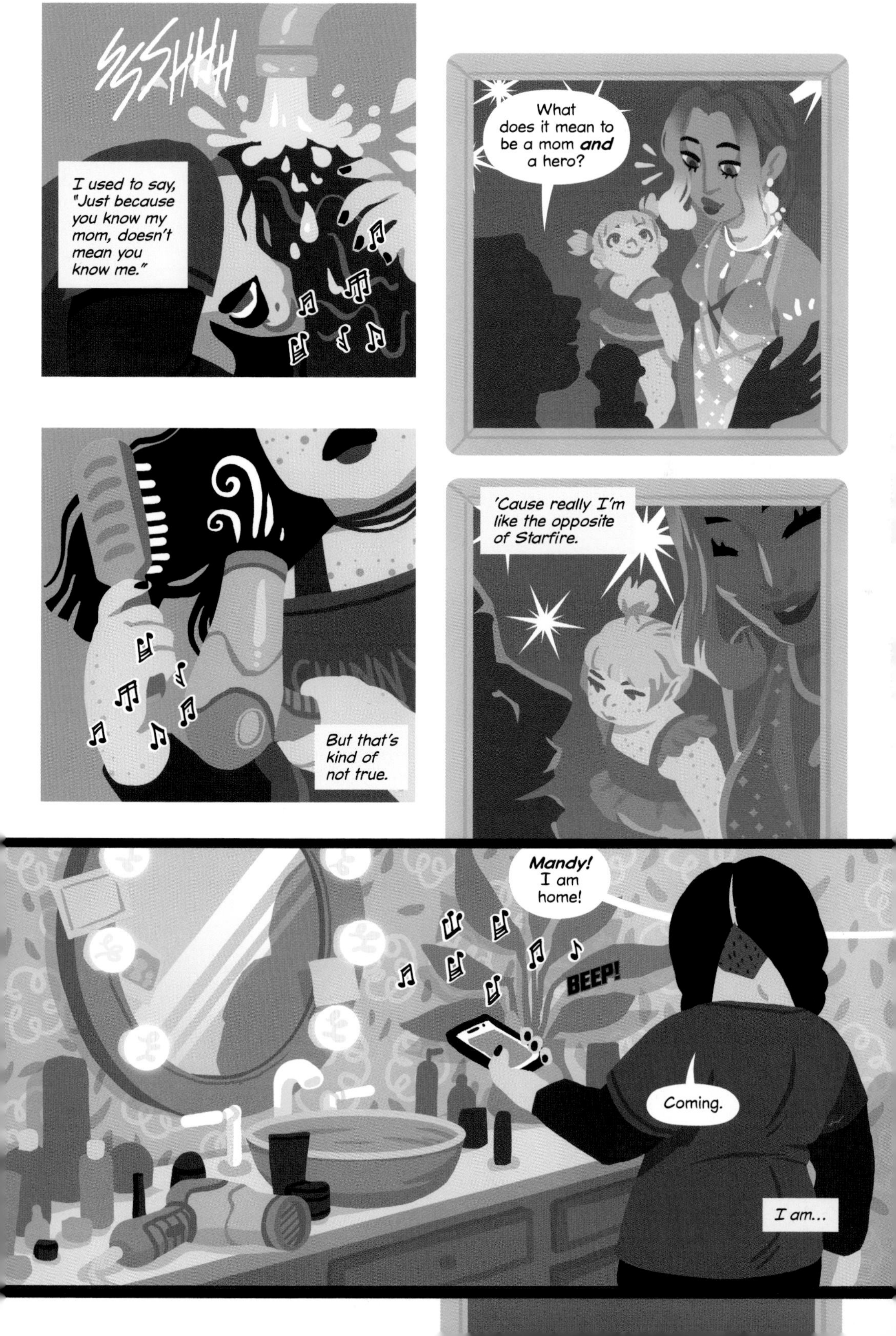
SSHHH
I used to say, "Just because you know my mom, doesn't mean you know me."
What does it mean to be a mom and a hero?
But that's kind of not true.
'Cause really I'm like the opposite of Starfire.
Mandy! I am home!
BEEP!
Coming.
I am...

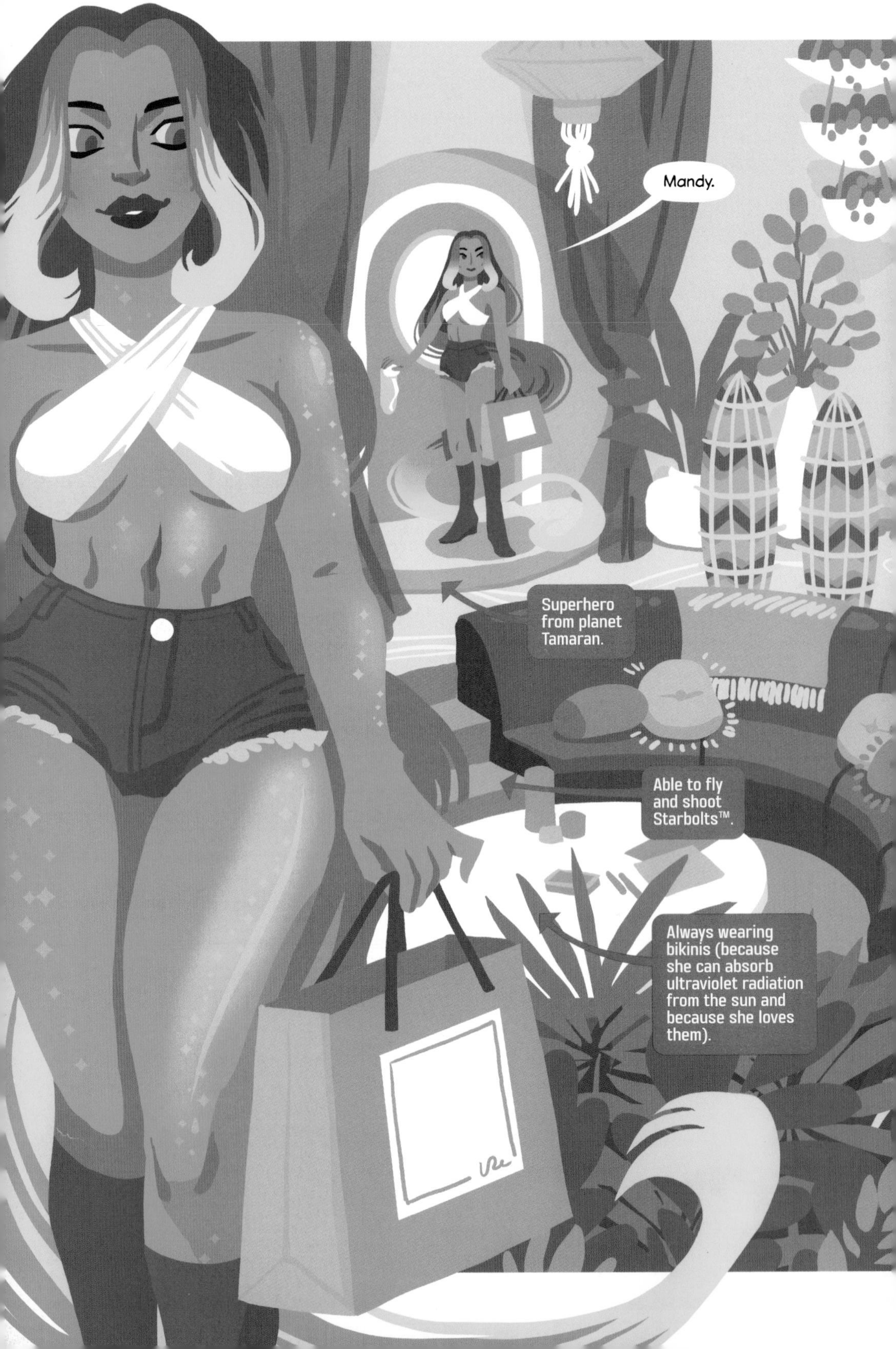
Mandy.
Superhero from planet Tamaran.
Able to fly and shoot Starbolts™.
Always wearing bikinis (because she can absorb ultraviolet radiation from the sun and because she loves them).

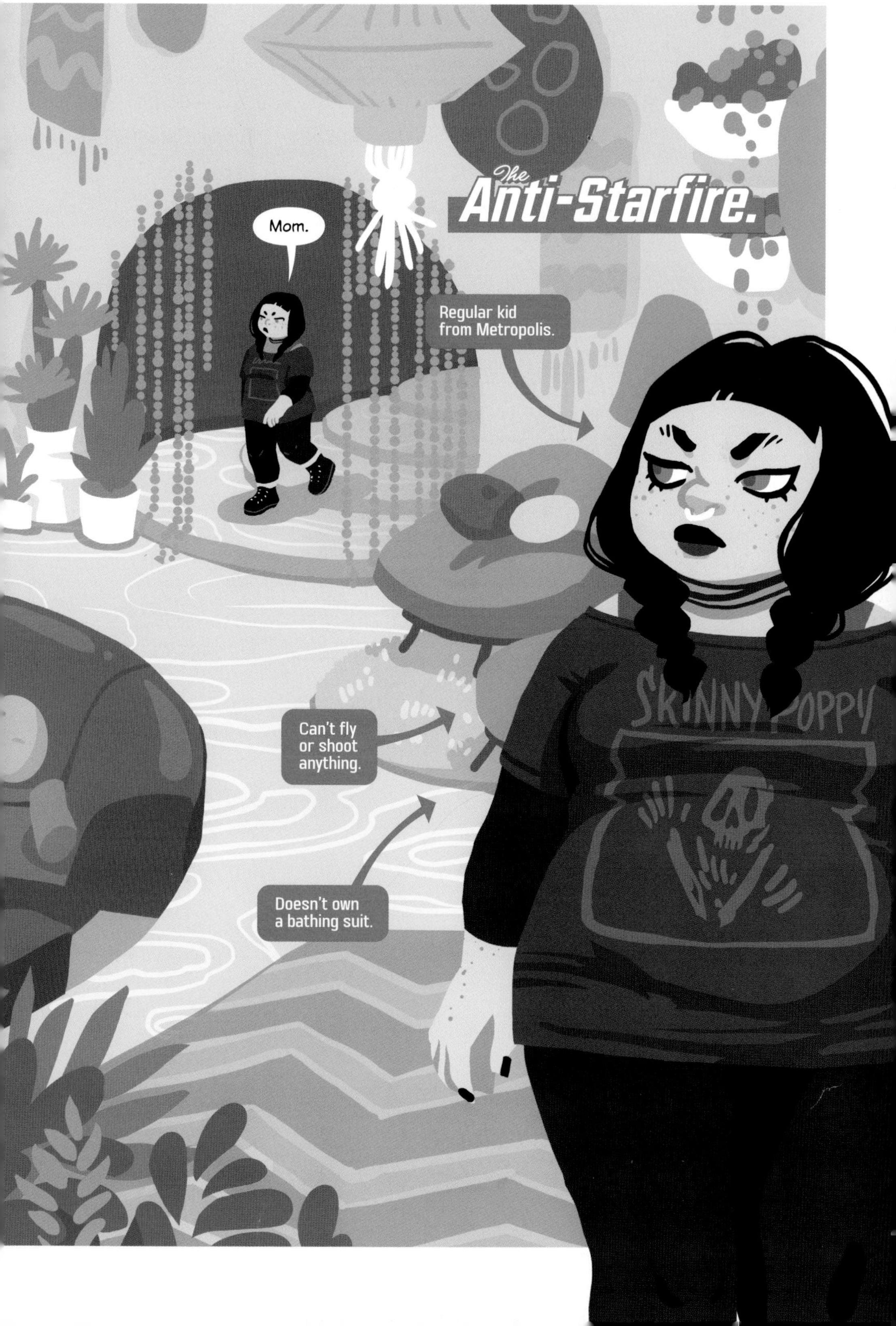
The Anti-Starfire.
Mom.
Regular kid from Metropolis.
Can't fly or shoot anything.
Doesn't own a bathing suit.
SKINNY PUPPY

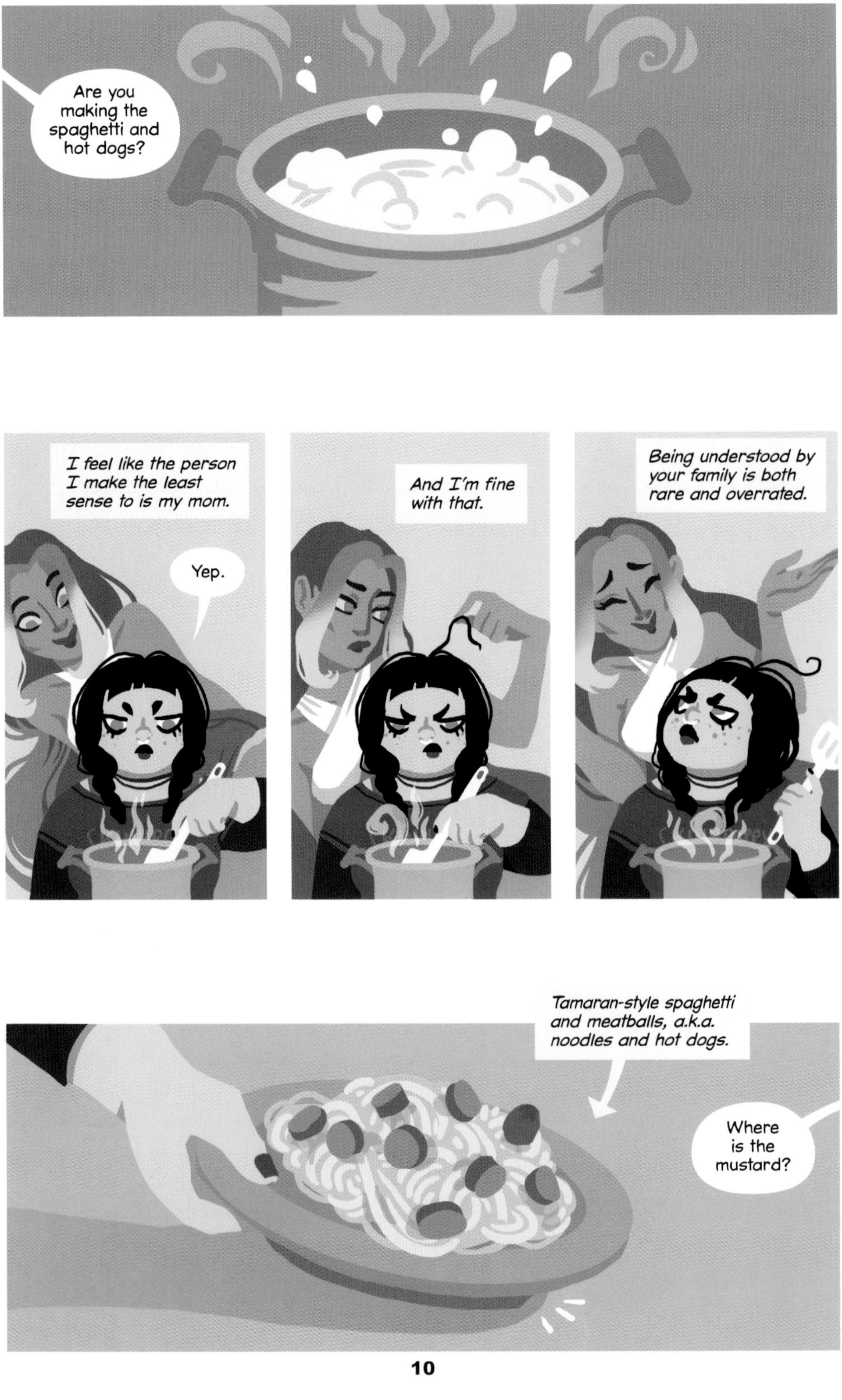
Are you making the spaghetti and hot dogs?
I feel like the person I make the least sense to is my mom.
Yep.
And I'm fine with that.
Being understood by your family is both rare and overrated.
Tamaran-style spaghetti and meatballs, a.k.a. noodles and hot dogs.
Where is the mustard?

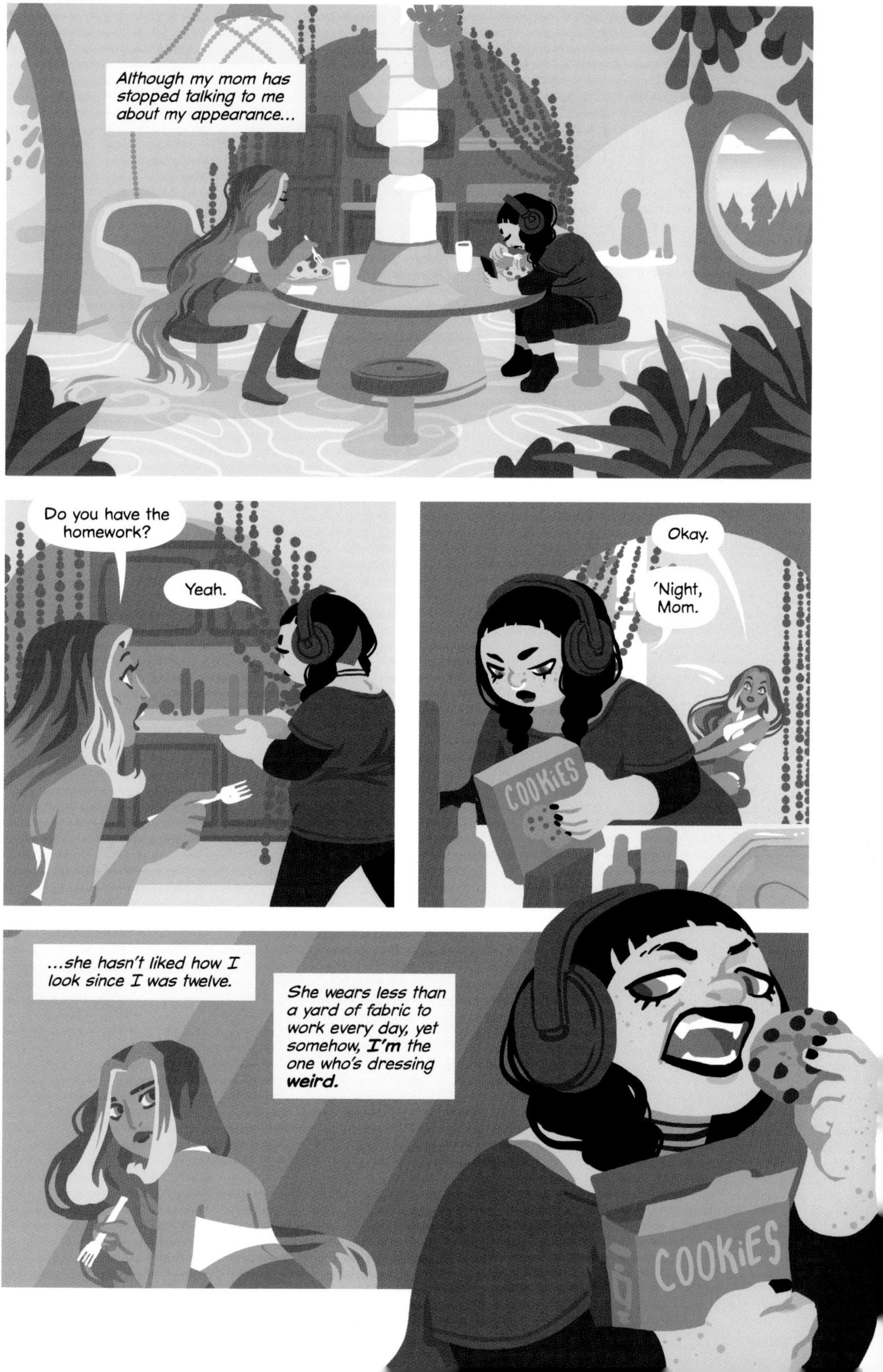
Although my mom has stopped talking to me about my appearance...
Do you have the homework?
Yeah.
Okay.
'Night, Mom.
COOKiES
...she hasn't liked how I look since I was twelve.
She wears less than a yard of fabric to work every day, yet somehow, **I'm** the one who's dressing **weird.**
COOKiES

SQUAAAK

KEEP OUT

CAUTION CAUTION CAUTION CAUTION CAUTION CAUTION

My friend Lincoln is convinced this is the cultural divide that happens between family generations born in different countries, or universes. His parents were born in Vietnam.

JooOoanie. Who's a smarty bird?

YOUAAH!

Lincoln and his sisters are all named after famous Americans. The hope of the next generation.

Also, Lincoln is an anarchist.

LINCOLN

Did you talk to your mom today? About recent events?

You can't set up future generations for success.

We'll screw you at every turn.

"I don't understand..."

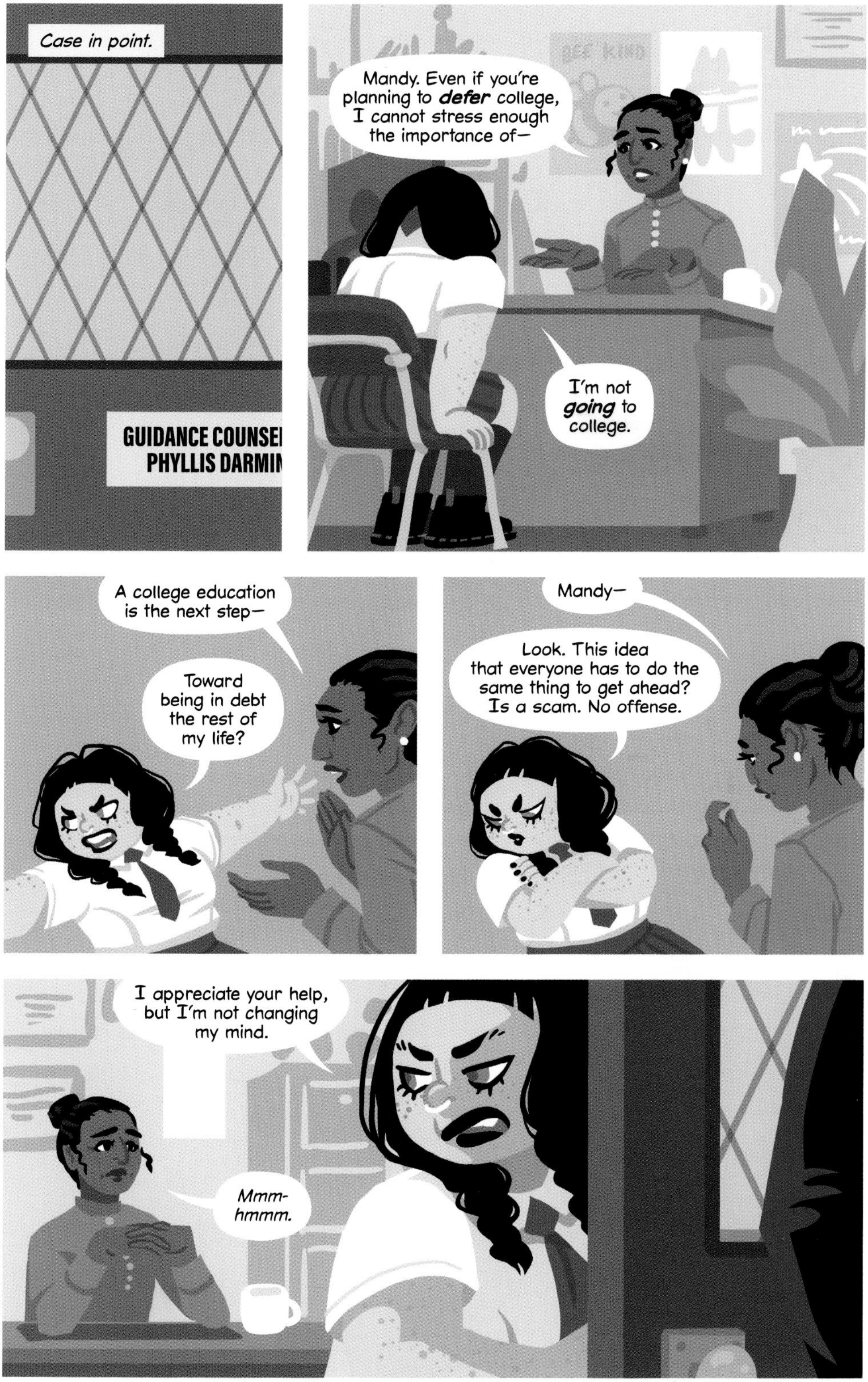

Case in point.
GUIDANCE COUNSEL
PHYLLIS DARMIN
BEE KIND
Mandy. Even if you're planning to *defer* college, I cannot stress enough the importance of—
I'm not *going* to college.
A college education is the next step—
Toward being in debt the rest of my life?
Mandy—
Look. This idea that everyone has to do the same thing to get ahead? Is a scam. No offense.
I appreciate your help, but I'm not changing my mind.
Mmm-hmmm.

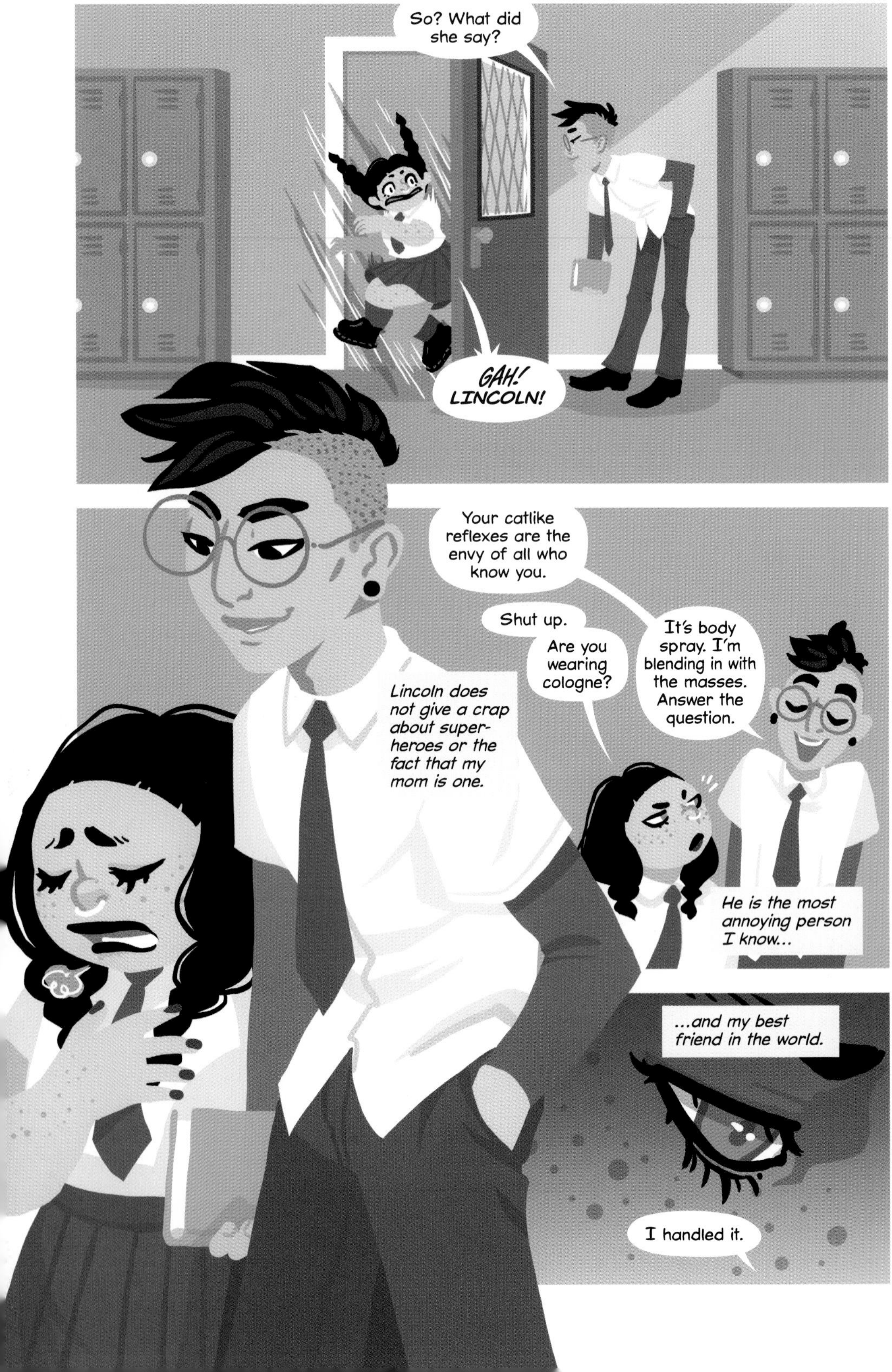
So? What did she say?
GAH! LINCOLN!
Your catlike reflexes are the envy of all who know you.
Lincoln does not give a crap about super-heroes or the fact that my mom is one.
Shut up.
Are you wearing cologne?
It's body spray. I'm blending in with the masses. Answer the question.
He is the most annoying person I know...
...and my best friend in the world.
I handled it.

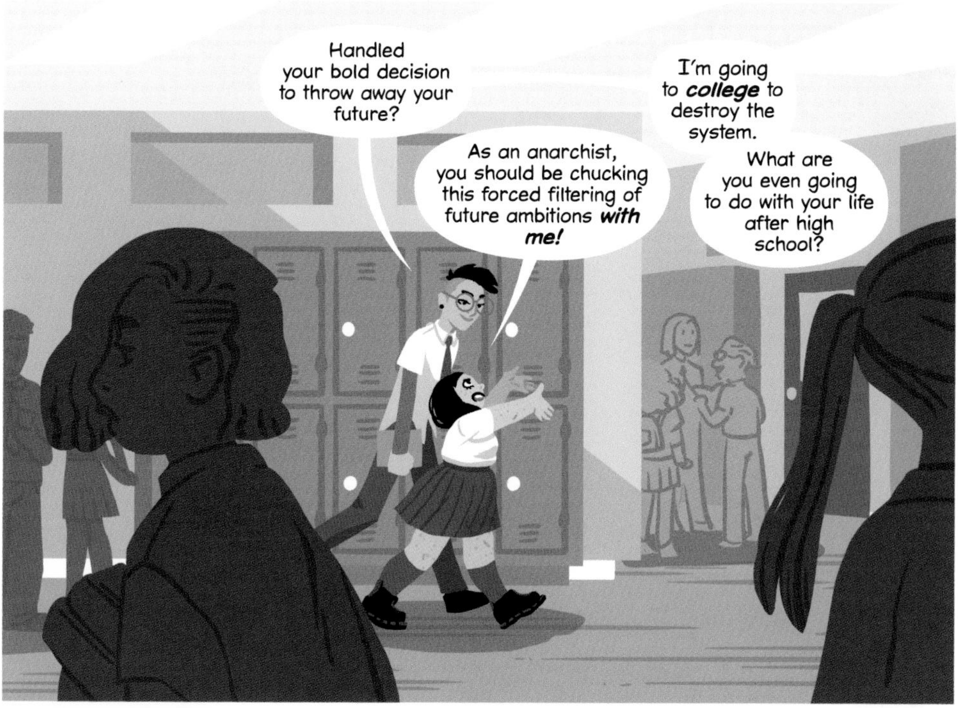
Handled your bold decision to throw away your future?
As an anarchist, you should be chucking this forced filtering of future ambitions ***with me!***
I'm going to ***college*** to destroy the system.
What are you even going to do with your life after high school?

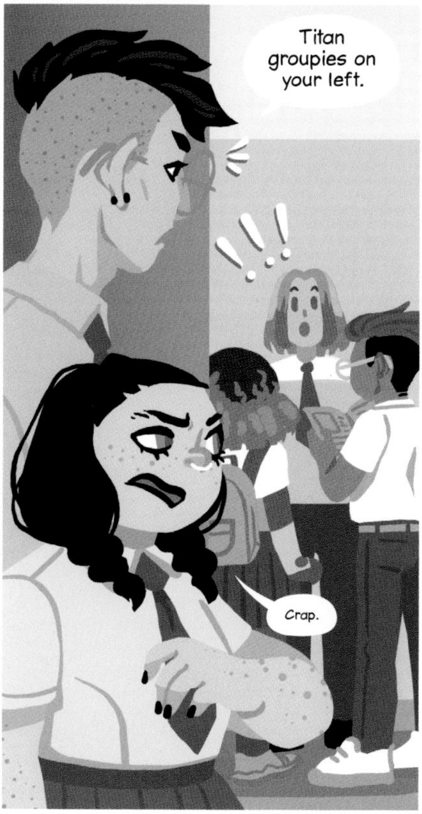
Titan groupies on your left.
Crap.

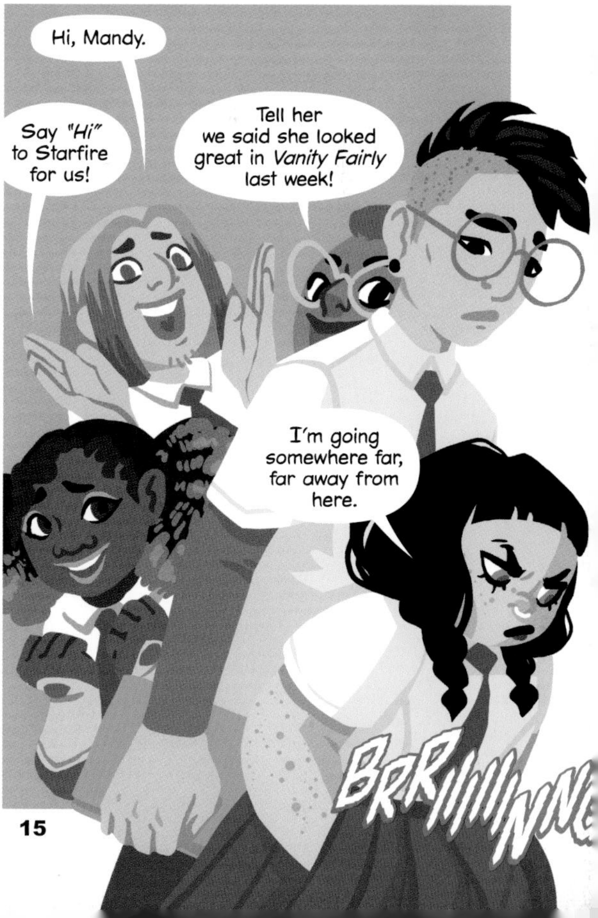
Hi, Mandy.
Say *"Hi"* to Starfire for us!
Tell her we said she looked great in *Vanity Fairly* last week!
I'm going somewhere far, far away from here.
BRRIIIINNG

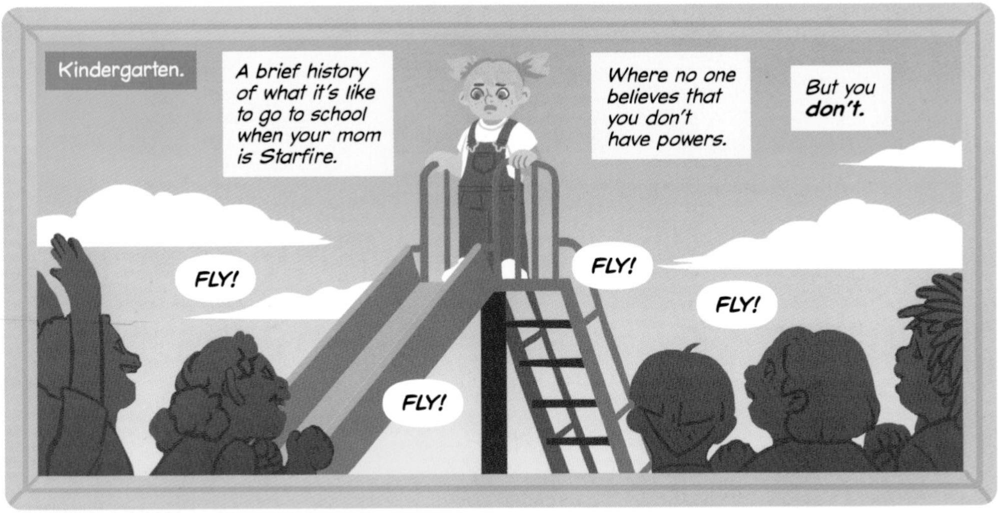
Kindergarten.
A brief history of what it's like to go to school when your mom is Starfire.
Where no one believes that you don't have powers.
But you **don't.**
FLY!
FLY!
FLY!
FLY!

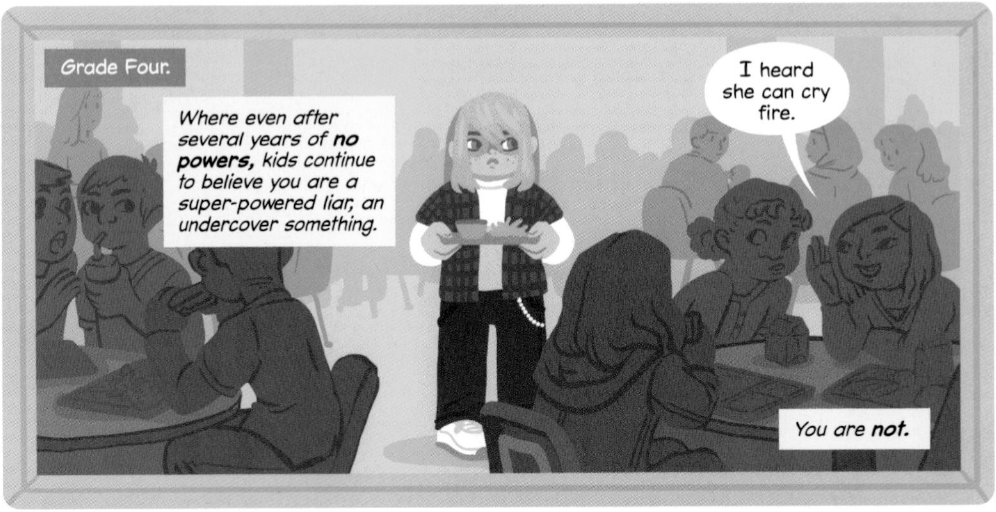
Grade Four.
Where even after several years of **no powers,** kids continue to believe you are a super-powered liar, an undercover something.
I heard she can cry fire.
You are **not.**

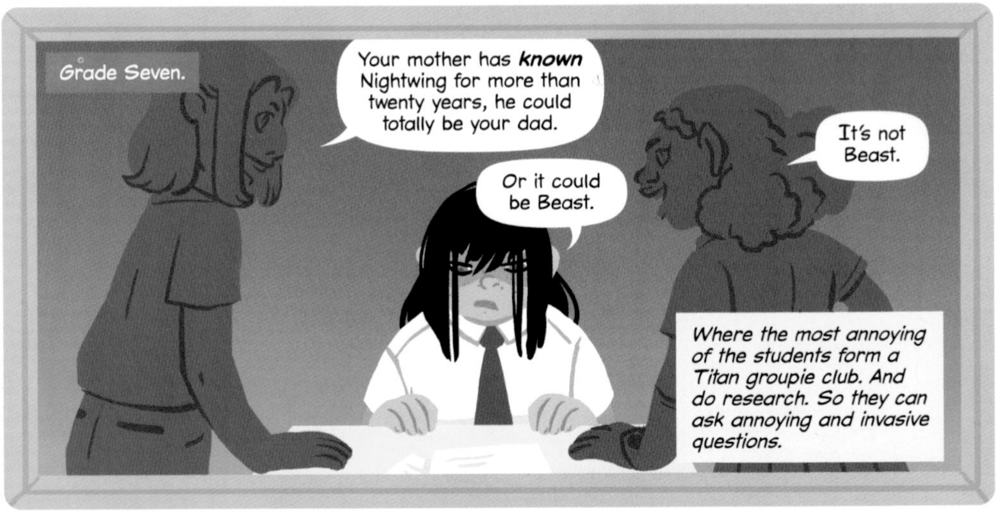
Grade Seven.
Your mother has ***known*** Nightwing for more than twenty years, he could totally be your dad.
Or it could be Beast.
It's not Beast.
Where the most annoying of the students form a Titan groupie club. And do research. So they can ask annoying and invasive questions.

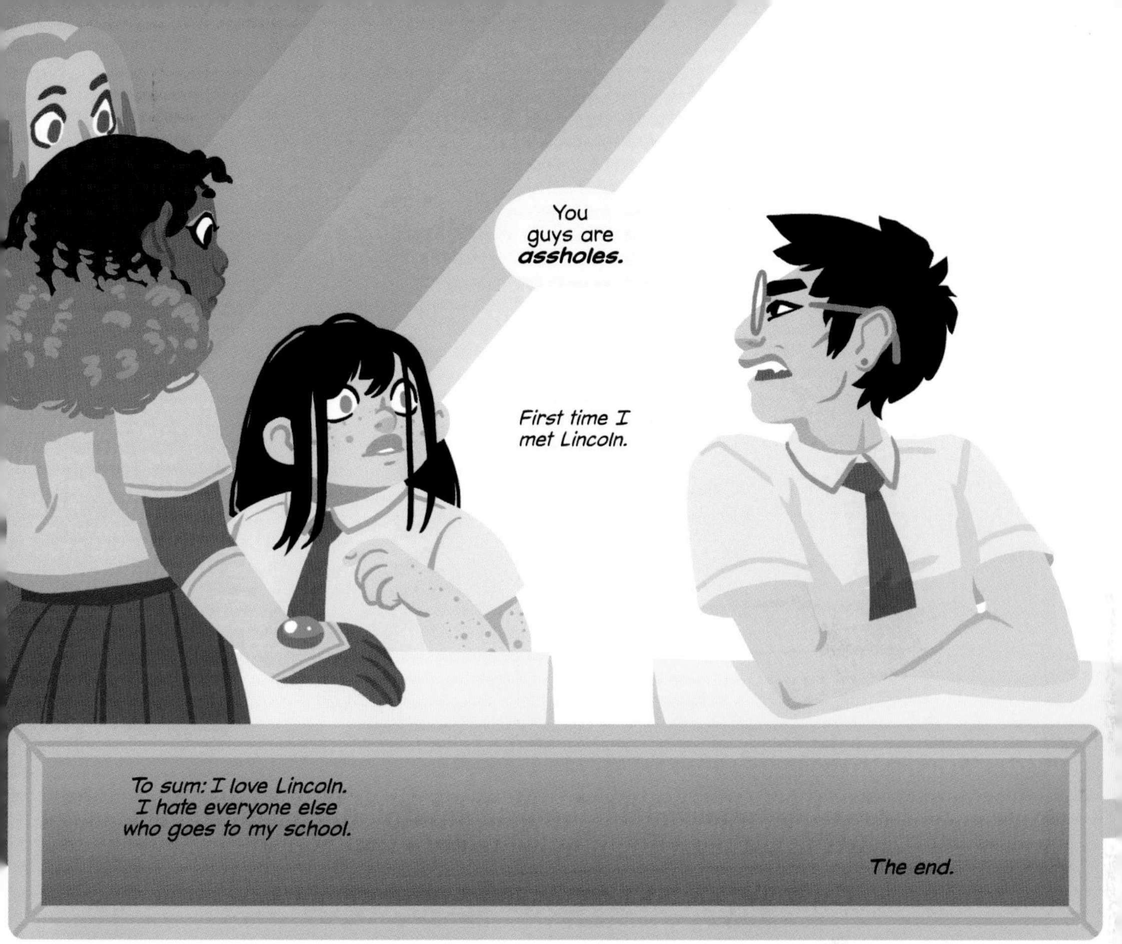
You guys are **assholes.**
First time I met Lincoln.
To sum: I love Lincoln. I hate everyone else who goes to my school.
The end.

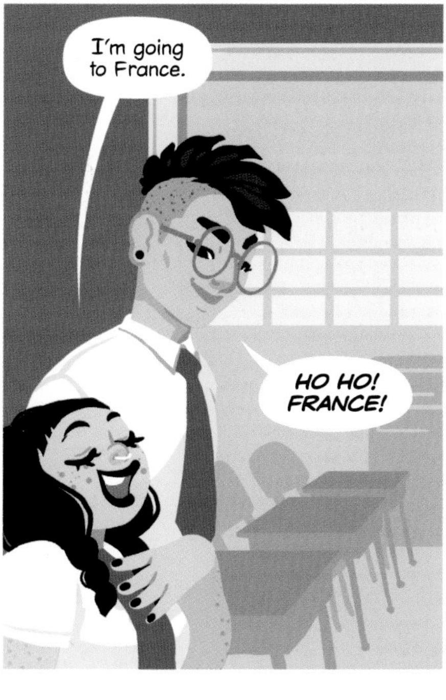
I'm going to France.
HO HO! FRANCE!

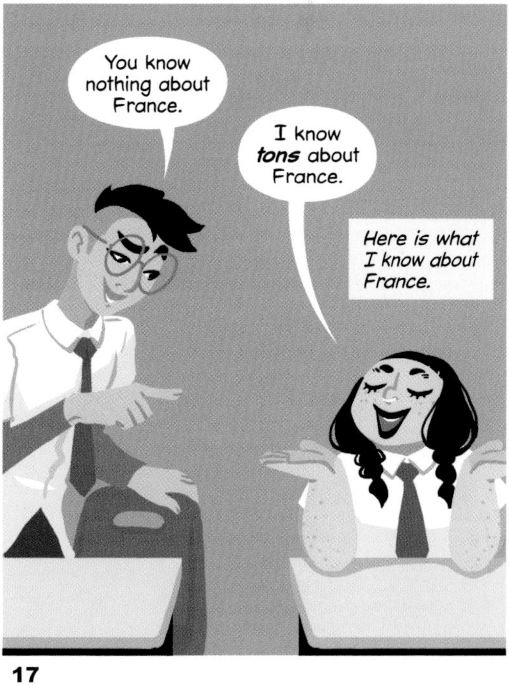
You know nothing about France.
I know **tons** about France.
Here is what I know about France.

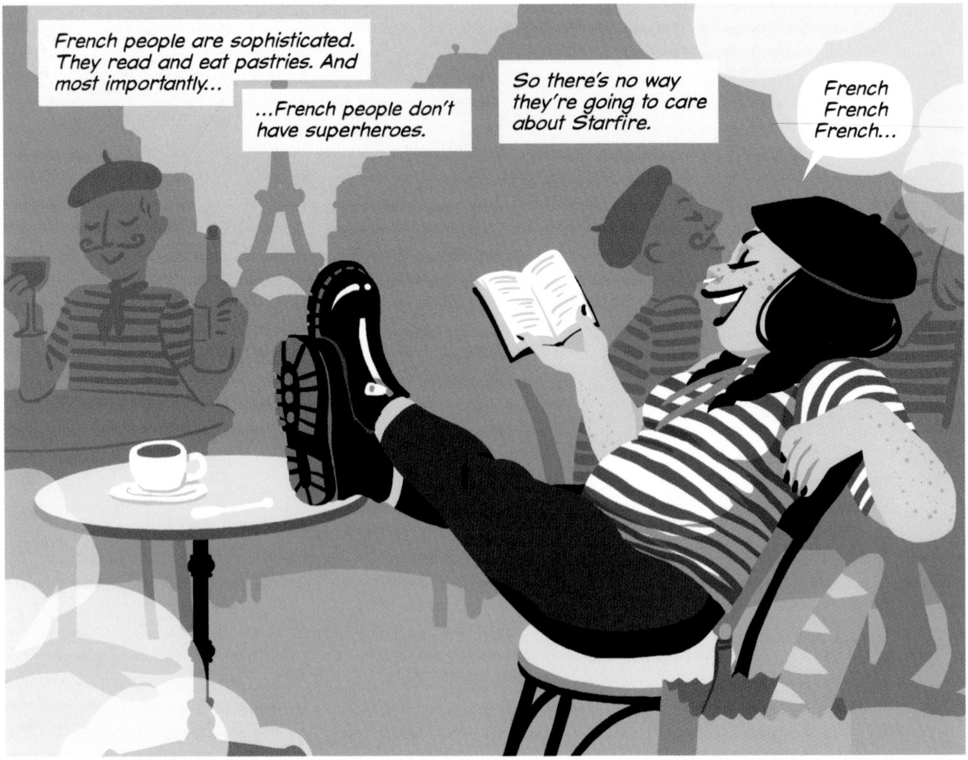
French people are sophisticated. They read and eat pastries. And most importantly...
...French people don't have superheroes.
So there's no way they're going to care about Starfire.
French French French...

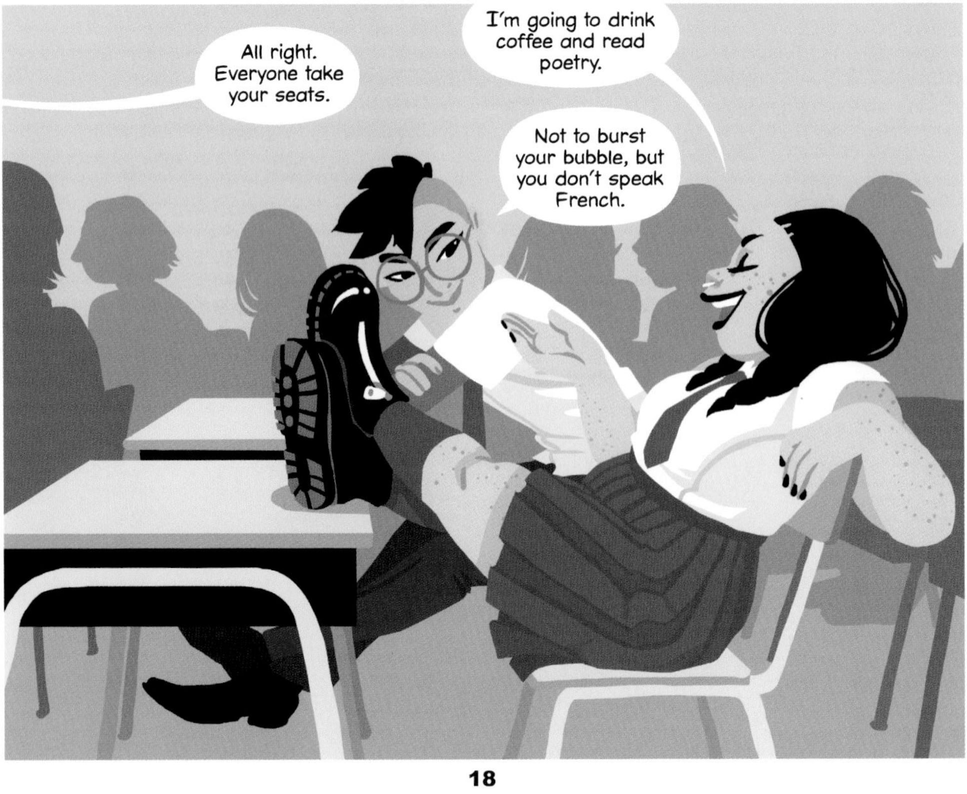
All right. Everyone take your seats.
I'm going to drink coffee and read poetry.
Not to burst your bubble, but you don't speak French.

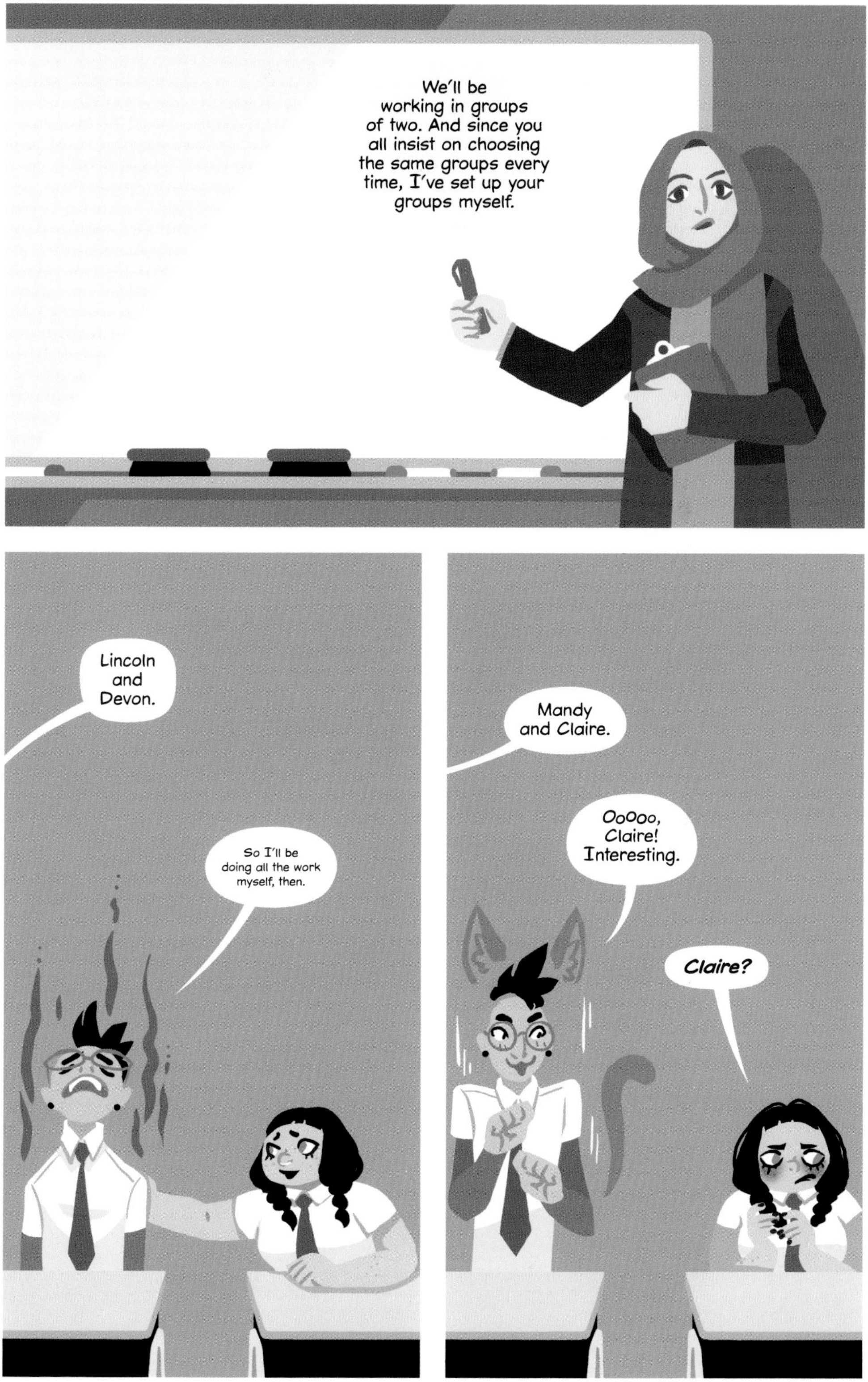
We'll be working in groups of two. And since you all insist on choosing the same groups every time, I've set up your groups myself.
Lincoln and Devon.
So I'll be doing all the work myself, then.
Mandy and Claire.
Ooooo, Claire! Interesting.
Claire?

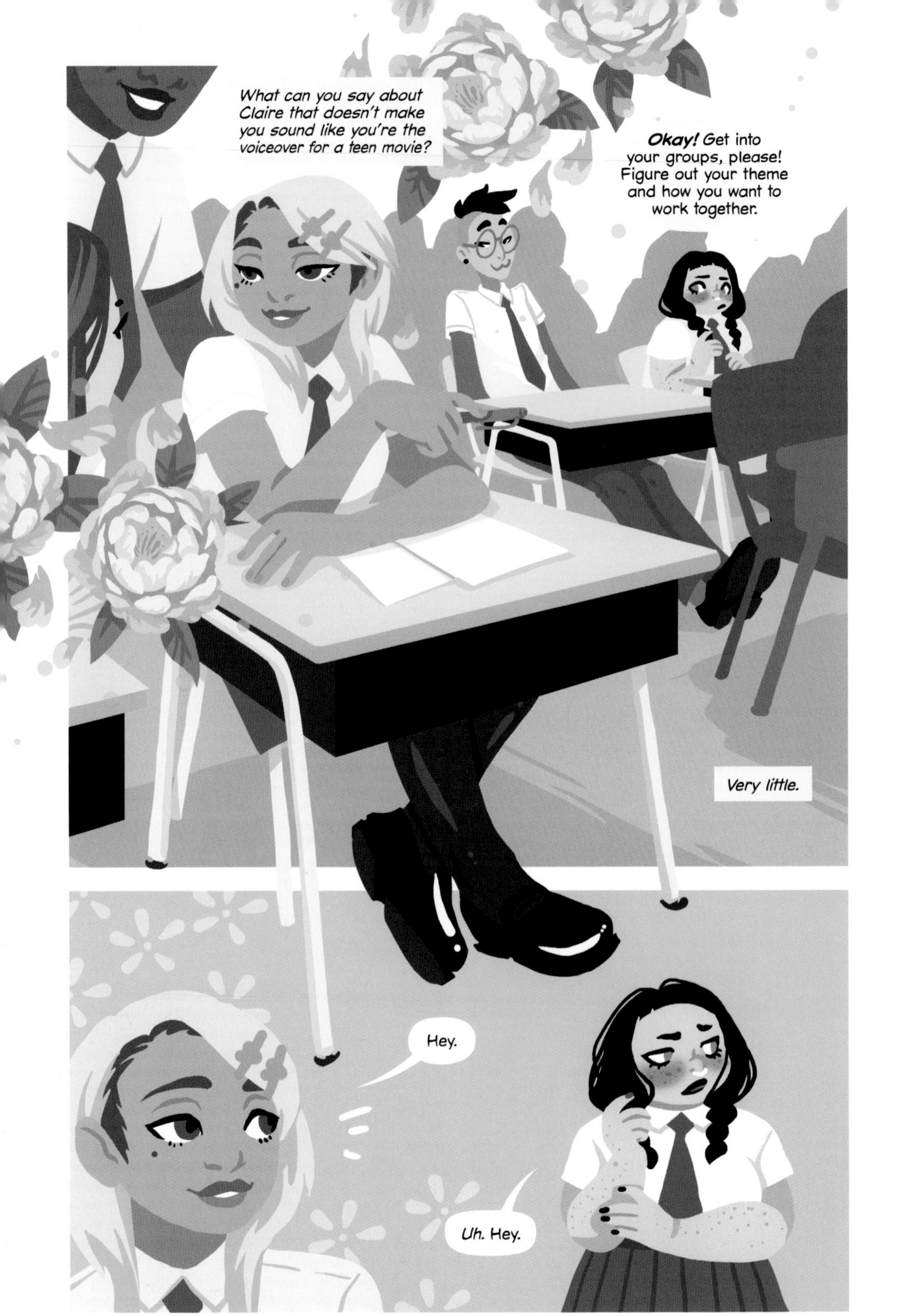
What can you say about Claire that doesn't make you sound like you're the voiceover for a teen movie?
Okay! Get into your groups, please! Figure out your theme and how you want to work together.
Very little.
Hey.
Uh. Hey.

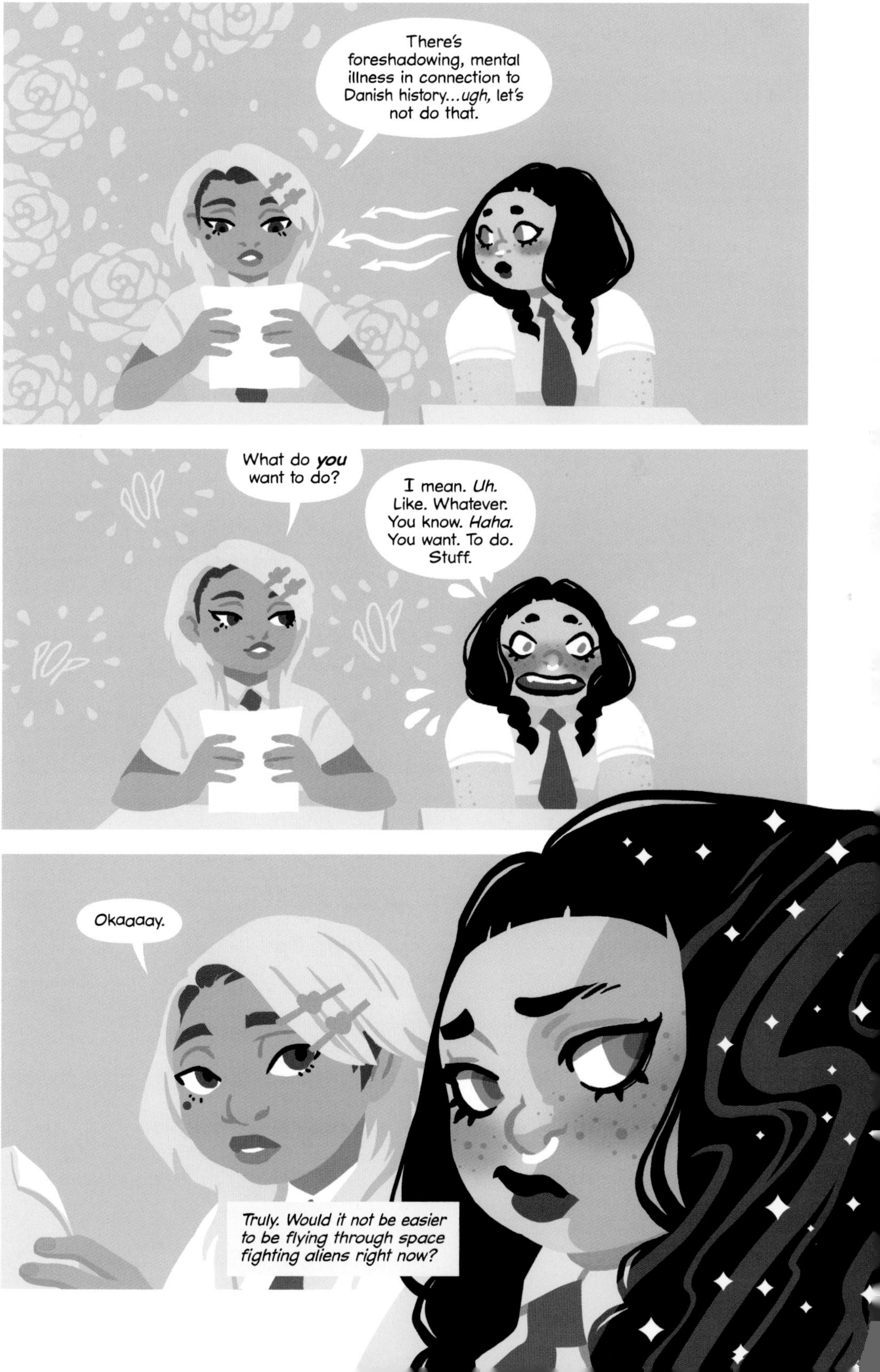
There's foreshadowing, mental illness in connection to Danish history...*ugh,* let's not do that.
What do ***you*** want to do?
I mean. *Uh.* Like. Whatever. You know. *Haha.* You want. To do. Stuff.
POP
POP
POP
Okaaaay.
Truly. Would it not be easier to be flying through space fighting aliens right now?

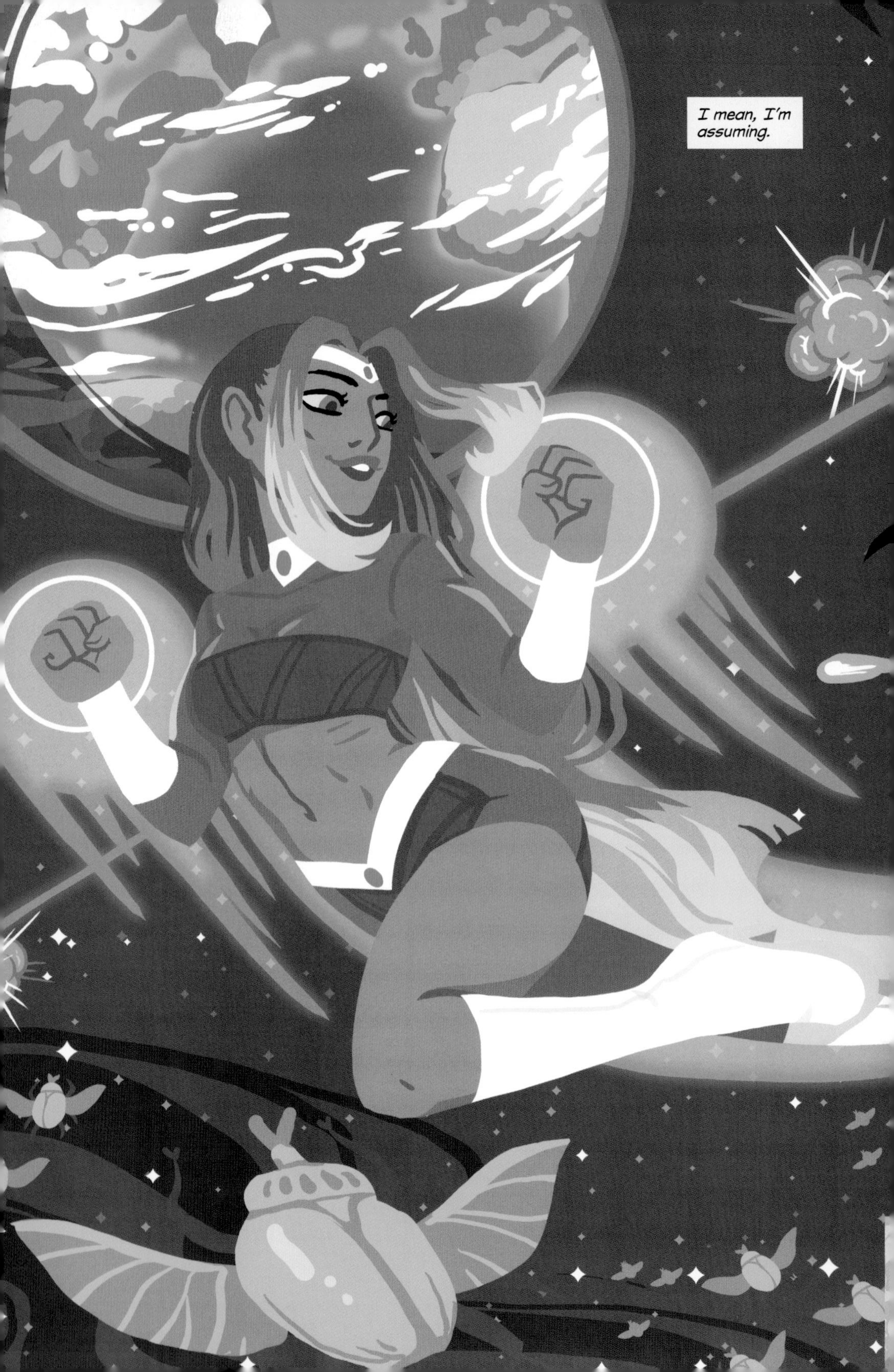
I mean, I'm assuming.

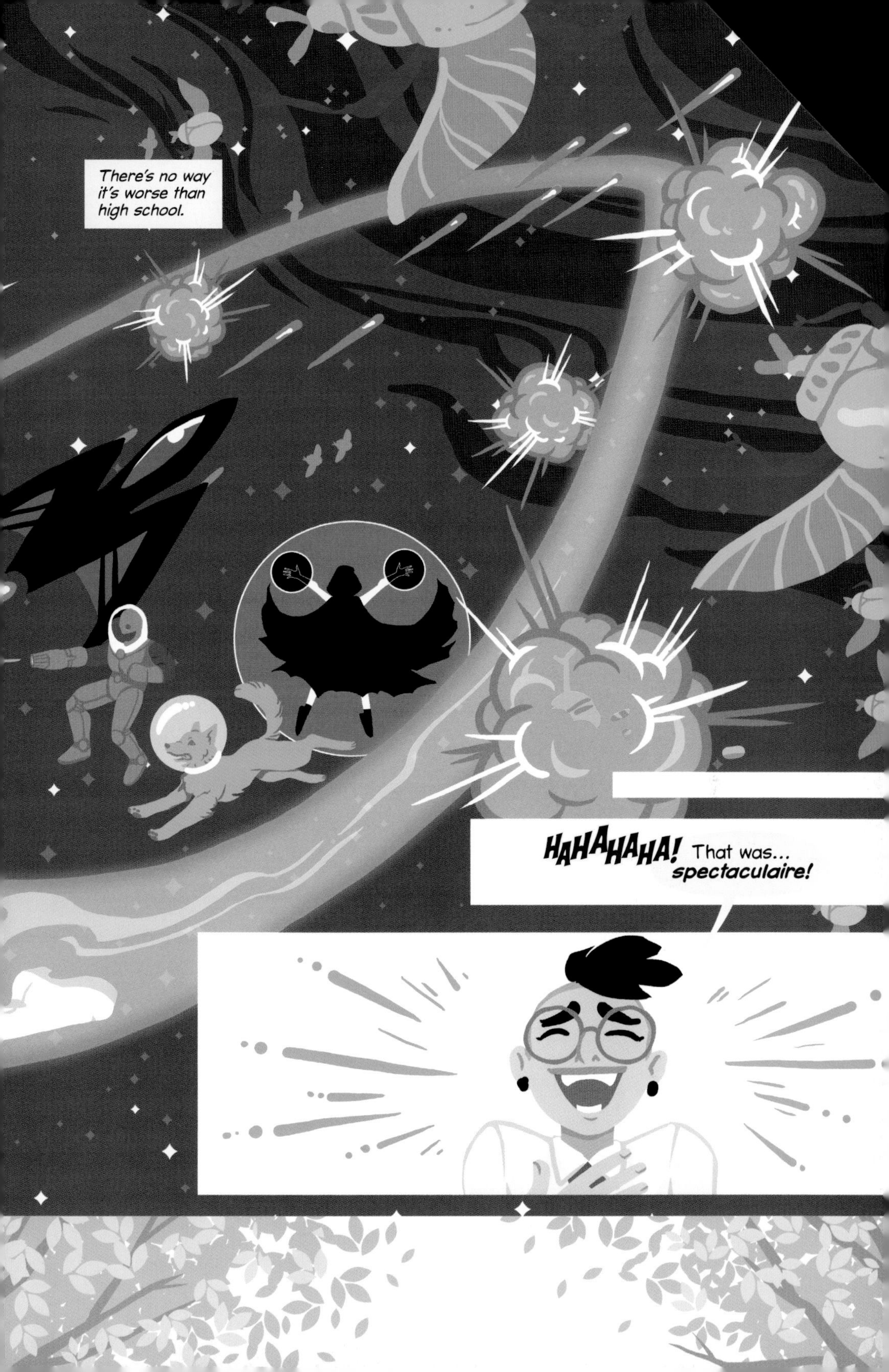
There's no way it's worse than high school.
HAHAHAHA! That was... spectaculaire!

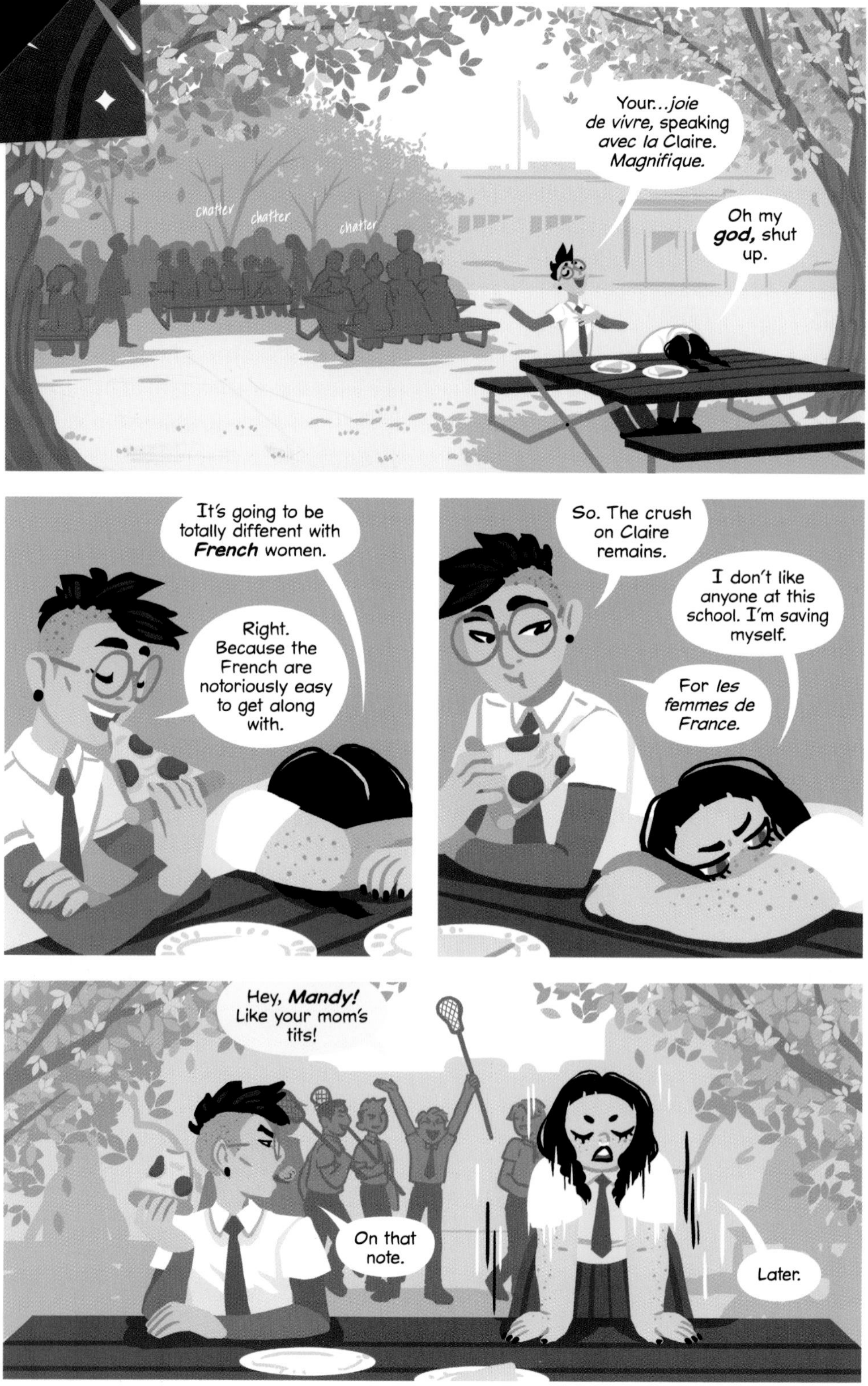
chatter
chatter
chatter
Your...*joie de vivre,* speaking *avec la Claire. Magnifique.*
Oh my ***god,*** shut up.
It's going to be totally different with ***French*** women.
Right. Because the French are notoriously easy to get along with.
So. The crush on Claire remains.
I don't like anyone at this school. I'm saving myself.
For *les femmes de France.*
Hey, ***Mandy!*** Like your mom's tits!
On that note.
Later.

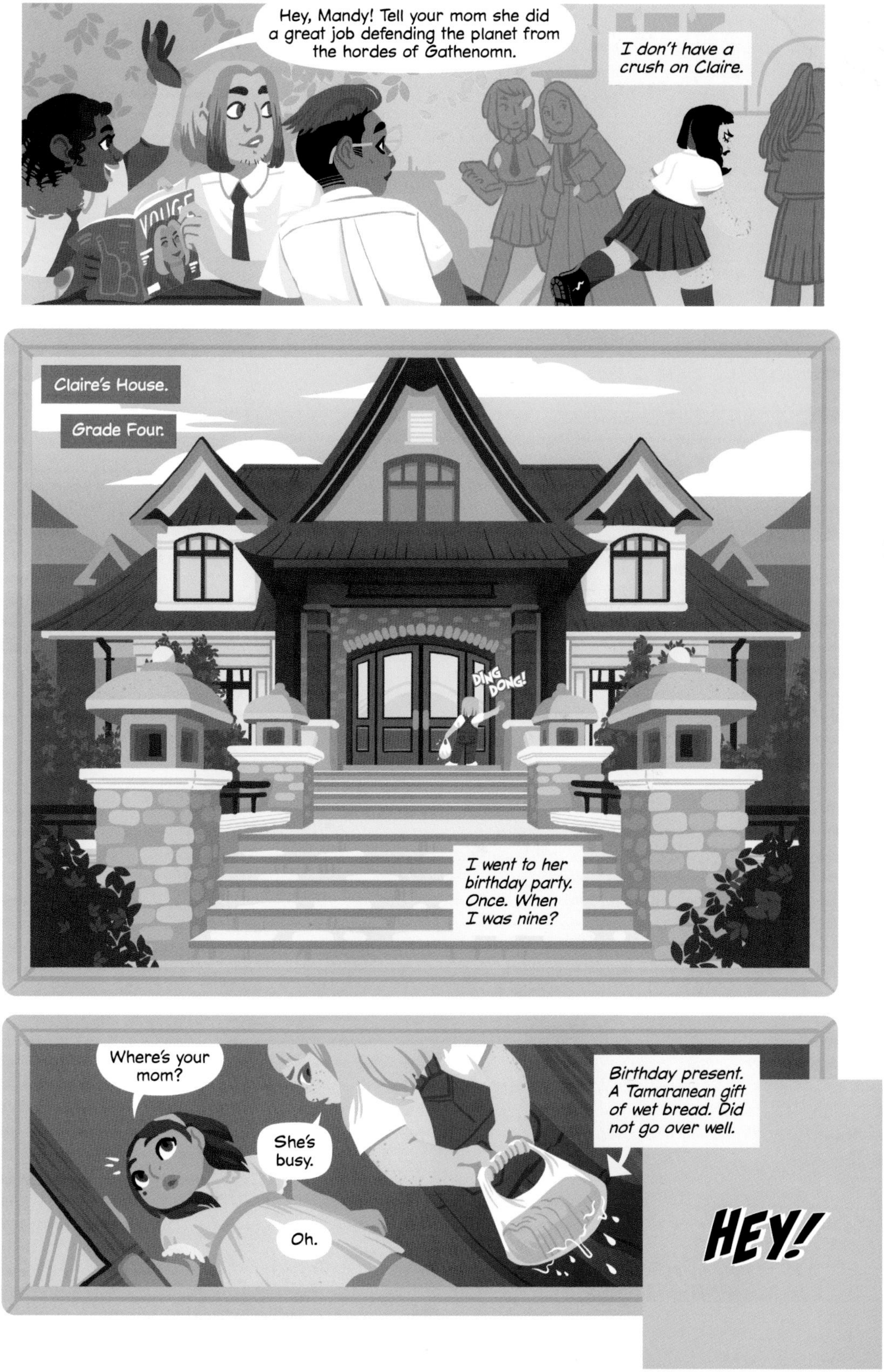
Hey, Mandy! Tell your mom she did a great job defending the planet from the hordes of Gathenomn.
I don't have a crush on Claire.
VOUGE
Claire's House.
Grade Four.
DING DONG!
I went to her birthday party. Once. When I was nine?
Where's your mom?
She's busy.
Oh.
Birthday present. A Tamaranean gift of wet bread. Did not go over well.
HEY!

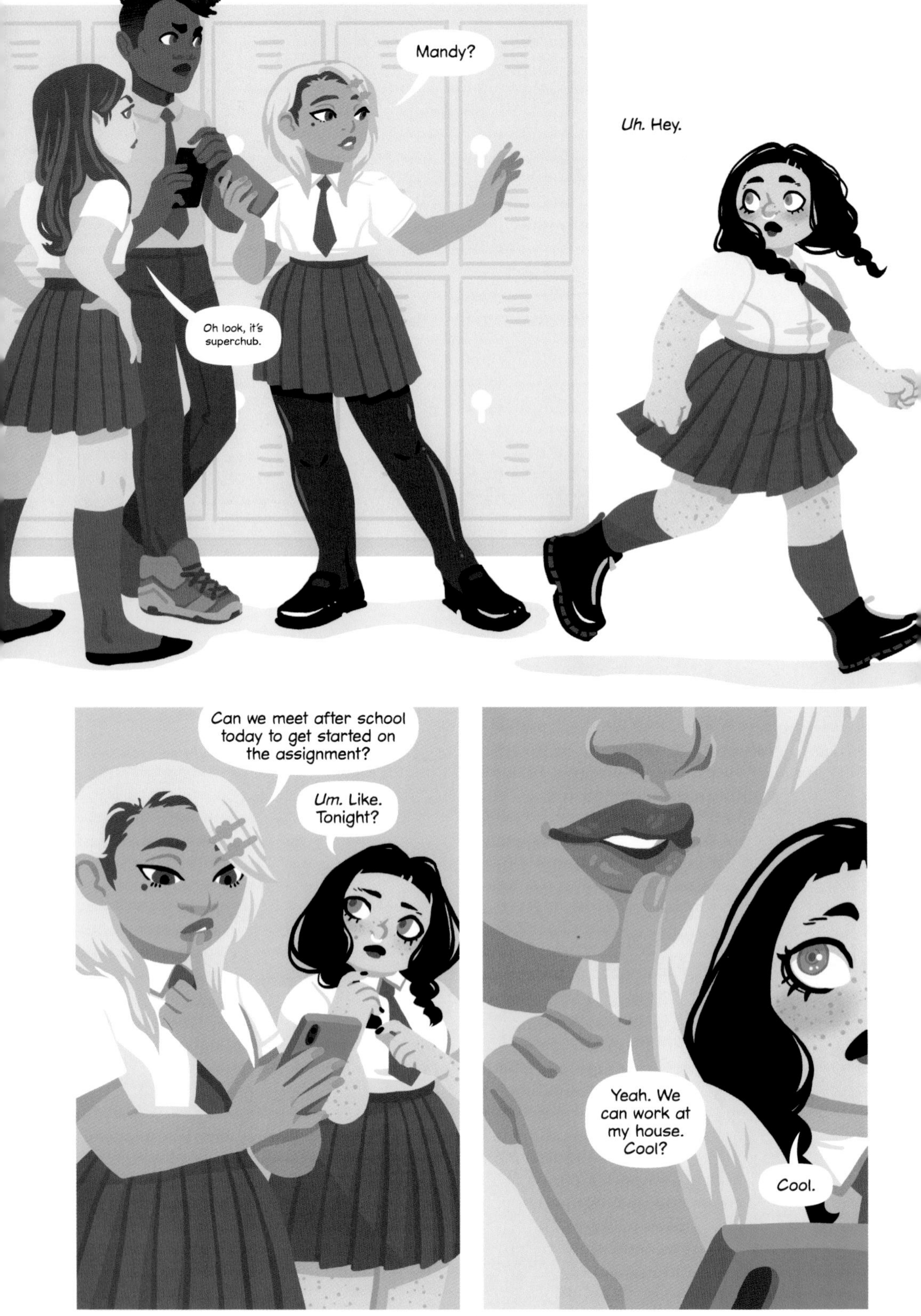
Mandy?
Oh look, it's superchub.
Uh. Hey.
Can we meet after school today to get started on the assignment?
Um. Like. Tonight?
Yeah. We can work at my house. Cool?
Cool.

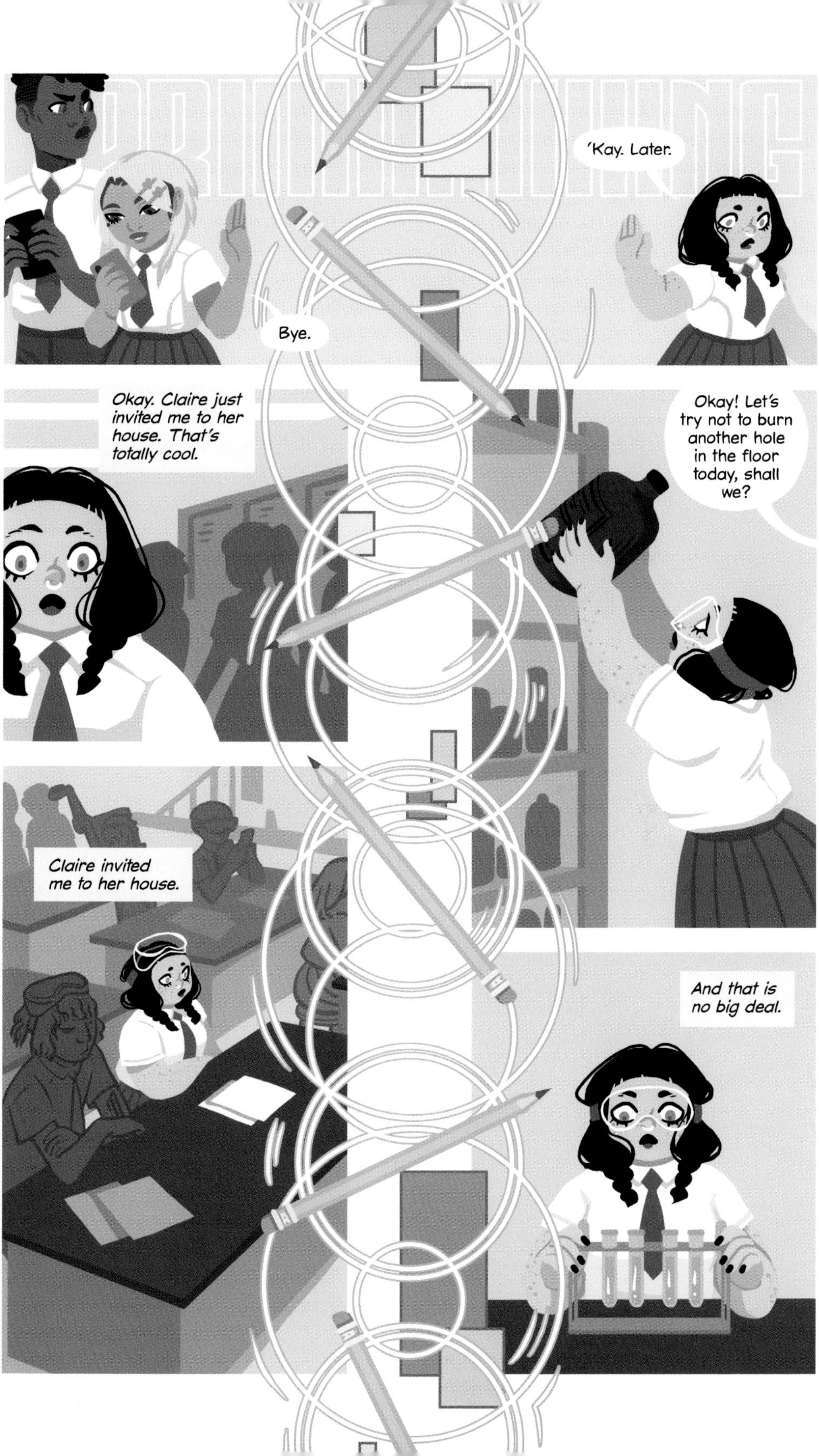

'Kay. Later.
Bye.
Okay. Claire just invited me to her house. That's totally cool.
Okay! Let's try not to burn another hole in the floor today, shall we?
Claire invited me to her house.
And that is no big deal.

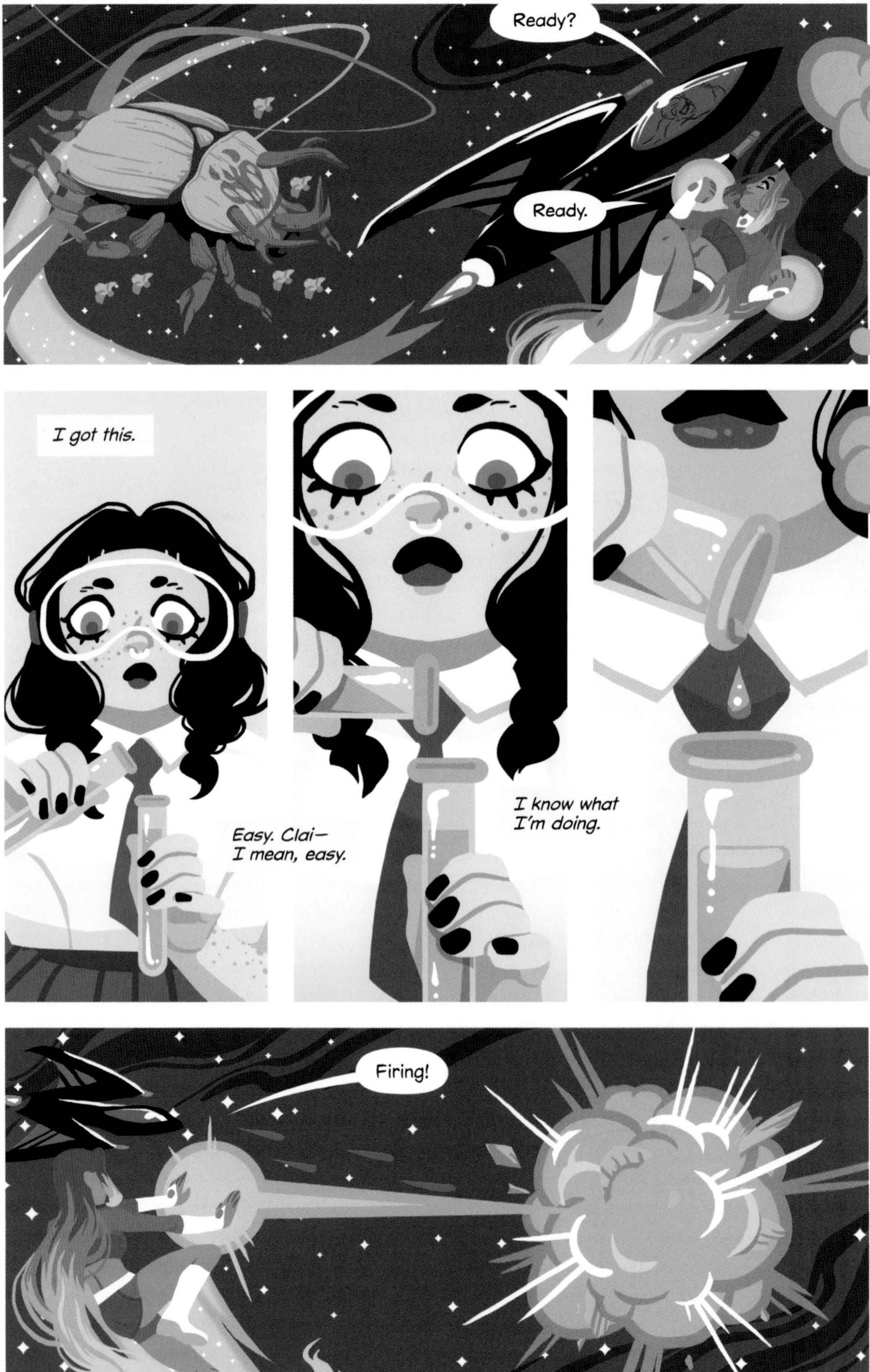
Ready?
Ready.
I got this.
Easy. Clai—
I mean, easy.
I know what
I'm doing.
Firing!

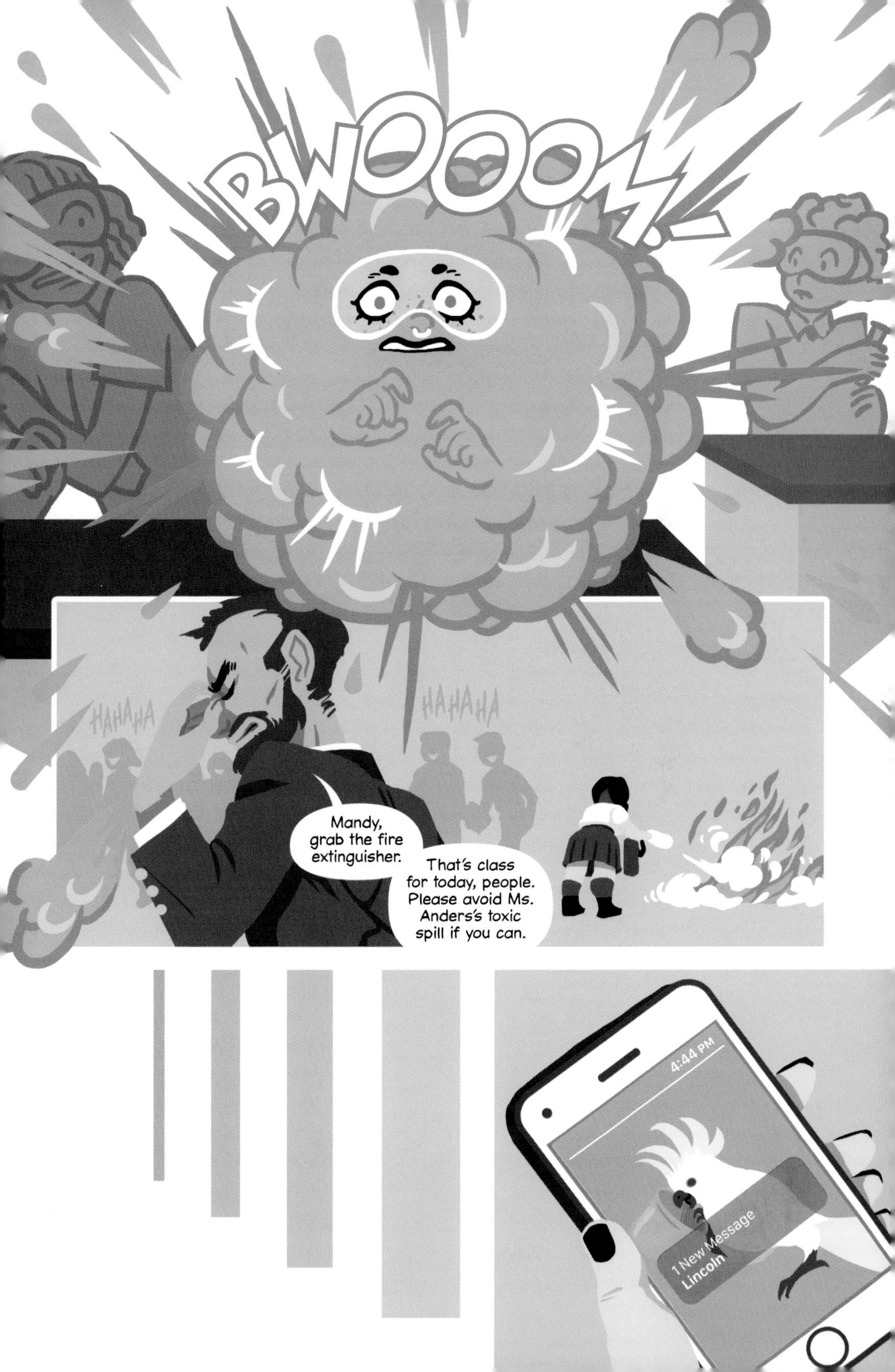
BWOOOM!
HAHAHA
HAHAHA
Mandy, grab the fire extinguisher.
That's class for today, people. Please avoid Ms. Anders's toxic spill if you can.
4:44 PM
1 New Message
Lincoln

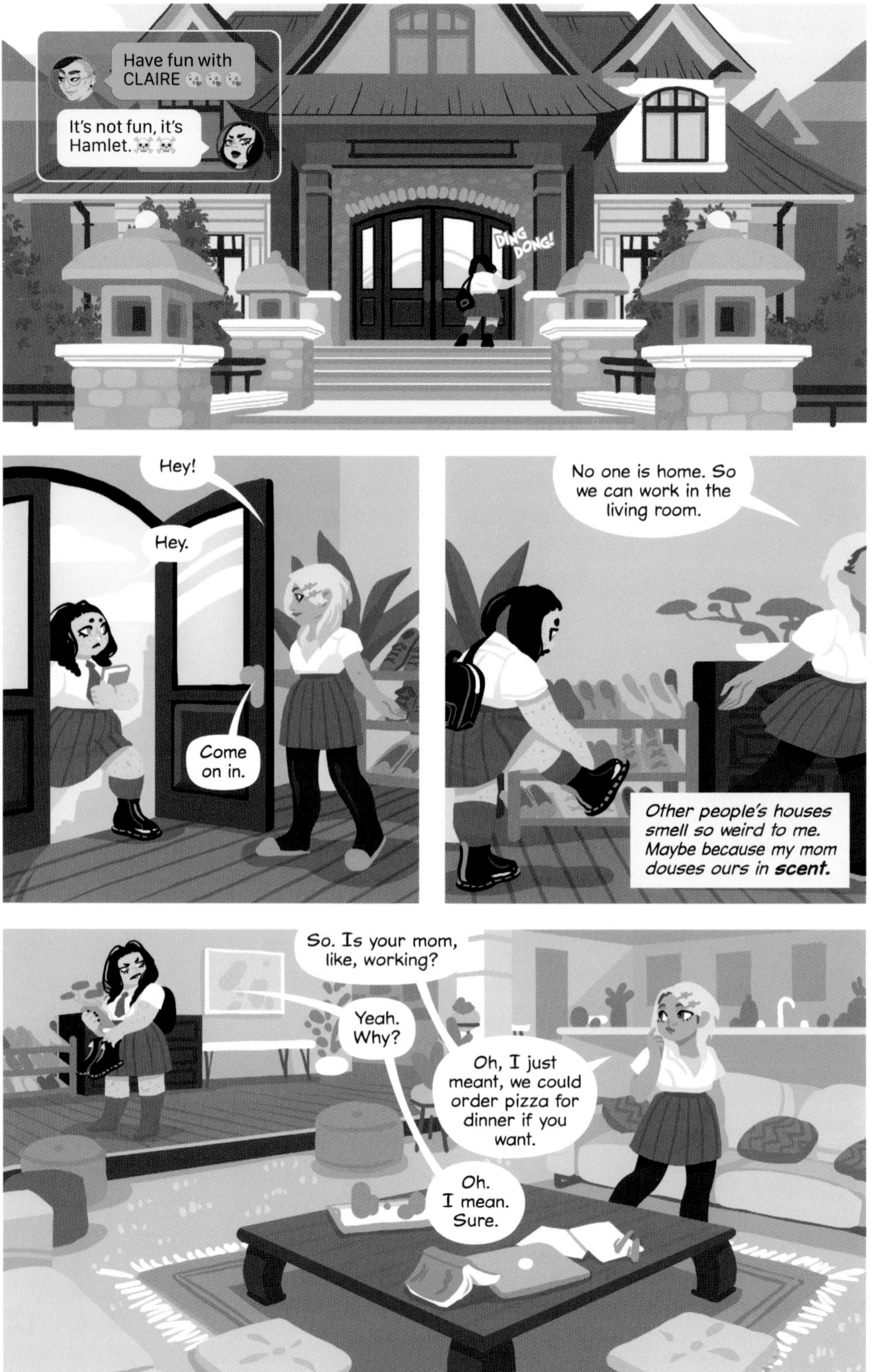
Have fun with CLAIRE 😘😘😘
It's not fun, it's Hamlet. ☠️☠️
DING DONG!
Hey!
Hey.
Come on in.
No one is home. So we can work in the living room.
Other people's houses smell so weird to me. Maybe because my mom douses ours in **scent.**
So. Is your mom, like, working?
Yeah. Why?
Oh, I just meant, we could order pizza for dinner if you want.
Oh. I mean. Sure.

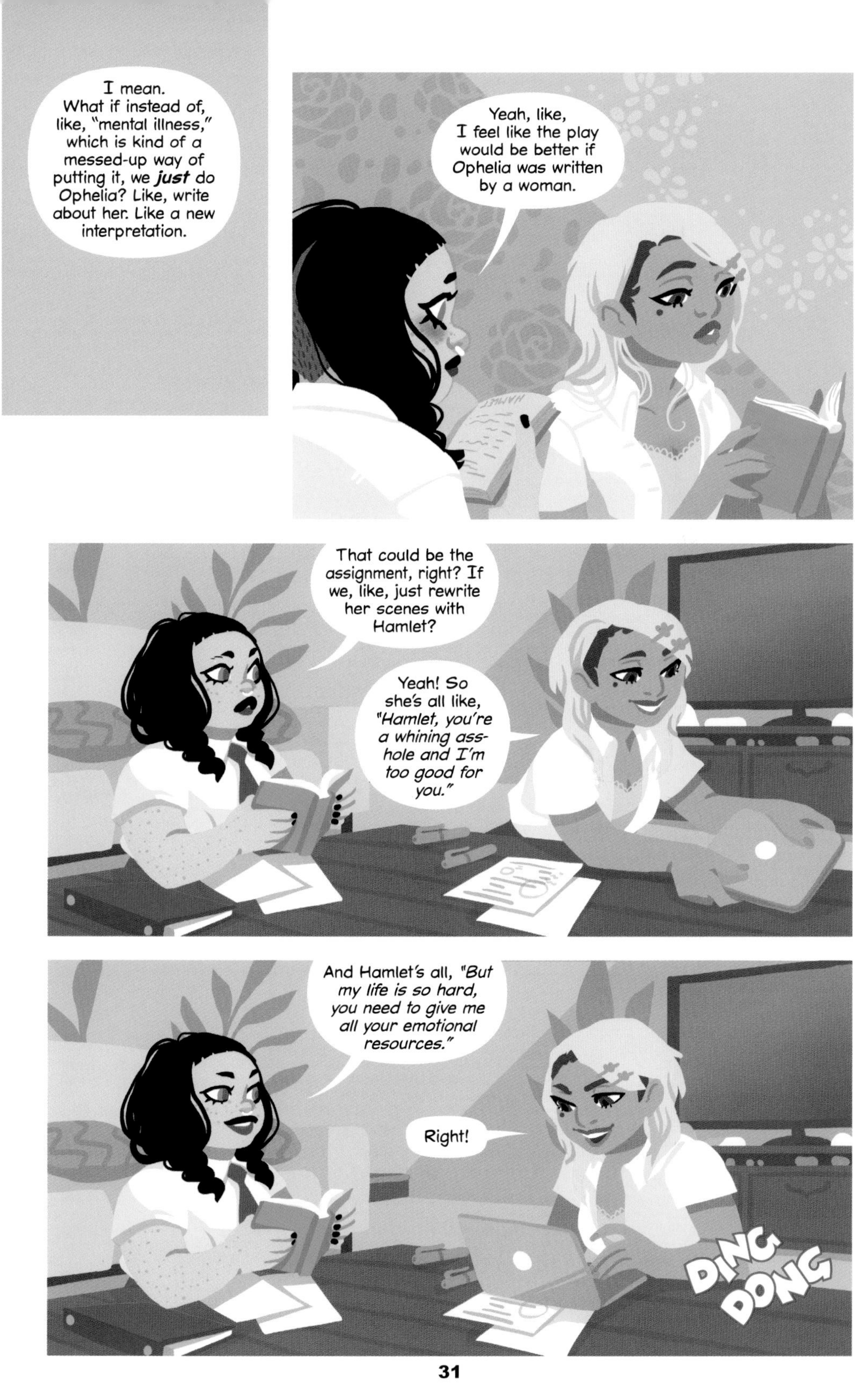
I mean. What if instead of, like, "mental illness," which is kind of a messed-up way of putting it, we ***just*** do Ophelia? Like, write about her. Like a new interpretation.
Yeah, like, I feel like the play would be better if Ophelia was written by a woman.
That could be the assignment, right? If we, like, just rewrite her scenes with Hamlet?
Yeah! So she's all like, *"Hamlet, you're a whining ass-hole and I'm too good for you."*
And Hamlet's all, *"But my life is so hard, you need to give me all your emotional resources."*
Right!
DING DONG

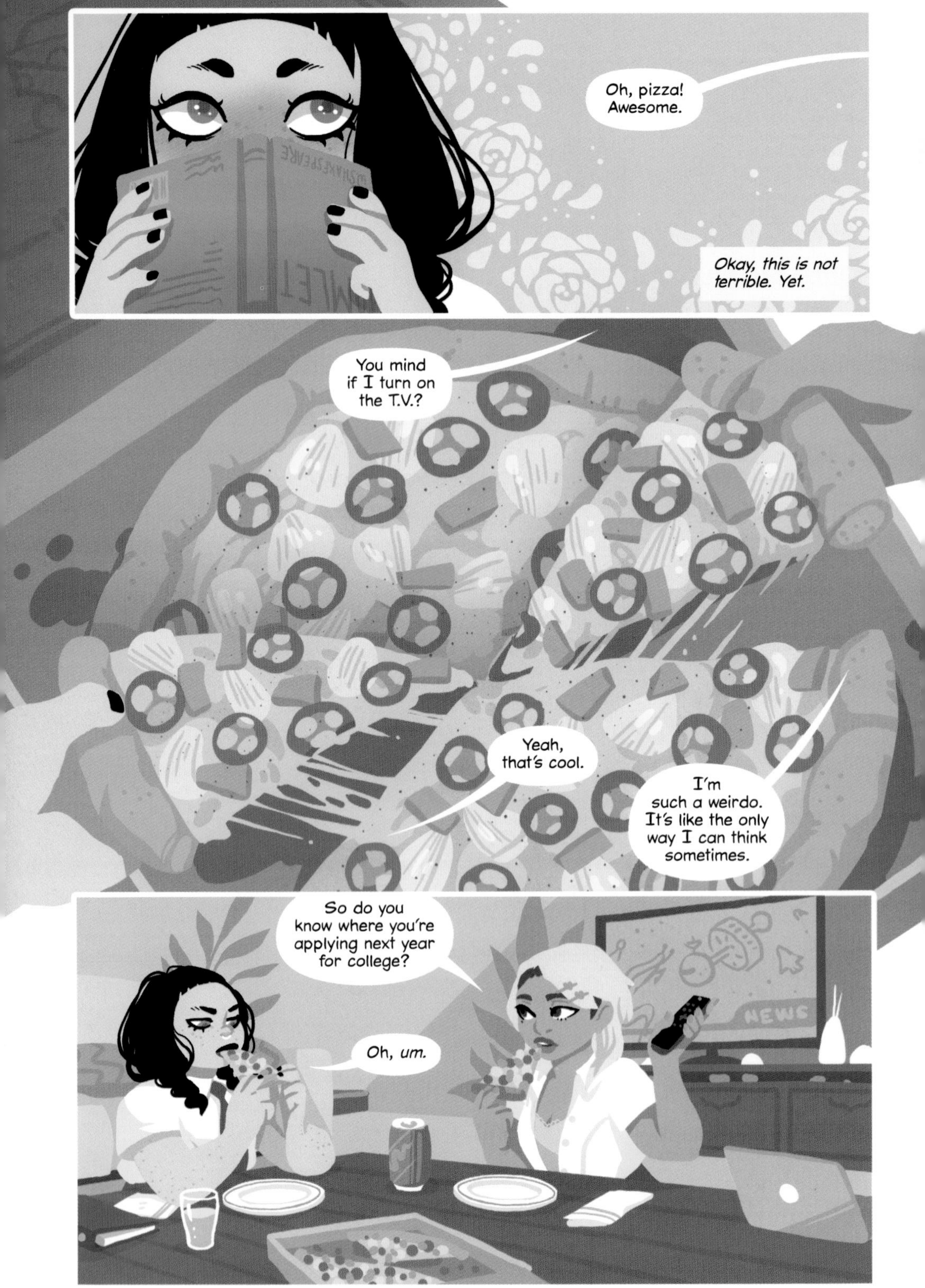
Oh, pizza! Awesome.
Okay, this is not terrible. Yet.
You mind if I turn on the T.V.?
Yeah, that's cool.
I'm such a weirdo. It's like the only way I can think sometimes.
So do you know where you're applying next year for college?
Oh, um.
NEWS

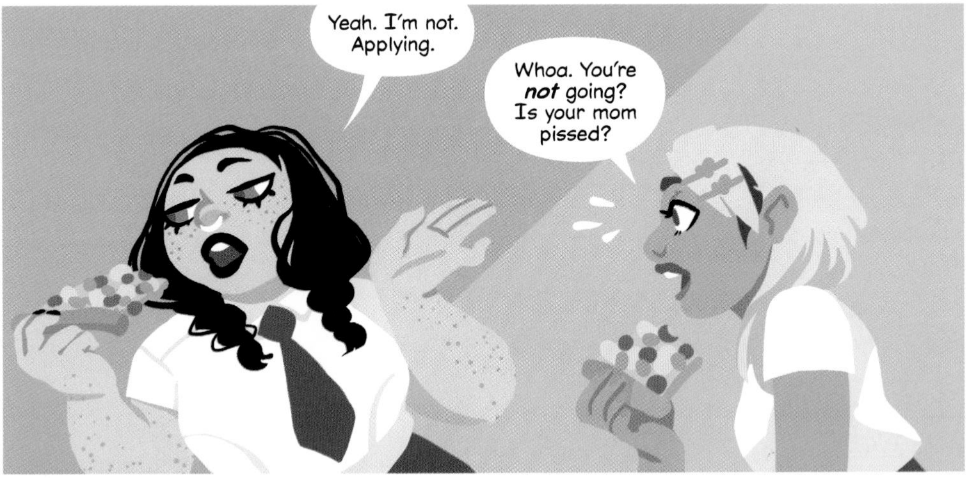
Yeah. I'm not. Applying.
Whoa. You're **not** going? Is your mom pissed?

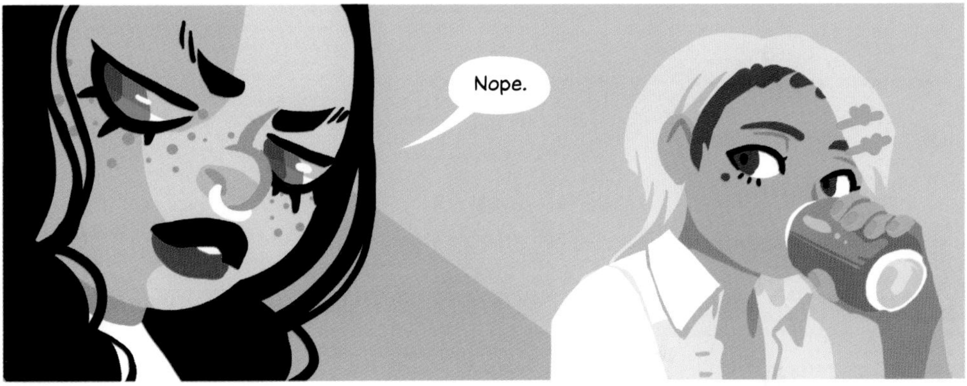
Nope.

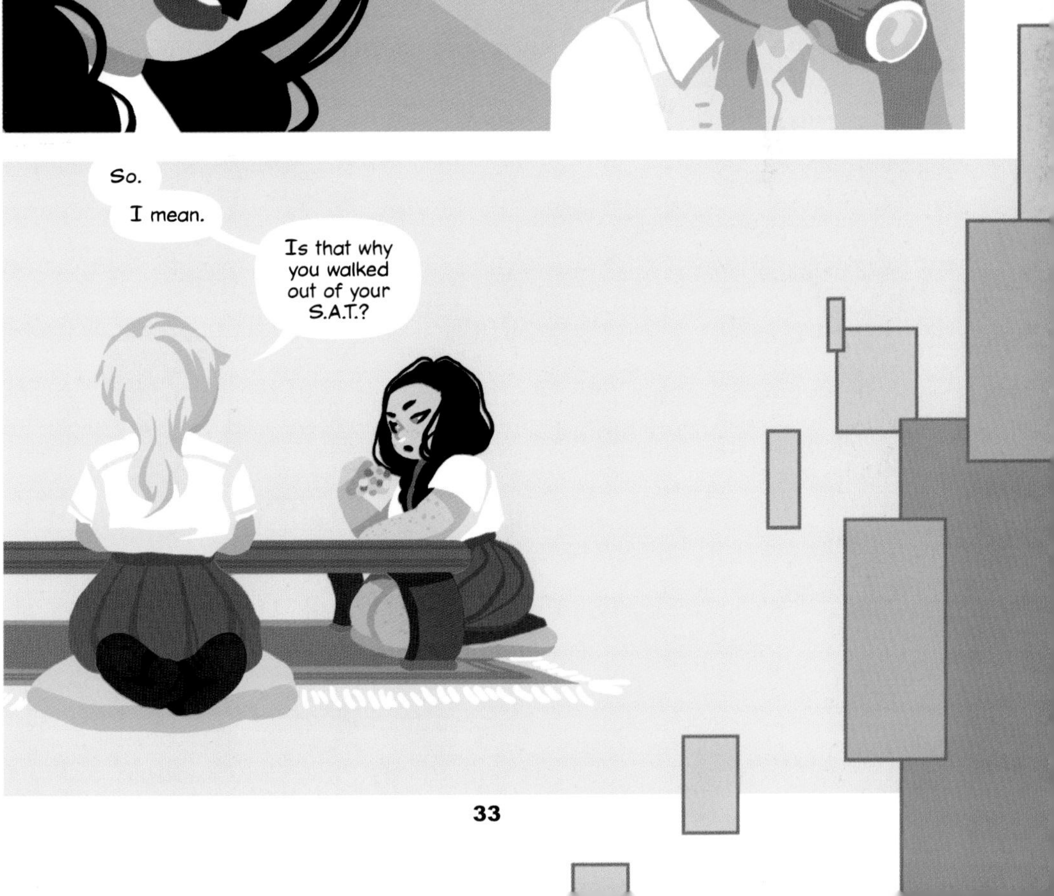
So.
I mean.
Is that why you walked out of your S.A.T.?

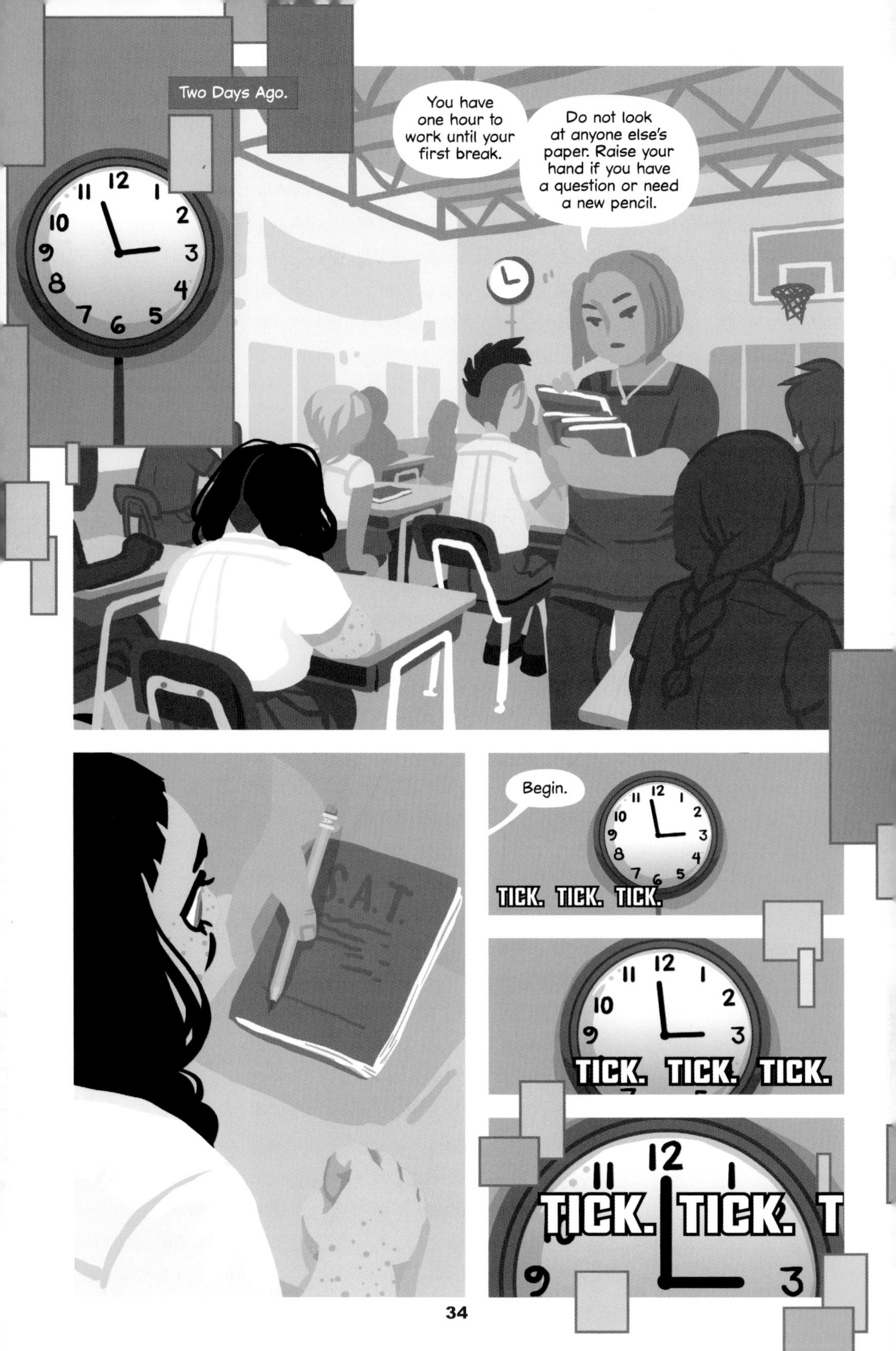
Two Days Ago.
You have one hour to work until your first break.
Do not look at anyone else's paper. Raise your hand if you have a question or need a new pencil.
S.A.T.
Begin.
TICK. TICK. TICK.
TICK. TICK. TICK.
TICK. TICK. T

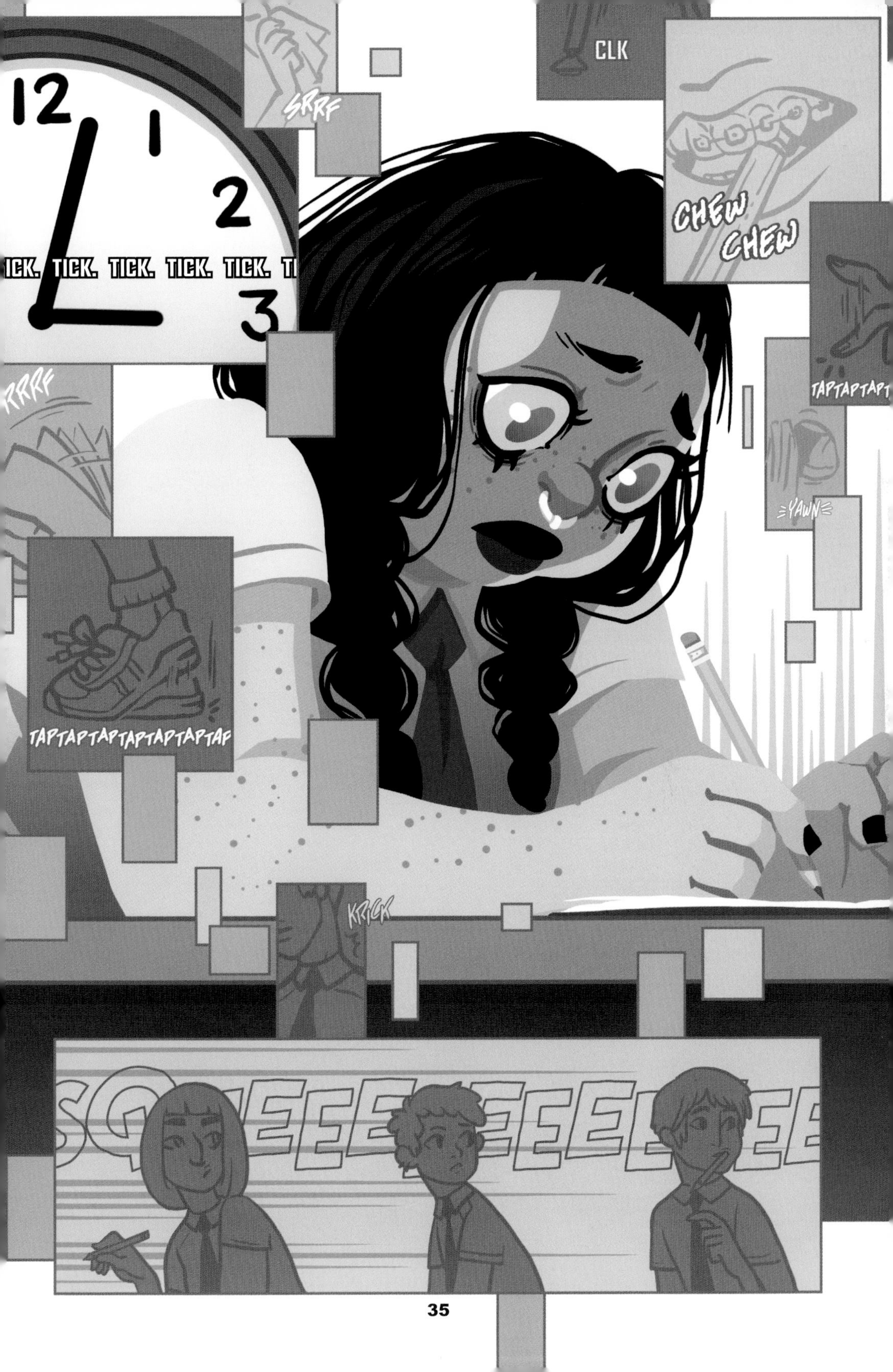
TICK. TICK. TICK. TICK. TICK.
SRRF
CLK
CHEW CHEW
TAPTAPTAPT
RRRF
YAWN
TAPTAPTAPTAPTAPTAPTAP
KRICK
SQEEEEEEEEEEE

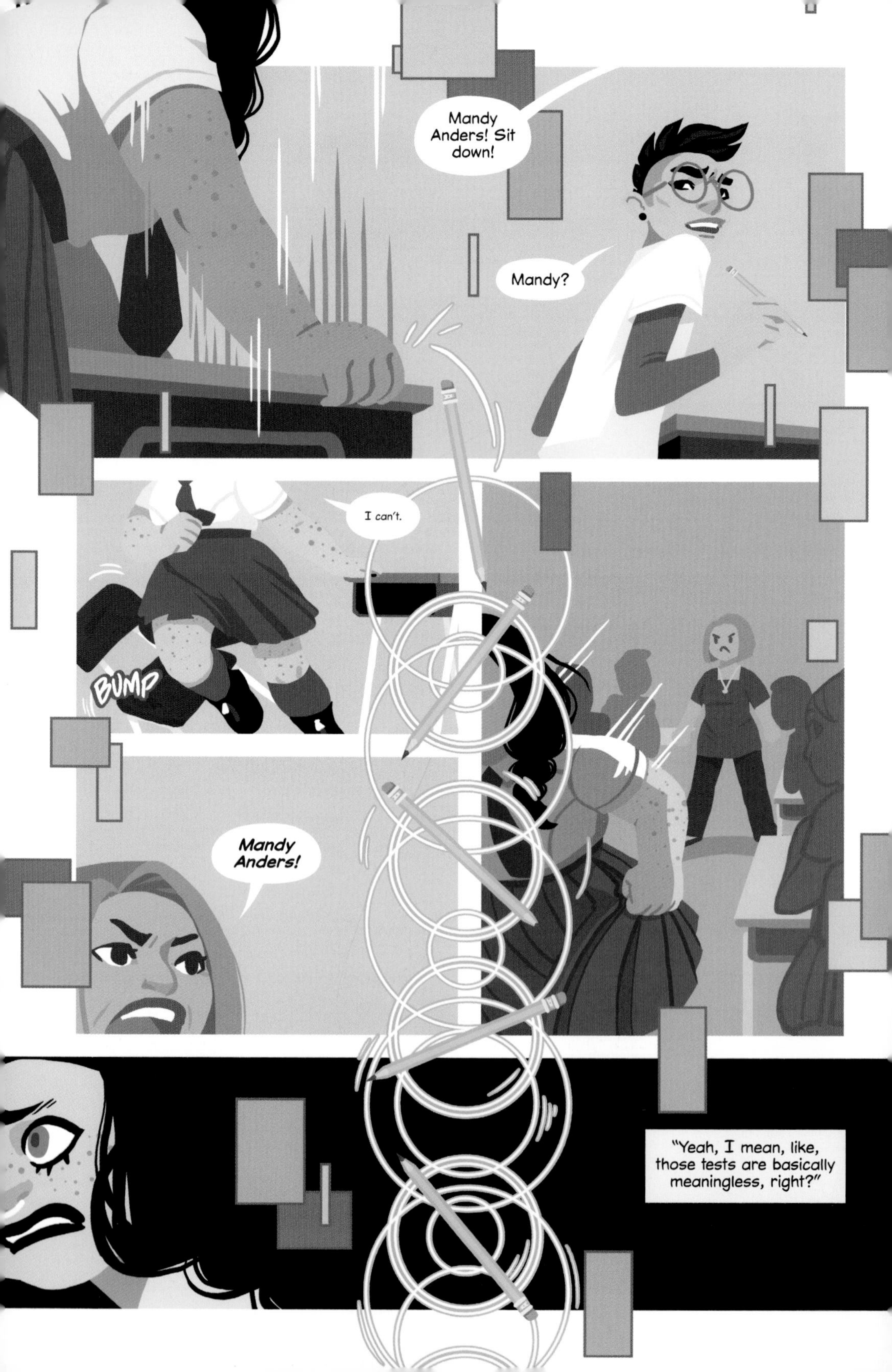
Mandy Anders! Sit down!
Mandy?
I can't.
BUMP
Mandy Anders!
"Yeah, I mean, like, those tests are basically meaningless, right?"

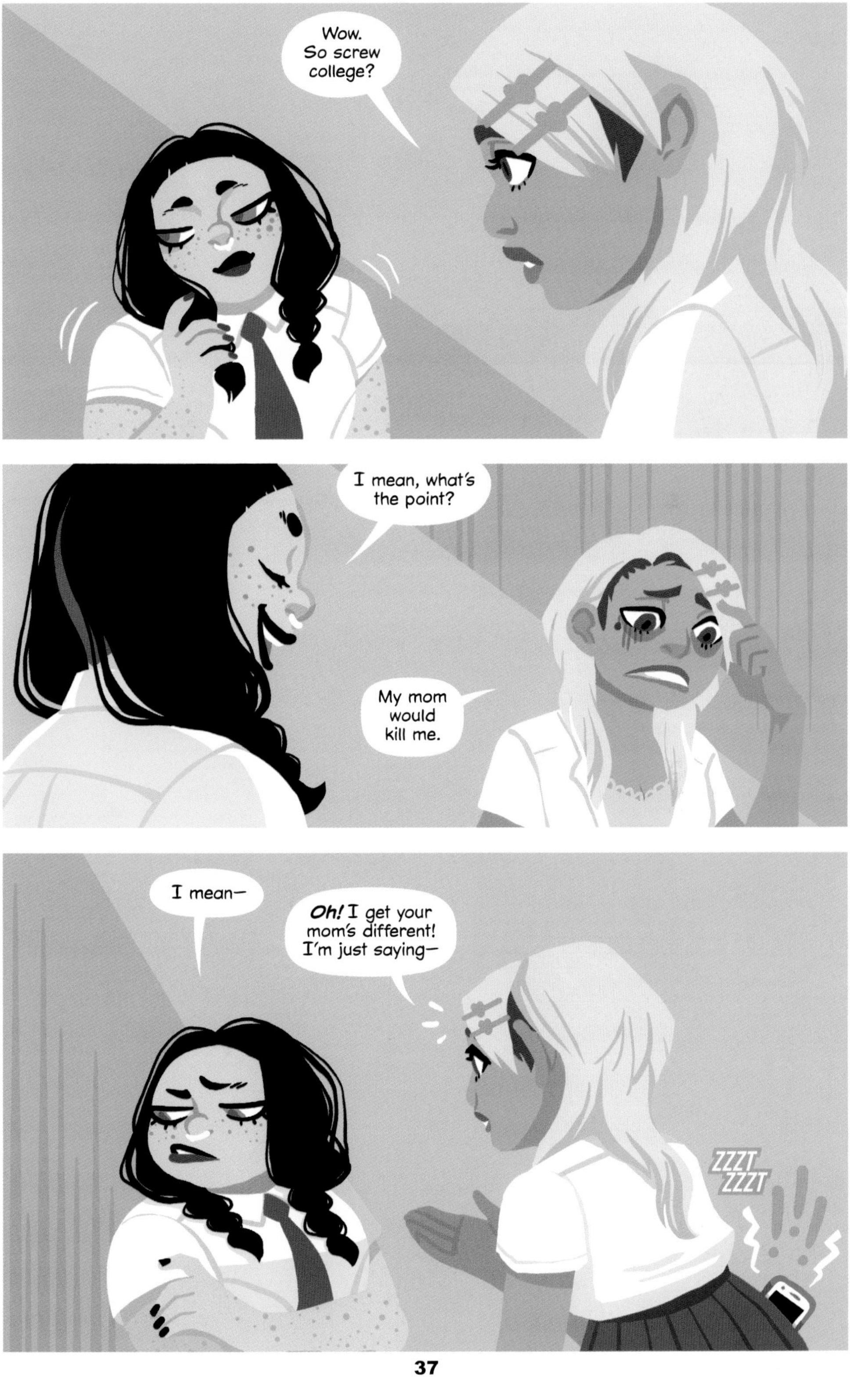
Wow. So screw college?
I mean, what's the point?
My mom would kill me.
I mean—
Oh! I get your mom's different! I'm just saying—
ZZZT ZZZT

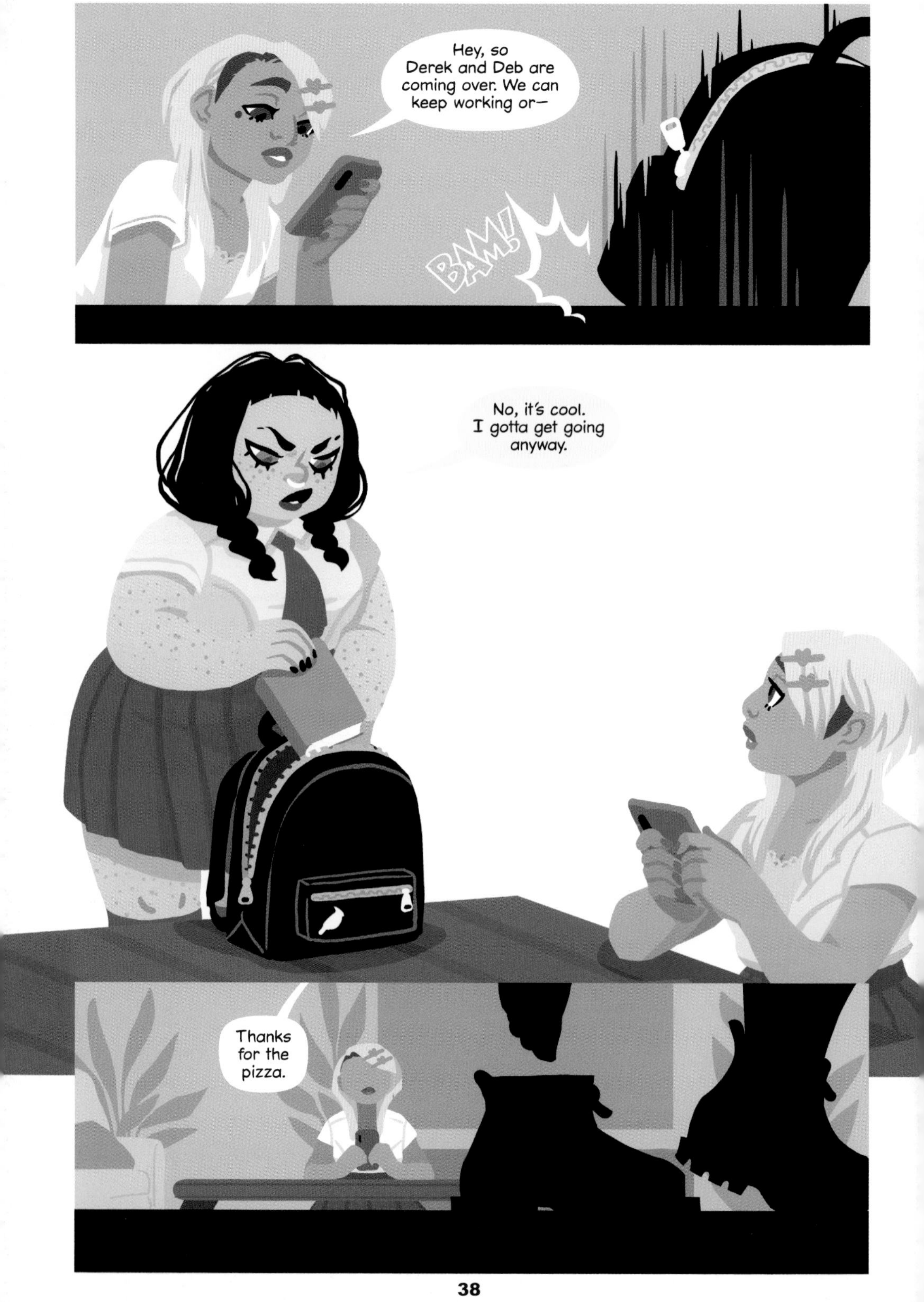
Hey, so Derek and Deb are coming over. We can keep working or—
BAM!
No, it's cool. I gotta get going anyway.
Thanks for the pizza.

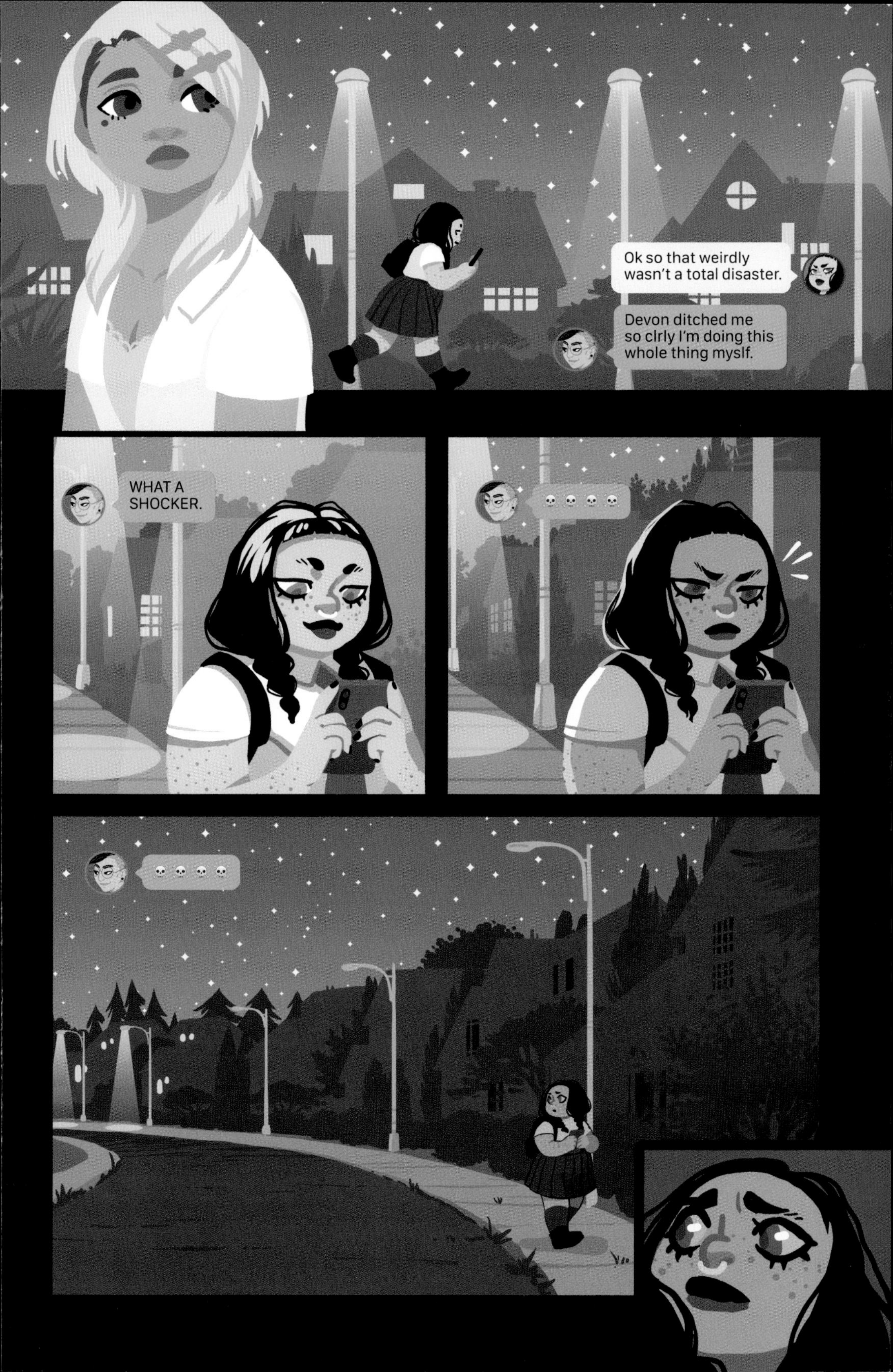
Ok so that weirdly wasn't a total disaster.
Devon ditched me so clrly I'm doing this whole thing myslf.
WHAT A SHOCKER.
💀💀💀💀
💀💀💀💀

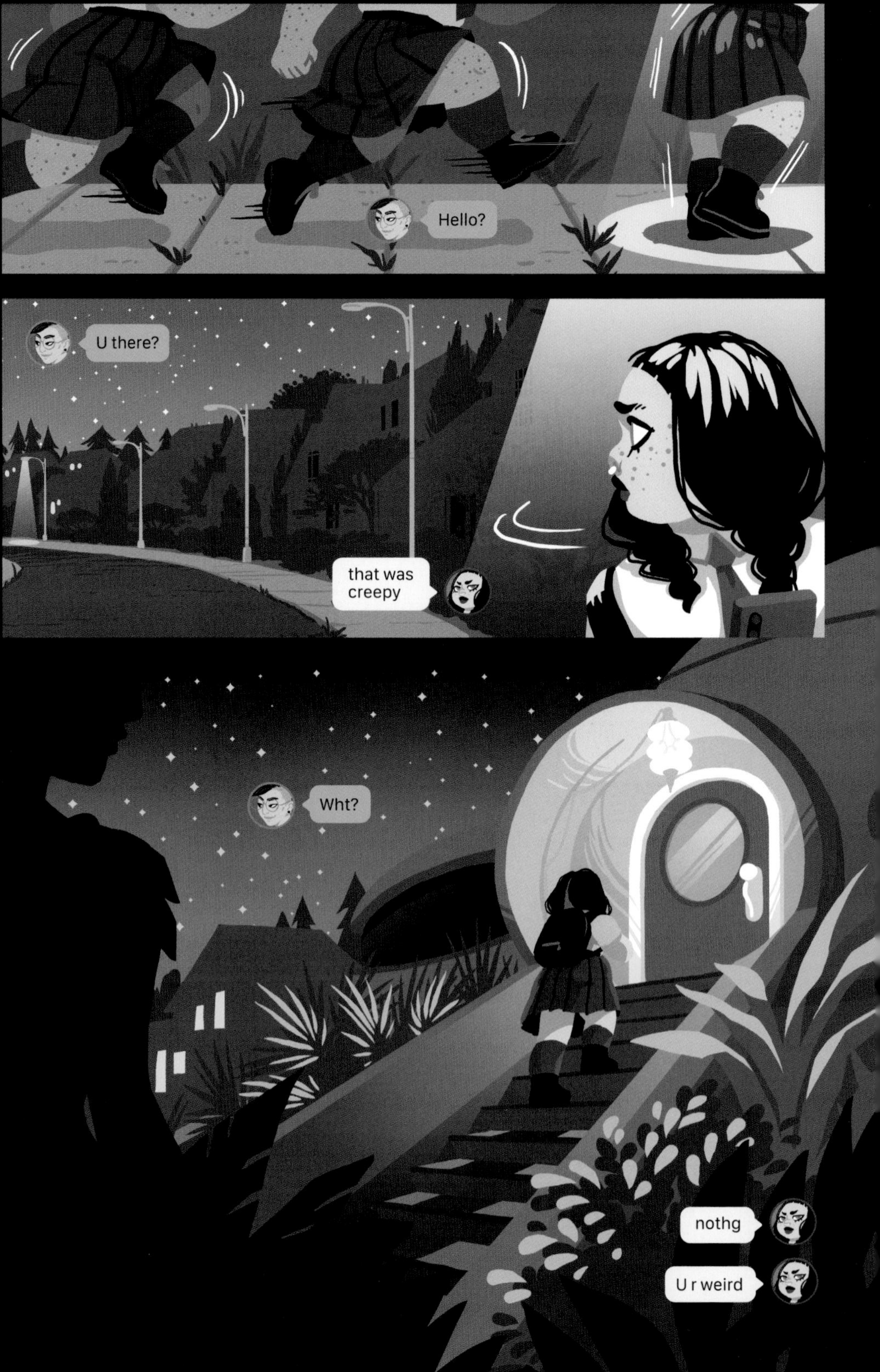
Hello?
U there?
that was creepy
Wht?
nothg
U r weird

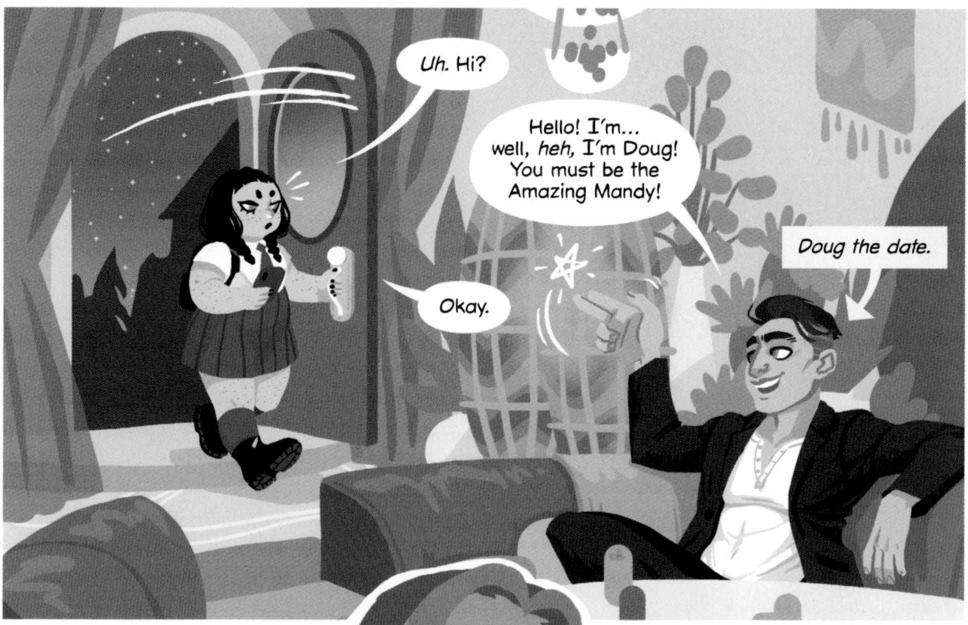
Uh. Hi?
Hello! I'm... well, *heh,* I'm Doug! You must be the Amazing Mandy!
Doug the date.
Okay.

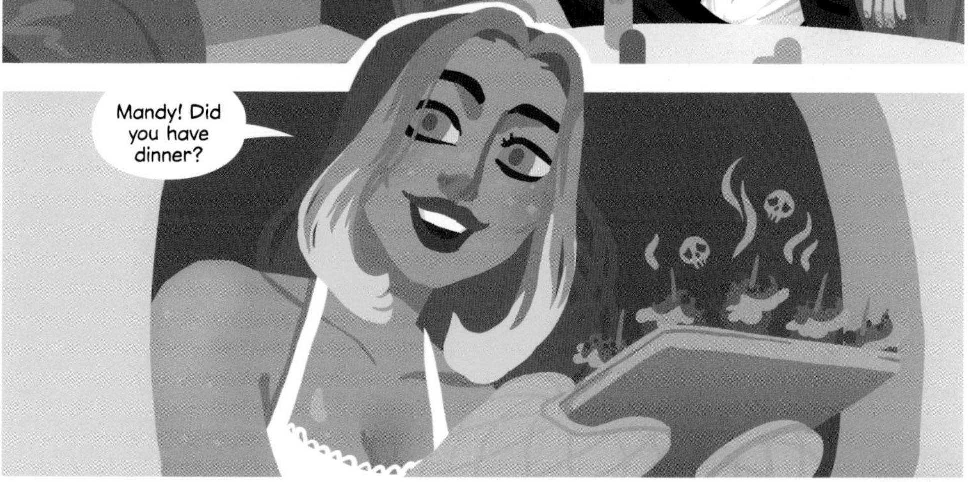
Mandy! Did you have dinner?

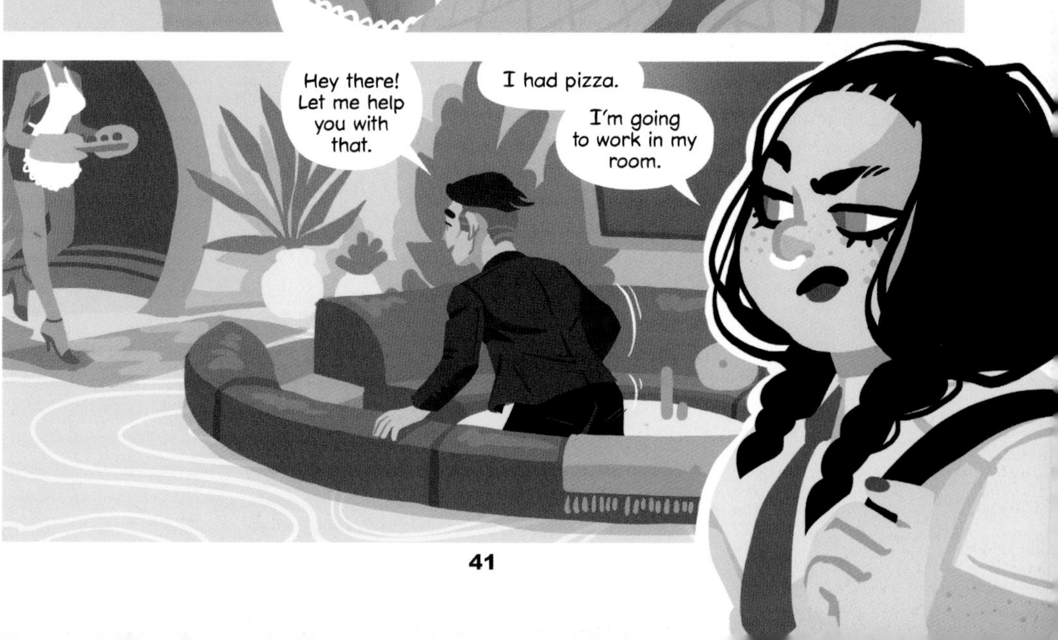
Hey there! Let me help you with that.
I had pizza.
I'm going to work in my room.

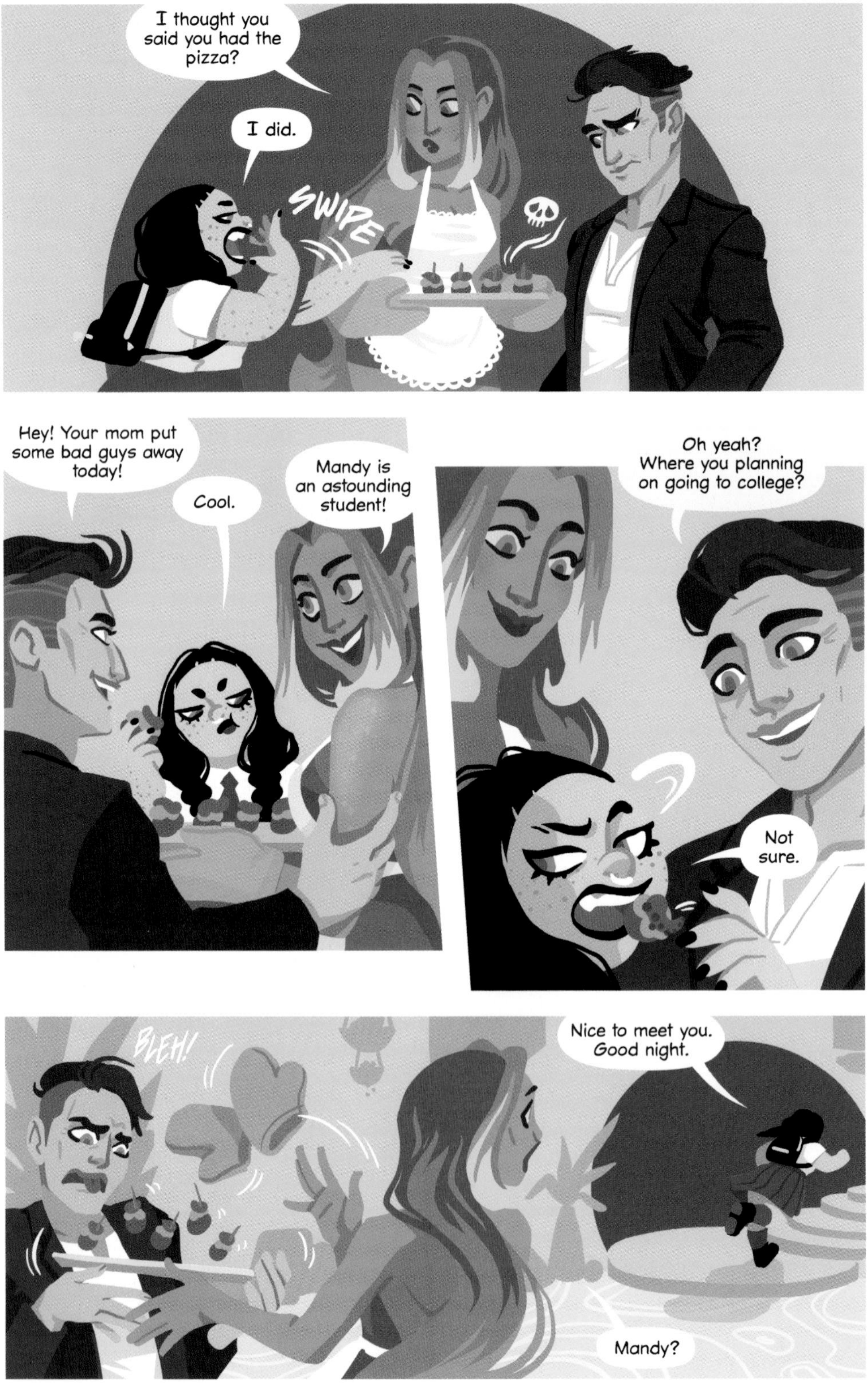
I thought you said you had the pizza?
I did.
SWIPE
Hey! Your mom put some bad guys away today!
Cool.
Mandy is an astounding student!
Oh yeah? Where you planning on going to college?
Not sure.
BLEH!
Nice to meet you. Good night.
Mandy?

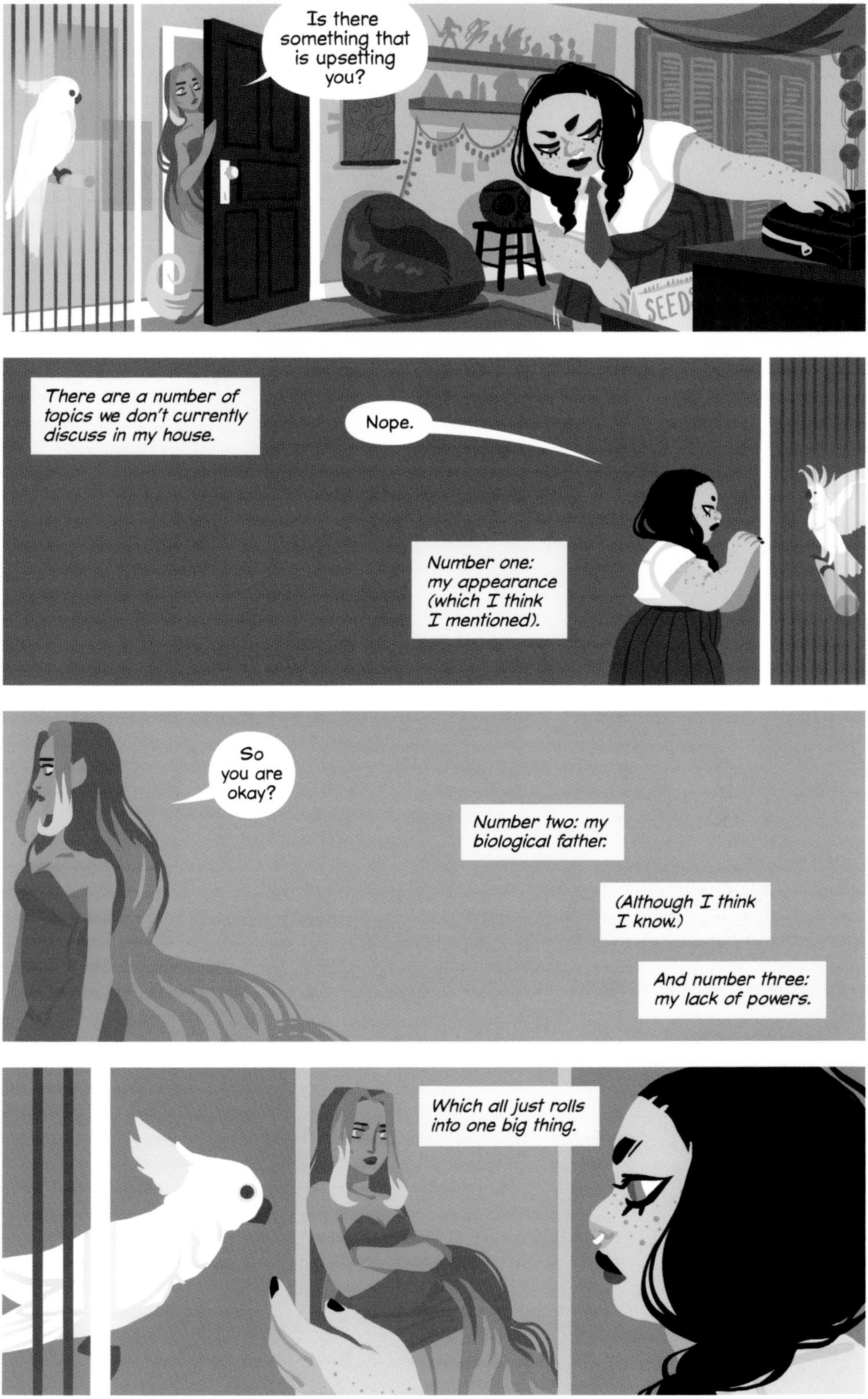
Is there something that is upsetting you?
There are a number of topics we don't currently discuss in my house.
Nope.
Number one: my appearance (which I think I mentioned).
So you are okay?
Number two: my biological father.
(Although I think I know.)
And number three: my lack of powers.
Which all just rolls into one big thing.

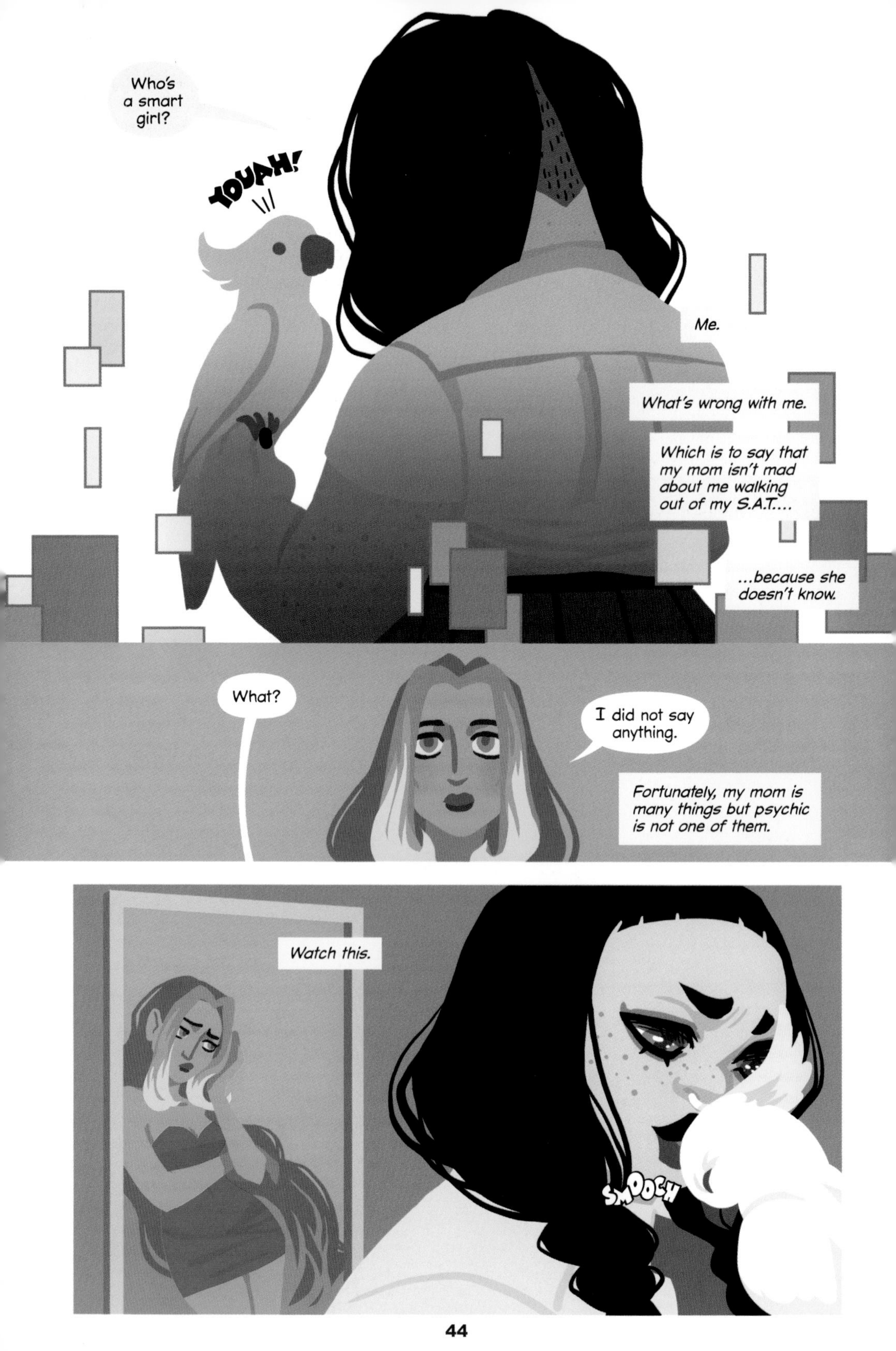

Who's a smart girl?
YOUAH!
Me.
What's wrong with me.
Which is to say that my mom isn't mad about me walking out of my S.A.T....
...because she doesn't know.
What?
I did not say anything.
Fortunately, my mom is many things but psychic is not one of them.
Watch this.
SMOOCH

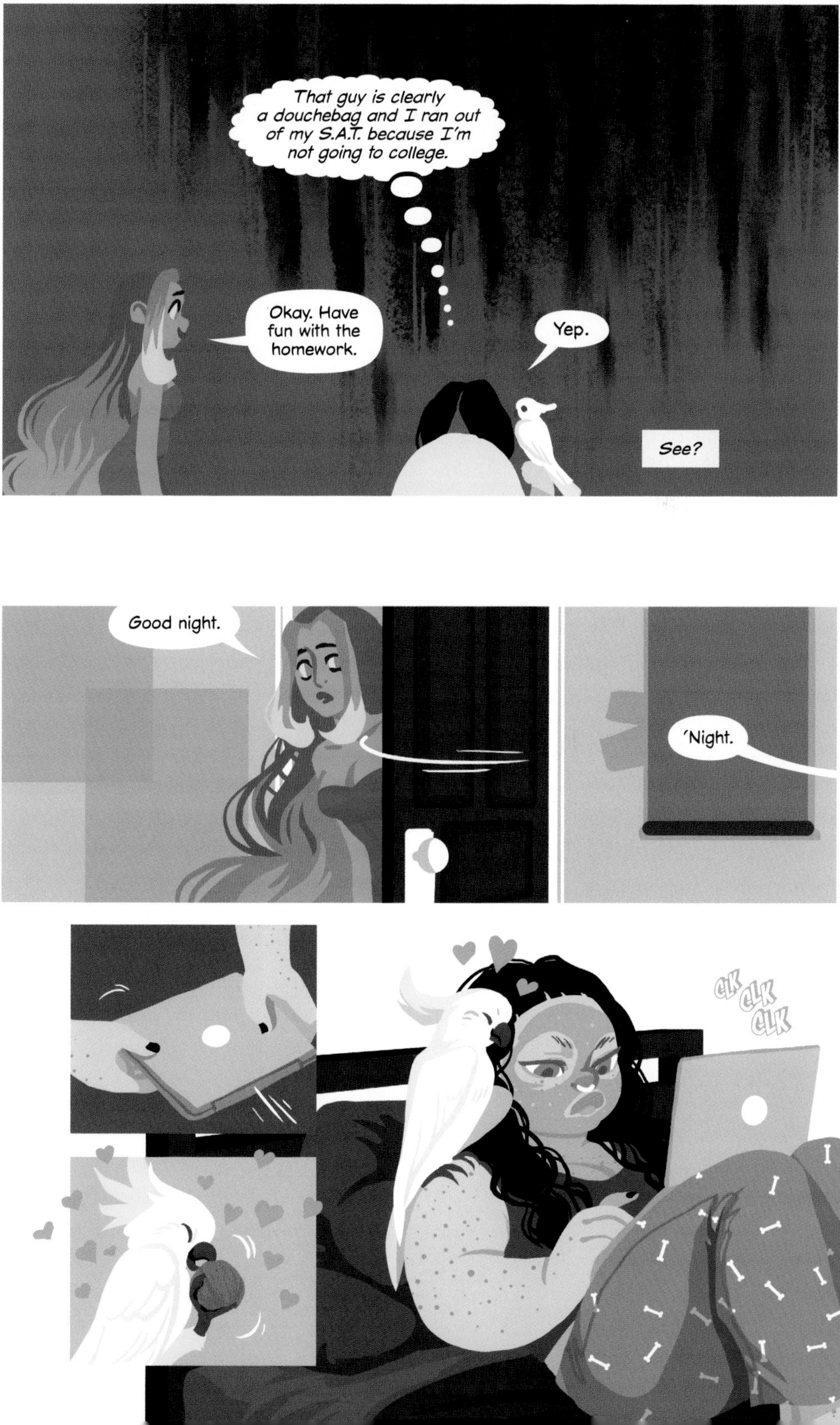
That guy is clearly a douchebag and I ran out of my S.A.T. because I'm not going to college.
Okay. Have fun with the homework.
Yep.
See?
Good night.
'Night.
CLK CLK CLK

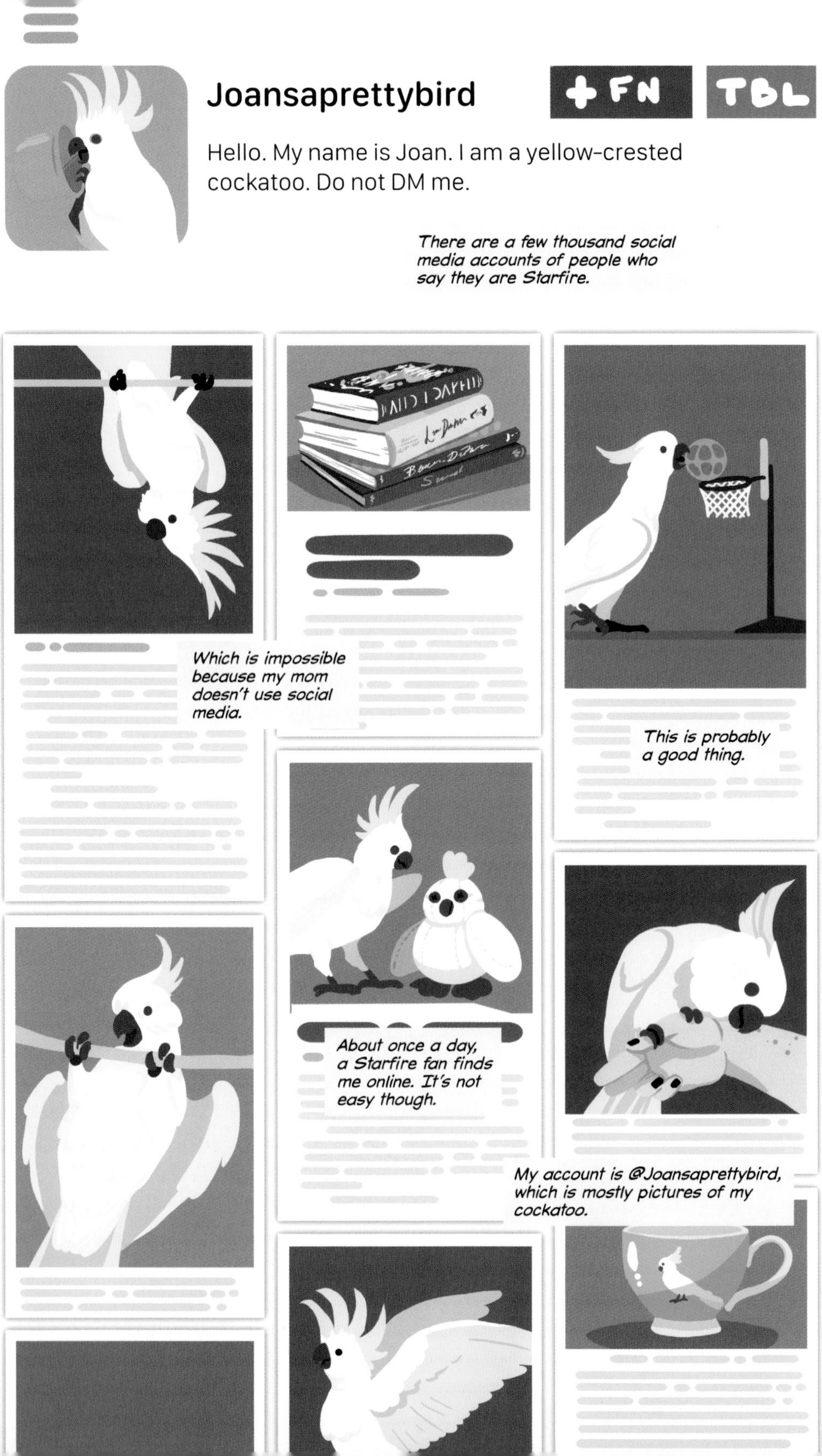

Joansaprettybird
+FN
TBL
Hello. My name is Joan. I am a yellow-crested cockatoo. Do not DM me.
There are a few thousand social media accounts of people who say they are Starfire.
Which is impossible because my mom doesn't use social media.
This is probably a good thing.
About once a day, a Starfire fan finds me online. It's not easy though.
My account is @Joansaprettybird, which is mostly pictures of my cockatoo.

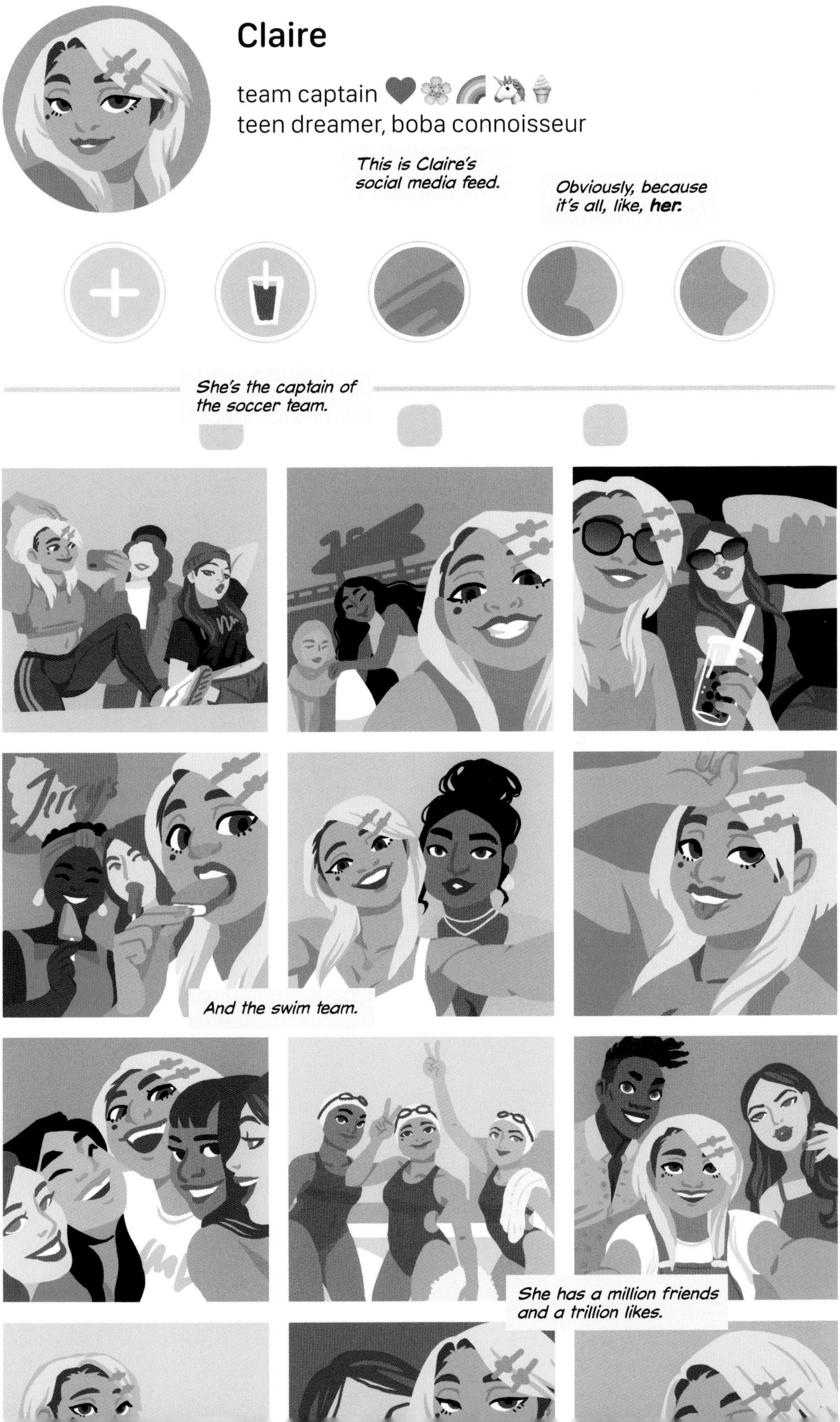
Claire
team captain
teen dreamer, boba connoisseur
This is Claire's social media feed.
Obviously, because it's all, like, **her.**
She's the captain of the soccer team.
And the swim team.
She has a million friends and a trillion likes.

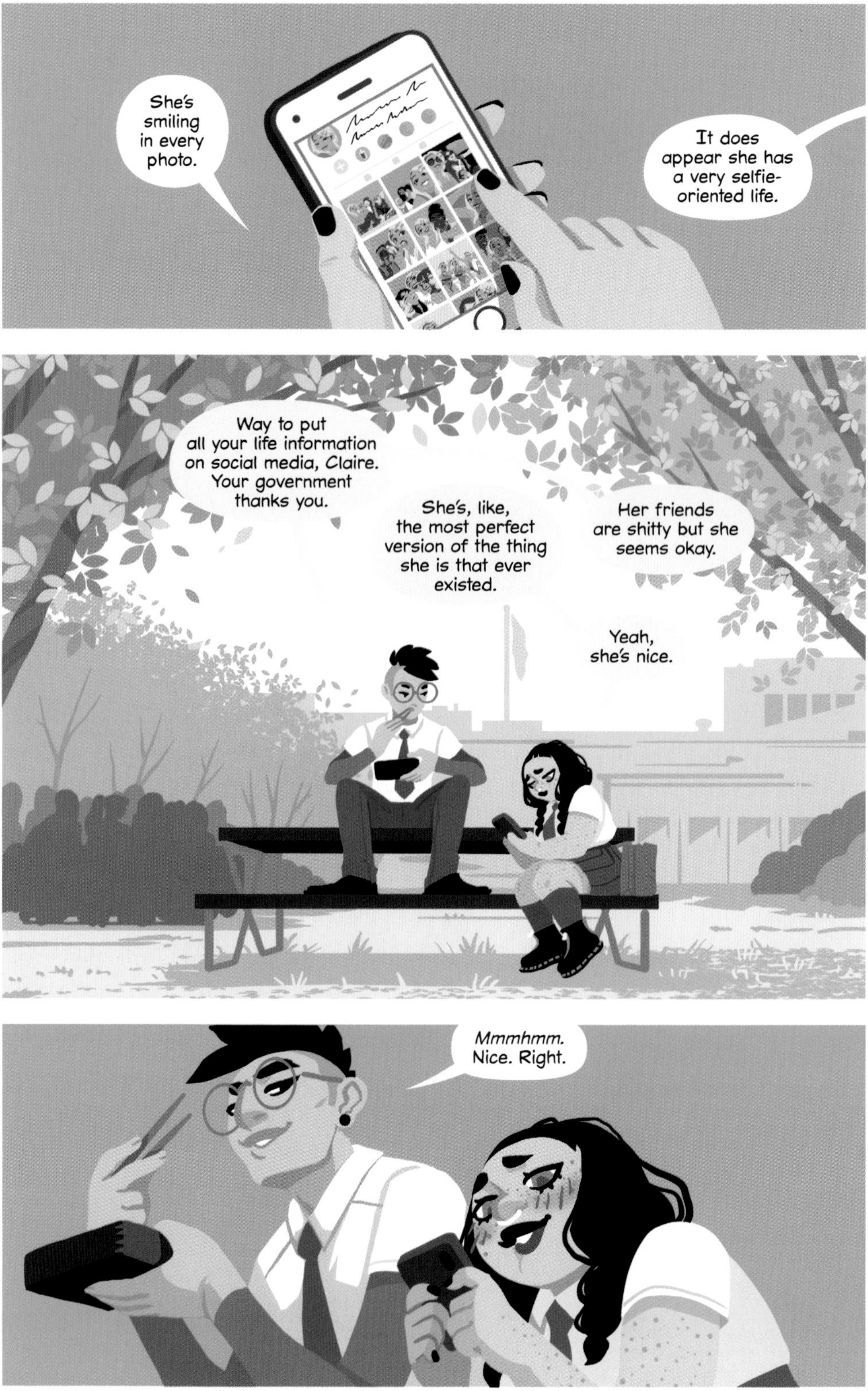
She's smiling in every photo.
It does appear she has a very selfie-oriented life.
Way to put all your life information on social media, Claire. Your government thanks you.
She's, like, the most perfect version of the thing she is that ever existed.
Her friends are shitty but she seems okay.
Yeah, she's nice.
Mmmhmm. Nice. Right.

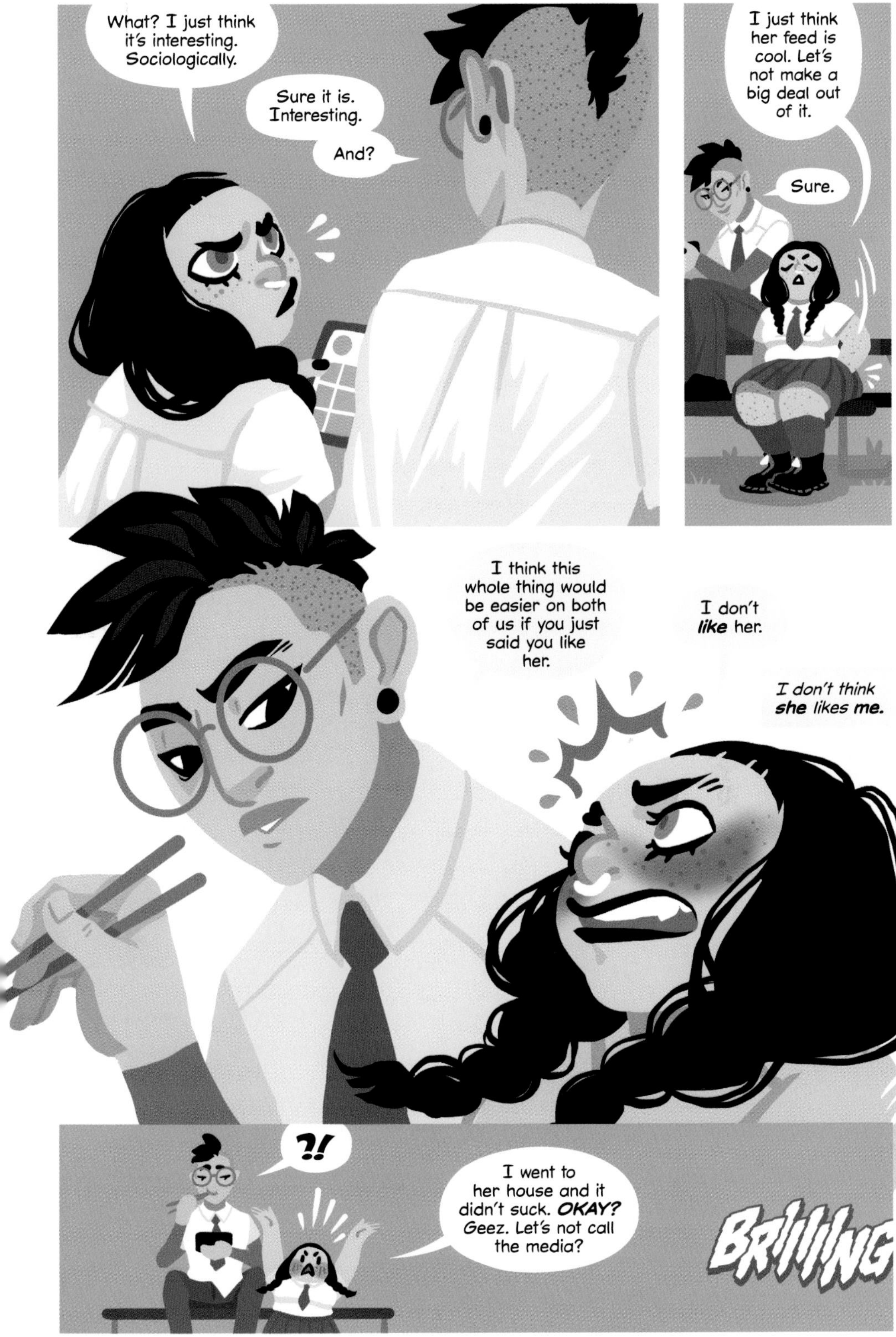
What? I just think it's interesting. Sociologically.
Sure it is. Interesting.
And?
I just think her feed is cool. Let's not make a big deal out of it.
Sure.
I think this whole thing would be easier on both of us if you just said you like her.
I don't ***like*** her.
*I don't think **she** likes **me.***
?!
I went to her house and it didn't suck. ***OKAY?*** Geez. Let's not call the media?
BRIIIING

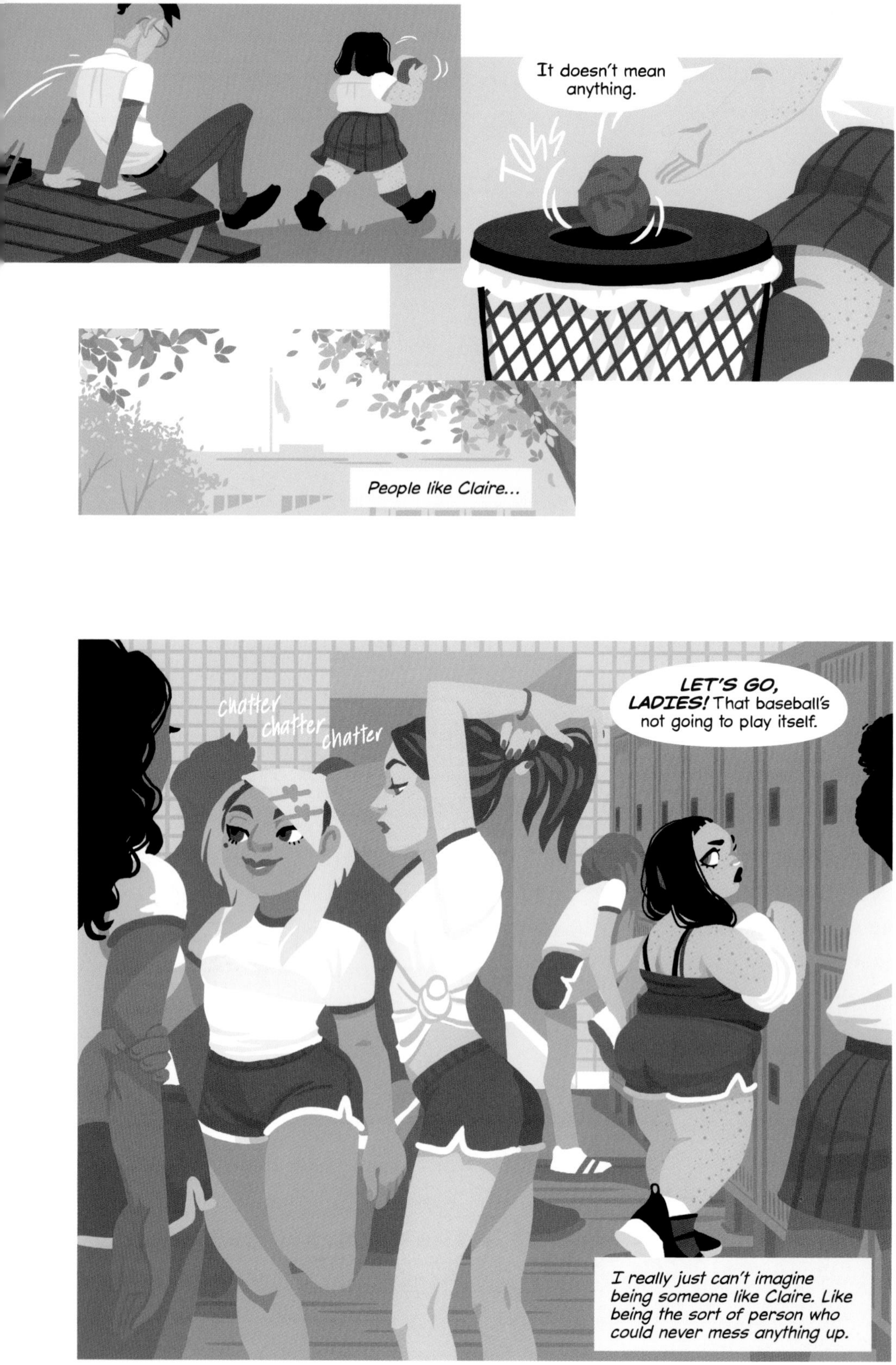

It doesn't mean anything.
TOSS
People like Claire...
chatter chatter chatter
LET'S GO, LADIES! That baseball's not going to play itself.
I really just can't imagine being someone like Claire. Like being the sort of person who could never mess anything up.

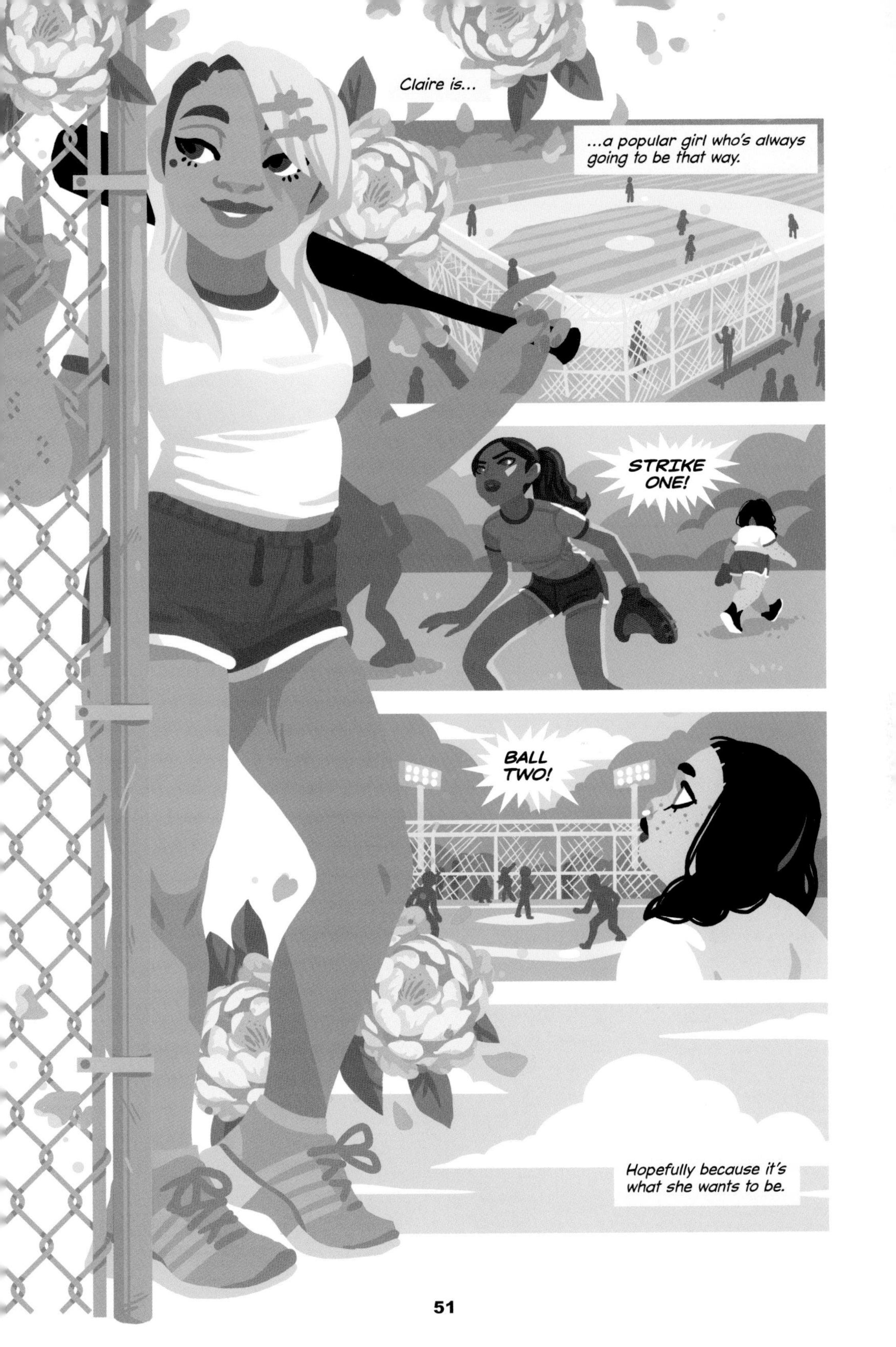
Claire is...
...a popular girl who's always going to be that way.
STRIKE ONE!
BALL TWO!
Hopefully because it's what she wants to be.

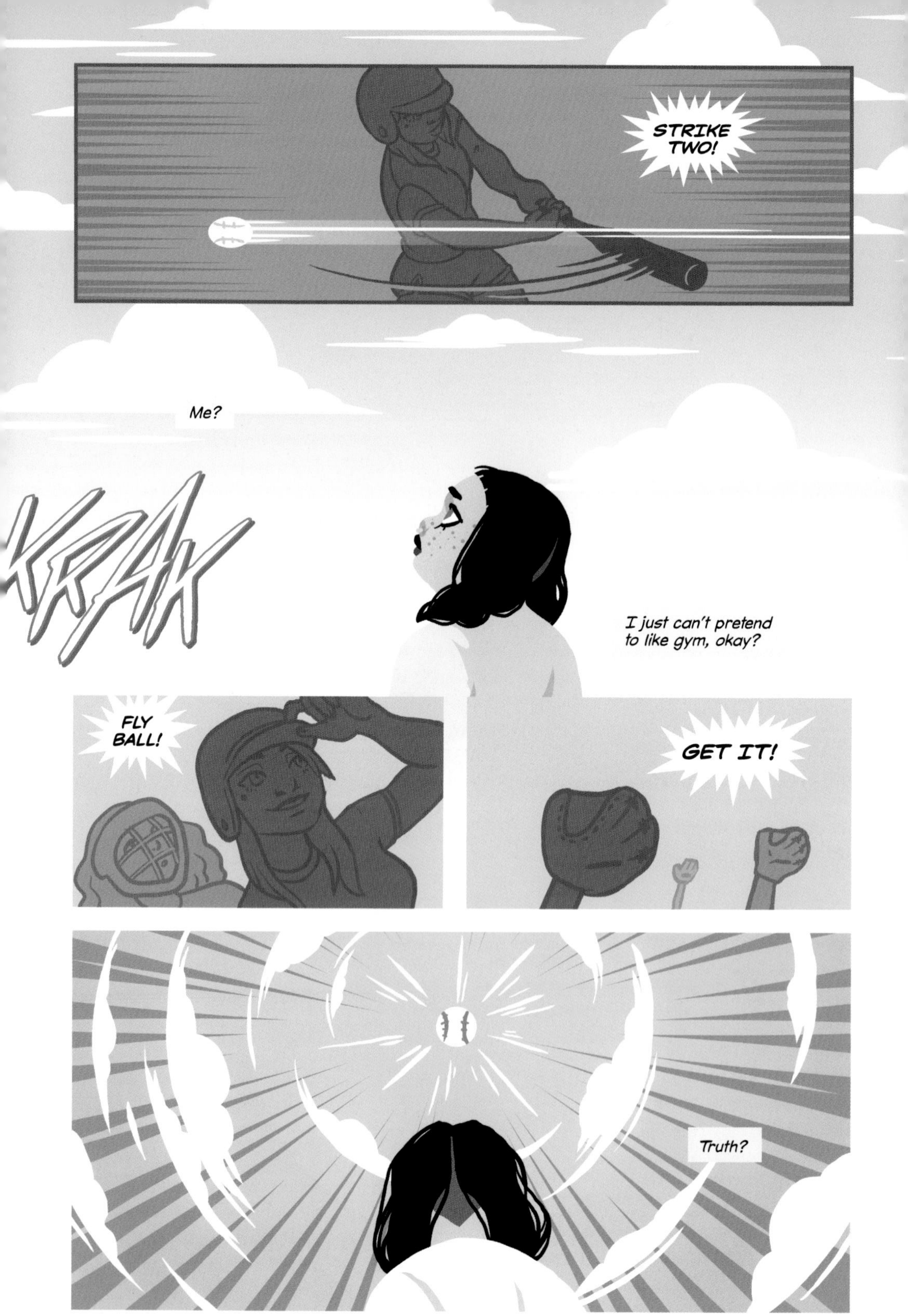
STRIKE TWO!
Me?
KRAK
I just can't pretend to like gym, okay?
FLY BALL!
GET IT!
Truth?

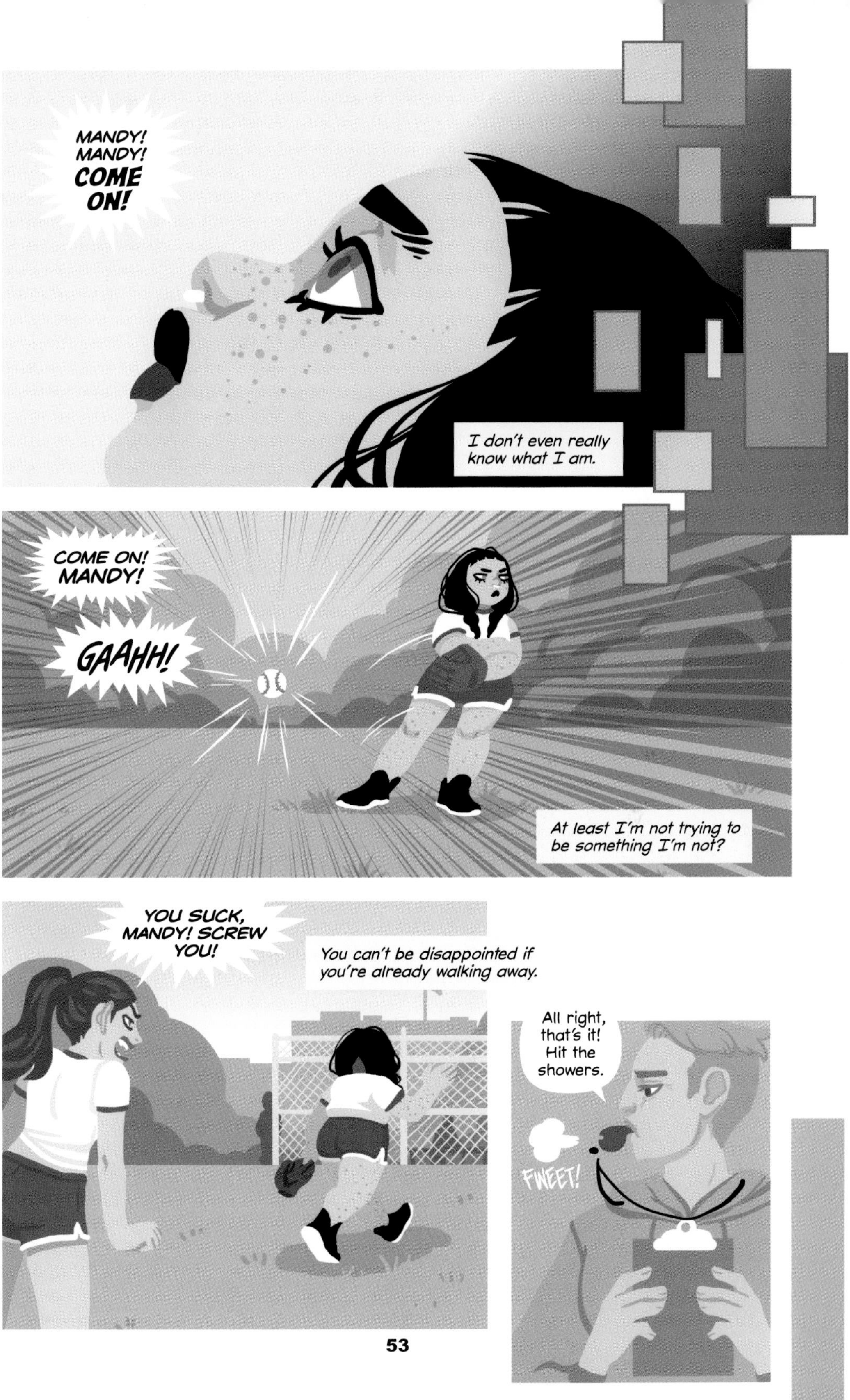
MANDY! MANDY! COME ON!
I don't even really know what I am.
COME ON! MANDY!
GAAHH!
At least I'm not trying to be something I'm not?
YOU SUCK, MANDY! SCREW YOU!
You can't be disappointed if you're already walking away.
All right, that's it! Hit the showers.
FWEET!

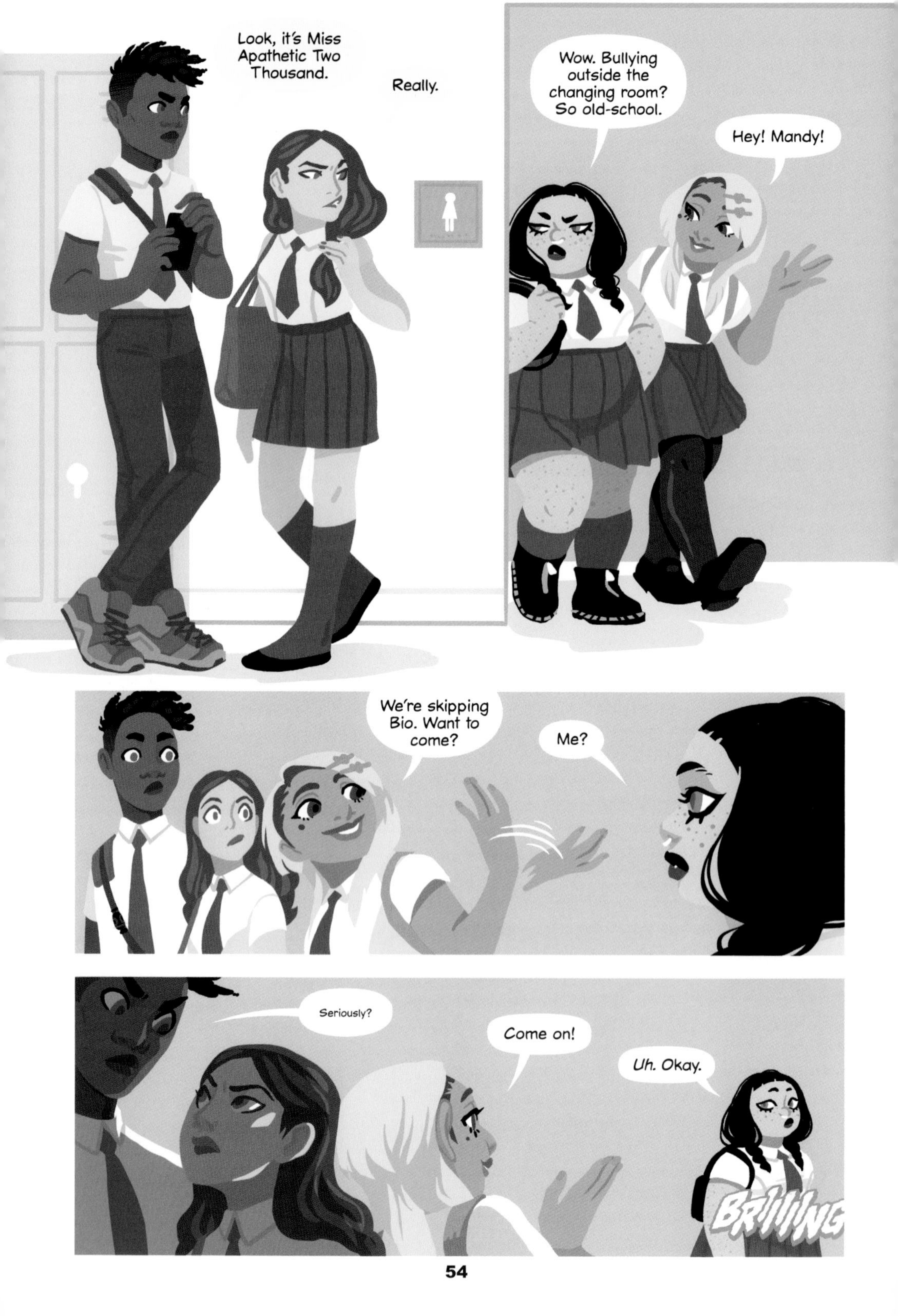

Look, it's Miss Apathetic Two Thousand.
Really.
Wow. Bullying outside the changing room? So old-school.
Hey! Mandy!
We're skipping Bio. Want to come?
Me?
Seriously?
Come on!
Uh. Okay.
BRIIIING

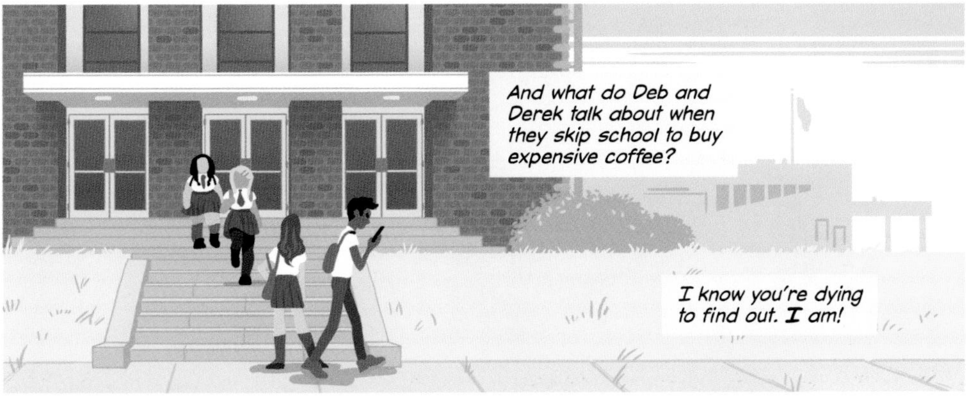
And what do Deb and Derek talk about when they skip school to buy expensive coffee?
I know you're dying to find out. I am!

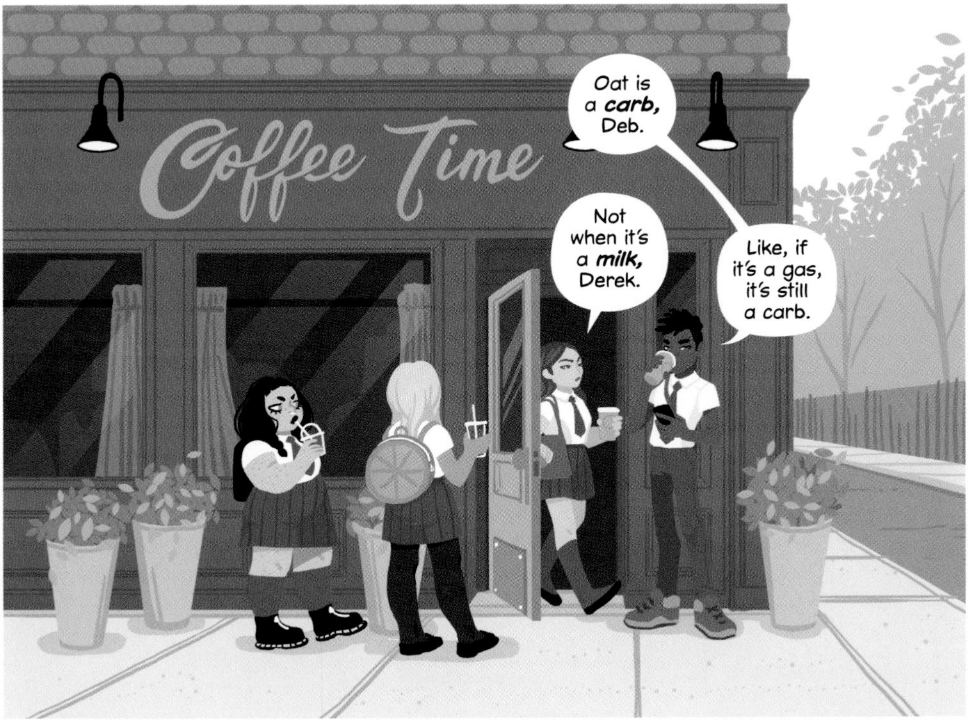
Coffee Time
Oat is a carb, Deb.
Not when it's a milk, Derek.
Like, if it's a gas, it's still a carb.

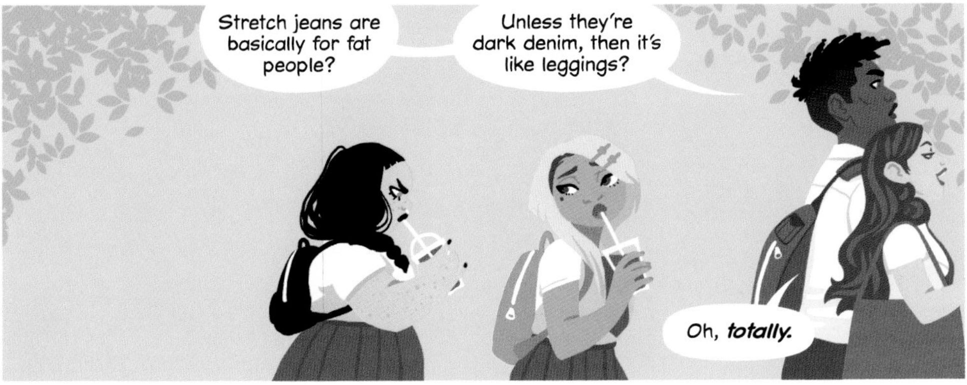
Stretch jeans are basically for fat people?
Unless they're dark denim, then it's like leggings?
Oh, totally.

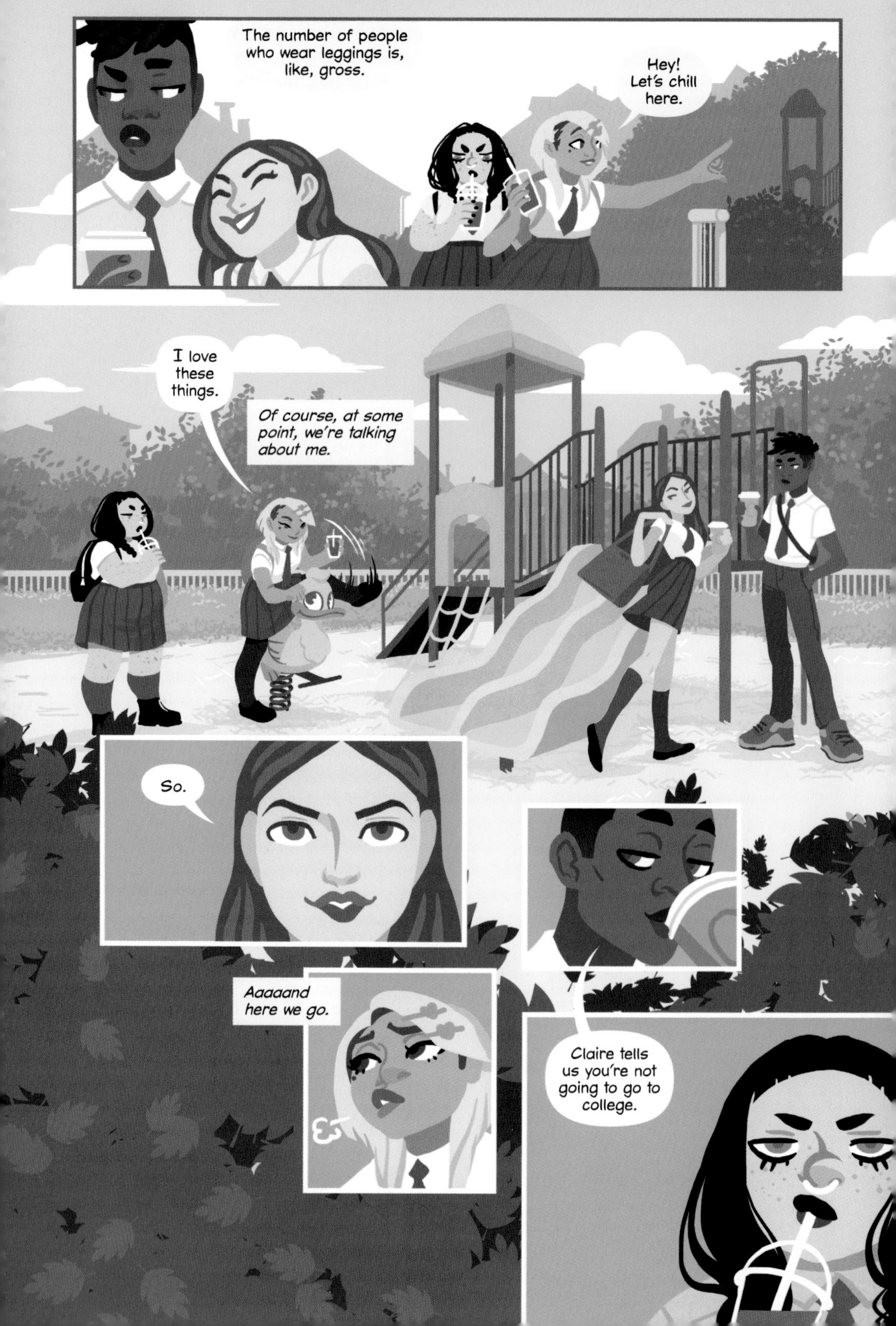
The number of people who wear leggings is, like, gross.
Hey! Let's chill here.
I love these things.
Of course, at some point, we're talking about me.
So.
Aaaaand here we go.
Claire tells us you're not going to go to college.

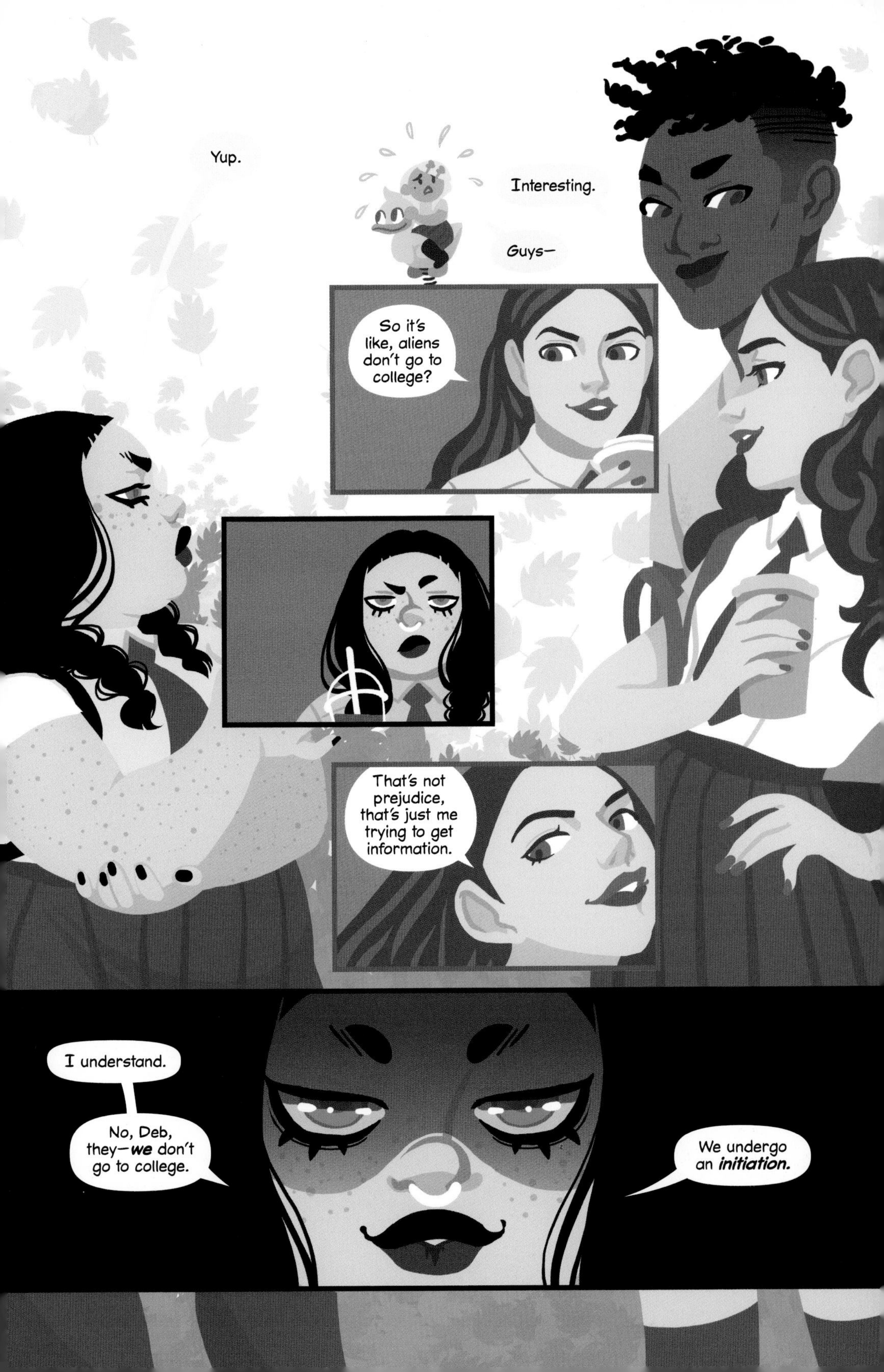
Yup.
Interesting.
Guys—
So it's like, aliens don't go to college?
That's not prejudice, that's just me trying to get information.
I understand.
No, Deb, they—*we* don't go to college.
We undergo an ***initiation.***

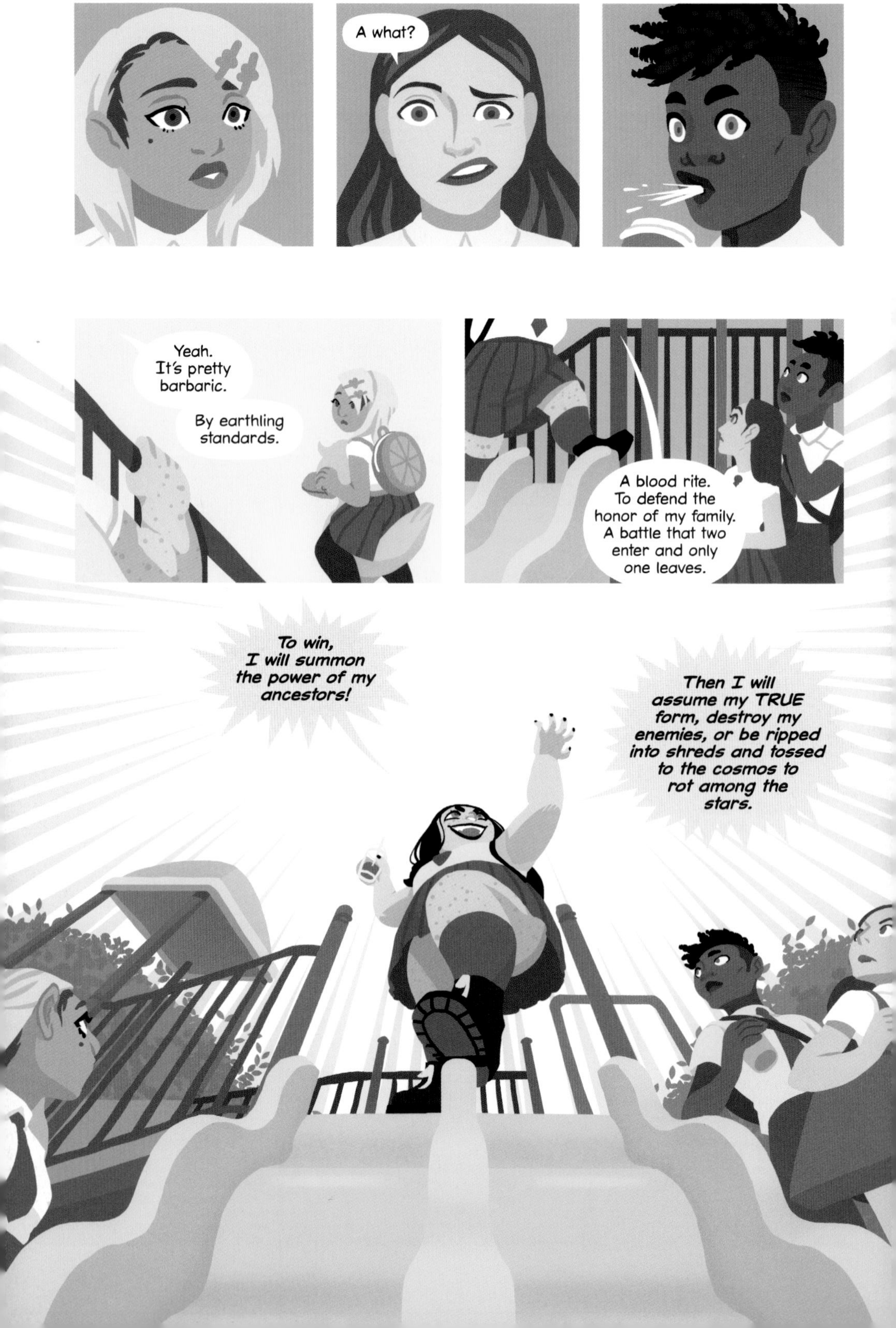
A what?
Yeah. It's pretty barbaric.
By earthling standards.
A blood rite. To defend the honor of my family. A battle that two enter and only one leaves.
To win, I will summon the power of my ancestors!
Then I will assume my TRUE form, destroy my enemies, or be ripped into shreds and tossed to the cosmos to rot among the stars.

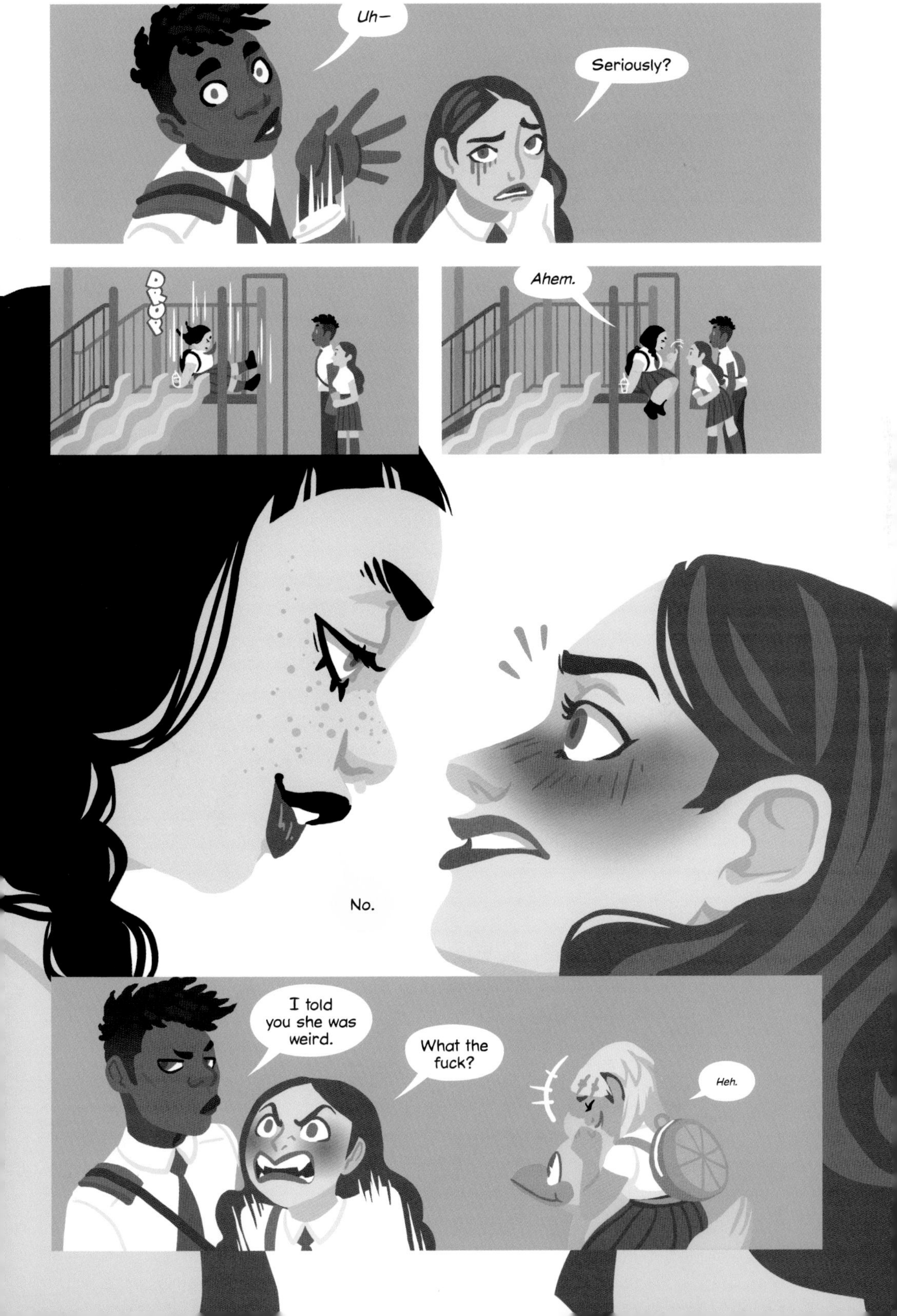
Uh—
Seriously?
DROP
Ahem.
No.
I told you she was weird.
What the fuck?
Heh.

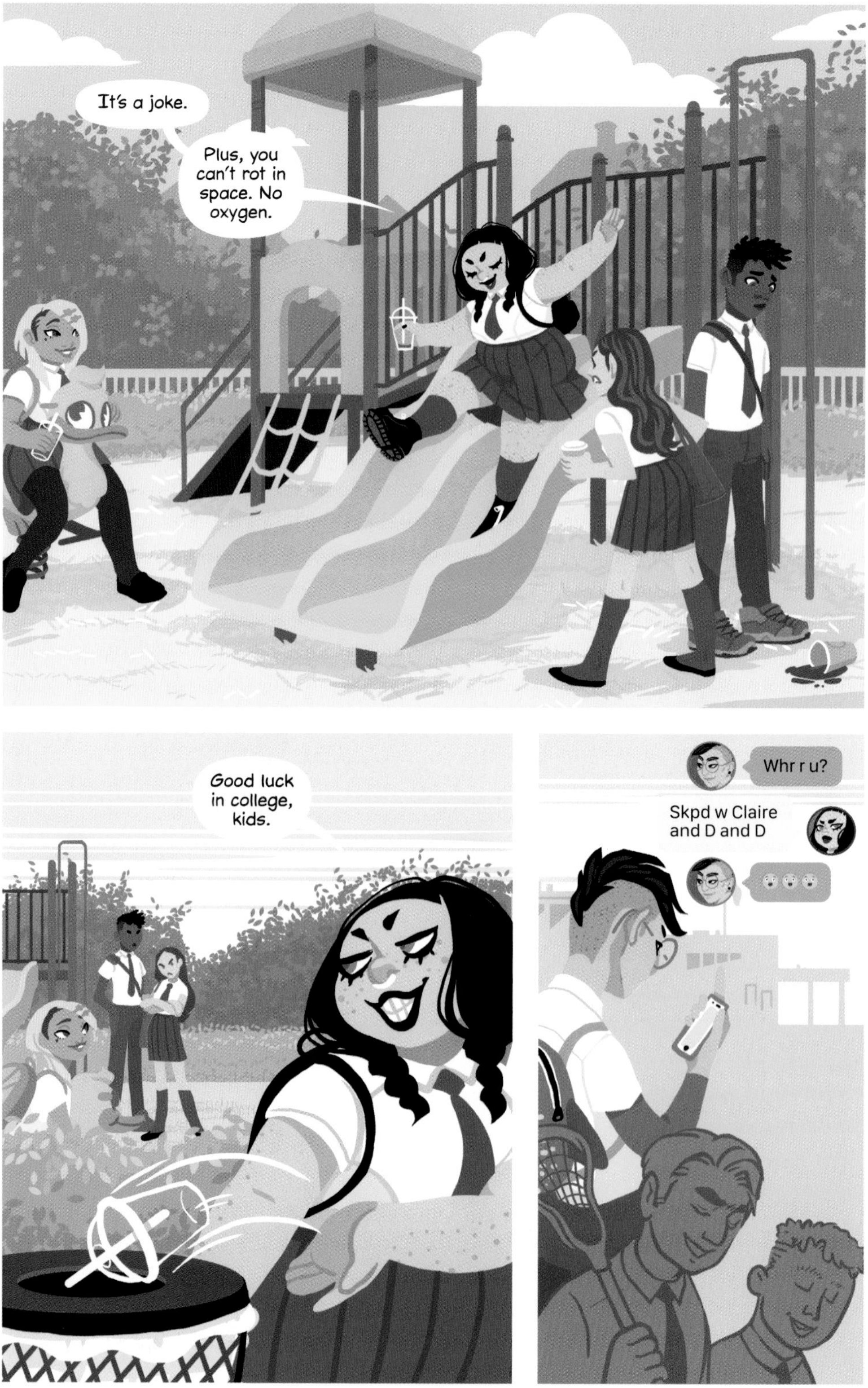
It's a joke.
Plus, you can't rot in space. No oxygen.
Good luck in college, kids.
Whr r u?
Skpd w Claire and D and D

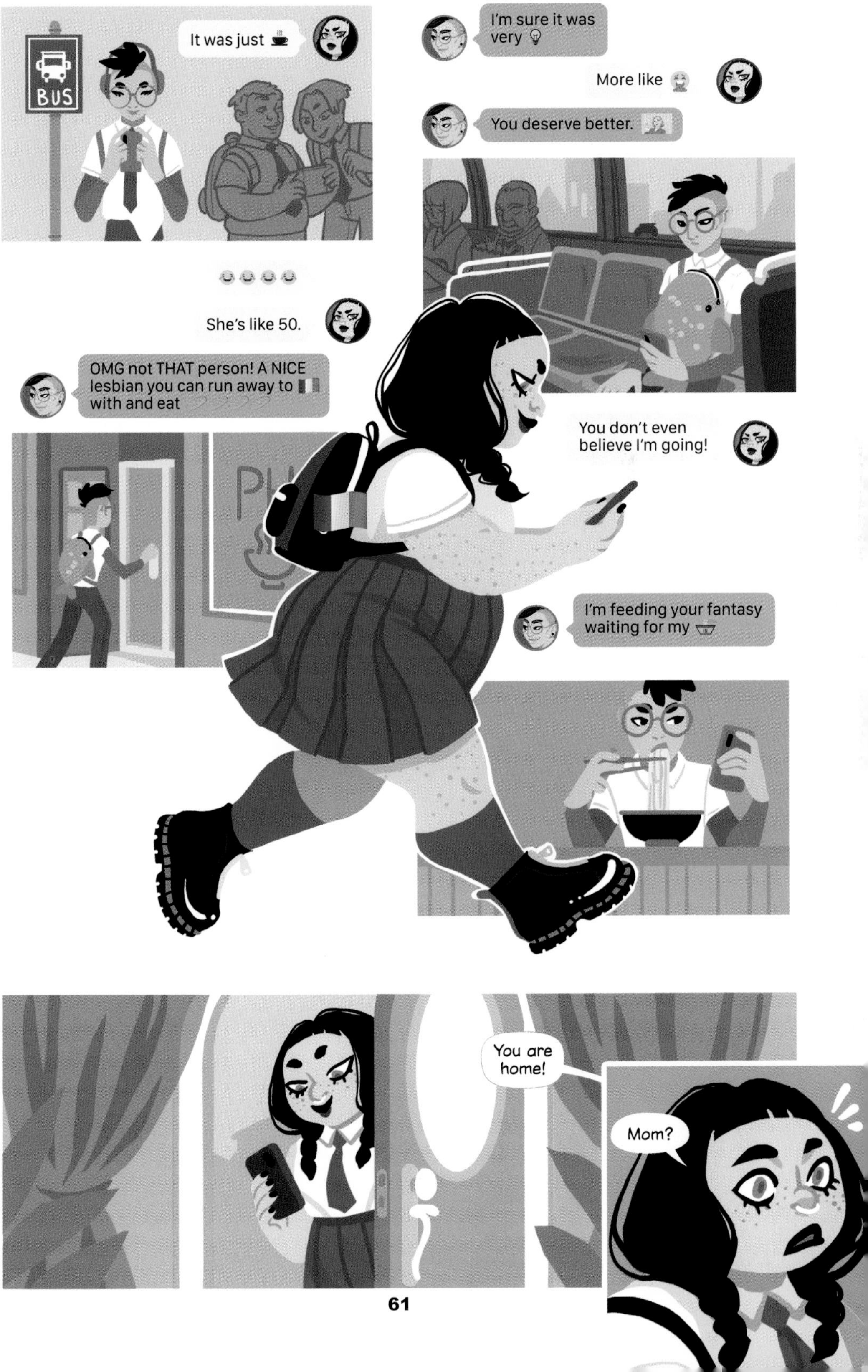

It was just
I'm sure it was very
More like
You deserve better.
She's like 50.
OMG not THAT person! A NICE lesbian you can run away to with and eat
You don't even believe I'm going!
I'm feeding your fantasy waiting for my
BUS
You are home!
Mom?

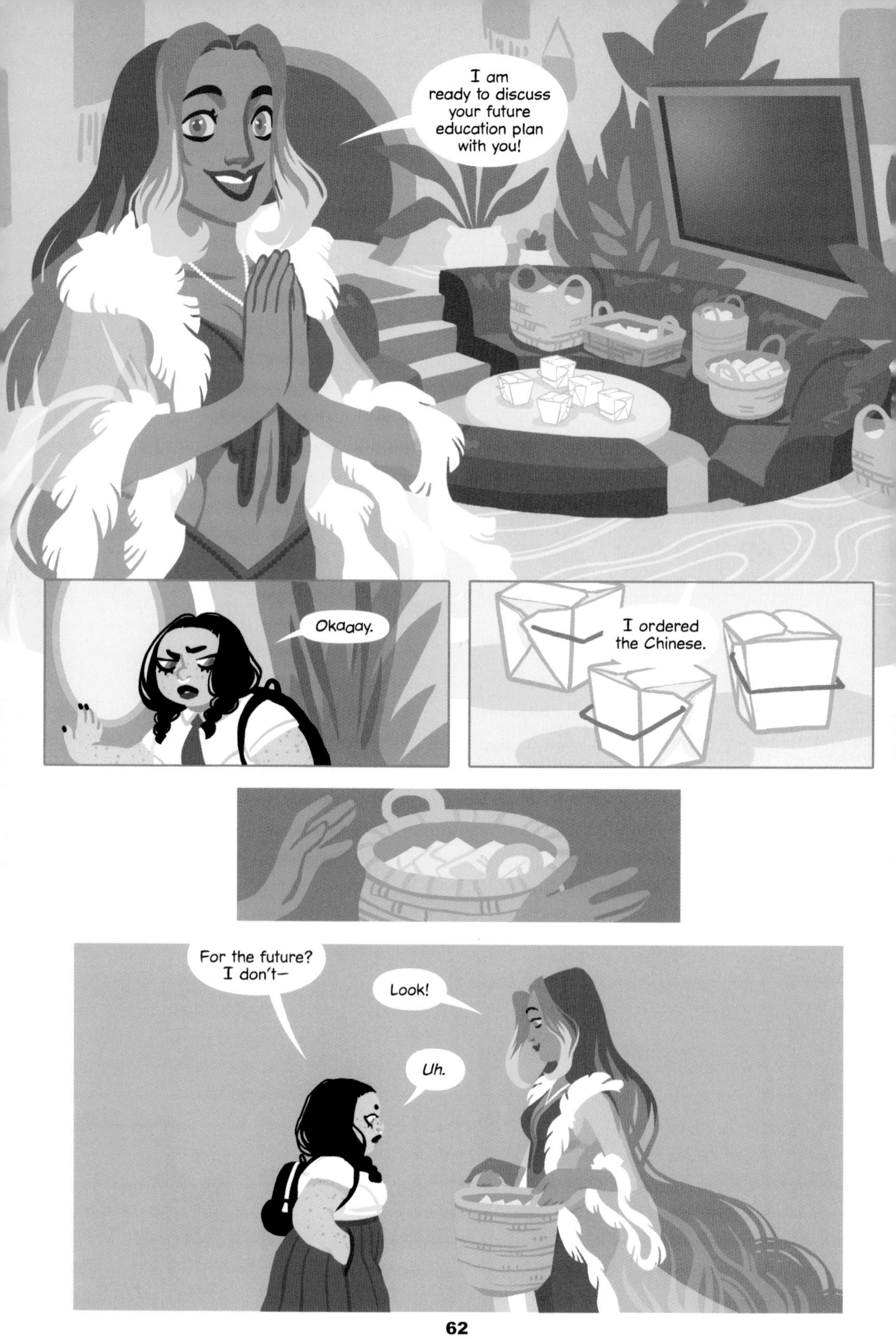
I am ready to discuss your future education plan with you!
Okaaay.
I ordered the Chinese.
For the future? I don't–
Look!
Uh.

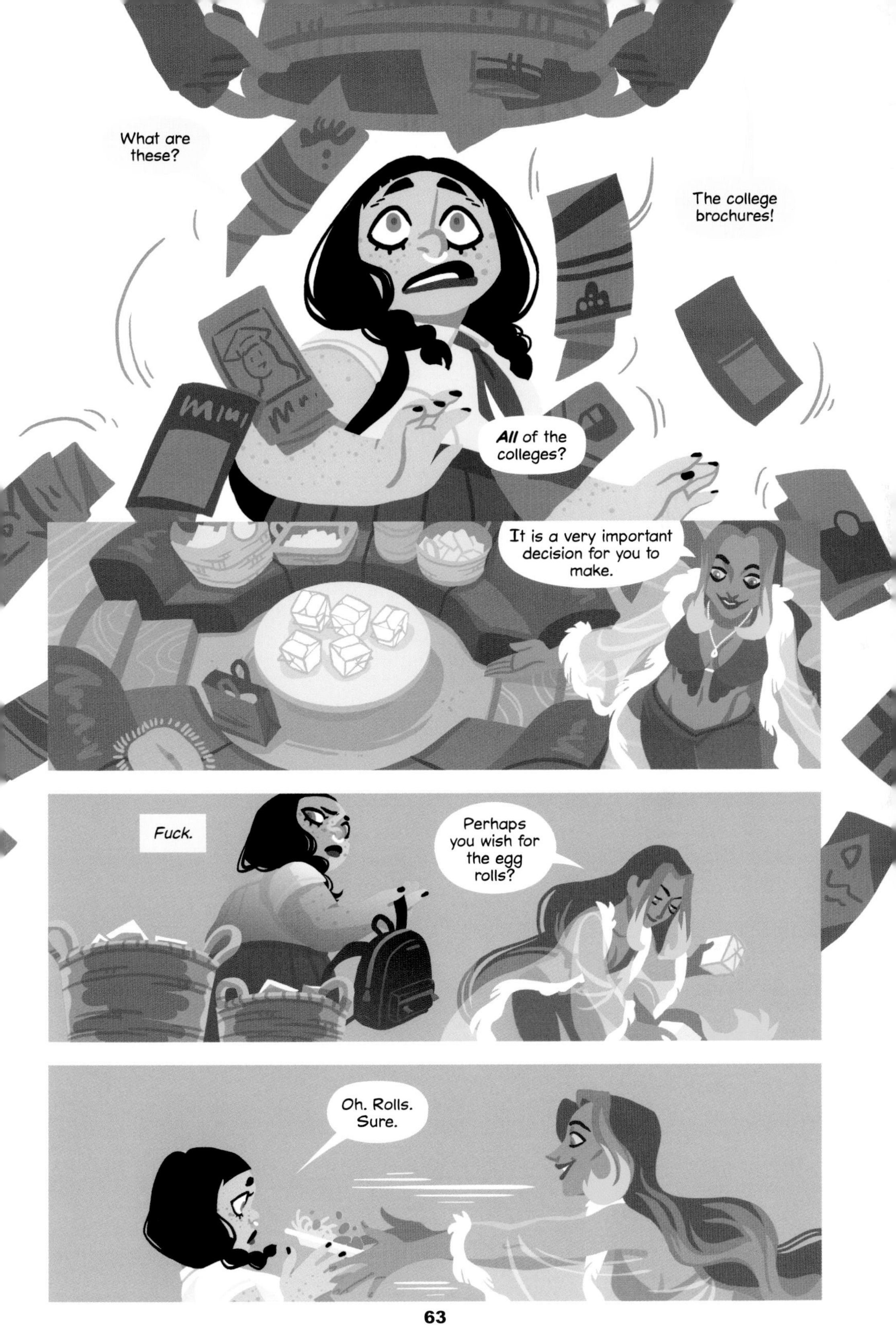
What are these?
The college brochures!
All of the colleges?
It is a very important decision for you to make.
Fuck.
Perhaps you wish for the egg rolls?
Oh. Rolls. Sure.

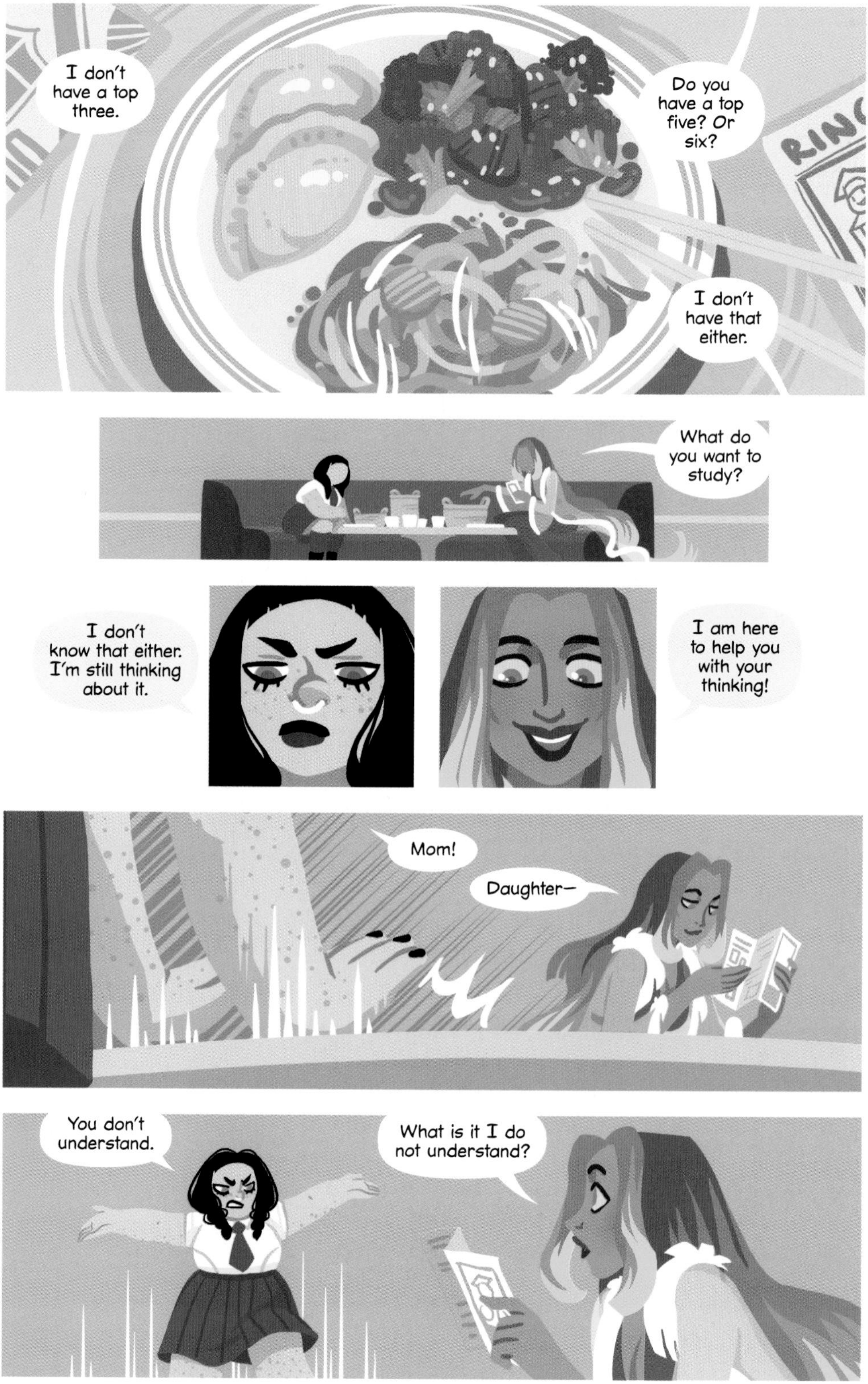
I don't have a top three.
Do you have a top five? Or six?
I don't have that either.
What do you want to study?
I don't know that either. I'm still thinking about it.
I am here to help you with your thinking!
Mom!
Daughter—
You don't understand.
What is it I do not understand?

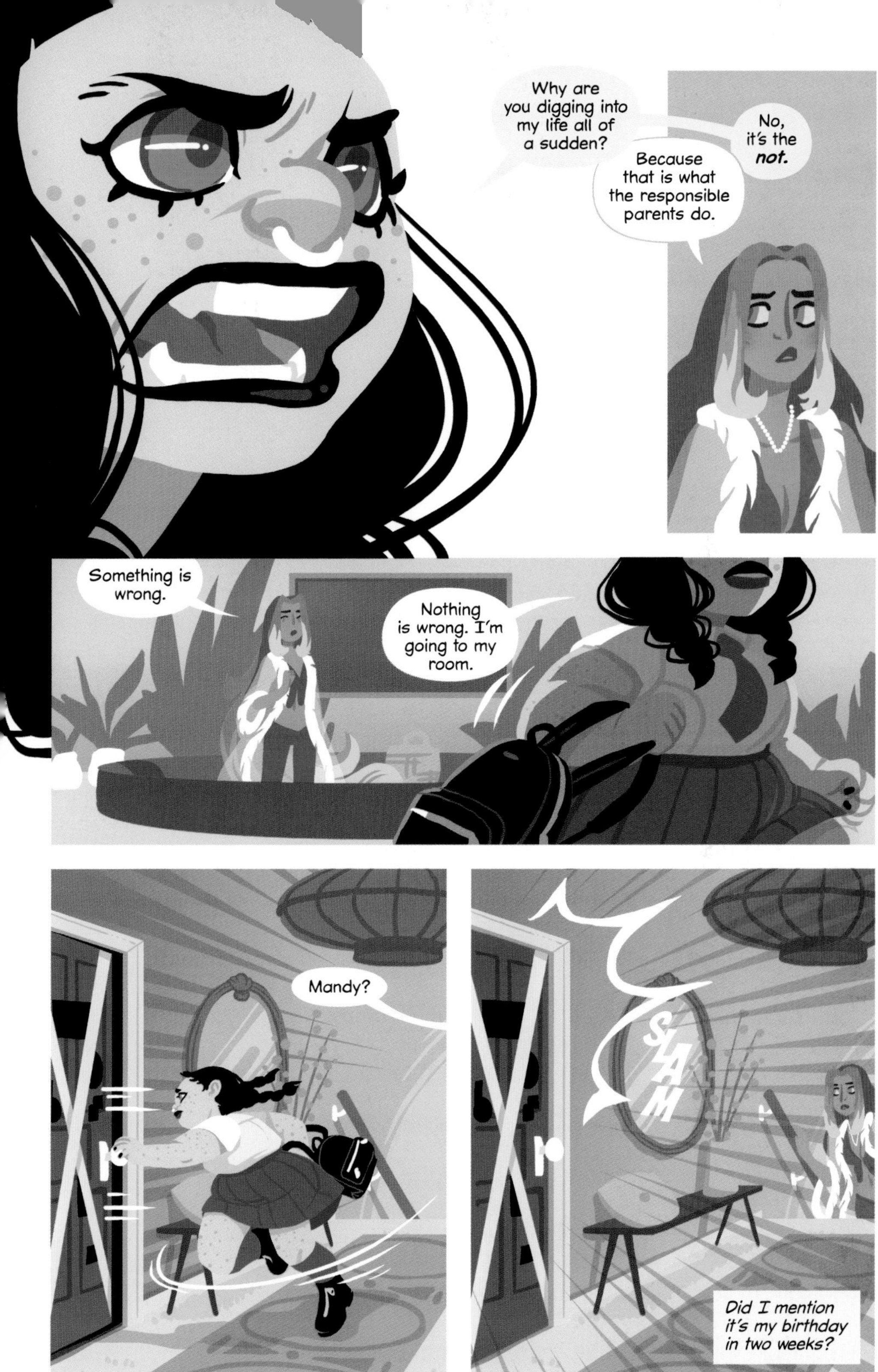
Why are you digging into my life all of a sudden?
Because that is what the responsible parents do.
No, it's the *not.*
Something is wrong.
Nothing is wrong. I'm going to my room.
Mandy?
SLAM
Did I mention it's my birthday in two weeks?

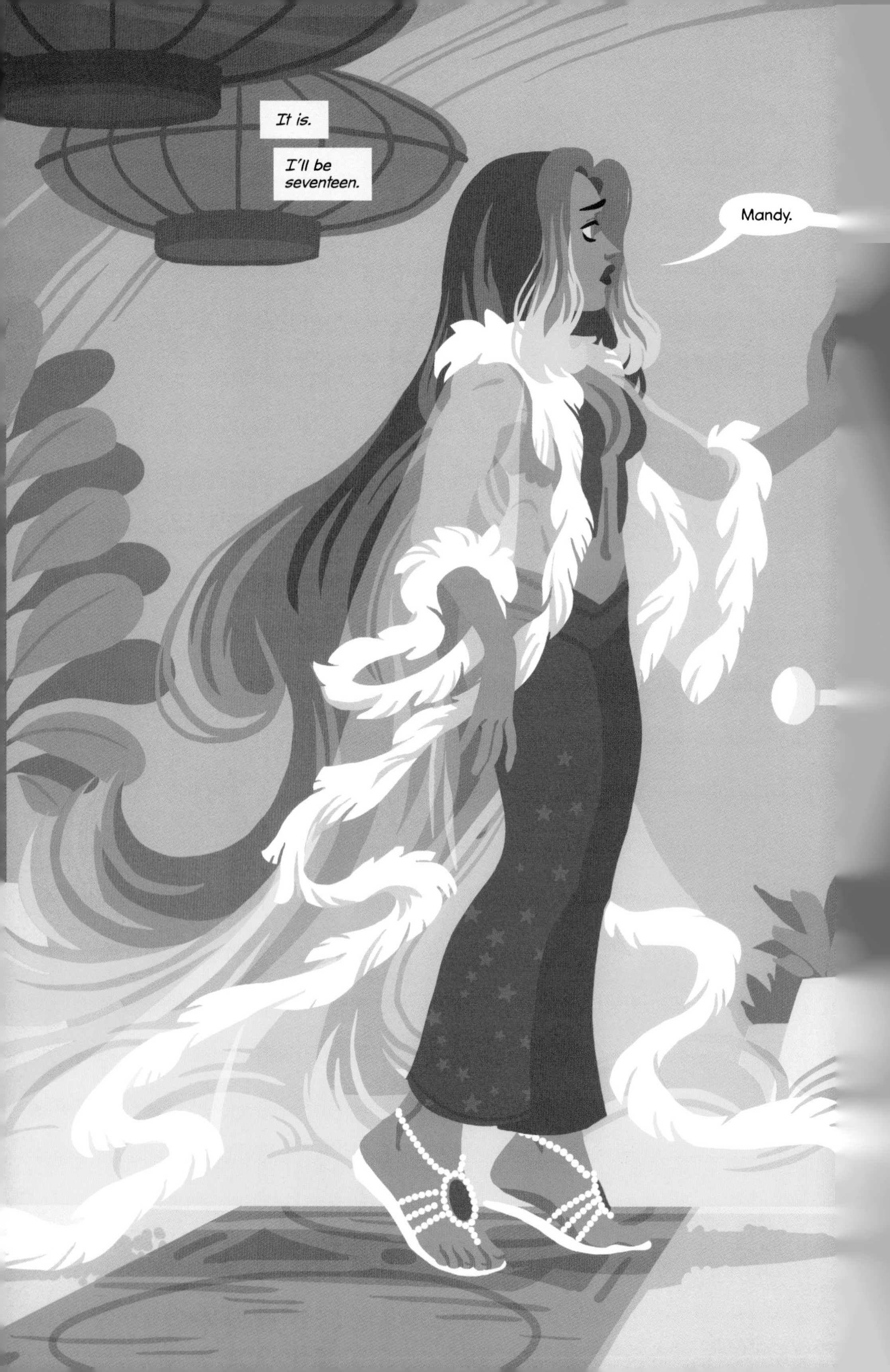
It is.
I'll be seventeen.
Mandy.

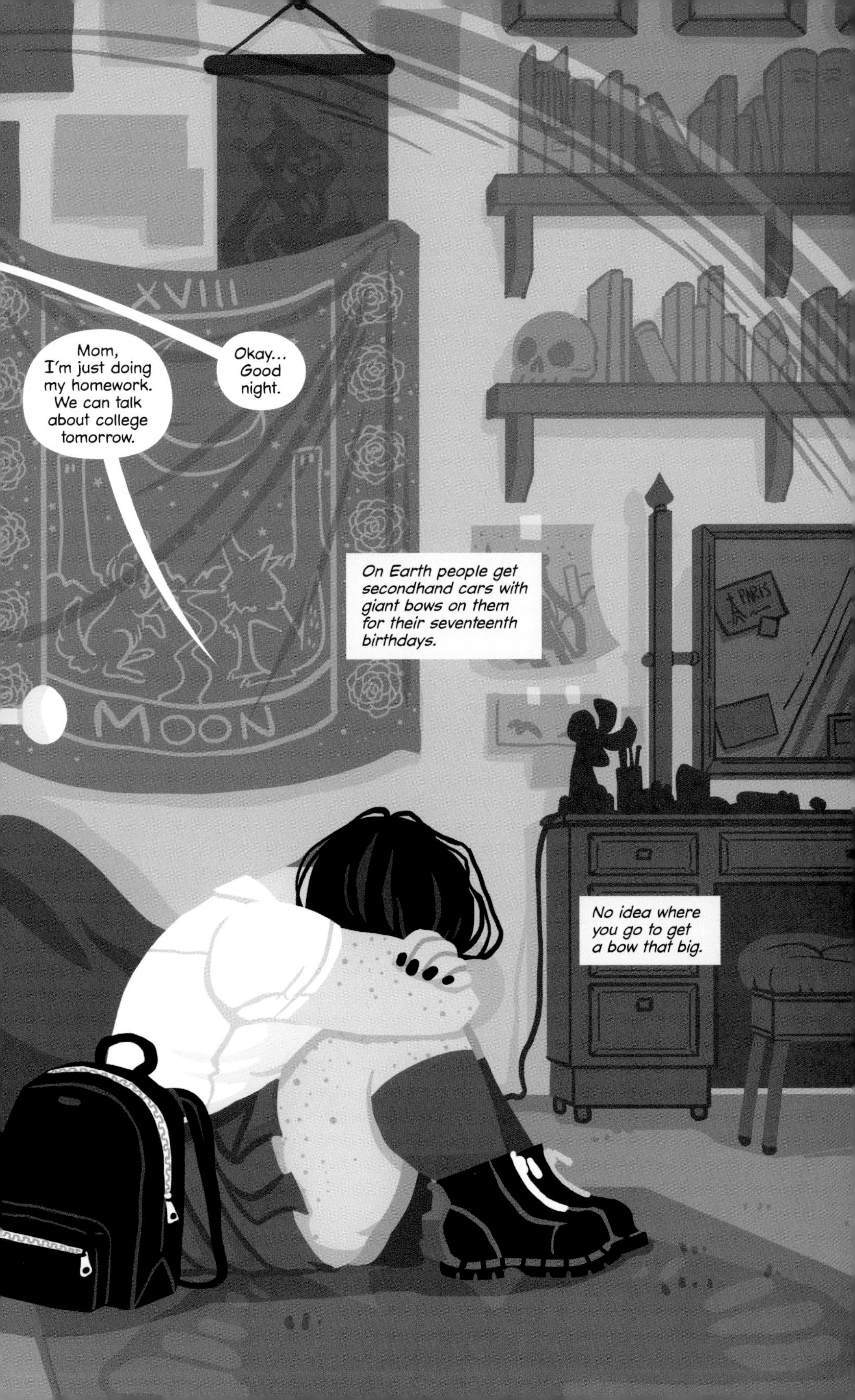
Mom, I'm just doing my homework. We can talk about college tomorrow.
Okay... Good night.
XVIII
MOON
On Earth people get secondhand cars with giant bows on them for their seventeenth birthdays.
PARIS
No idea where you go to get a bow that big.

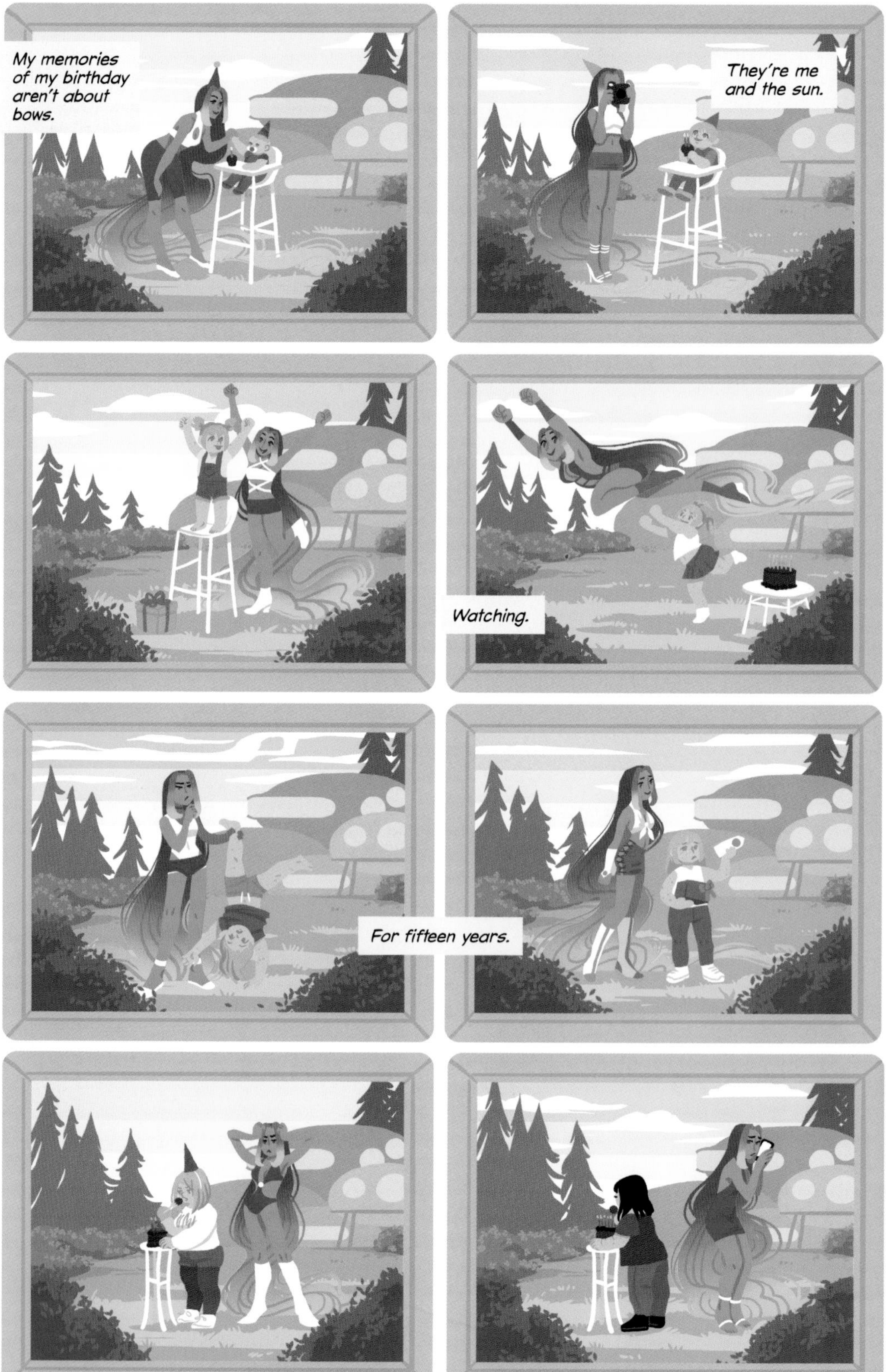
My memories of my birthday aren't about bows.
They're me and the sun.
Watching.
For fifteen years.

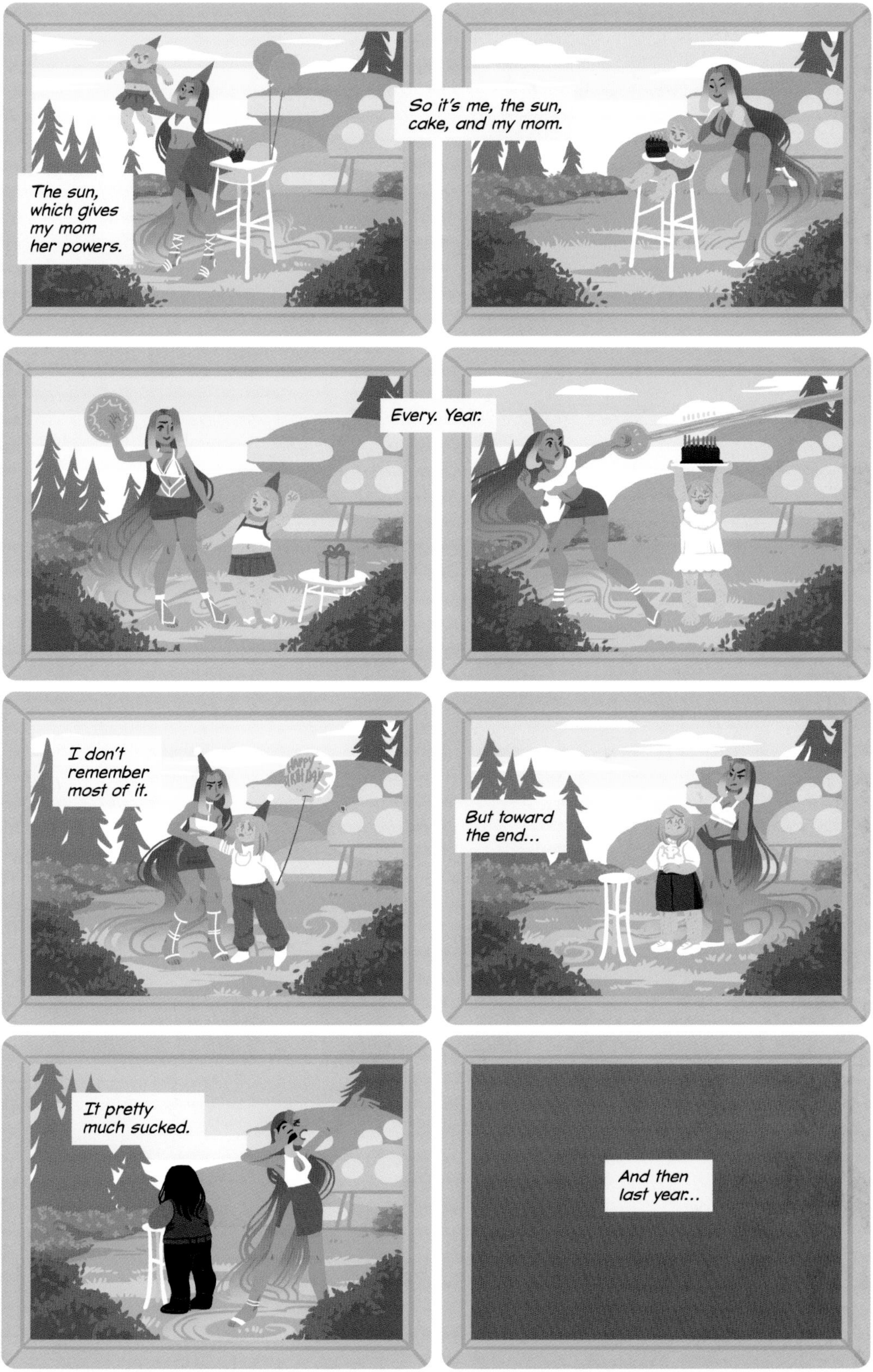
The sun, which gives my mom her powers.
So it's me, the sun, cake, and my mom.
Every. Year.
I don't remember most of it.
But toward the end...
It pretty much sucked.
And then last year...

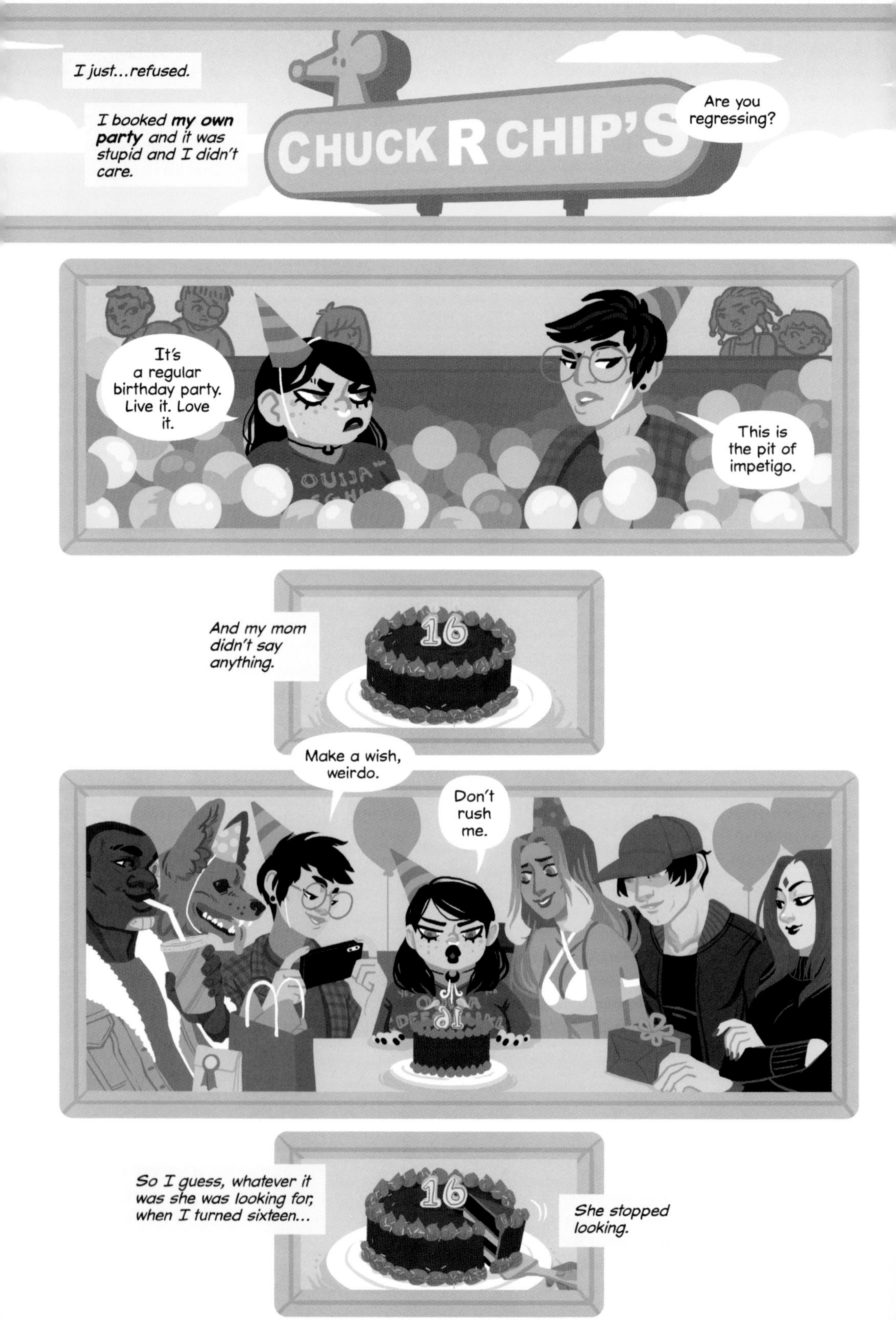

I just...refused.
I booked **my own party** and it was stupid and I didn't care.
CHUCK R CHIP'S
Are you regressing?
It's a regular birthday party. Live it. Love it.
This is the pit of impetigo.
And my mom didn't say anything.
16
Make a wish, weirdo.
Don't rush me.
So I guess, whatever it was she was looking for, when I turned sixteen...
16
She stopped looking.

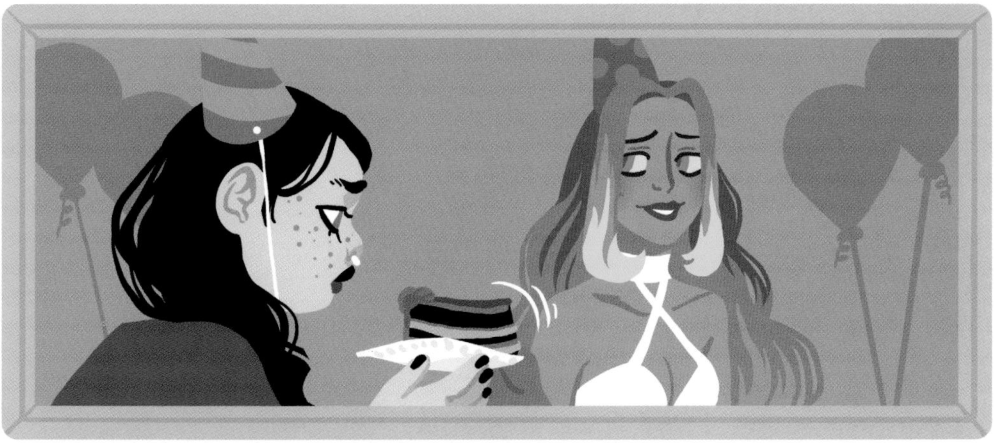

I don't actually know anything about how people on my mother's home planet, my motherland, celebrate birthdays.

If they even have birthdays...

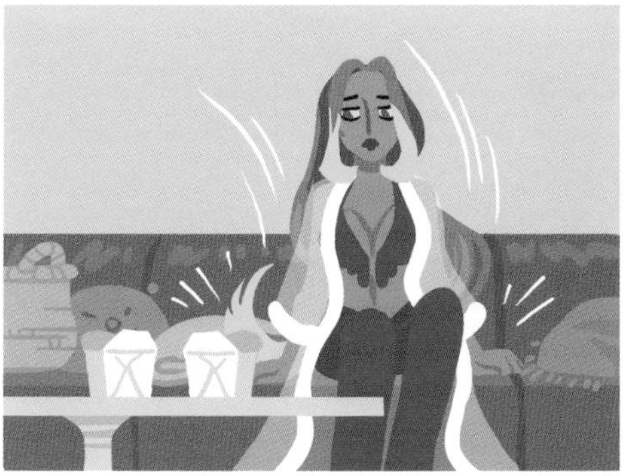

Since they probably don't have regular Earth years.

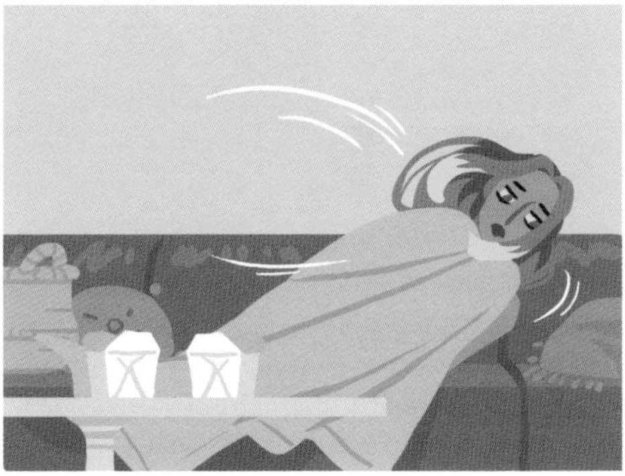

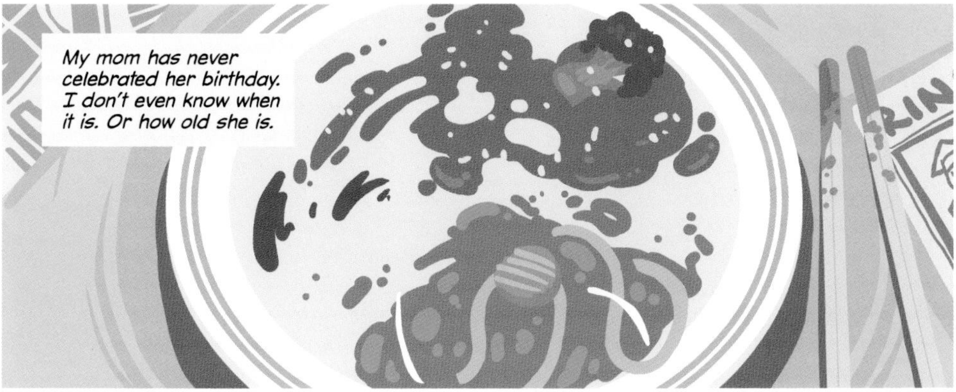
My mom has never celebrated her birthday. I don't even know when it is. Or how old she is.

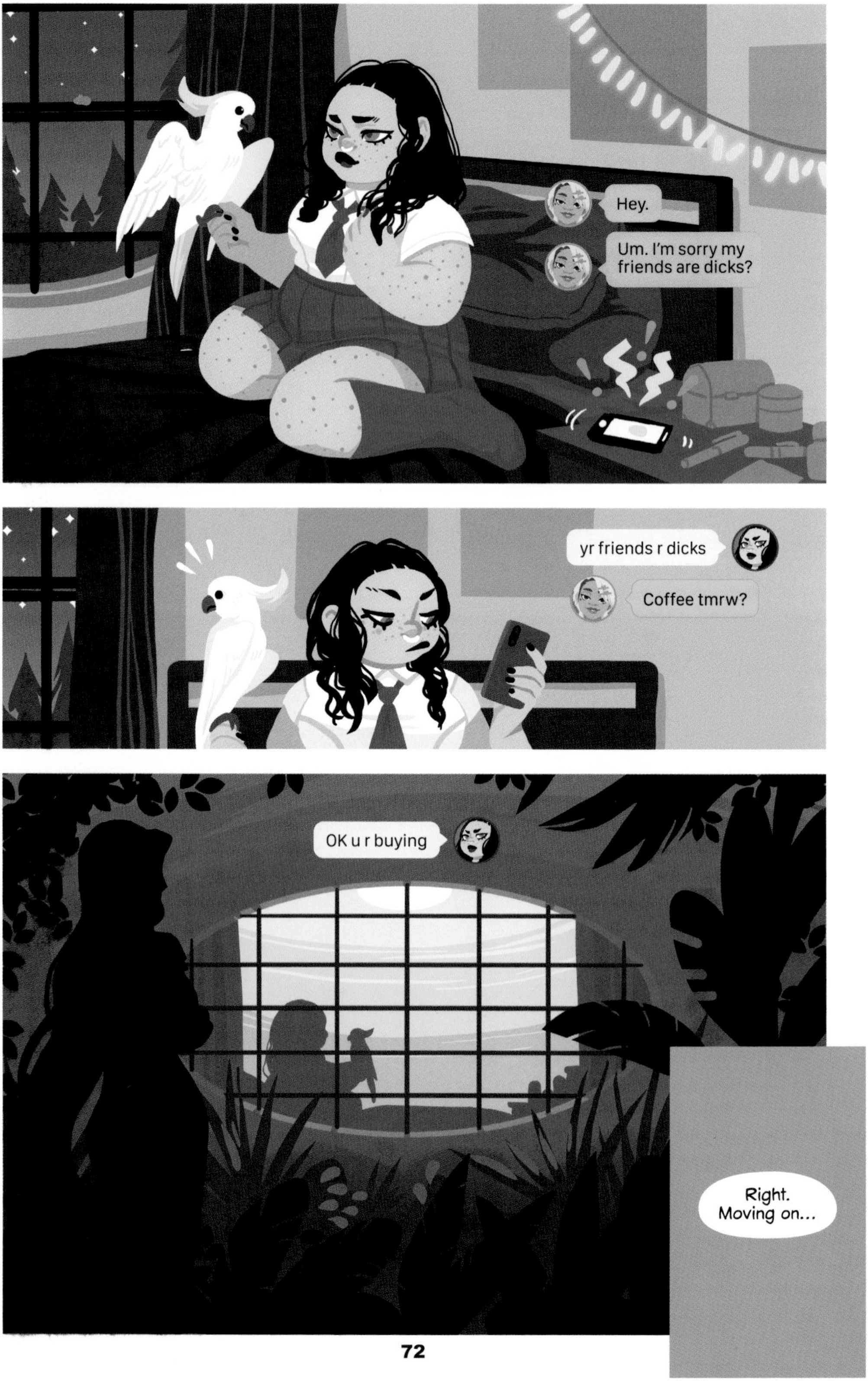
Hey.
Um. I'm sorry my friends are dicks?
yr friends r dicks
Coffee tmrw?
OK u r buying
Right. Moving on...

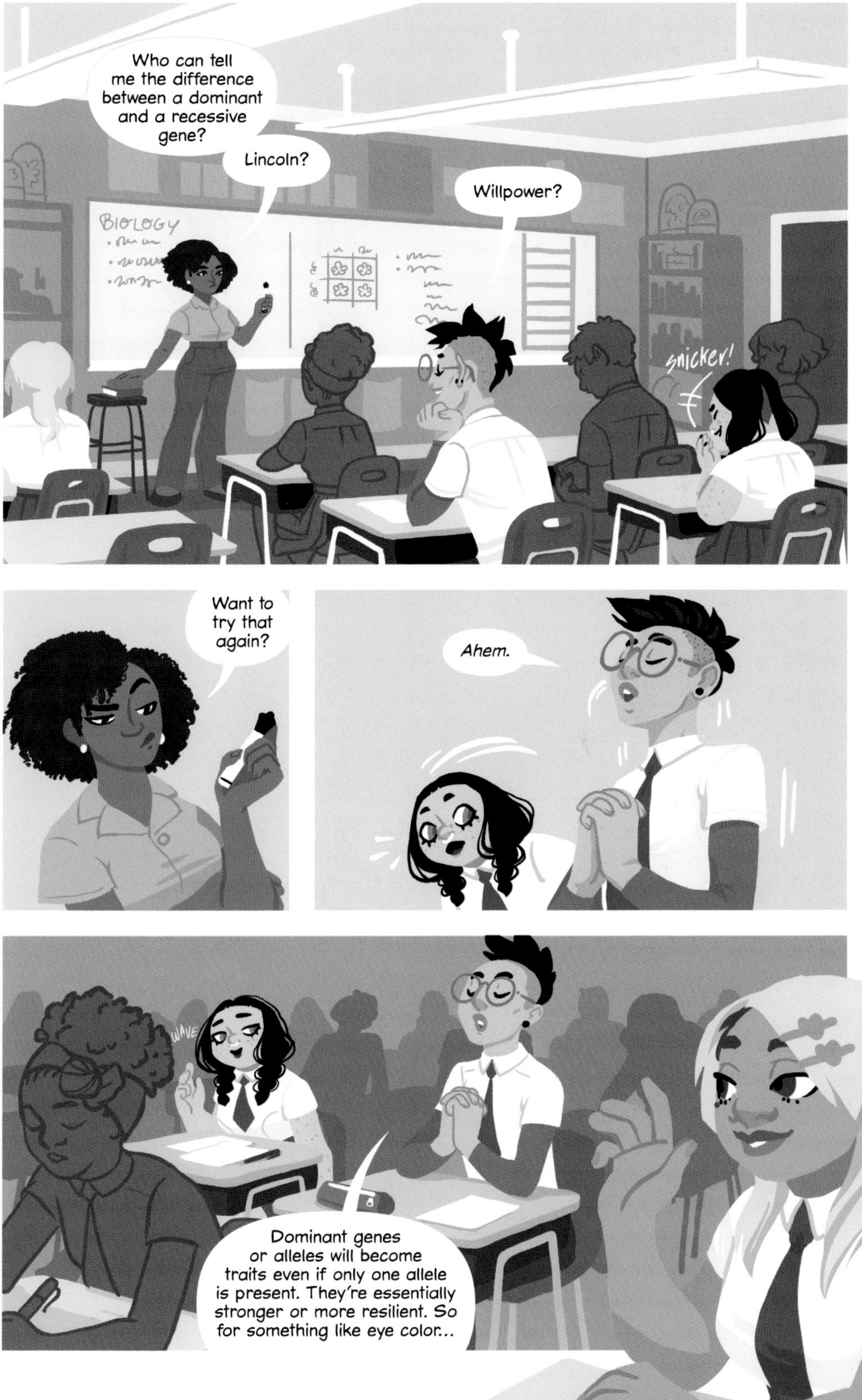
Who can tell me the difference between a dominant and a recessive gene?
Lincoln?
Willpower?
BIOLOGY
SNICKER!
Want to try that again?
Ahem.
WAVE
Dominant genes or alleles will become traits even if only one allele is present. They're essentially stronger or more resilient. So for something like eye color...

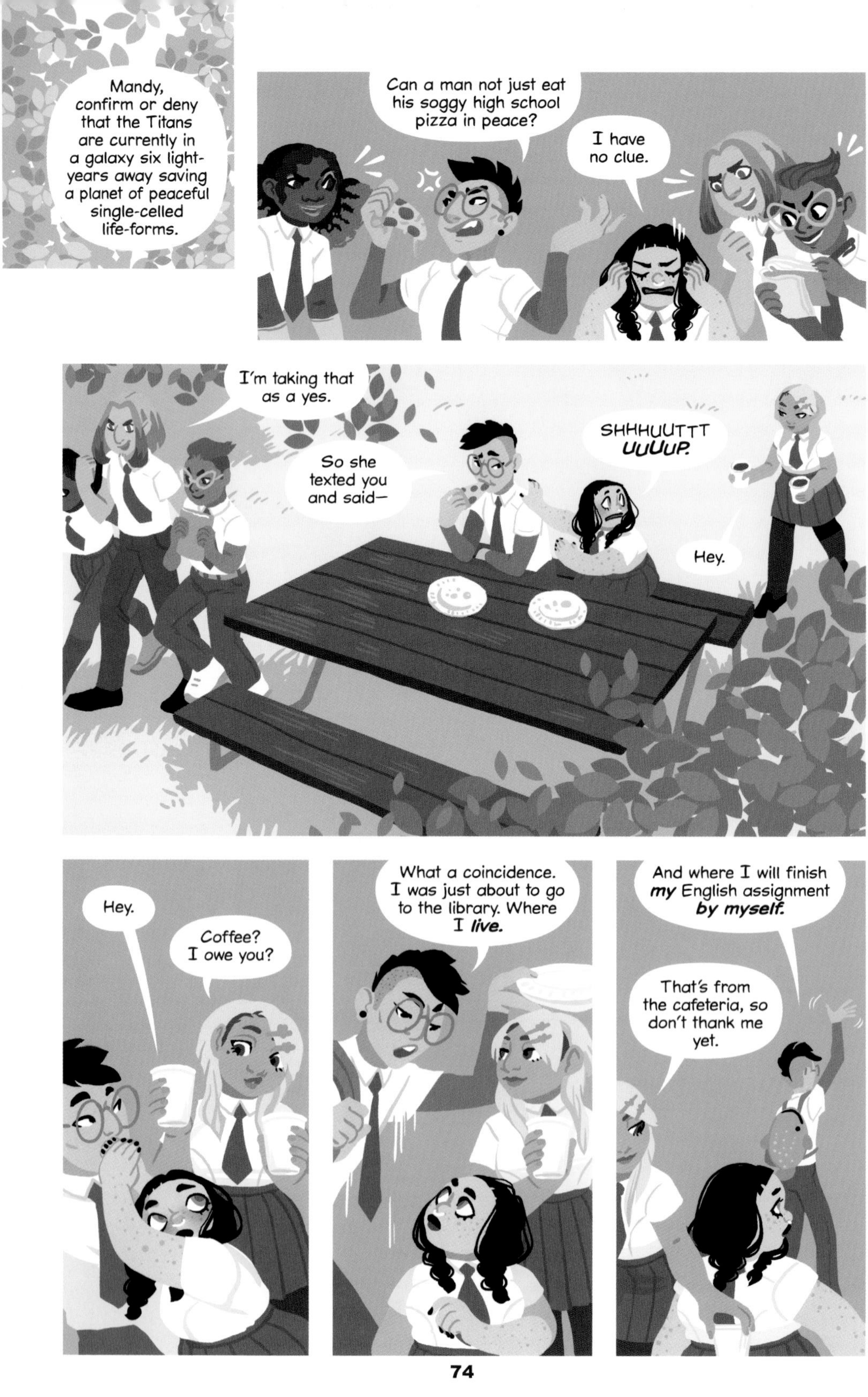

Mandy, confirm or deny that the Titans are currently in a galaxy six light-years away saving a planet of peaceful single-celled life-forms.
Can a man not just eat his soggy high school pizza in peace?
I have no clue.
I'm taking that as a yes.
So she texted you and said—
SHHHUUTTT UUUUP.
Hey.
Hey.
Coffee? I owe you?
What a coincidence. I was just about to go to the library. Where I *live.*
And where I will finish ***my*** English assignment ***by myself.***
That's from the cafeteria, so don't thank me yet.

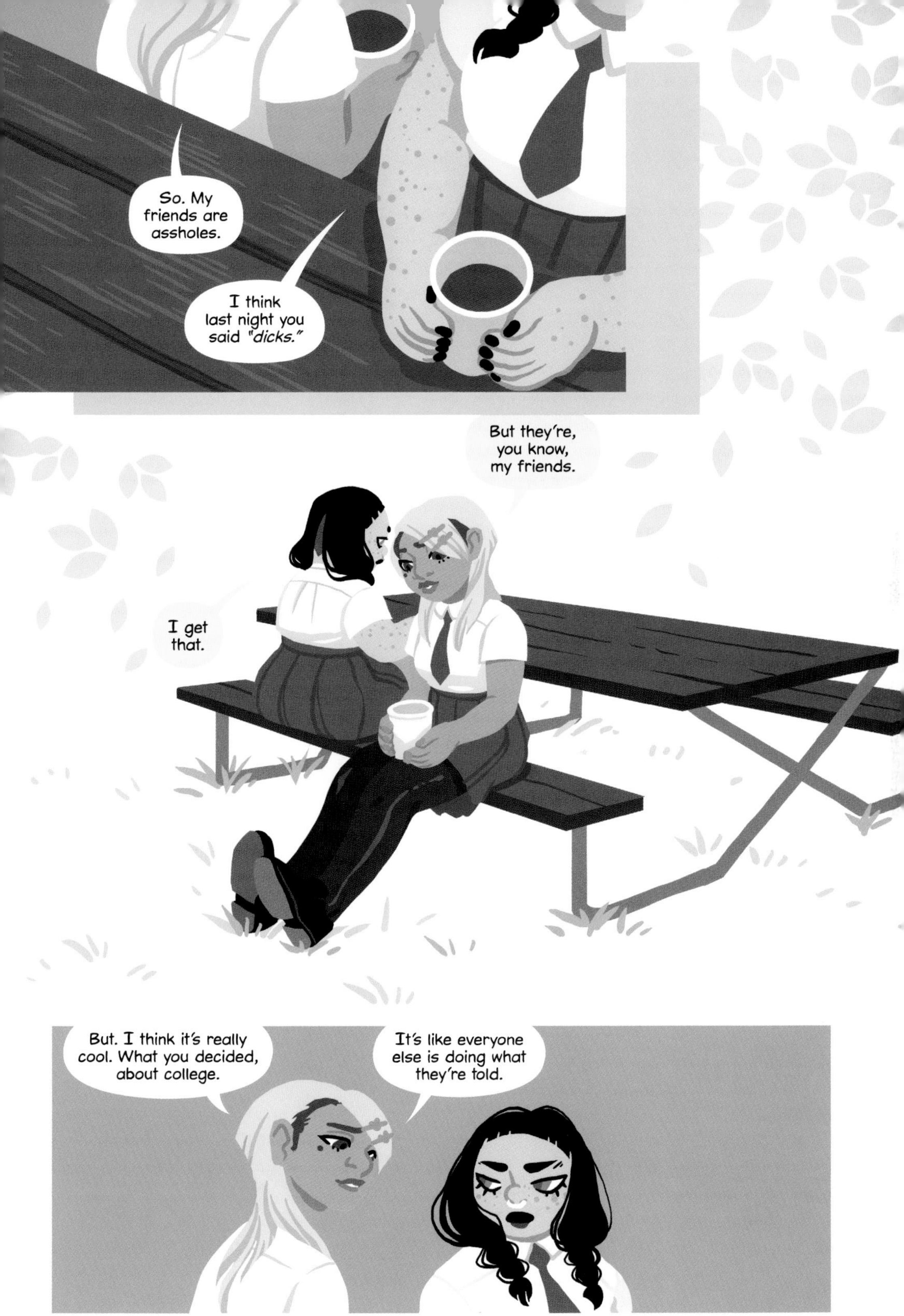
So. My friends are assholes.
I think last night you said *"dicks."*
But they're, you know, my friends.
I get that.
But. I think it's really cool. What you decided, about college.
It's like everyone else is doing what they're told.

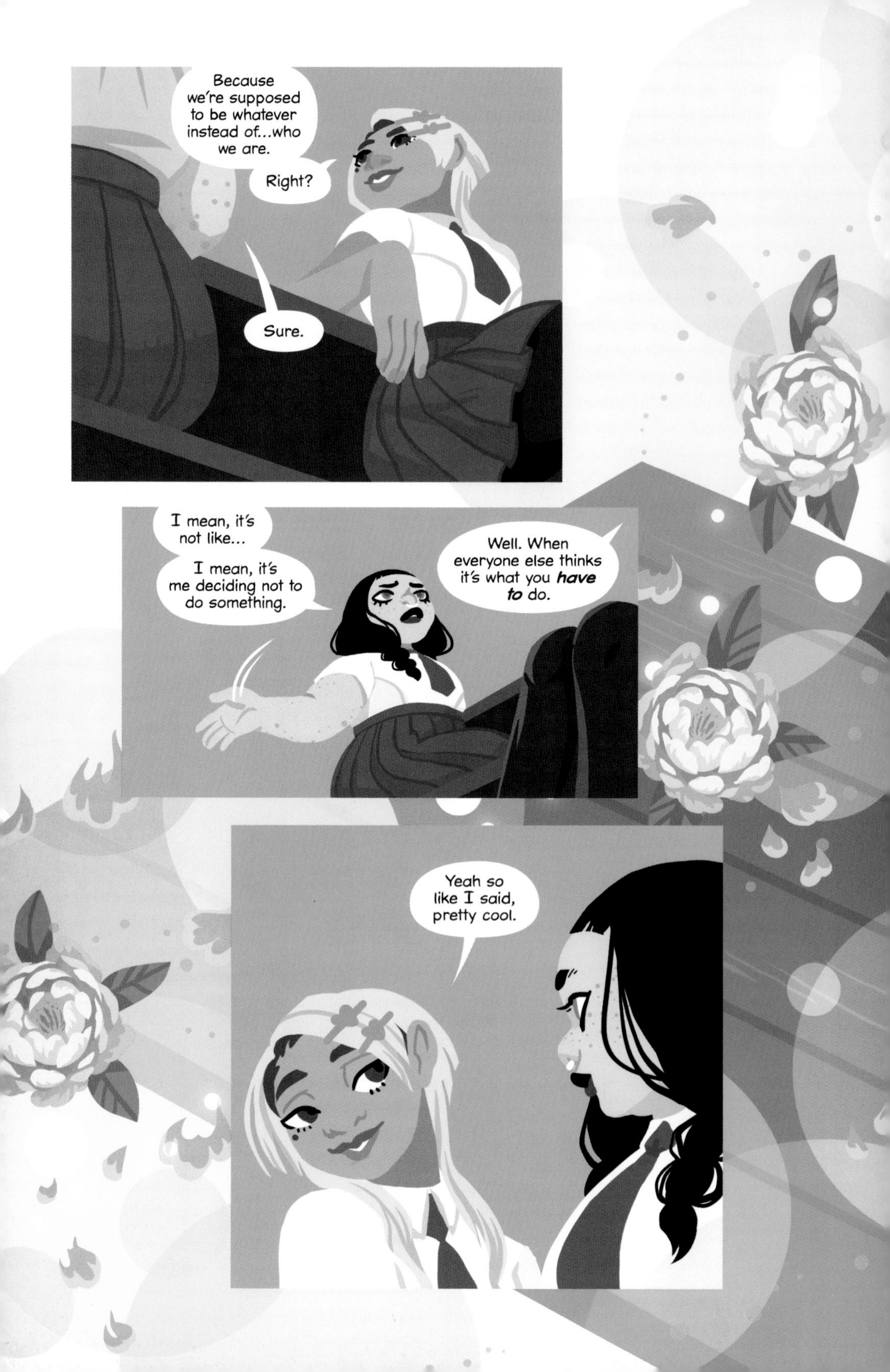
Because we're supposed to be whatever instead of...who we are.
Right?
Sure.
I mean, it's not like...
I mean, it's me deciding not to do something.
Well. When everyone else thinks it's what you *have to* do.
Yeah so like I said, pretty cool.

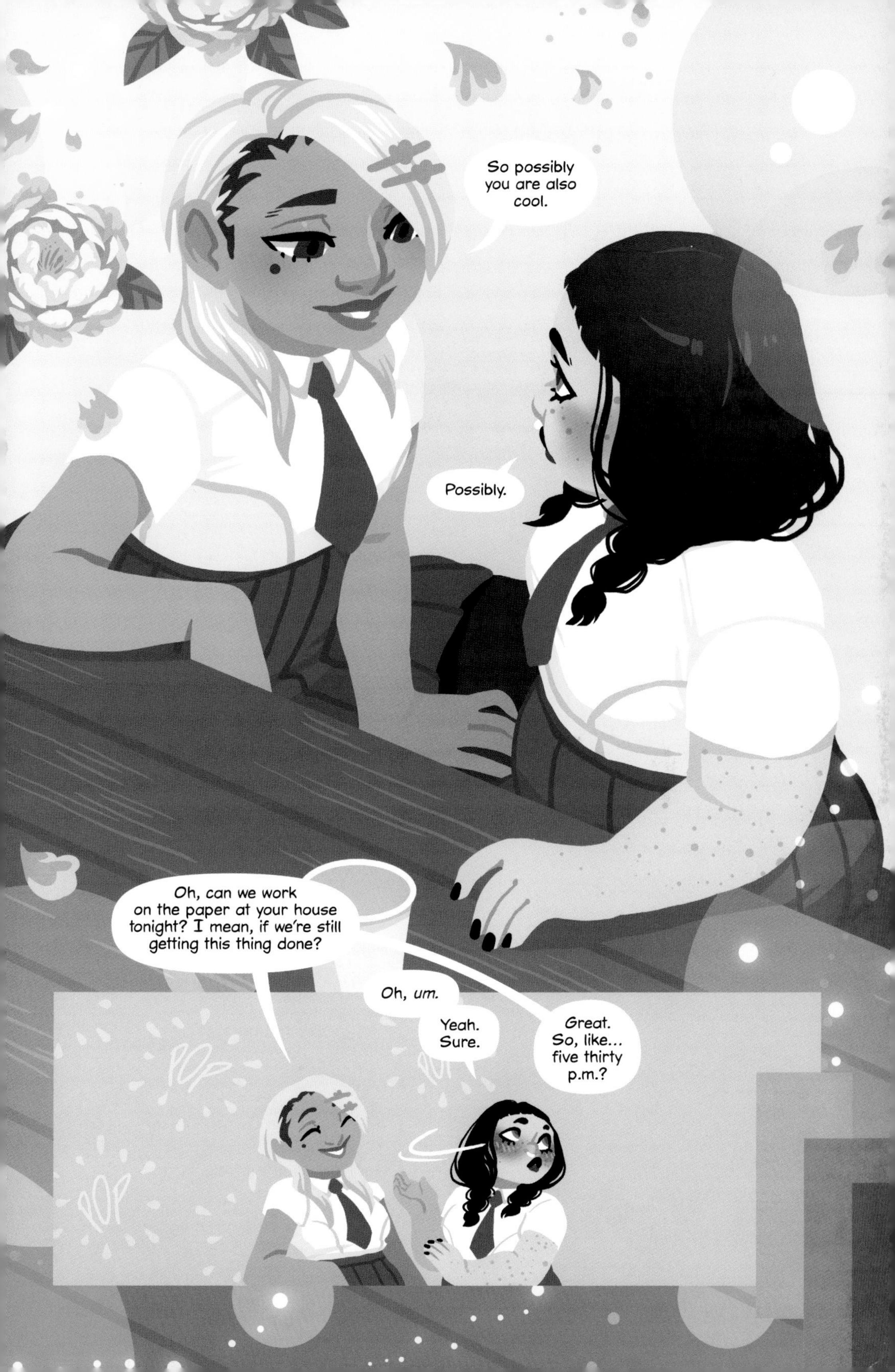
So possibly you are also cool.
Possibly.
Oh, can we work on the paper at your house tonight? I mean, if we're still getting this thing done?
Oh, *um.*
Yeah. Sure.
Great. So, like... five thirty p.m.?
POP
POP
POP

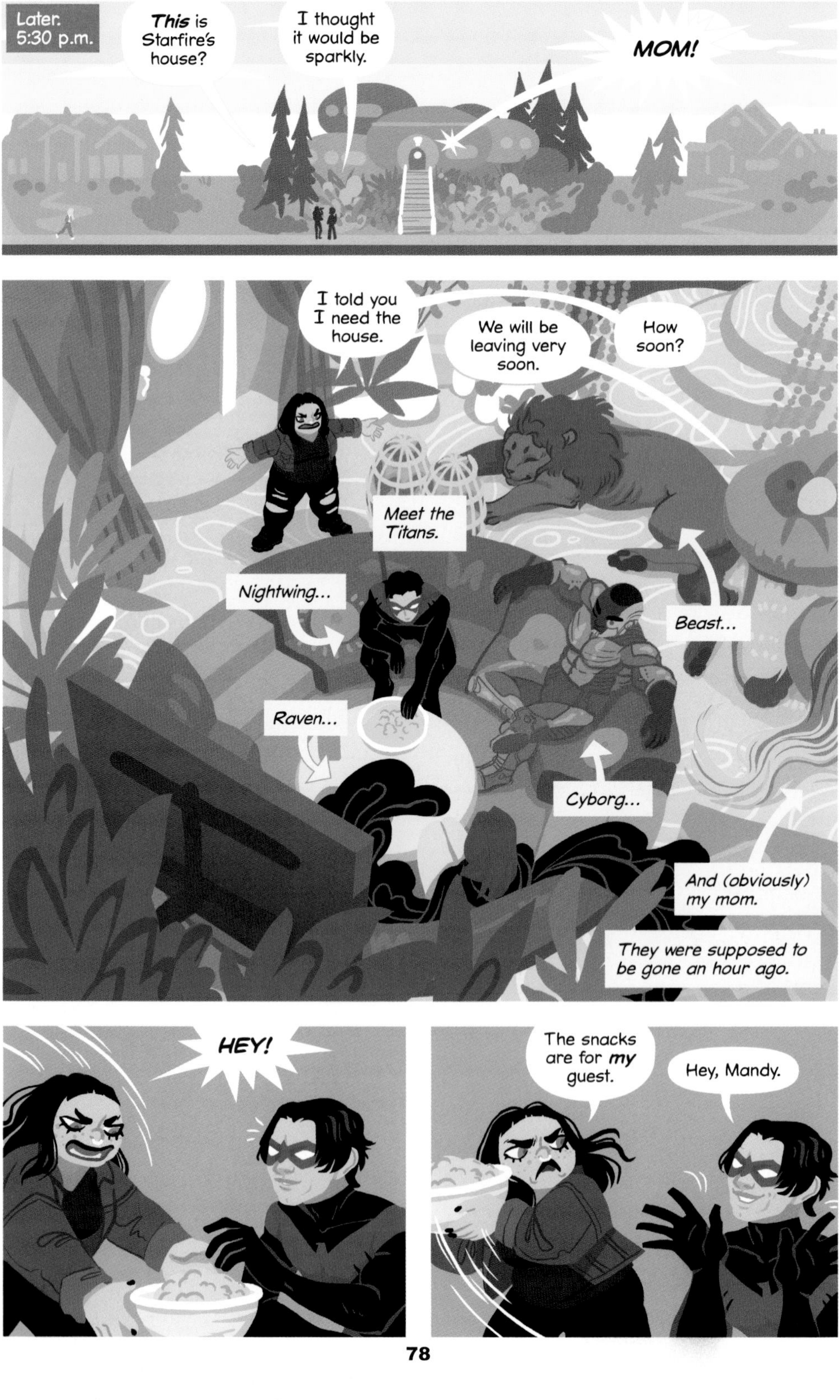
Later. 5:30 p.m.
This is Starfire's house?
I thought it would be sparkly.
MOM!
I told you I need the house.
We will be leaving very soon.
How soon?
Meet the Titans.
Nightwing...
Beast...
Raven...
Cyborg...
And (obviously) my mom.
They were supposed to be gone an hour ago.
HEY!
The snacks are for my guest.
Hey, Mandy.

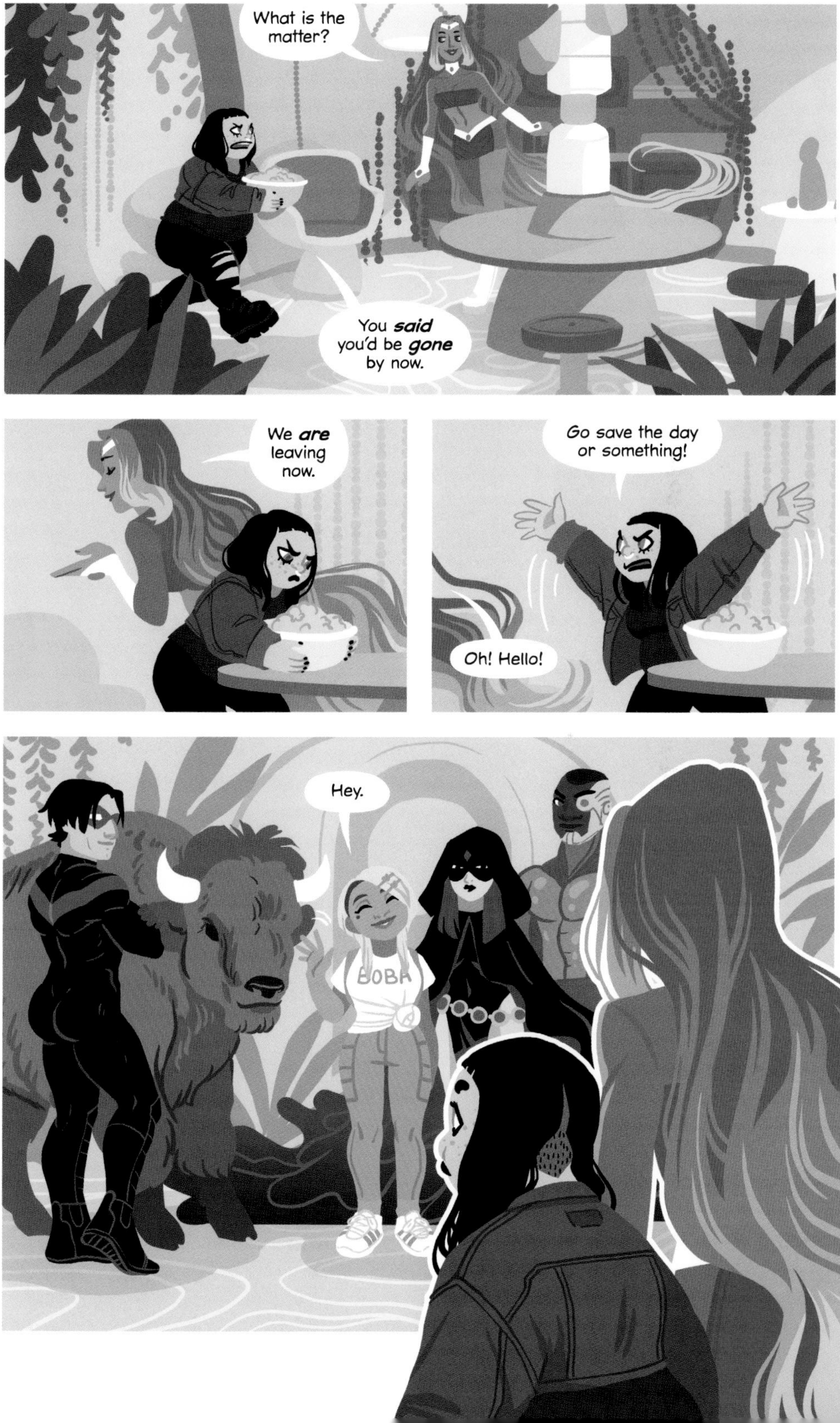
What is the matter?
You *said* you'd be *gone* by now.
We *are* leaving now.
Go save the day or something!
Oh! Hello!
Hey.
BOBA

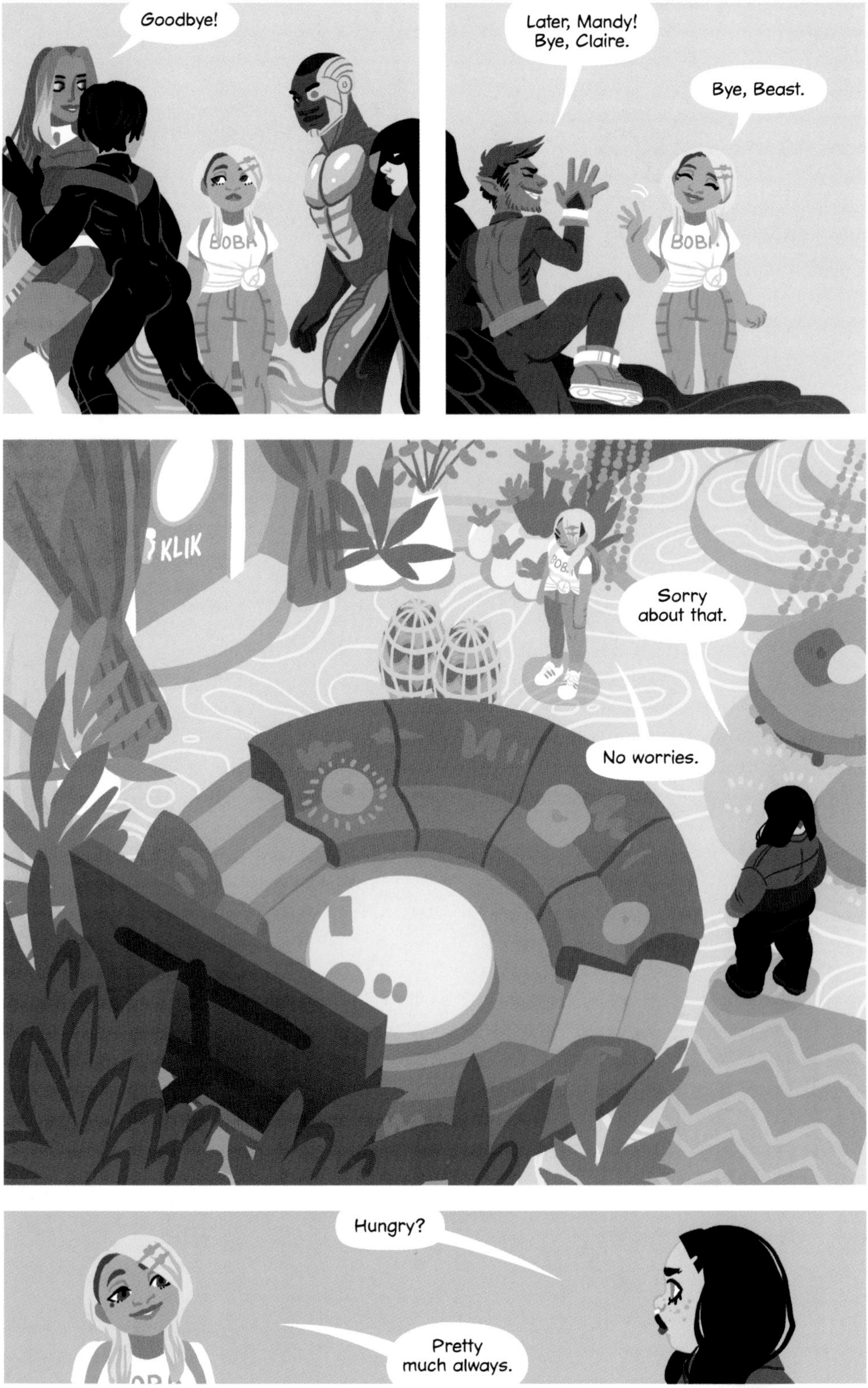
Goodbye!
Later, Mandy! Bye, Claire.
Bye, Beast.
KLIK
Sorry about that.
No worries.
Hungry?
Pretty much always.

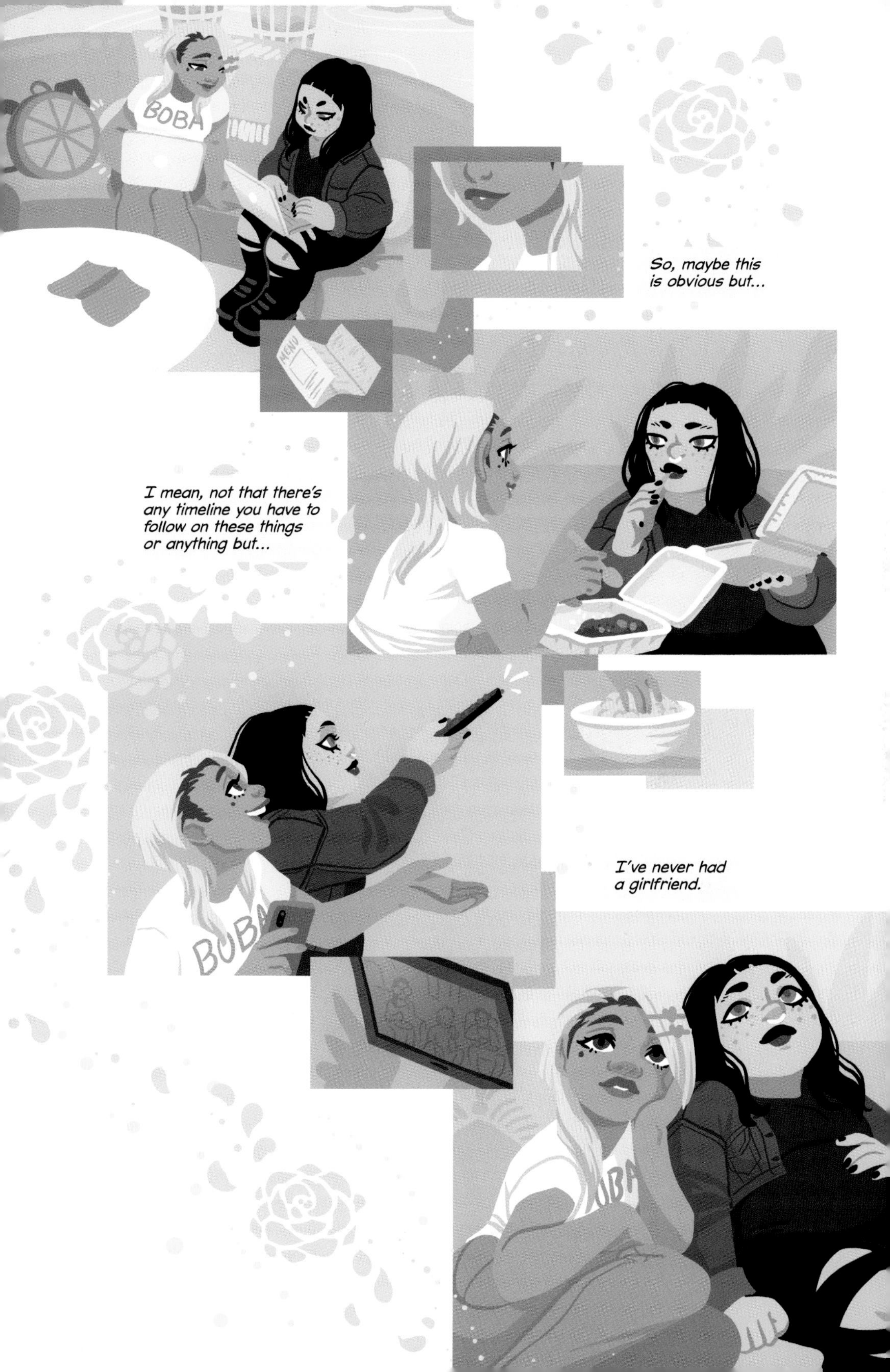
BOBA
So, maybe this is obvious but...
MENU
I mean, not that there's any timeline you have to follow on these things or anything but...
BOBA
I've never had a girlfriend.
BOBA

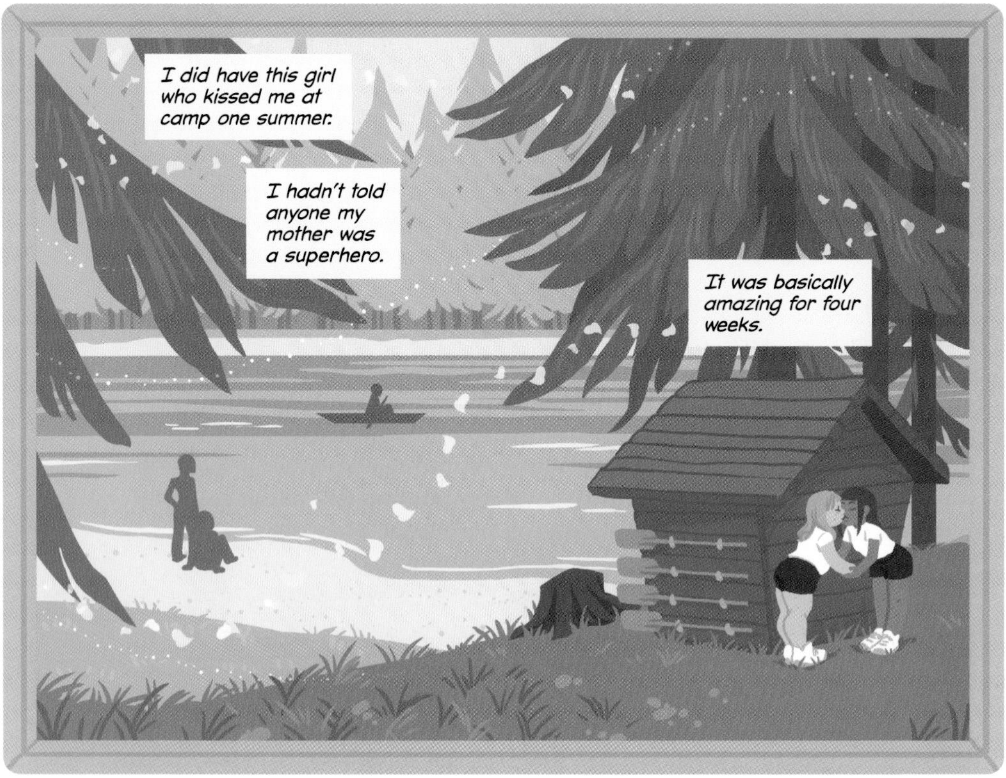
I did have this girl who kissed me at camp one summer.
I hadn't told anyone my mother was a superhero.
It was basically amazing for four weeks.

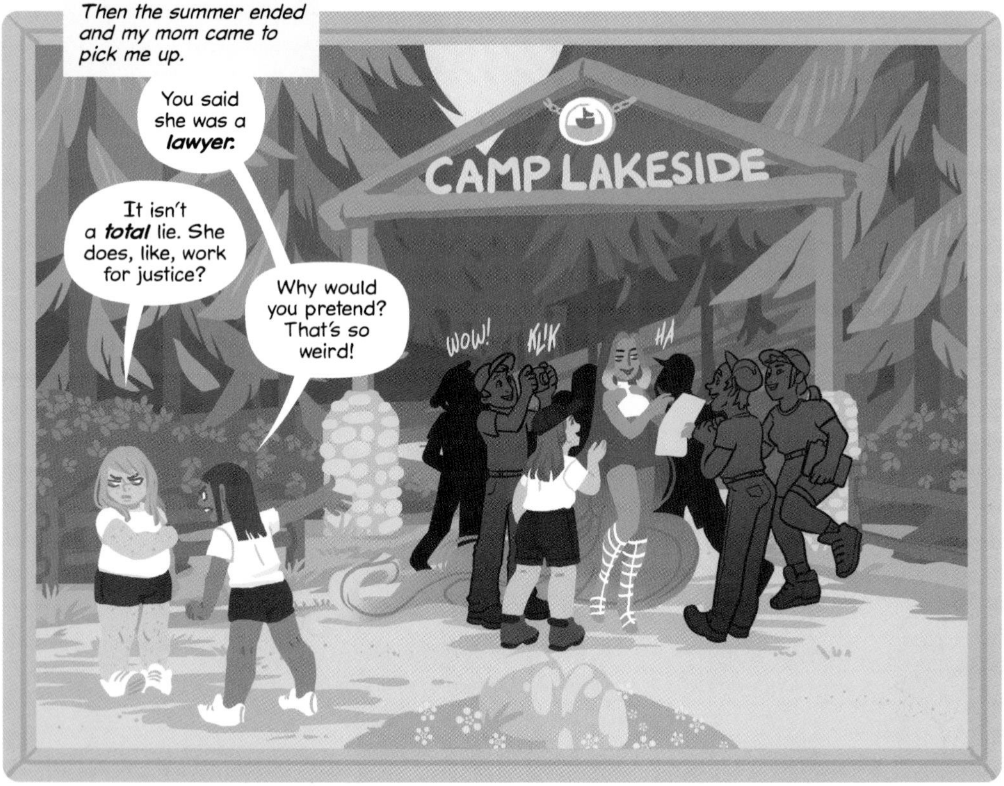
Then the summer ended and my mom came to pick me up.
CAMP LAKESIDE
You said she was a ***lawyer.***
It isn't a ***total*** lie. She does, like, work for justice?
Why would you pretend? That's so weird!
WOW!
KLIK
HA

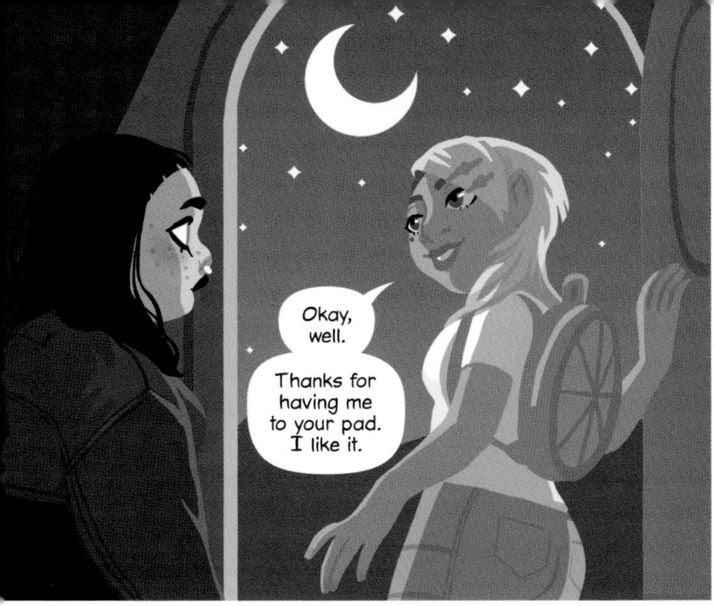
Okay, well.
Thanks for having me to your pad. I like it.

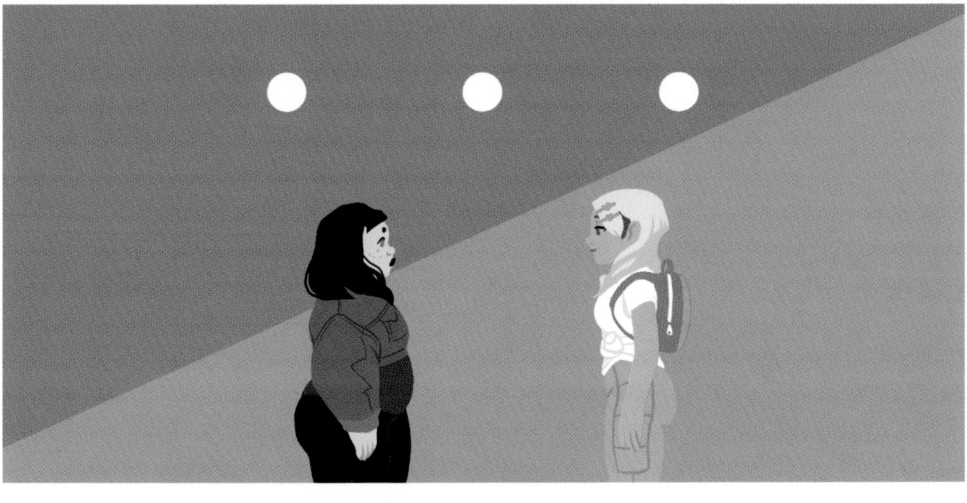

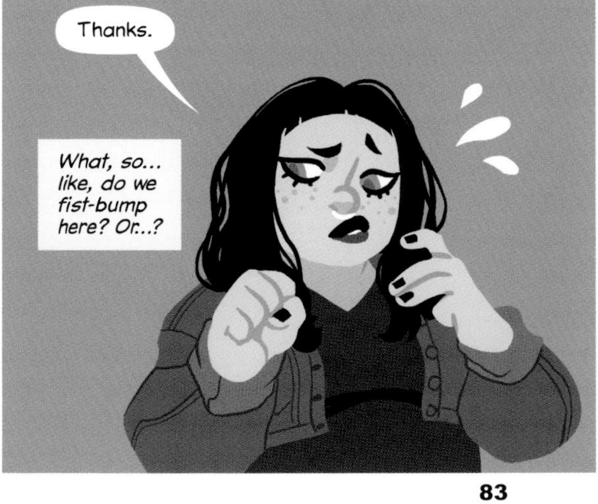
Thanks.
What, so... like, do we fist-bump here? Or...?

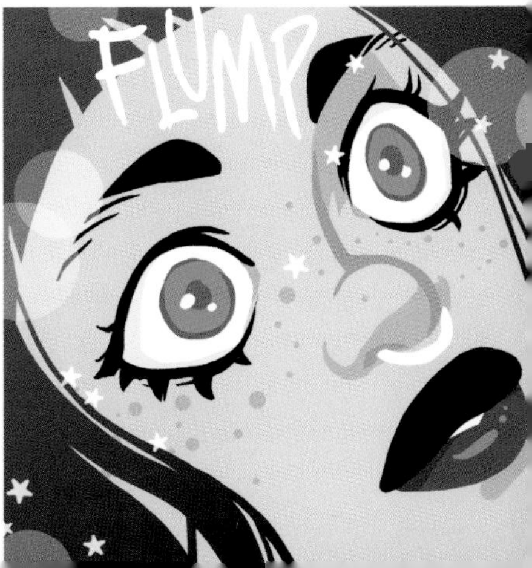
FLUMP

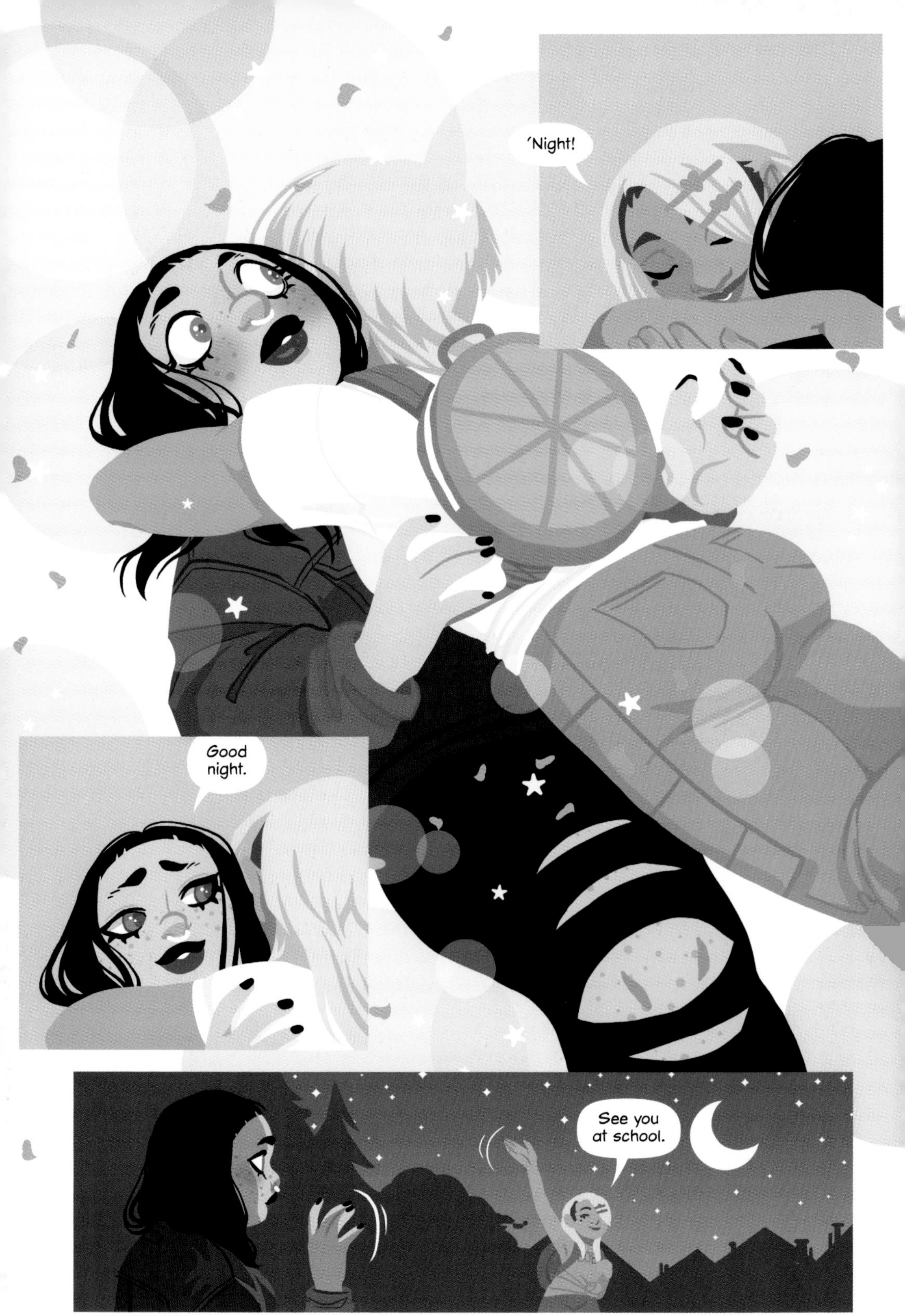
'Night!
Good night.
See you at school.

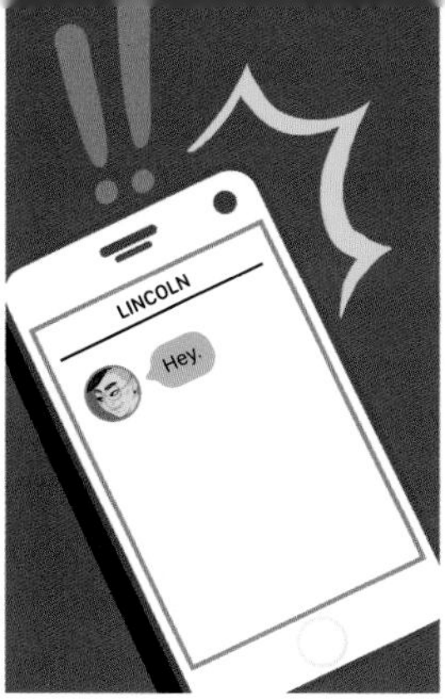
LINCOLN
Hey.

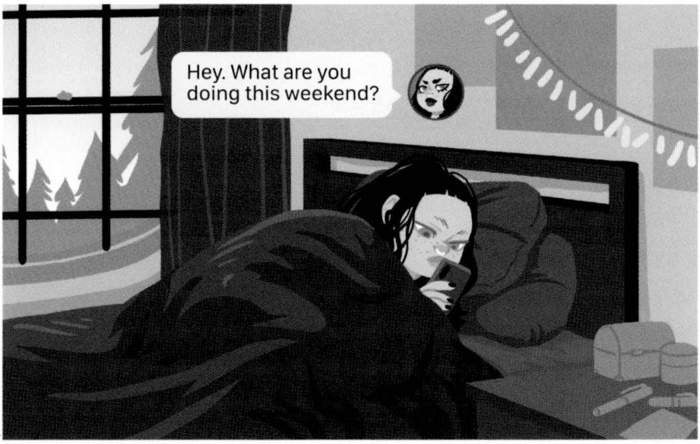
Hey. What are you doing this weekend?

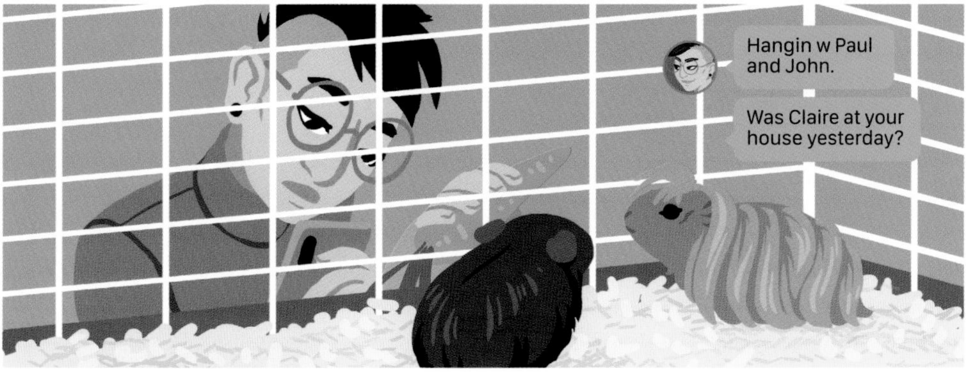
Hangin w Paul and John.
Was Claire at your house yesterday?

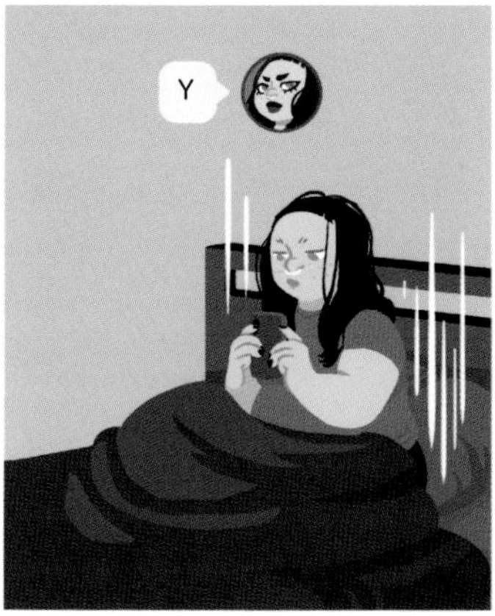
Y

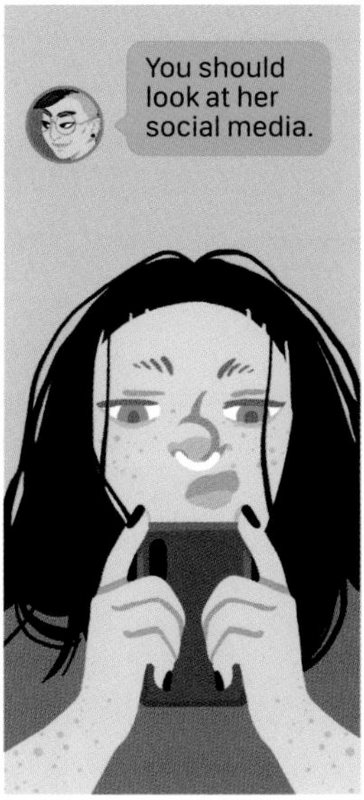
You should look at her social media.

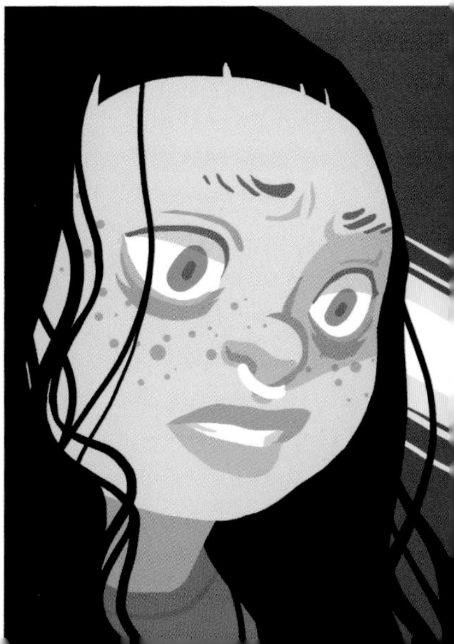

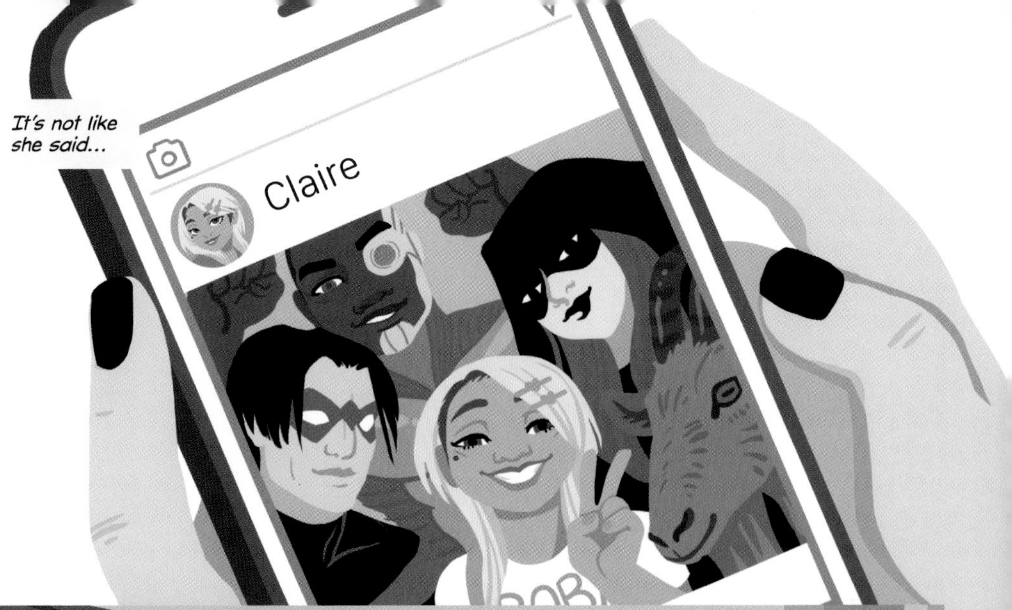

It's not like
she said...
Claire

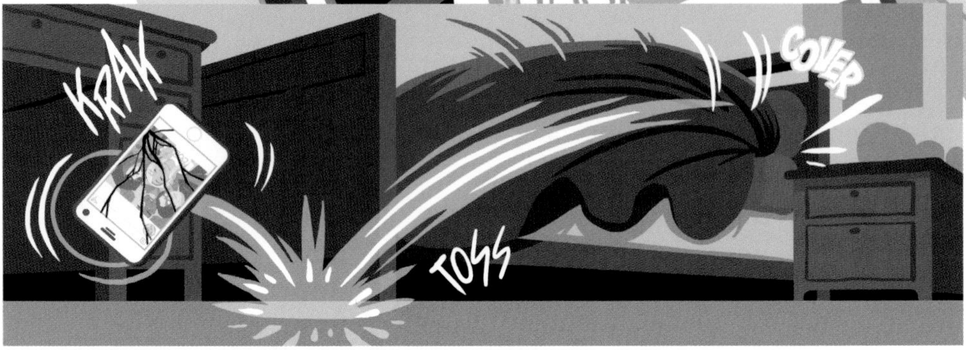

KRAK
TOSS
COVER

It's not like she said she didn't care about the Titans stuff. The superhero stuff.

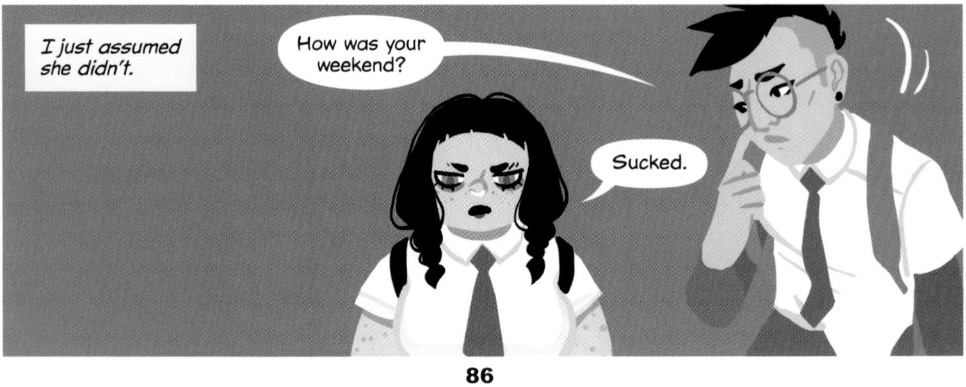

I just assumed she didn't.
How was your weekend?
Sucked.

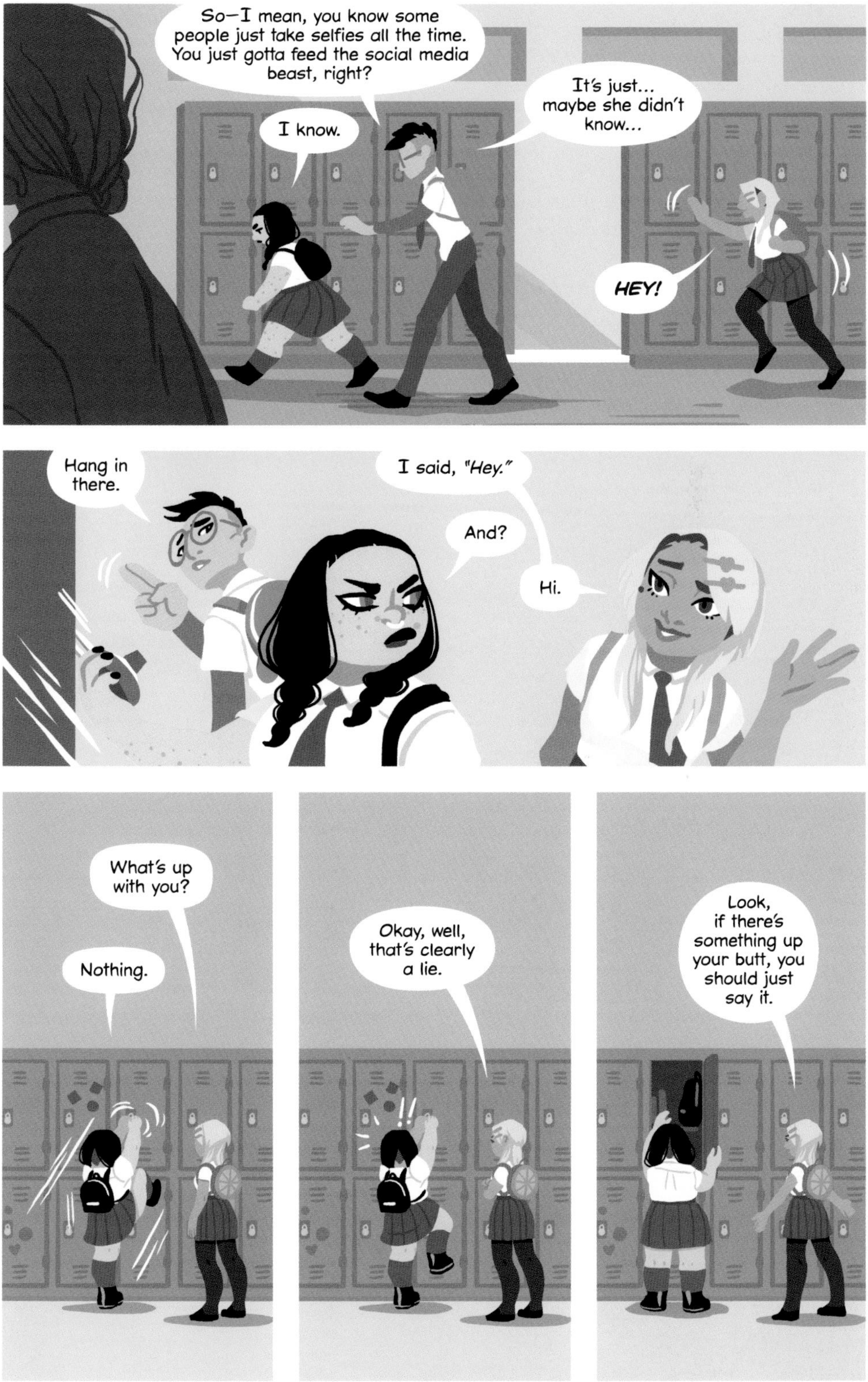
So—I mean, you know some people just take selfies all the time. You just gotta feed the social media beast, right?
I know.
It's just... maybe she didn't know...
HEY!
Hang in there.
I said, "Hey."
And?
Hi.
What's up with you?
Nothing.
Okay, well, that's clearly a lie.
Look, if there's something up your butt, you should just say it.

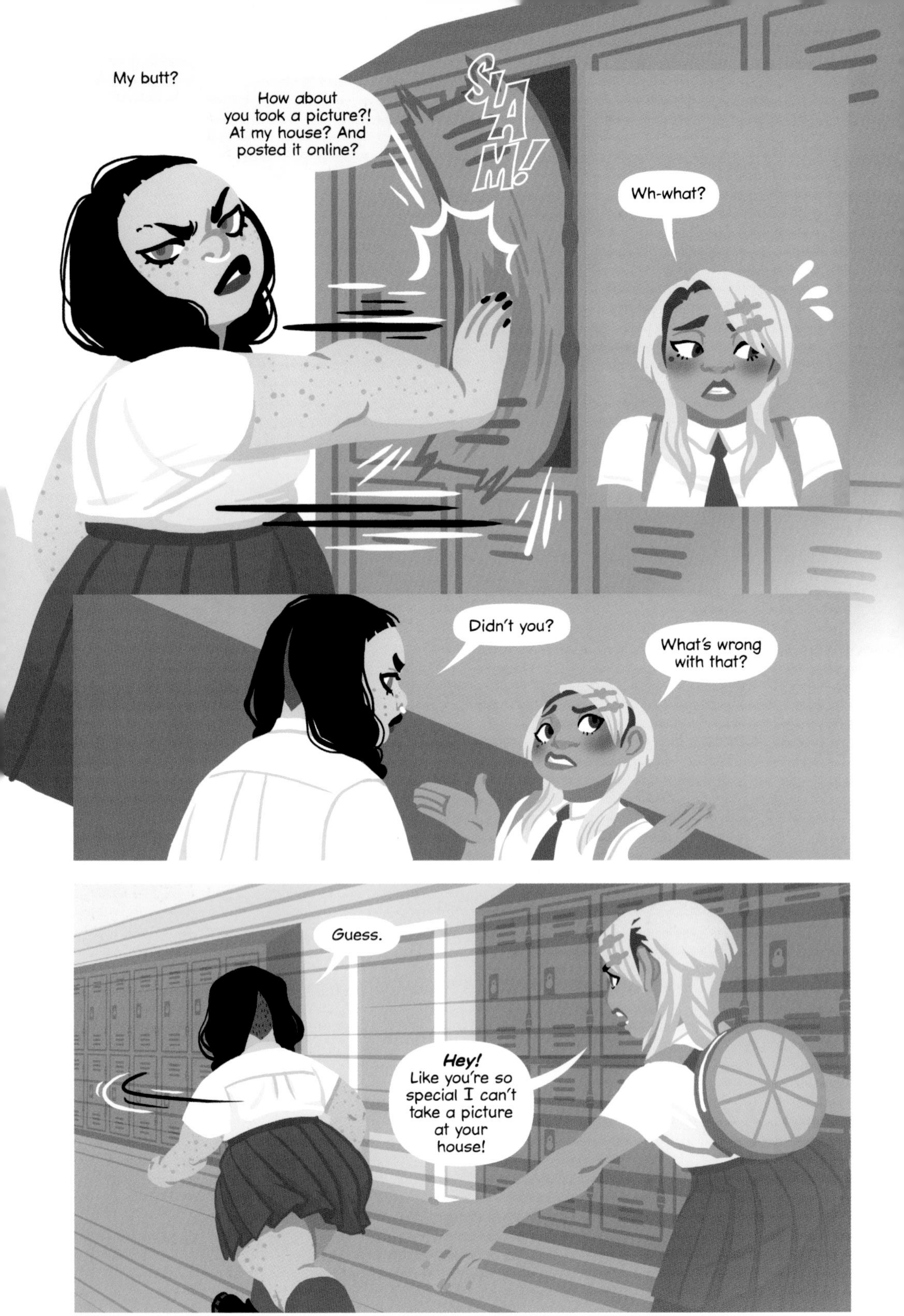
My butt?
How about you took a picture?! At my house? And posted it online?
SLAM!
Wh-what?
Didn't you?
What's wrong with that?
Guess.
Hey!
Like you're so special I can't take a picture at your house!

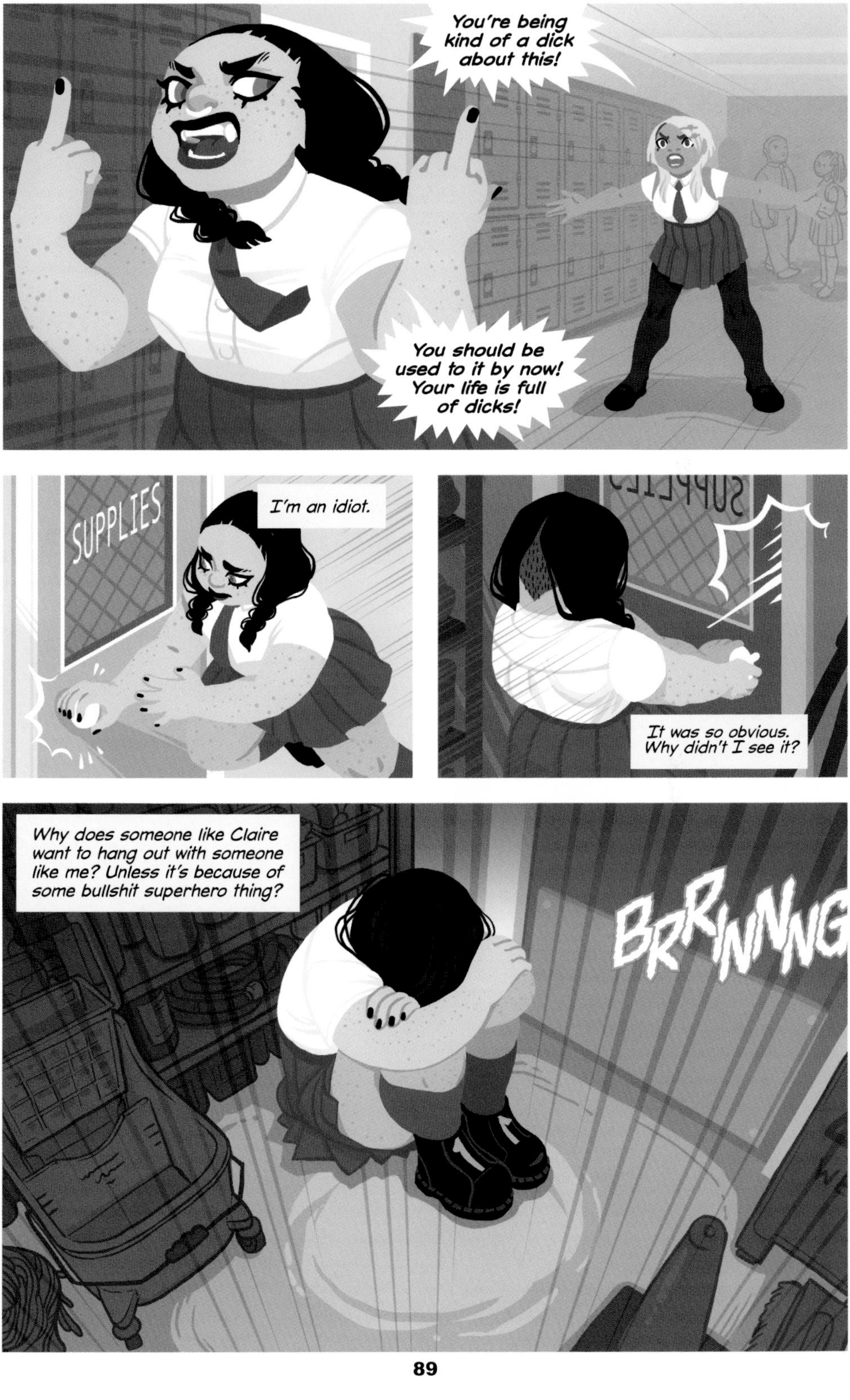
You're being kind of a dick about this!
You should be used to it by now! Your life is full of dicks!
SUPPLIES
I'm an idiot.
SUPPLIES
It was so obvious. Why didn't I see it?
Why does someone like Claire want to hang out with someone like me? Unless it's because of some bullshit superhero thing?
BRRINNNG

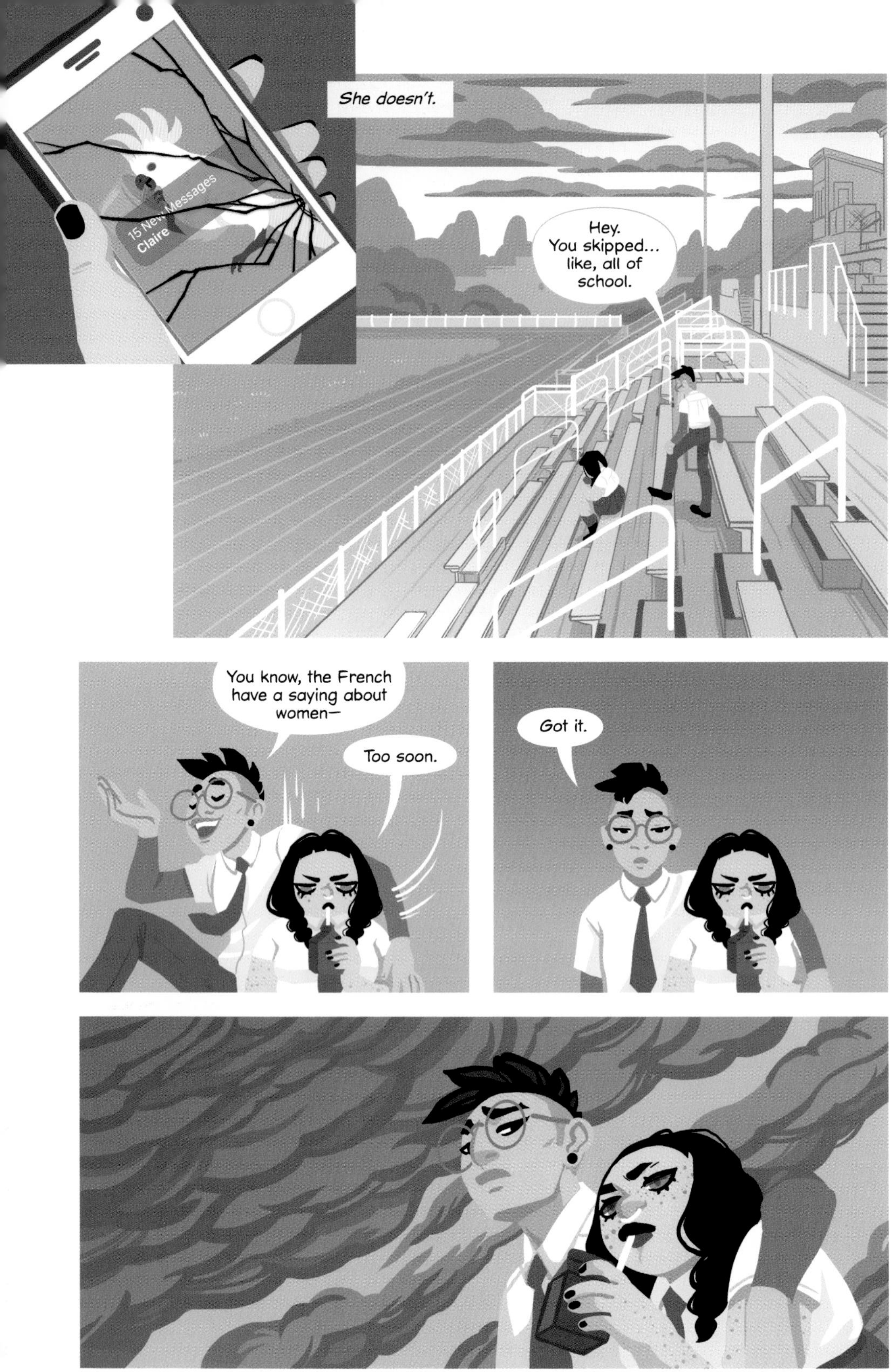
15 New Messages
Claire
She doesn't.
Hey. You skipped... like, all of school.
You know, the French have a saying about women—
Too soon.
Got it.

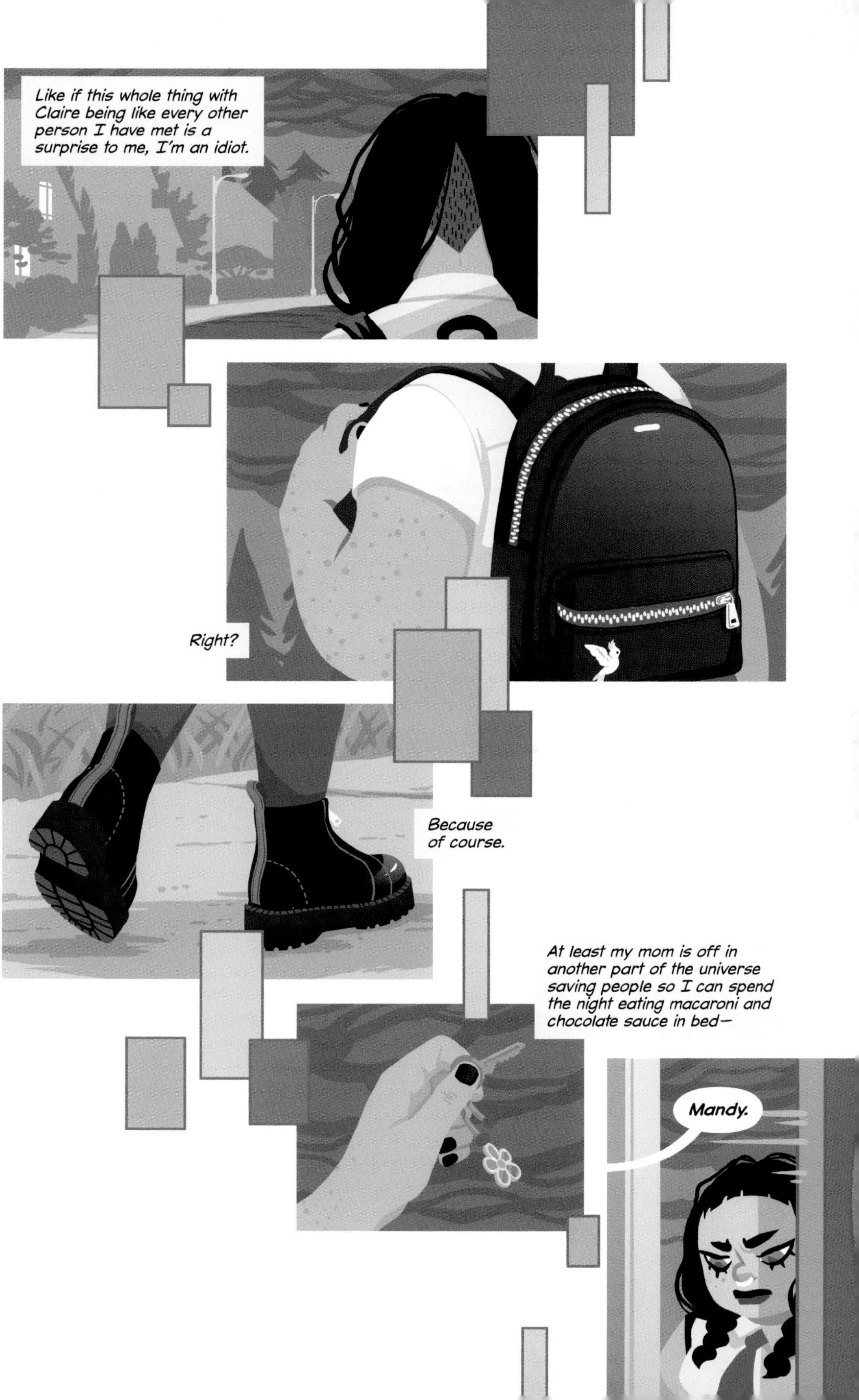
Like if this whole thing with Claire being like every other person I have met is a surprise to me, I'm an idiot.
Right?
Because of course.
At least my mom is off in another part of the universe saving people so I can spend the night eating macaroni and chocolate sauce in bed—
Mandy.

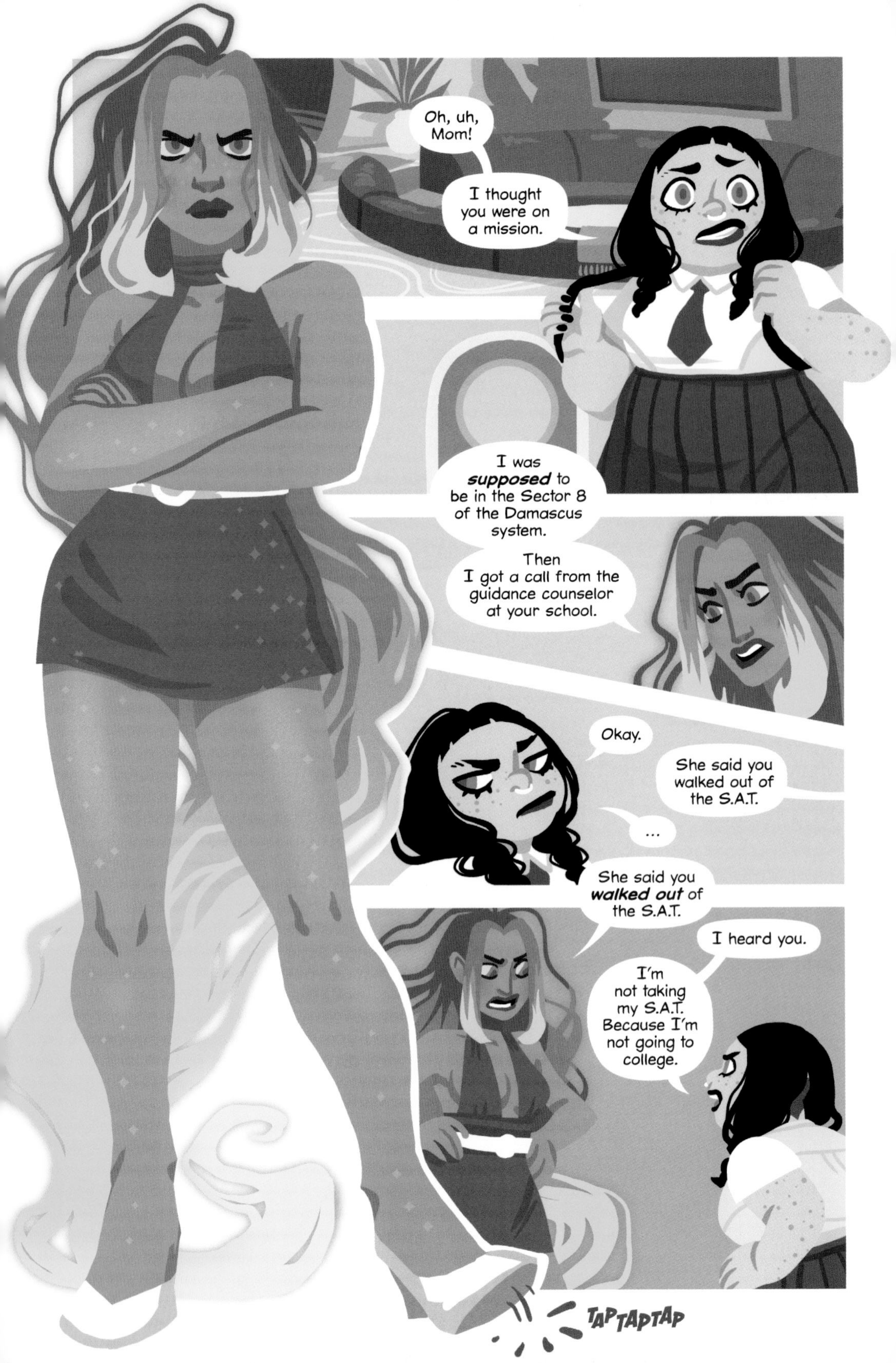

Oh, uh, Mom!
I thought you were on a mission.
I was ***supposed*** to be in the Sector 8 of the Damascus system.
Then I got a call from the guidance counselor at your school.
Okay.
She said you walked out of the S.A.T.
...
She said you ***walked out*** of the S.A.T.
I heard you.
I'm not taking my S.A.T. Because I'm not going to college.
TAPTAPTAP

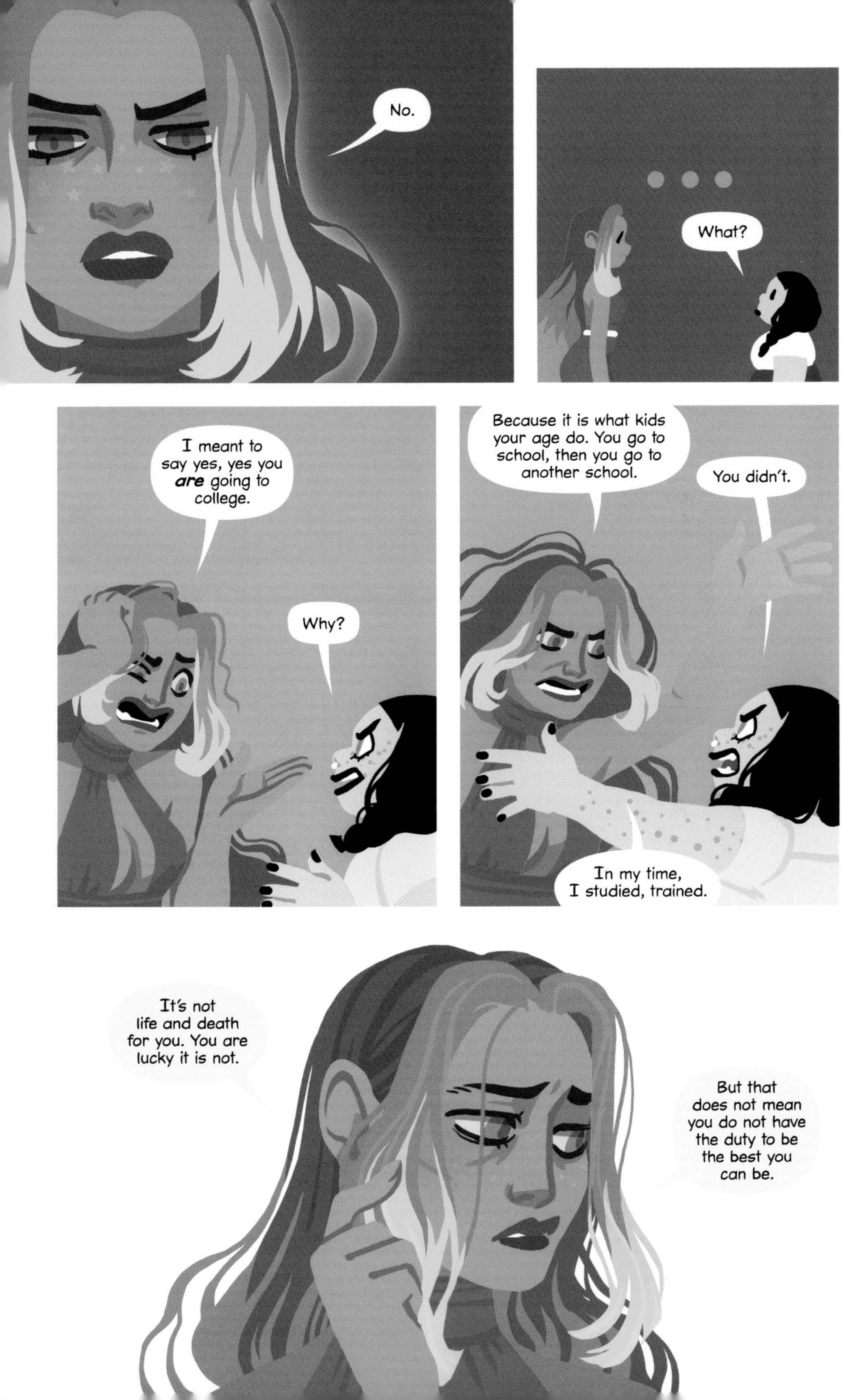
No.
What?
I meant to say yes, yes you ***are*** going to college.
Why?
Because it is what kids your age do. You go to school, then you go to another school.
You didn't.
In my time, I studied, trained.
It's not life and death for you. You are lucky it is not.
But that does not mean you do not have the duty to be the best you can be.

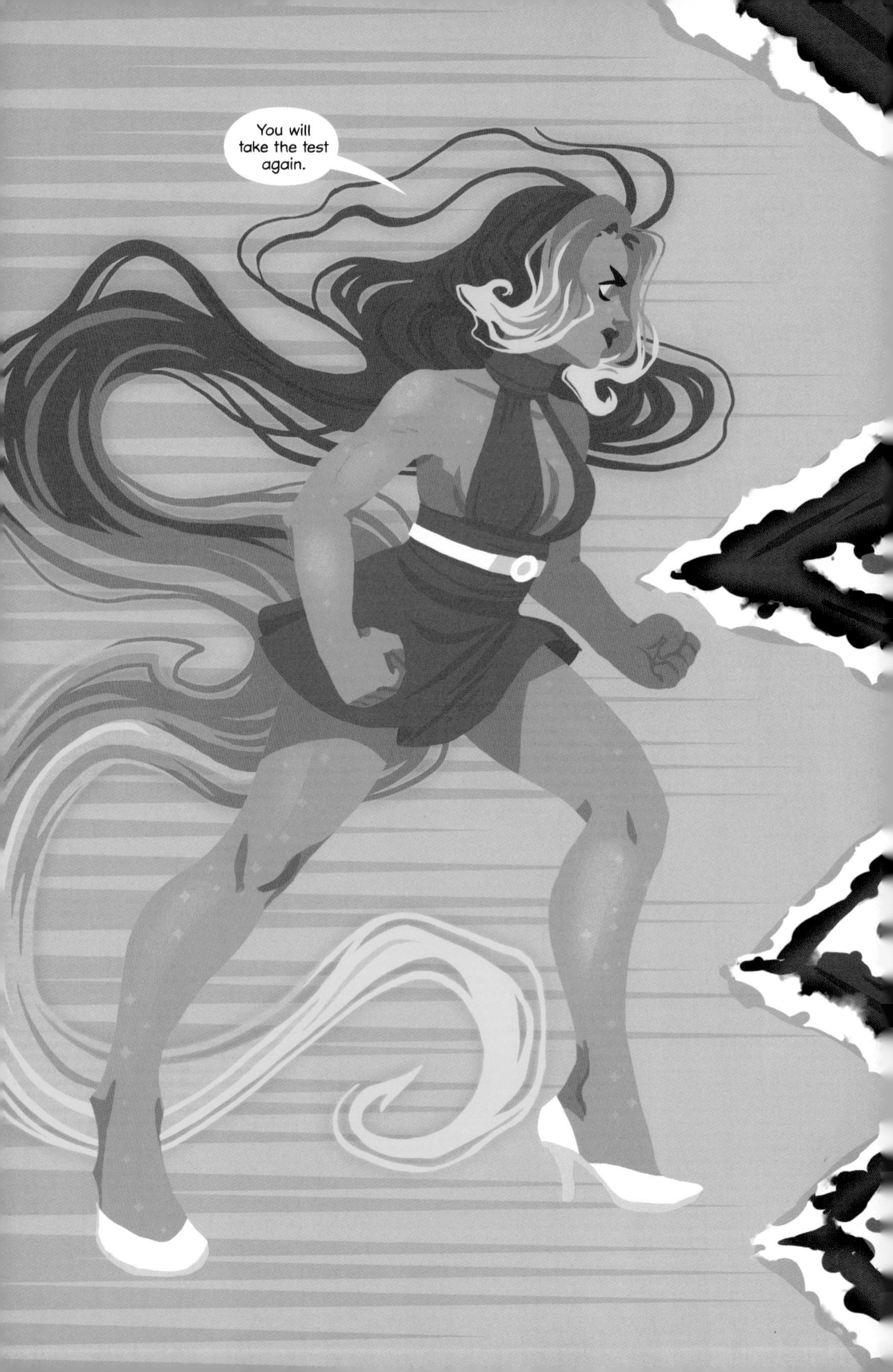
You will take the test again.

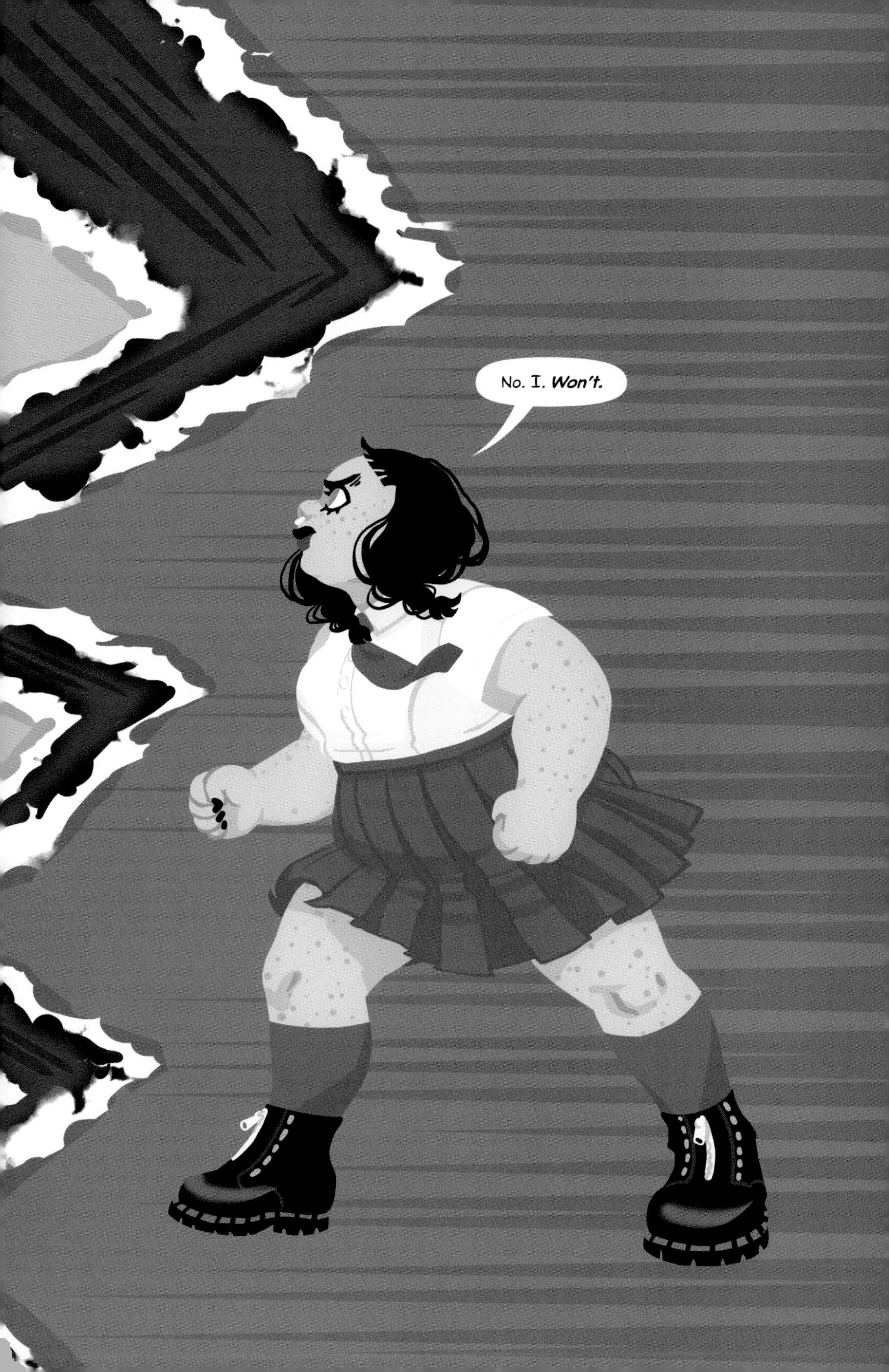
No. I. *Won't.*

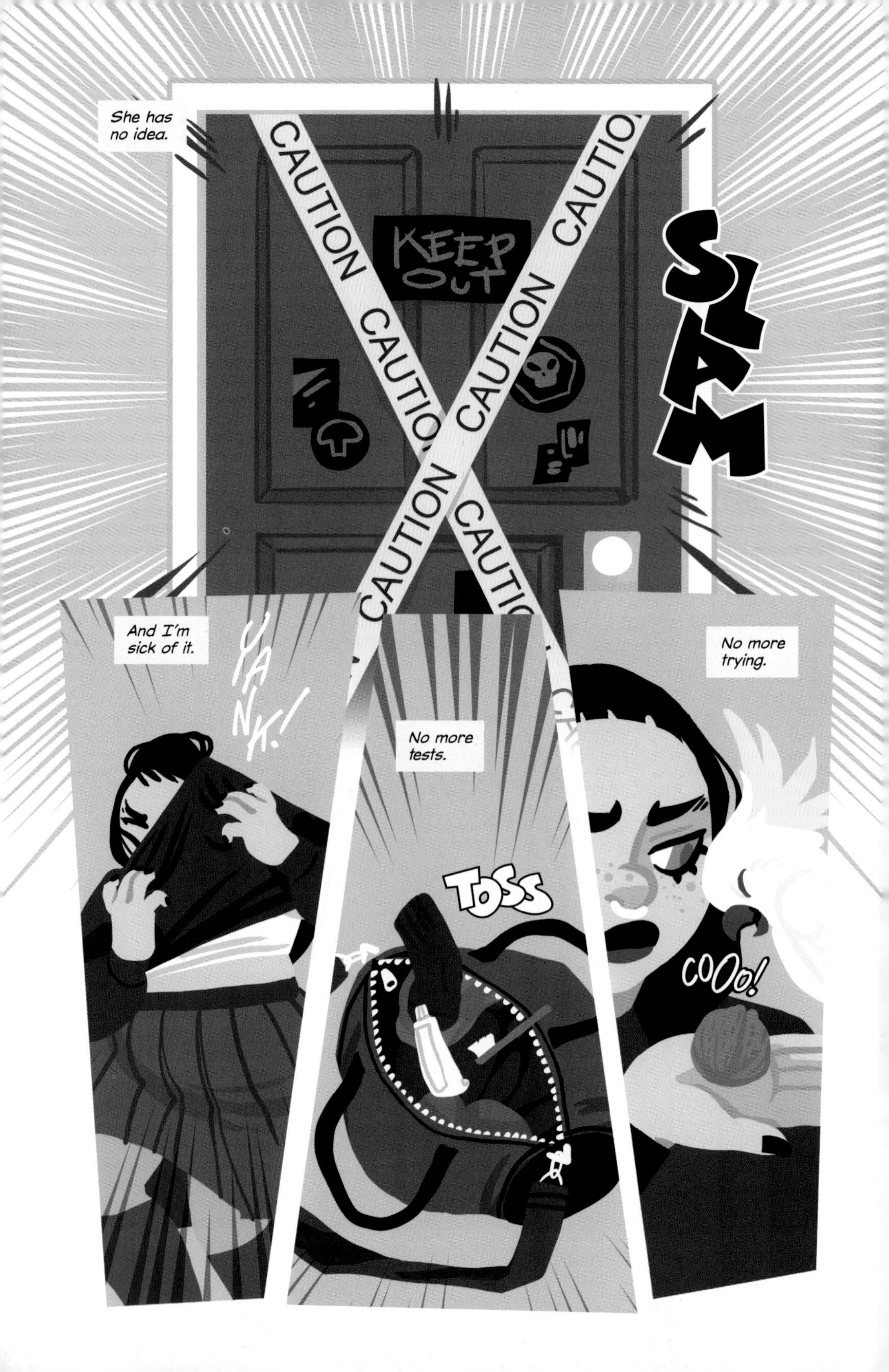

She has no idea.
CAUTION
KEEP OUT
SLAM
And I'm sick of it.
YANK!
No more tests.
TOSS
No more trying.
COOO!

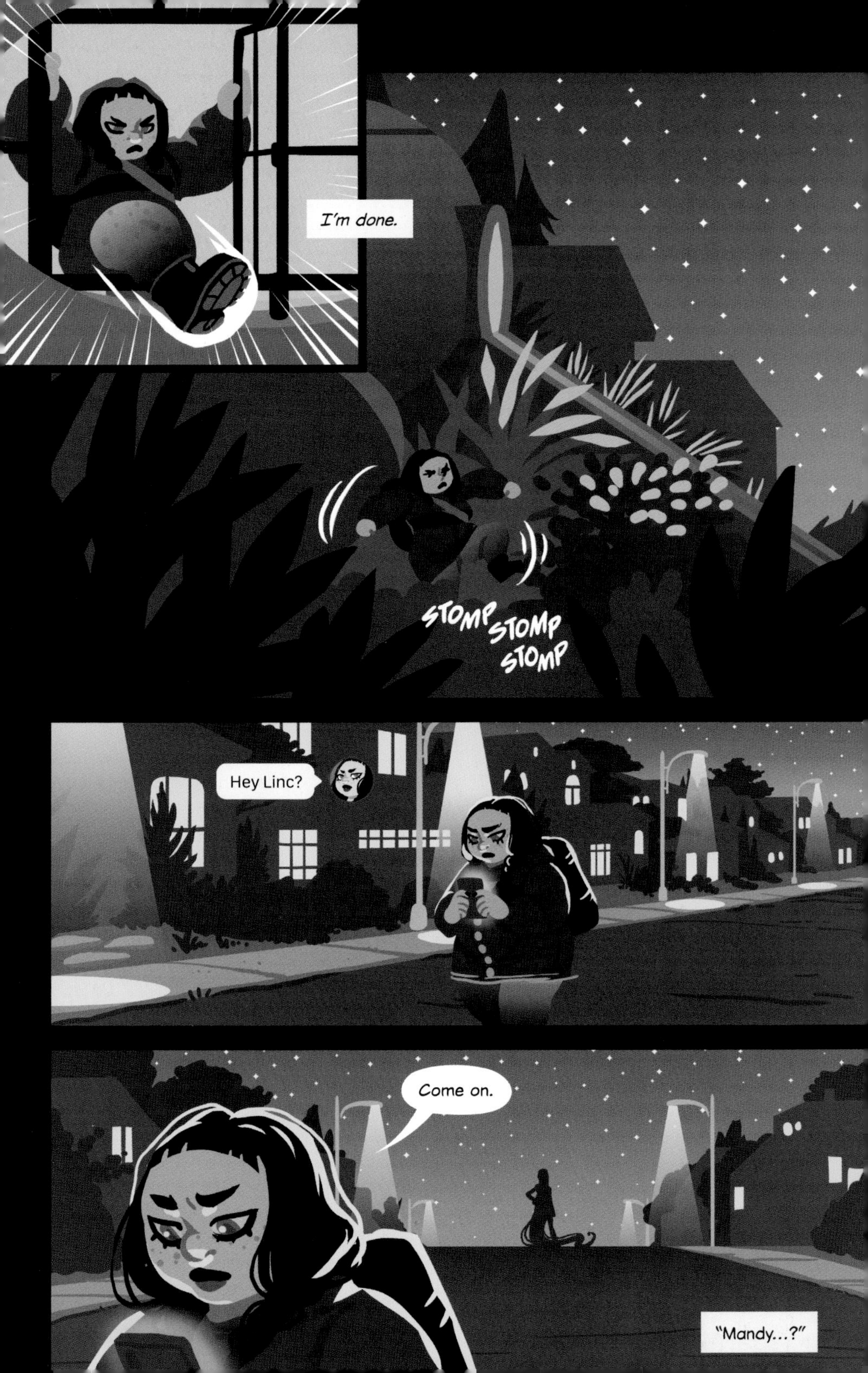
I'm done.
STOMP STOMP STOMP
Hey Linc?
Come on.
"Mandy...?"

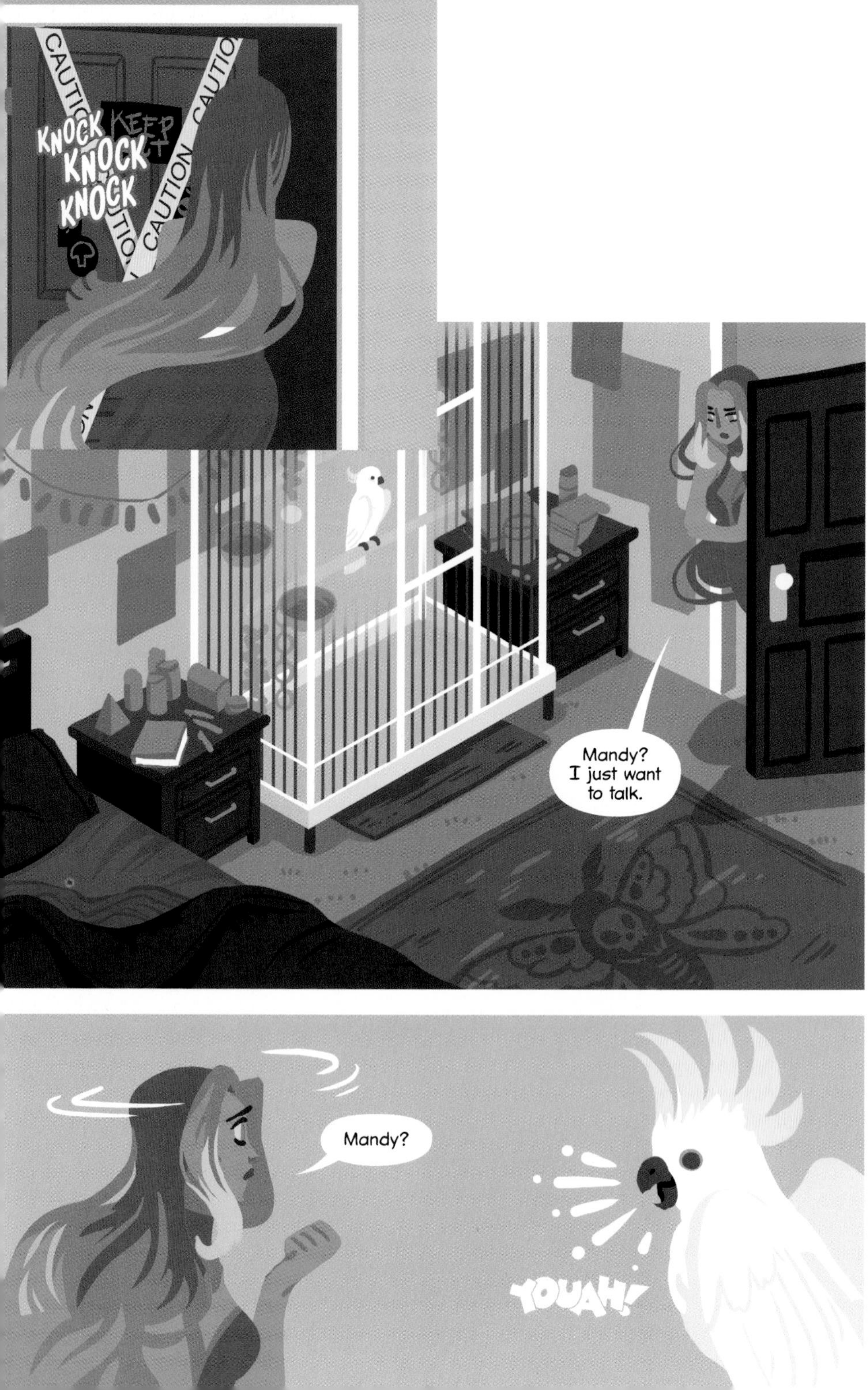
CAUTION
KEEP
KNOCK
KNOCK
KNOCK
Mandy? I just want to talk.
Mandy?
YOUAH!

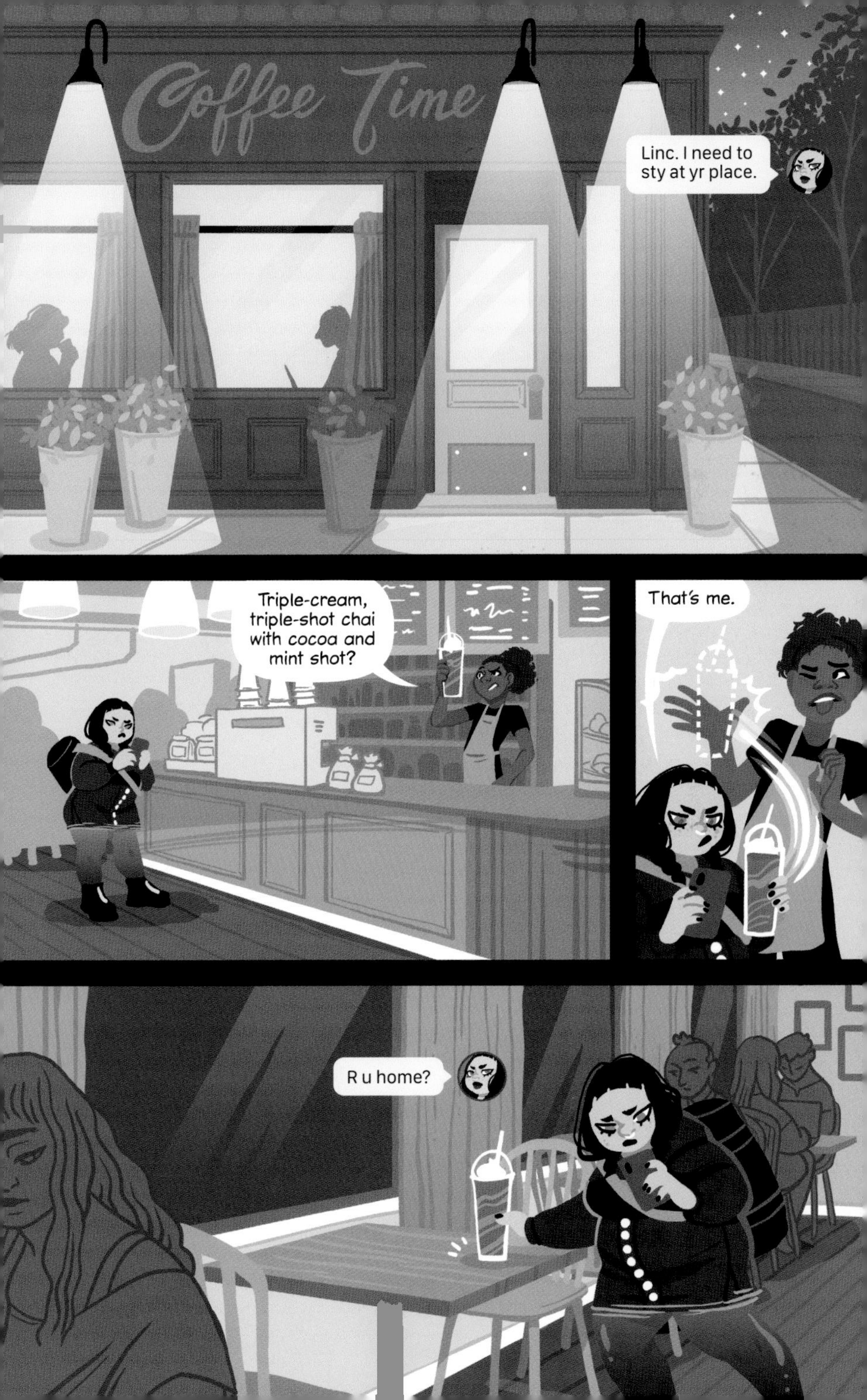
Coffee Time
Linc. I need to sty at yr place.
Triple-cream, triple-shot chai with cocoa and mint shot?
That's me.
R u home?

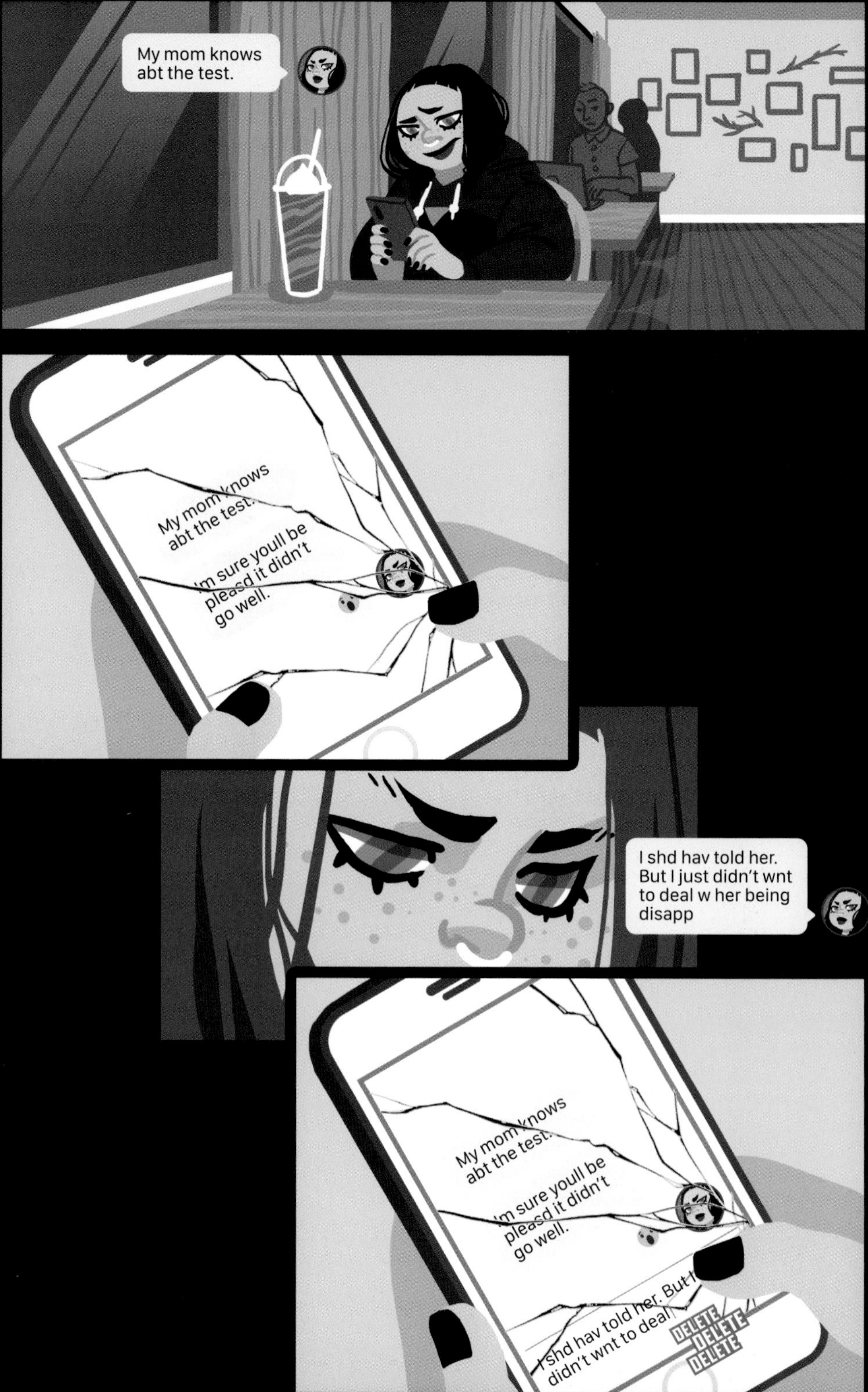

My mom knows abt the test.
My mom knows abt the test.
Im sure youll be pleasd it didn't go well.
I shd hav told her. But I just didn't wnt to deal w her being disapp
My mom knows abt the test.
Im sure youll be pleasd it didn't go well.
I shd hav told her. But I didn't wnt to deal
DELETE DELETE DELETE

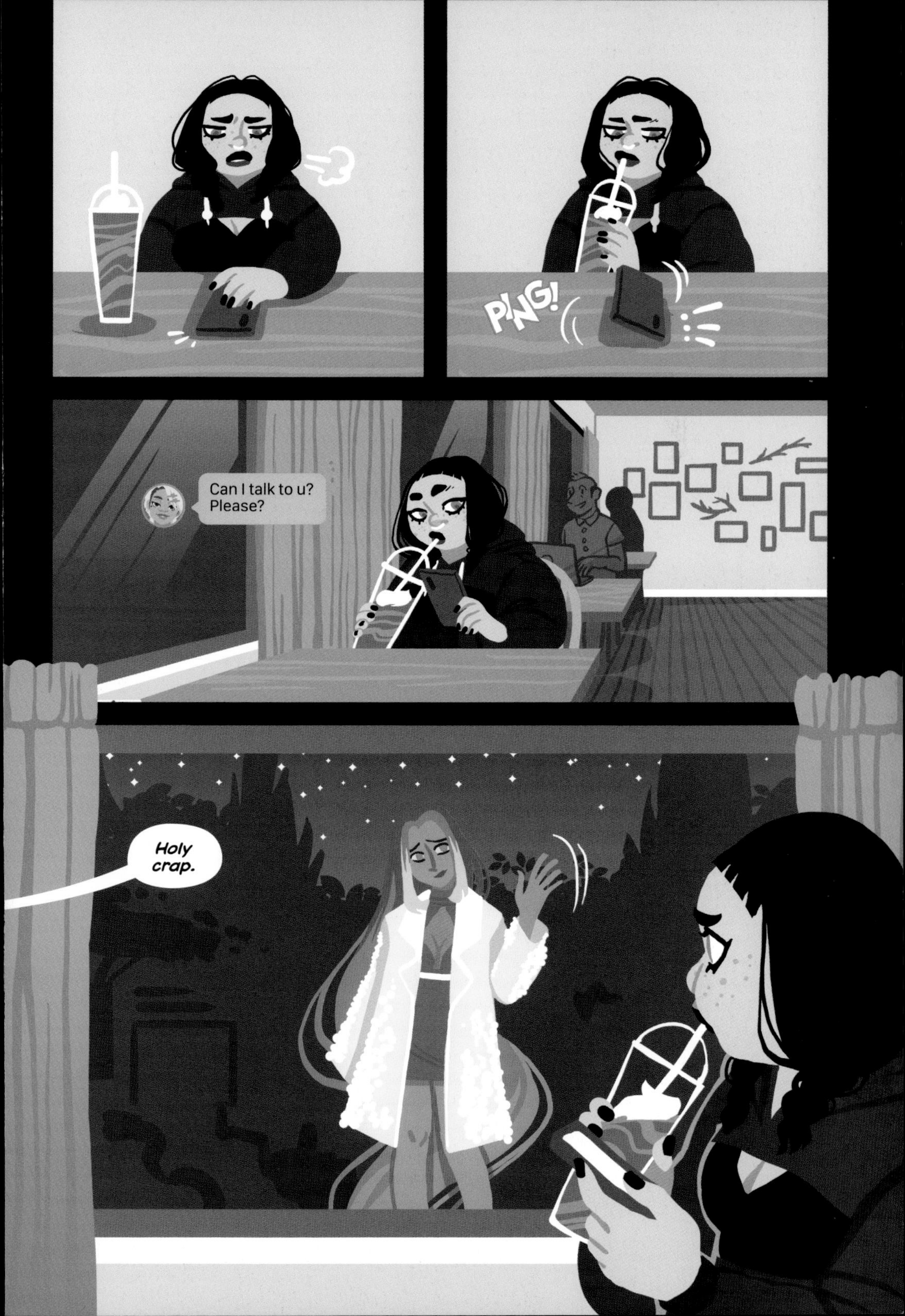
PING!
Can I talk to u?
Please?
Holy crap.

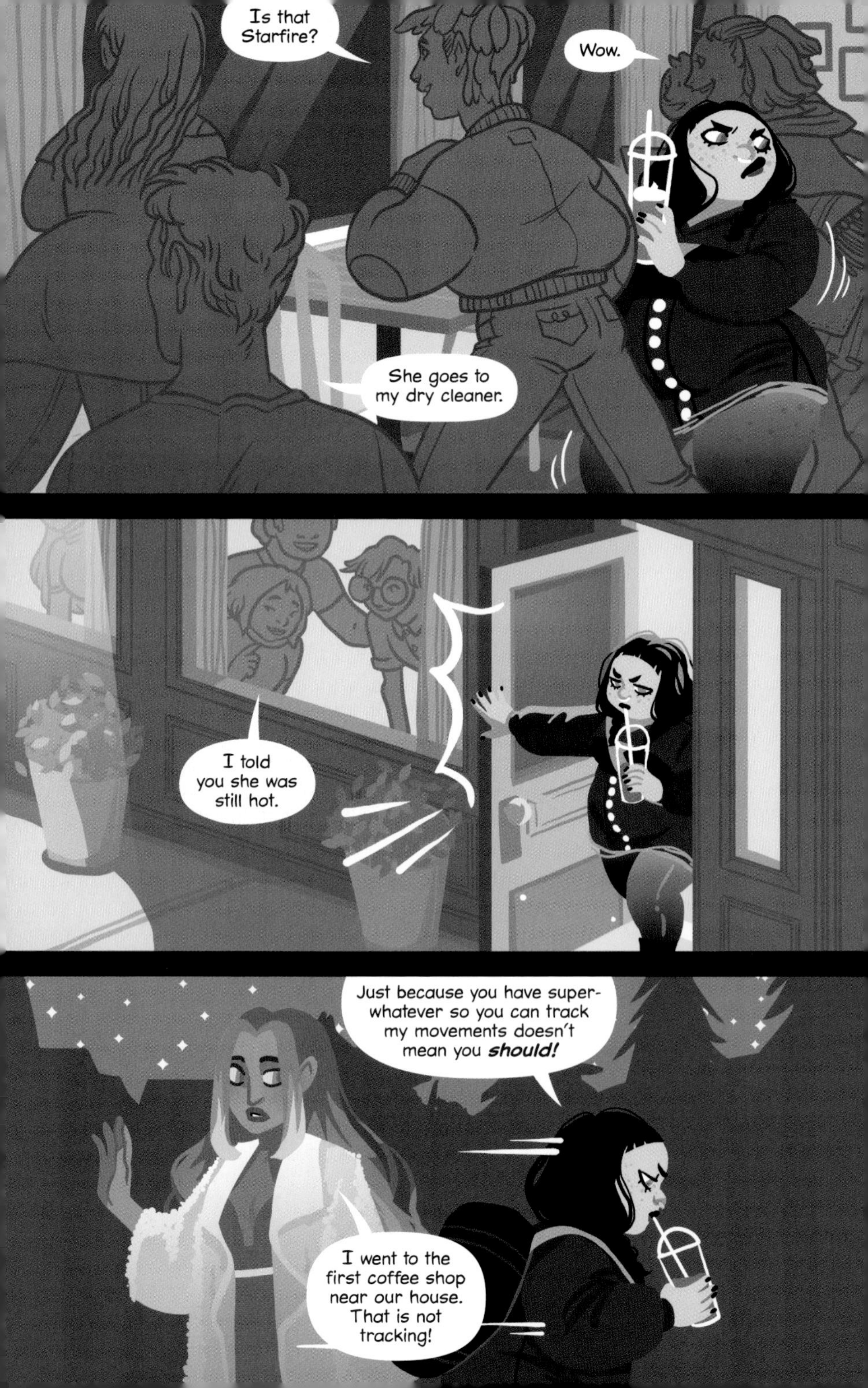
Is that Starfire?
Wow.
She goes to my dry cleaner.
I told you she was still hot.
Just because you have super-whatever so you can track my movements doesn't mean you ***should!***
I went to the first coffee shop near our house. That is not tracking!

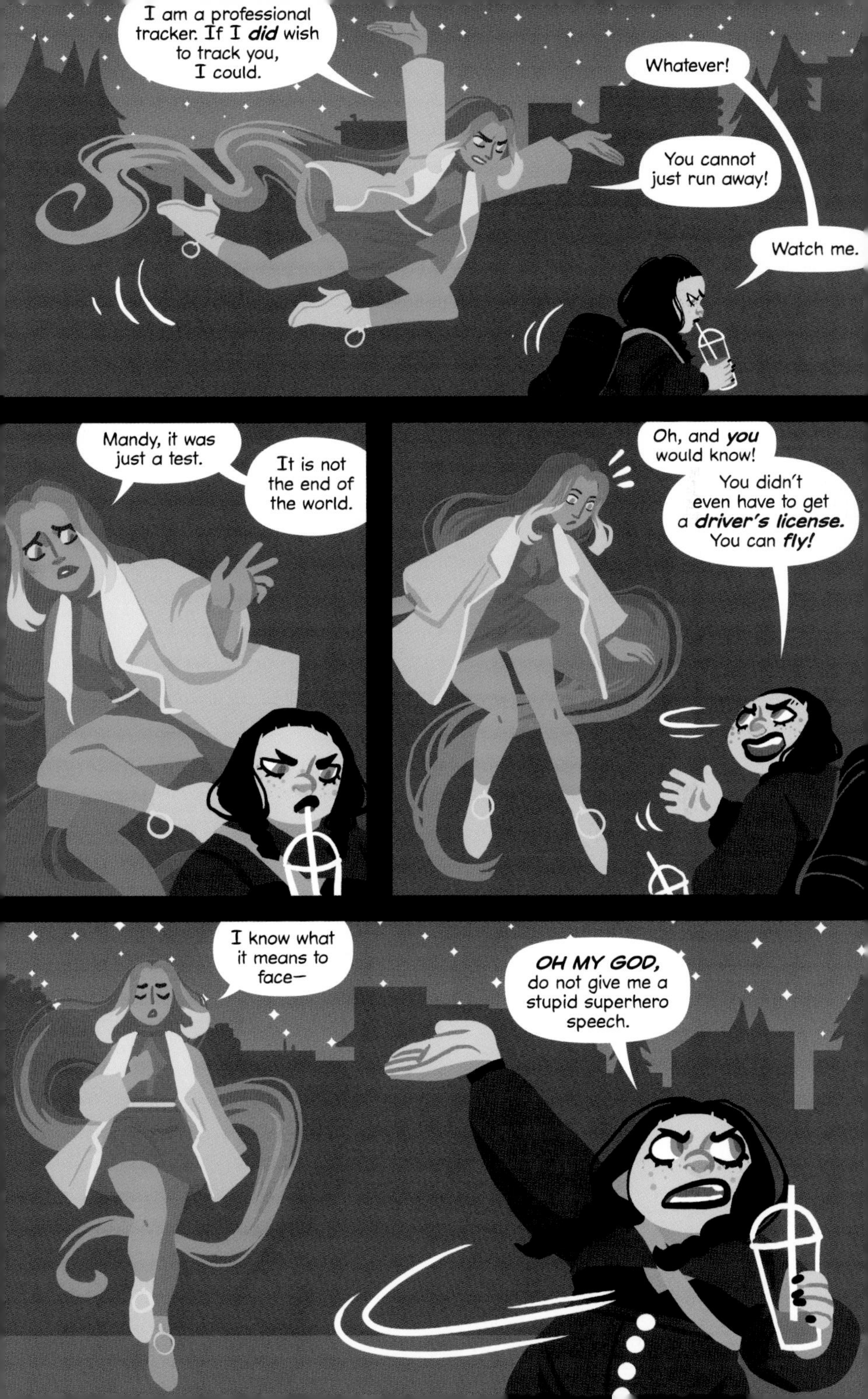
I am a professional tracker. If I *did* wish to track you, I could.
Whatever!
You cannot just run away!
Watch me.
Mandy, it was just a test.
It is not the end of the world.
Oh, and *you* would know!
You didn't even have to get a *driver's license.* You can *fly!*
I know what it means to face—
OH MY GOD, do not give me a stupid superhero speech.

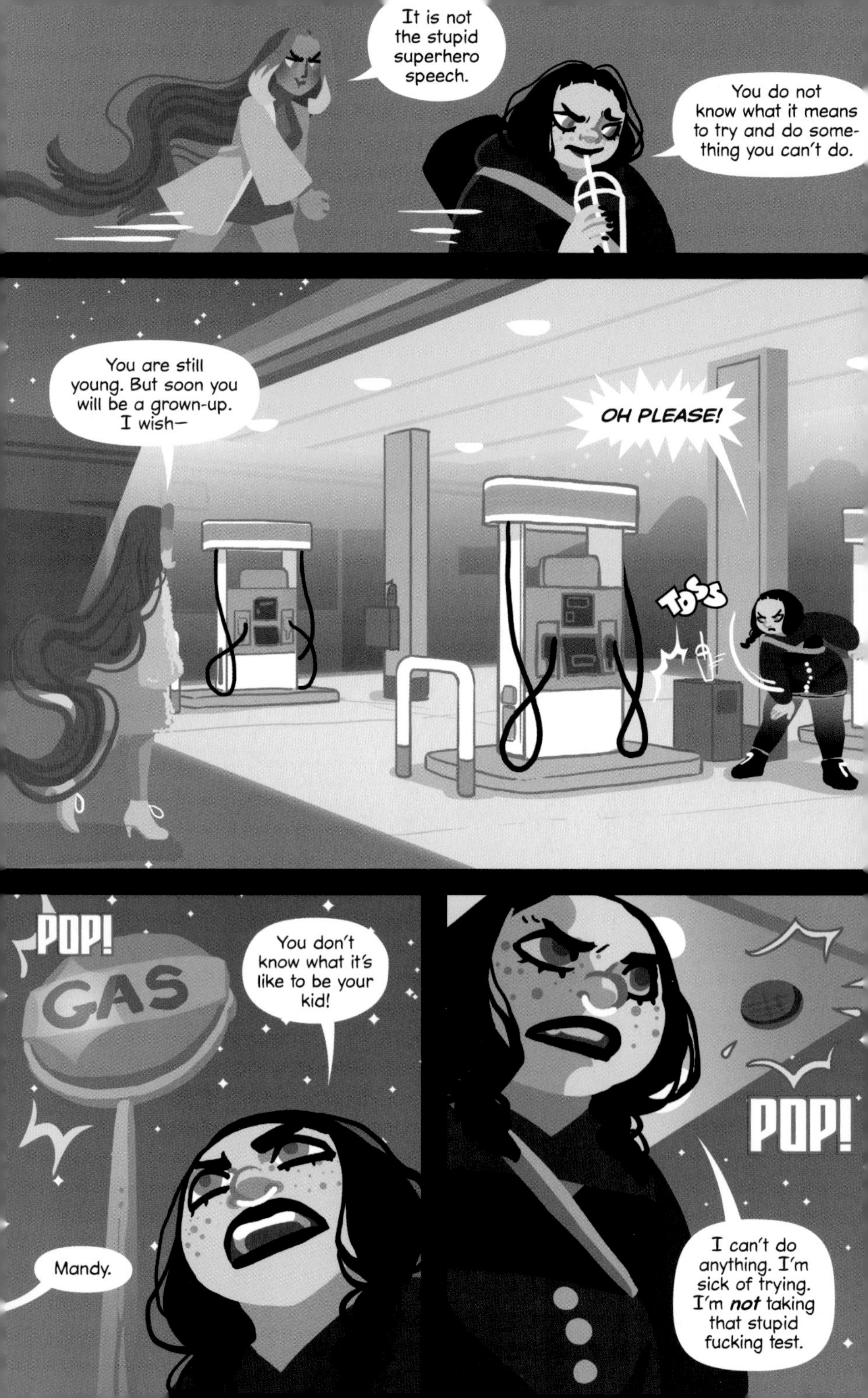
It is not the stupid superhero speech.
You do not know what it means to try and do something you can't do.
You are still young. But soon you will be a grown-up. I wish—
OH PLEASE!
TOSS
POP!
GAS
You don't know what it's like to be your kid!
Mandy.
POP!
I can't do anything. I'm sick of trying. I'm *not* taking that stupid fucking test.

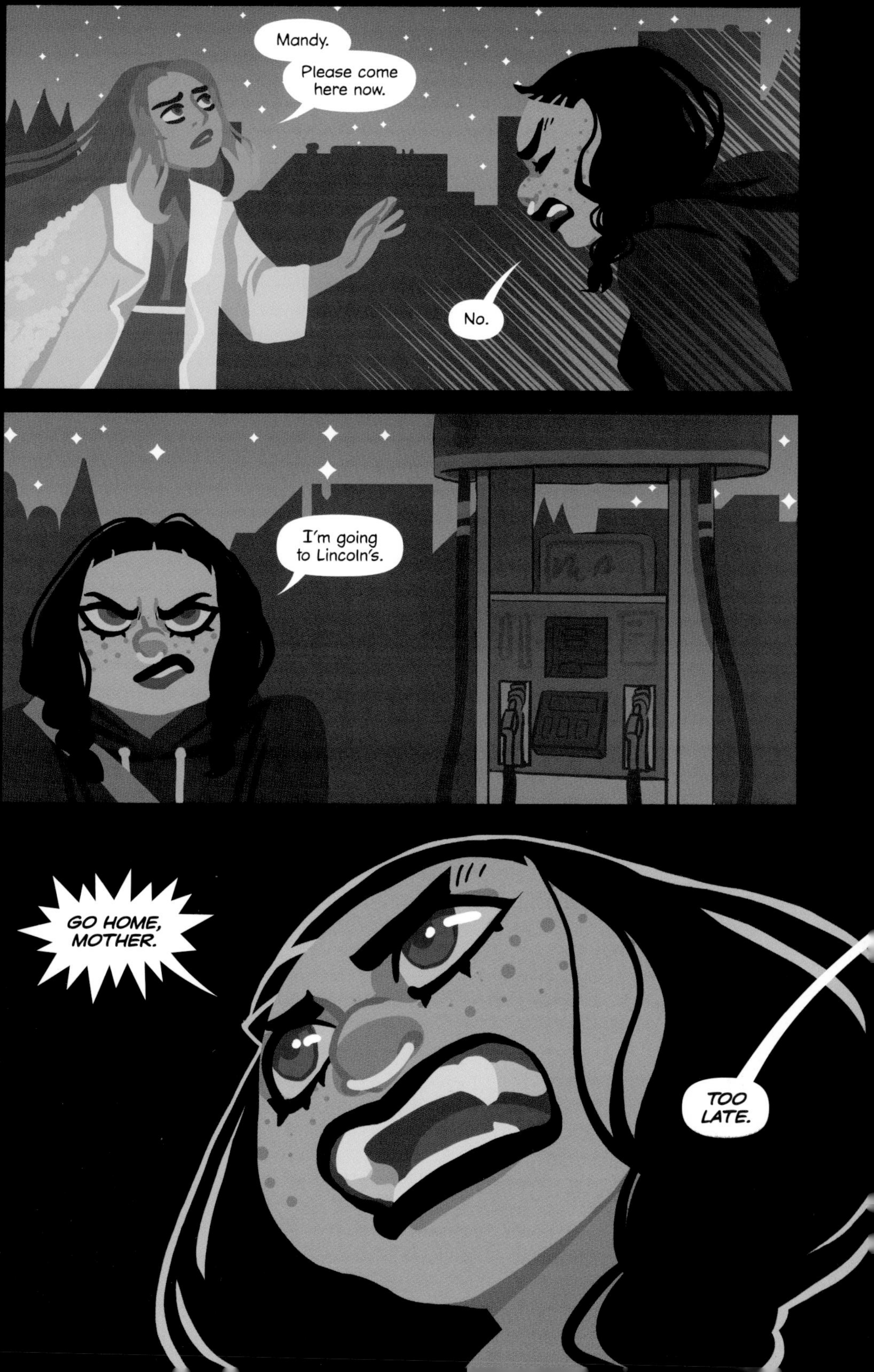
Mandy.
Please come here now.
No.
I'm going to Lincoln's.
GO HOME, MOTHER.
TOO LATE.

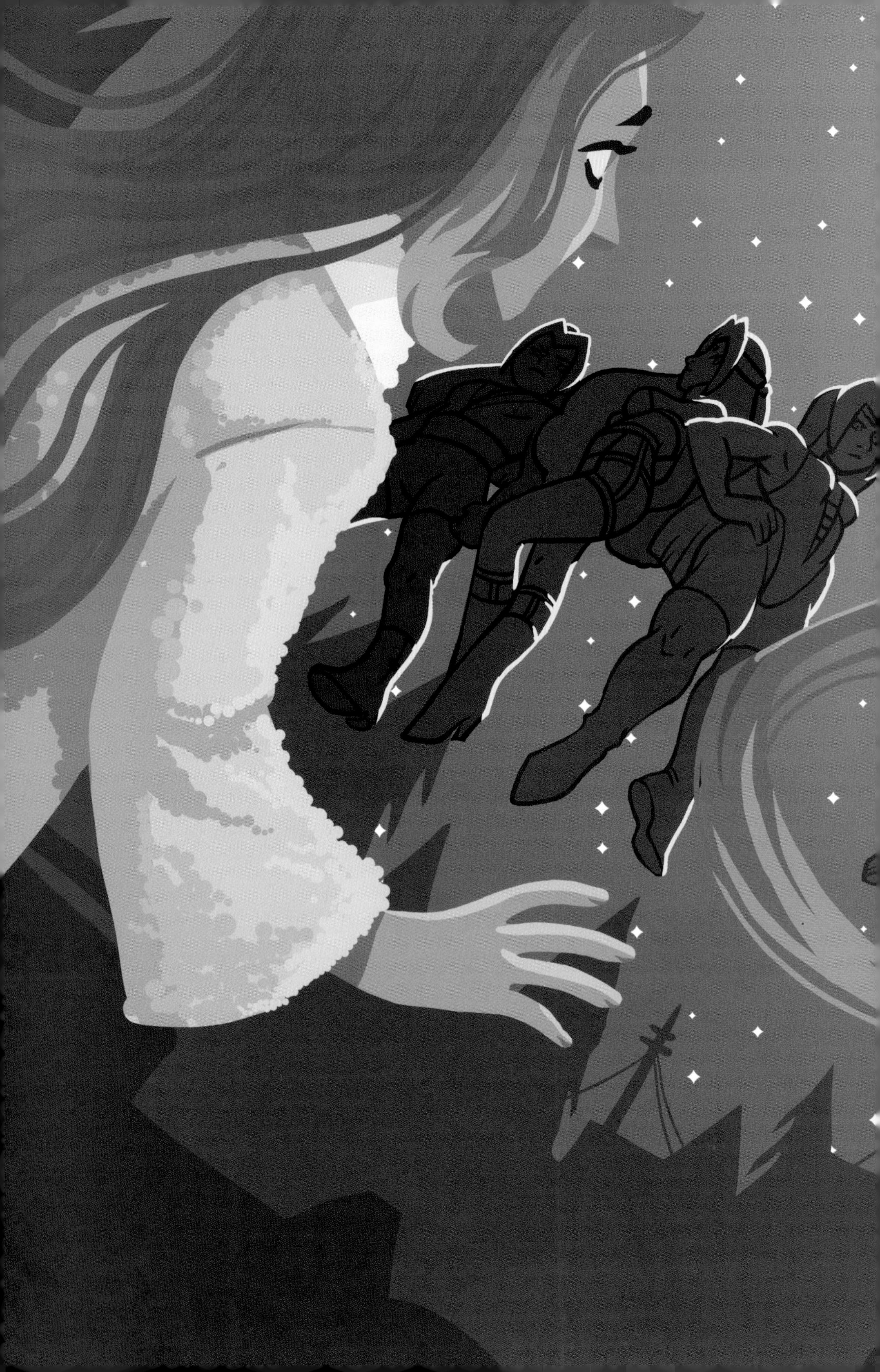

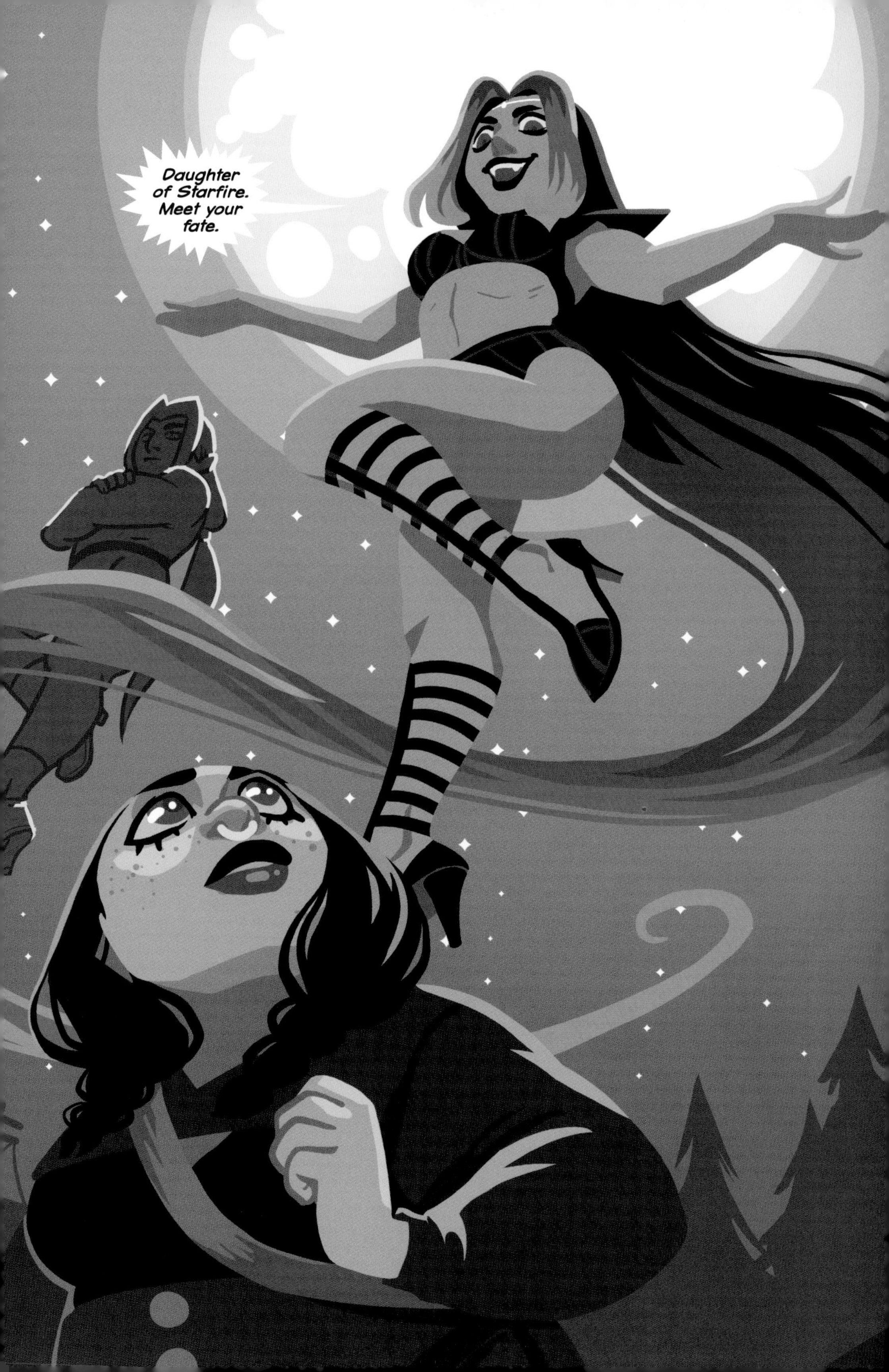
Daughter of Starfire. Meet your fate.

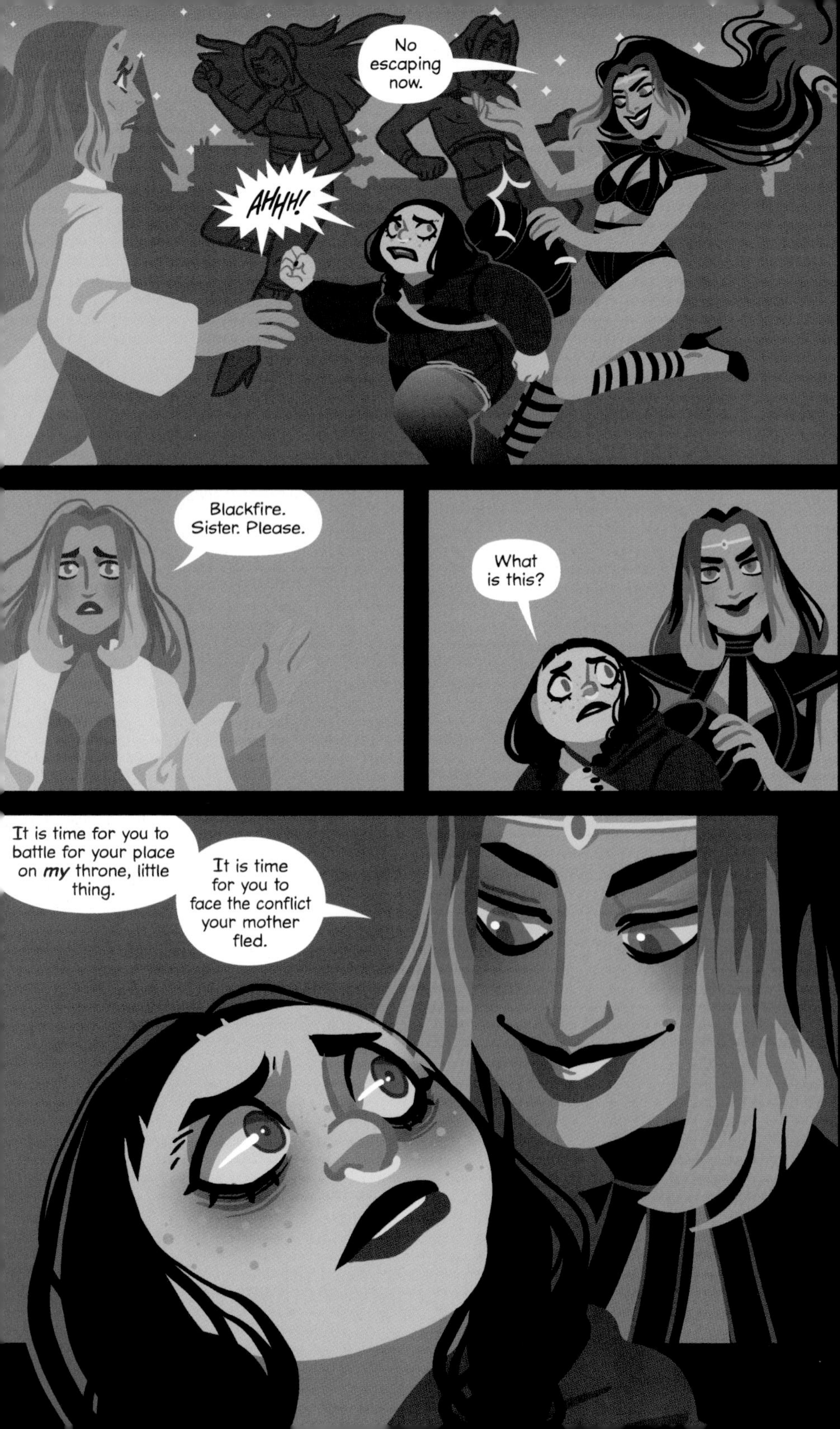
No escaping now.
AHHH!
Blackfire. Sister. Please.
What is this?
It is time for you to battle for your place on *my* throne, little thing.
It is time for you to face the conflict your mother fled.

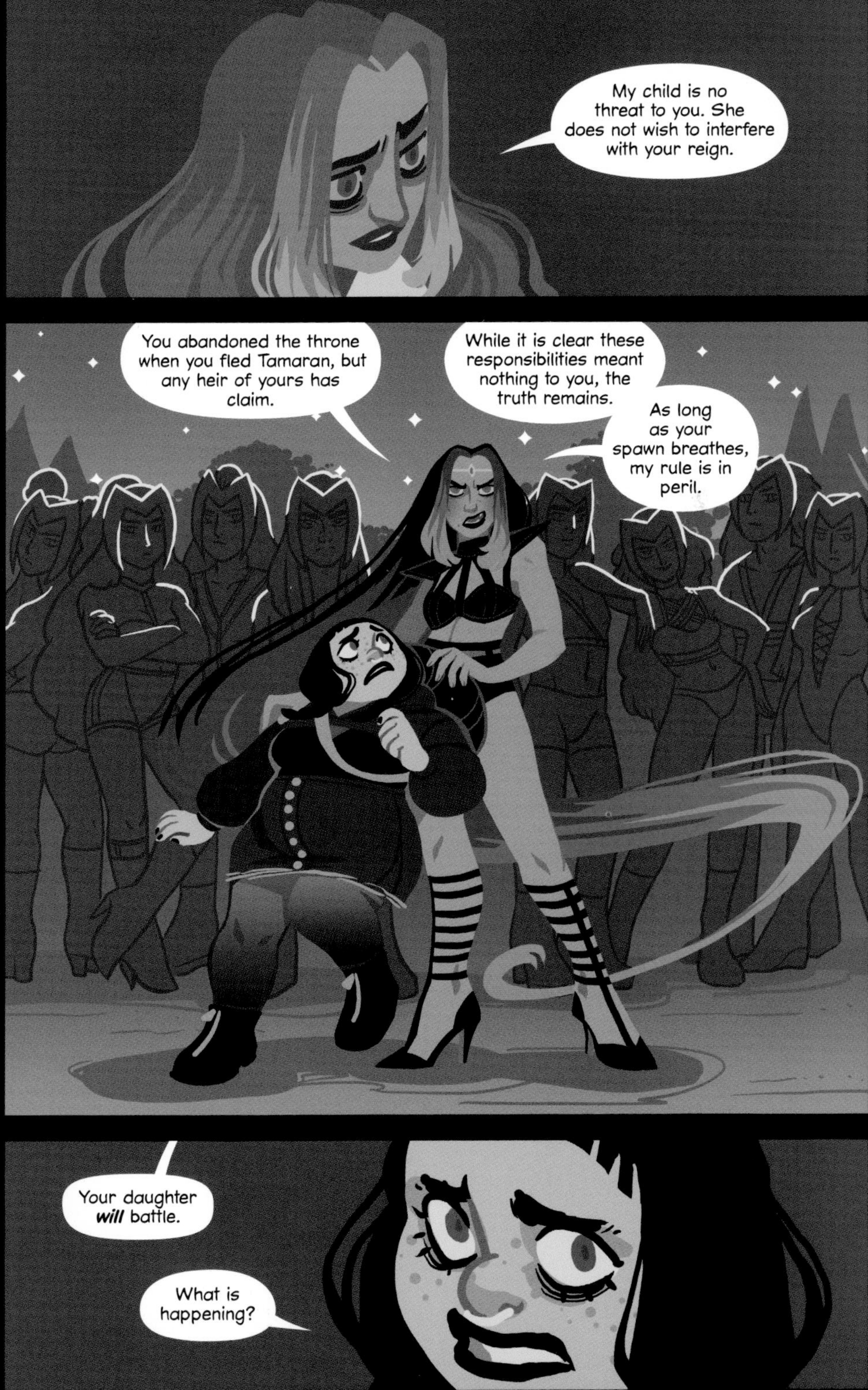
My child is no threat to you. She does not wish to interfere with your reign.
You abandoned the throne when you fled Tamaran, but any heir of yours has claim.
While it is clear these responsibilities meant nothing to you, the truth remains.
As long as your spawn breathes, my rule is in peril.
Your daughter *will* battle.
What is happening?

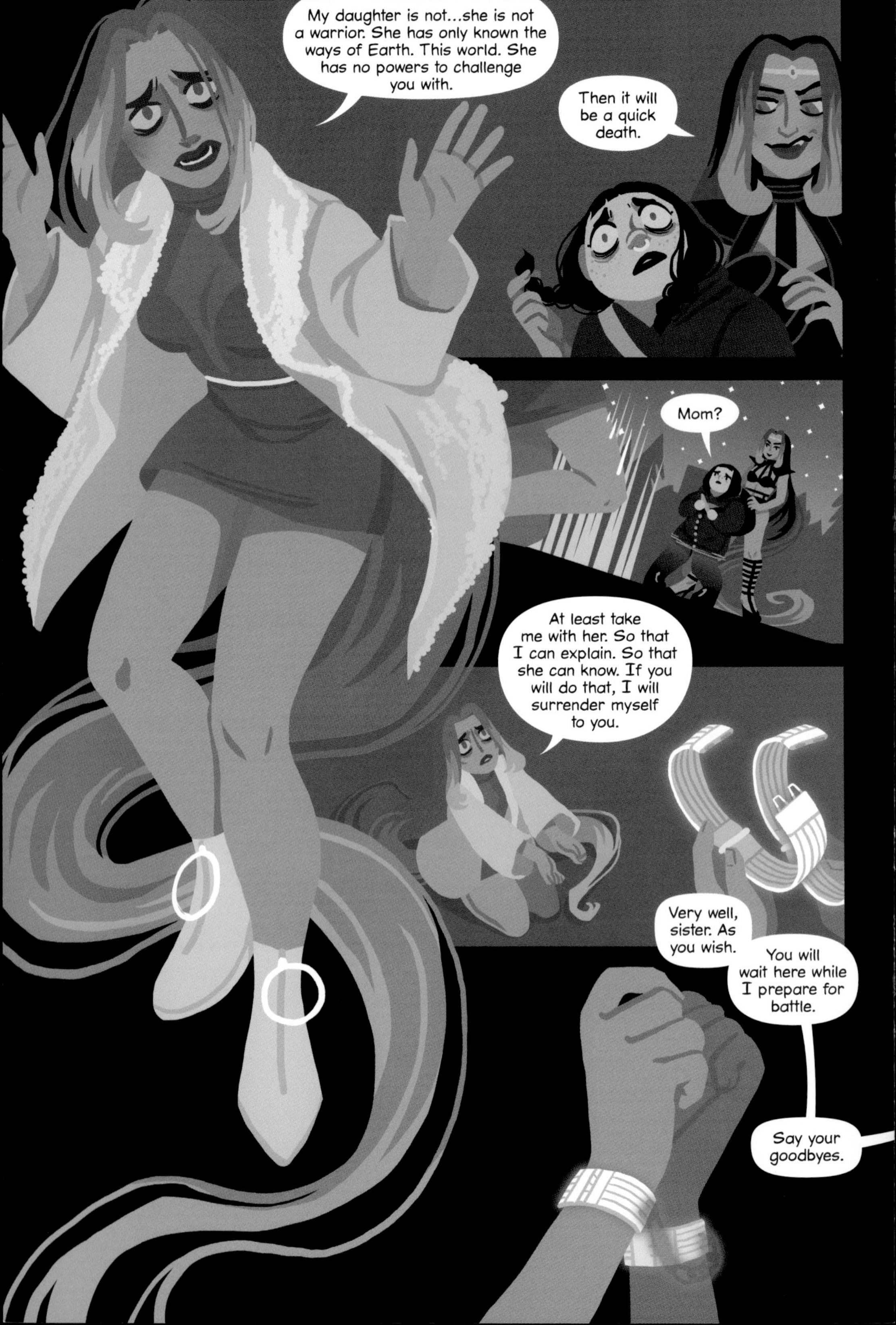
My daughter is not...she is not a warrior. She has only known the ways of Earth. This world. She has no powers to challenge you with.
Then it will be a quick death.
Mom?
At least take me with her. So that I can explain. So that she can know. If you will do that, I will surrender myself to you.
Very well, sister. As you wish.
You will wait here while I prepare for battle.
Say your goodbyes.

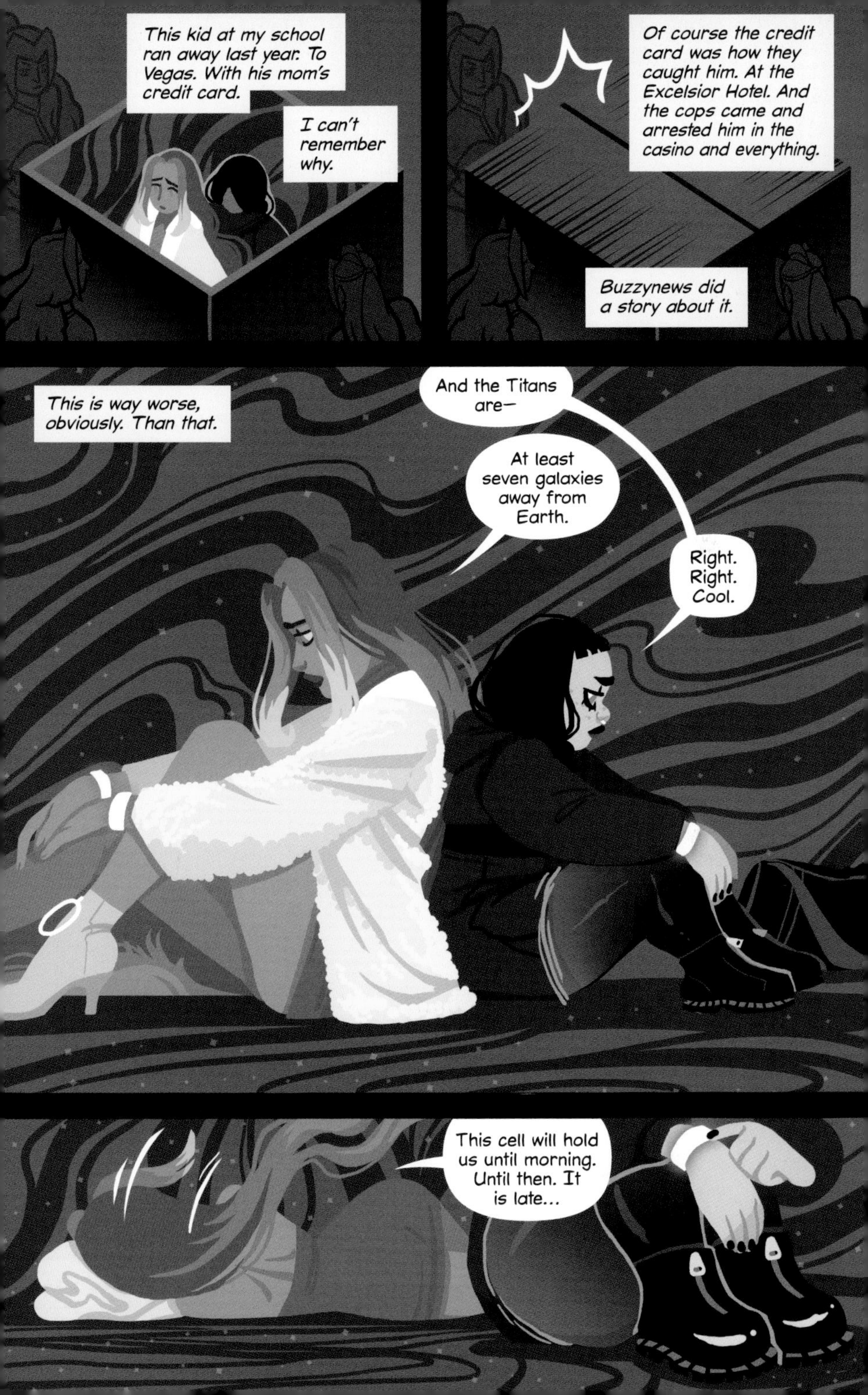
This kid at my school ran away last year. To Vegas. With his mom's credit card.
I can't remember why.
Of course the credit card was how they caught him. At the Excelsior Hotel. And the cops came and arrested him in the casino and everything.
Buzzynews did a story about it.
This is way worse, obviously. Than that.
And the Titans are—
At least seven galaxies away from Earth.
Right. Right. Cool.
This cell will hold us until morning. Until then. It is late...

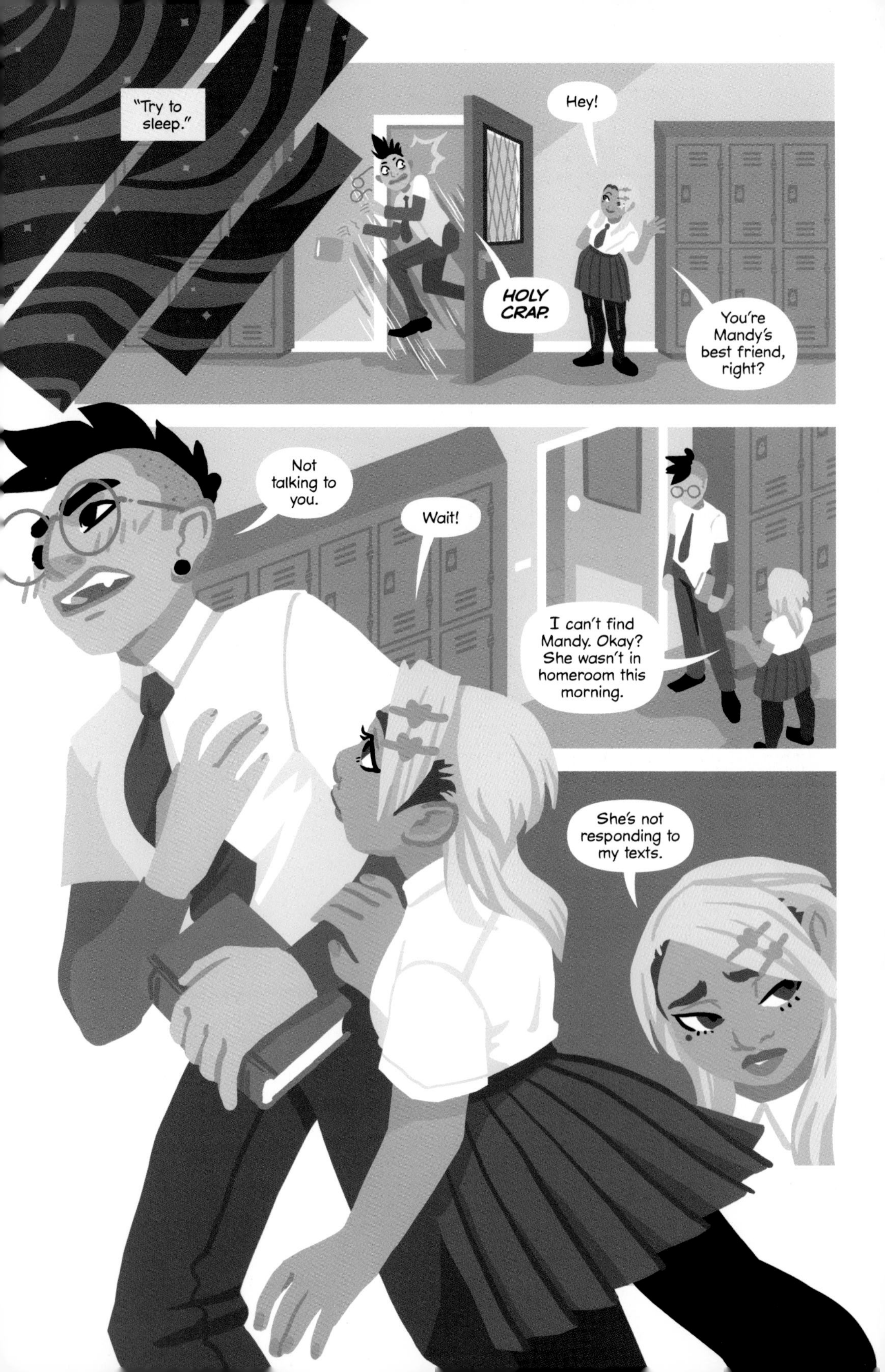
"Try to sleep."
Hey!
HOLY CRAP.
You're Mandy's best friend, right?
Not talking to you.
Wait!
I can't find Mandy. Okay? She wasn't in homeroom this morning.
She's not responding to my texts.

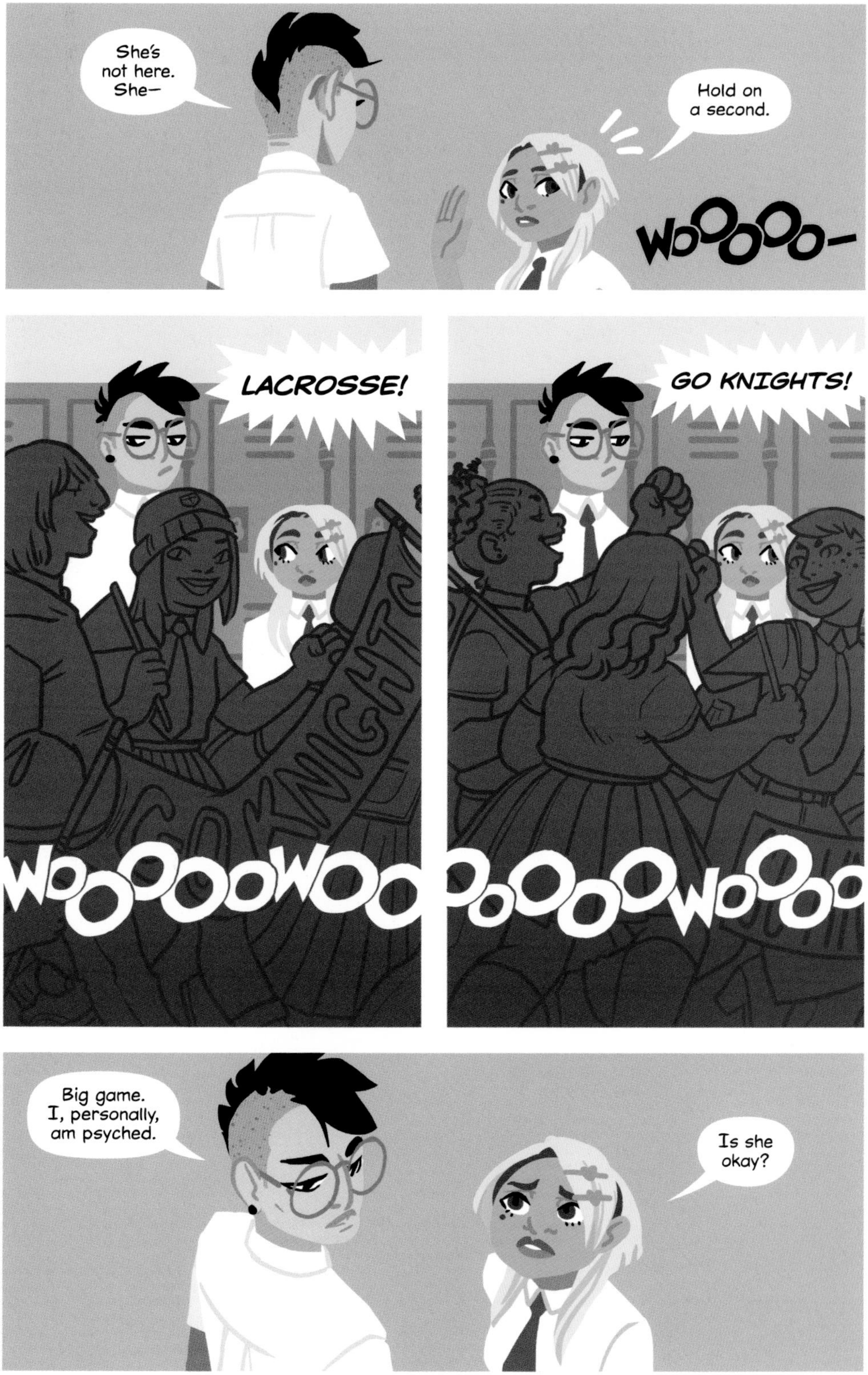
She's not here. She—
Hold on a second.
WOOOOO-
LACROSSE!
WOOOOOWOOO
GO KNIGHTS!
OOOOOOOWOOOO
Big game. I, personally, am psyched.
Is she okay?

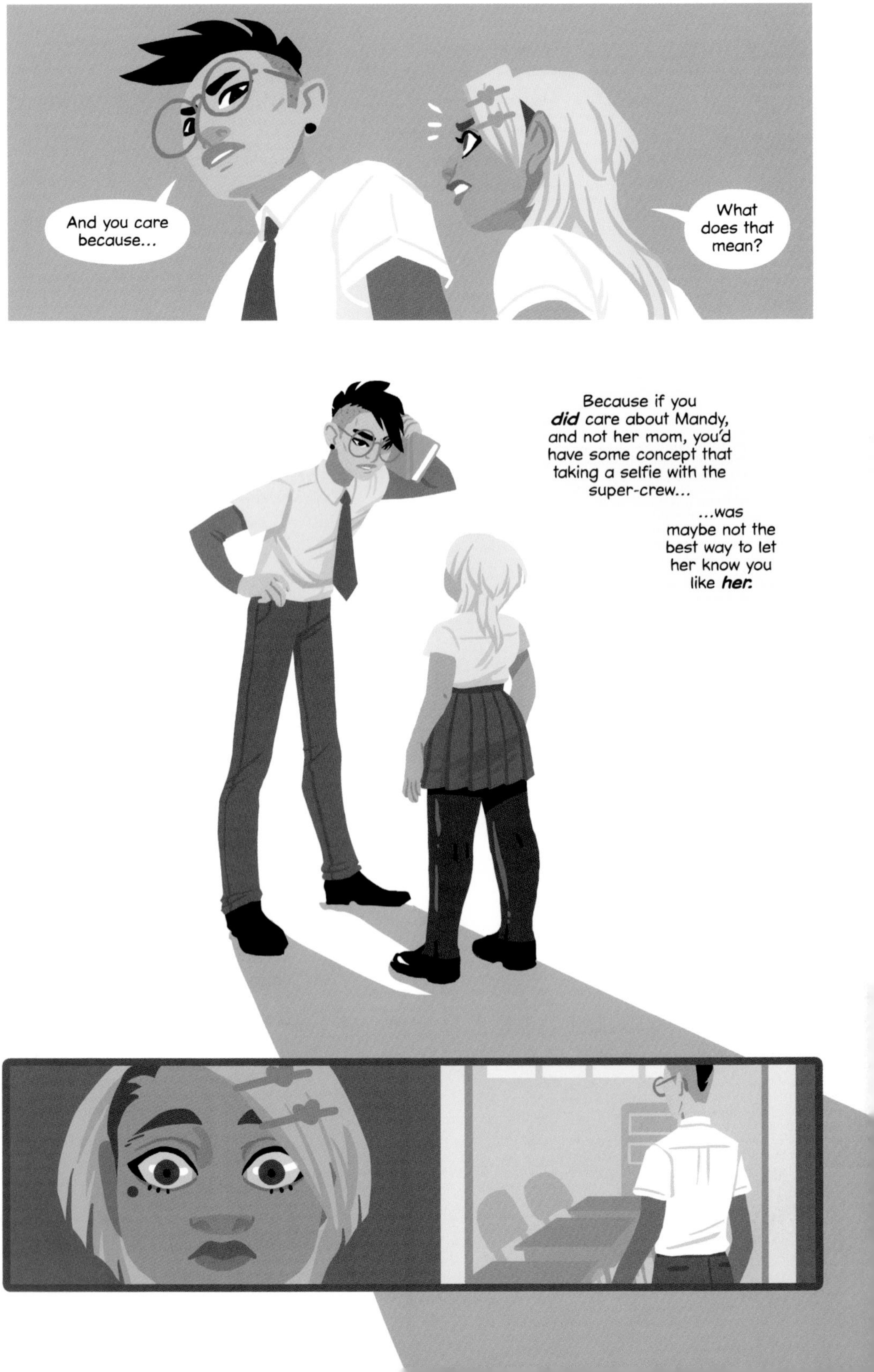
And you care because...
What does that mean?
Because if you *did* care about Mandy, and not her mom, you'd have some concept that taking a selfie with the super-crew...
...was maybe not the best way to let her know you like *her*.

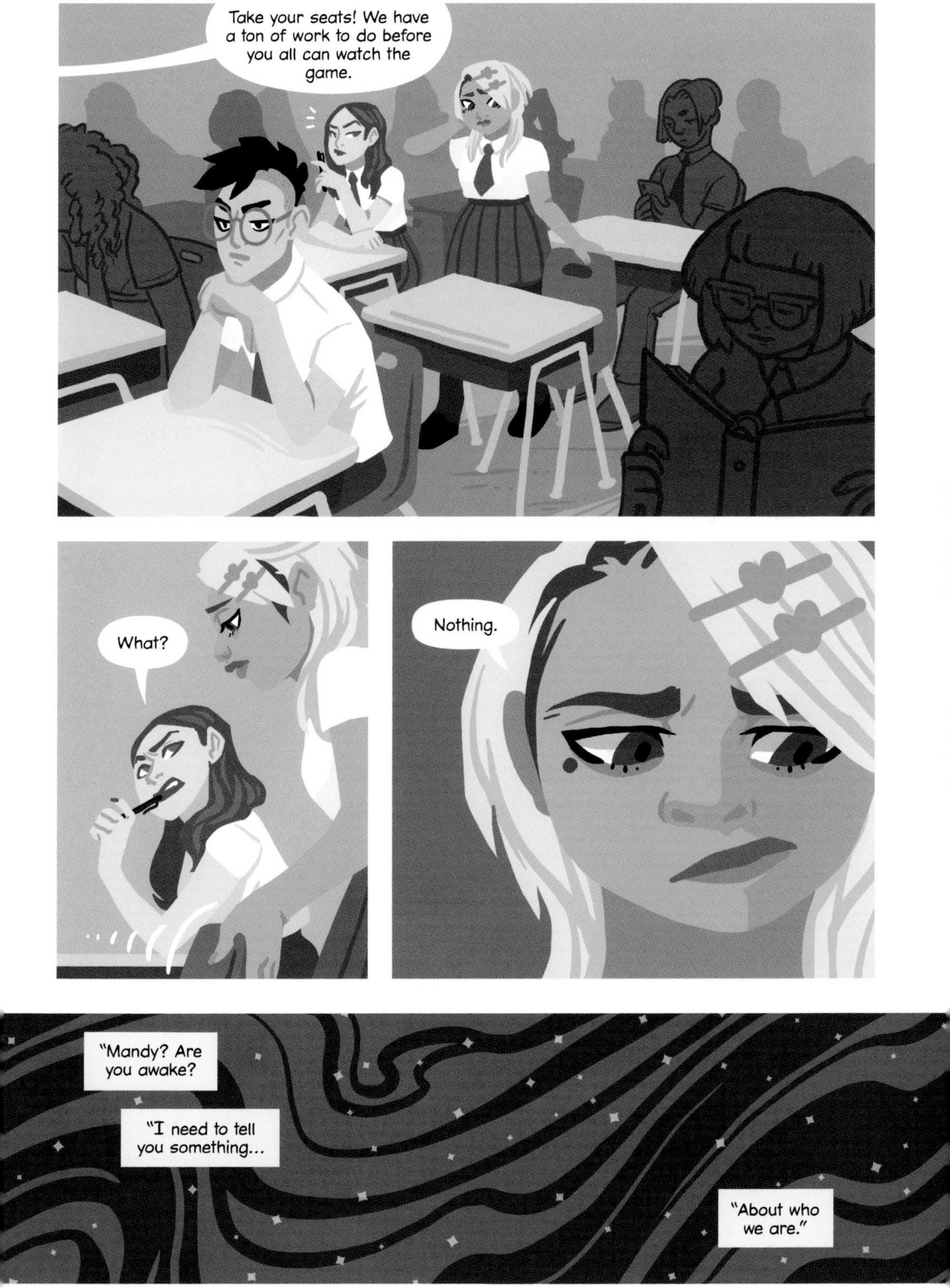
Take your seats! We have a ton of work to do before you all can watch the game.
What?
Nothing.
"Mandy? Are you awake?
"I need to tell you something...
"About who we are."

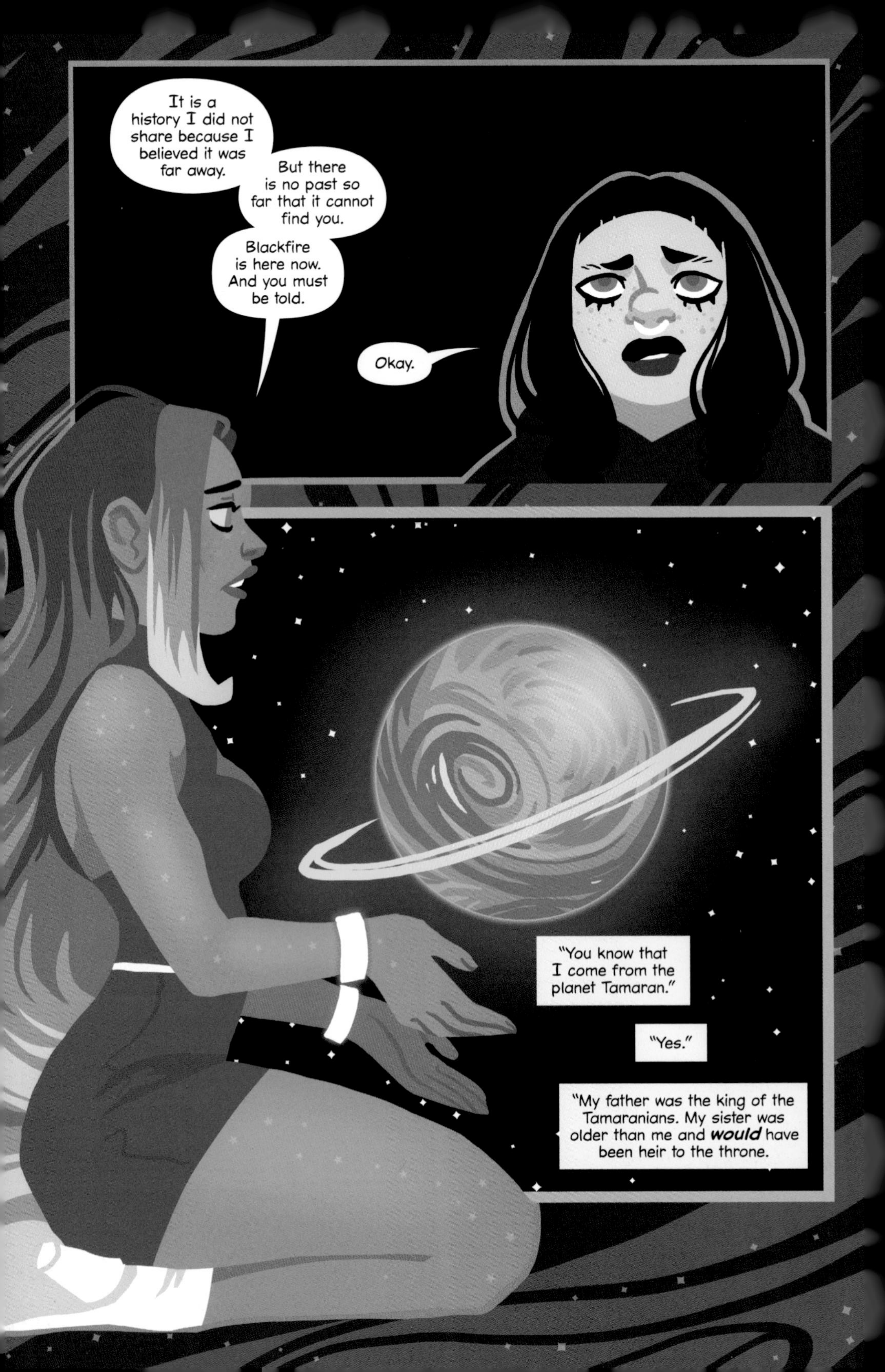
It is a history I did not share because I believed it was far away.
But there is no past so far that it cannot find you.
Blackfire is here now. And you must be told.
Okay.
"You know that I come from the planet Tamaran."
"Yes."
"My father was the king of the Tamaranians. My sister was older than me and ***would*** have been heir to the throne.

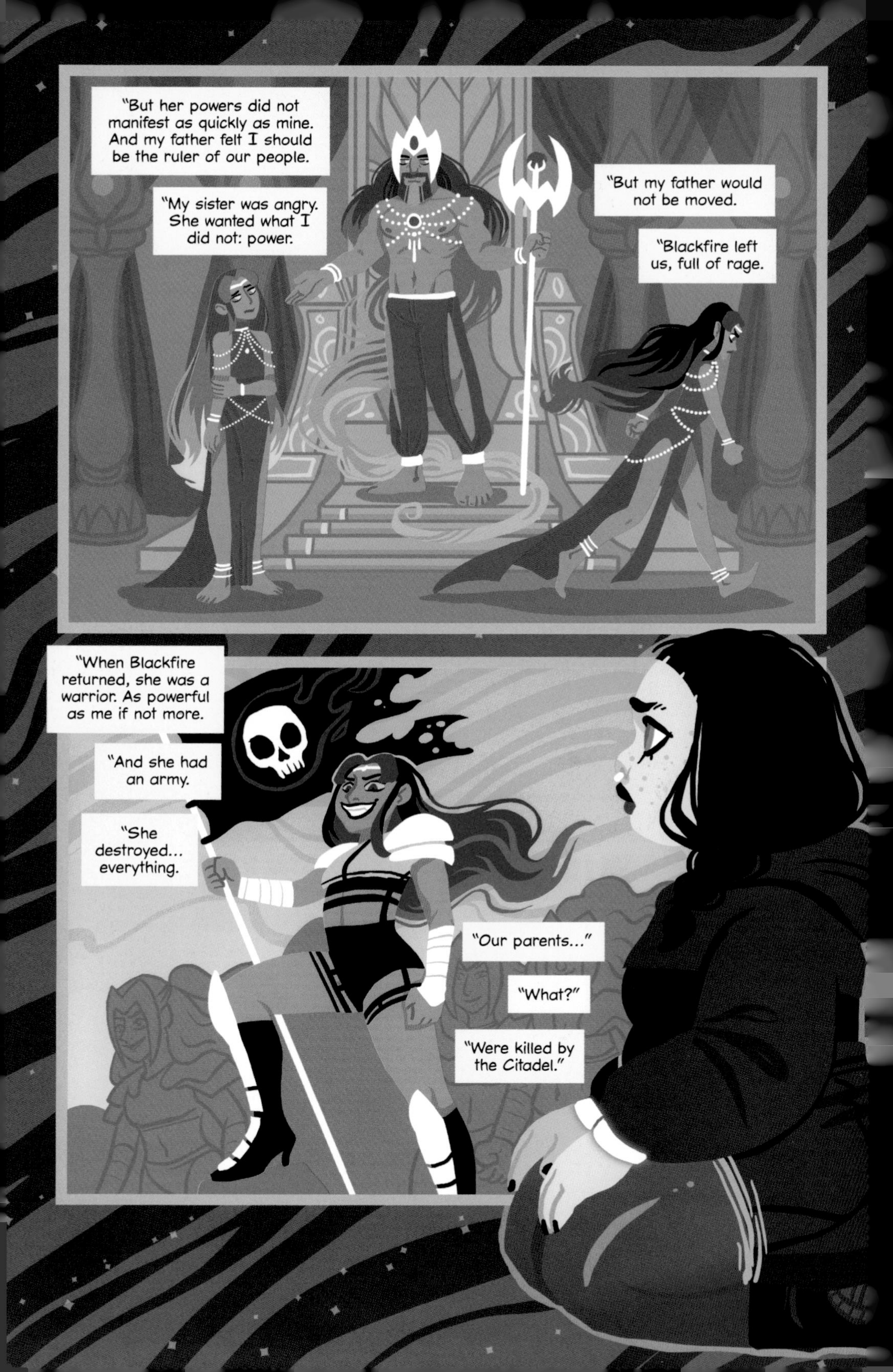
"But her powers did not manifest as quickly as mine. And my father felt I should be the ruler of our people.
"My sister was angry. She wanted what I did not: power.
"But my father would not be moved.
"Blackfire left us, full of rage.
"When Blackfire returned, she was a warrior. As powerful as me if not more.
"And she had an army.
"She destroyed... everything.
"Our parents..."
"What?"
"Were killed by the Citadel."

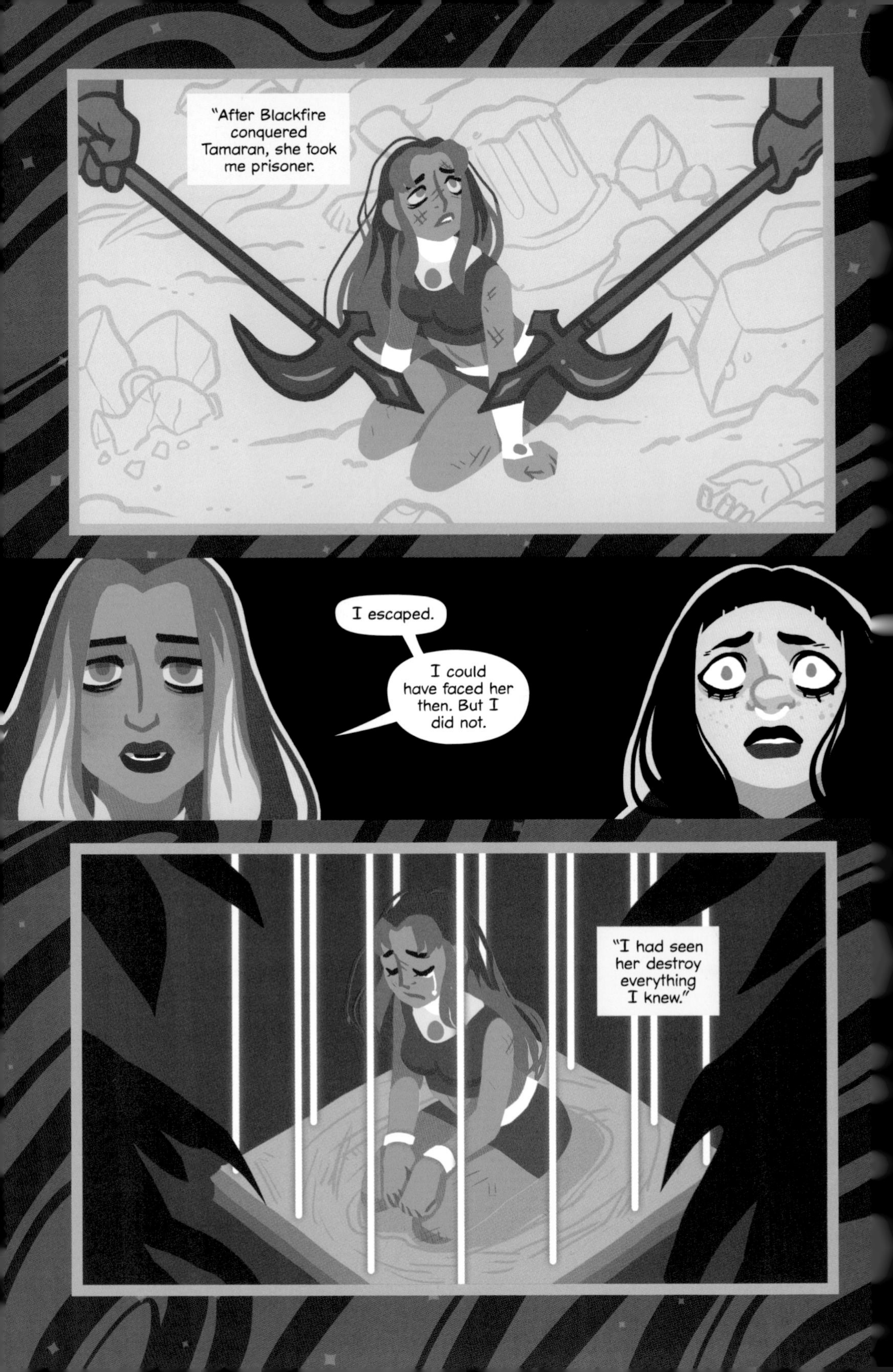
"After Blackfire conquered Tamaran, she took me prisoner.
I escaped.
I could have faced her then. But I did not.
"I had seen her destroy everything I knew."

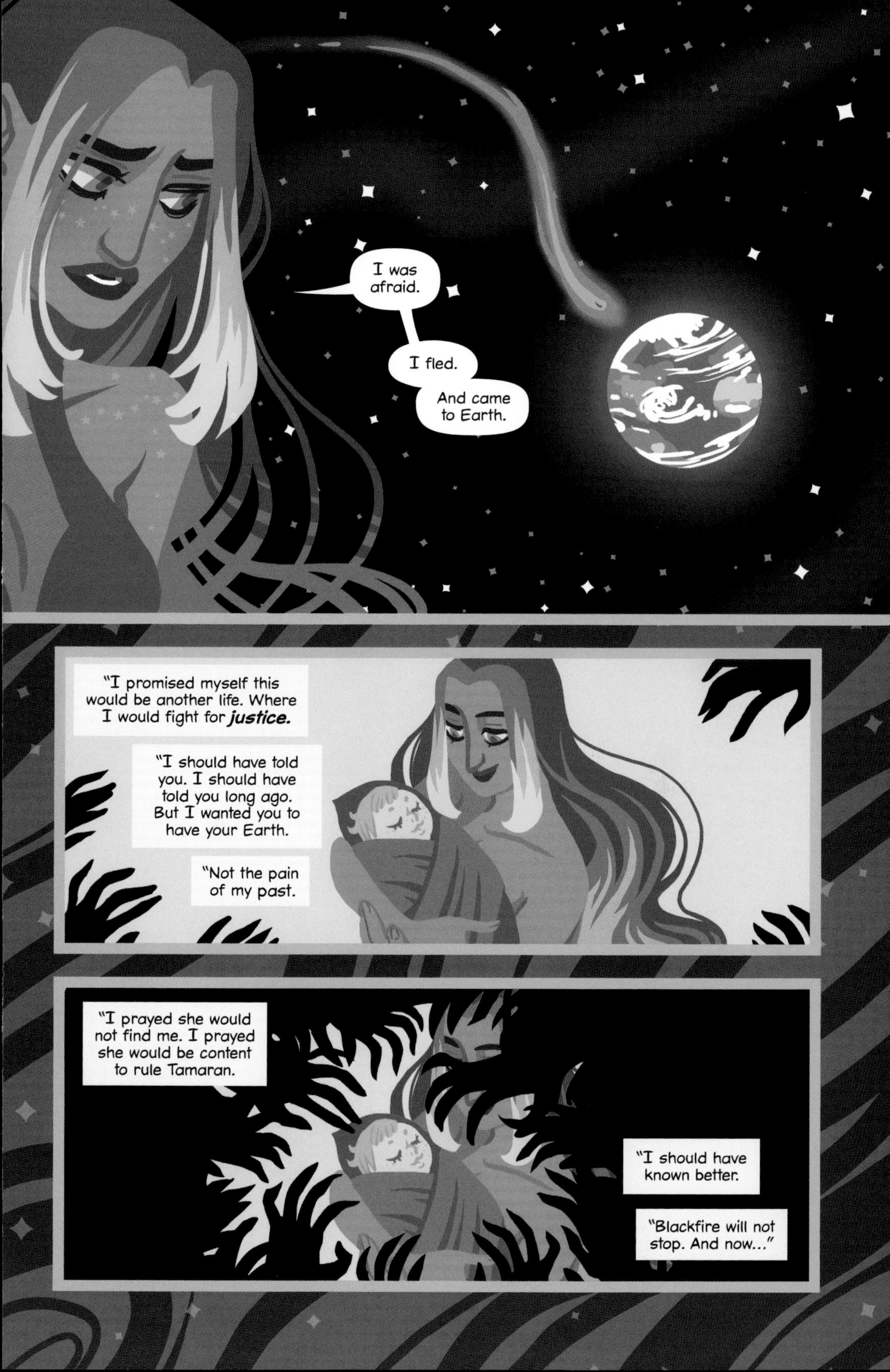
I was afraid.
I fled.
And came to Earth.
"I promised myself this would be another life. Where I would fight for ***justice.***
"I should have told you. I should have told you long ago. But I wanted you to have your Earth.
"Not the pain of my past.
"I prayed she would not find me. I prayed she would be content to rule Tamaran.
"I should have known better.
"Blackfire will not stop. And now..."

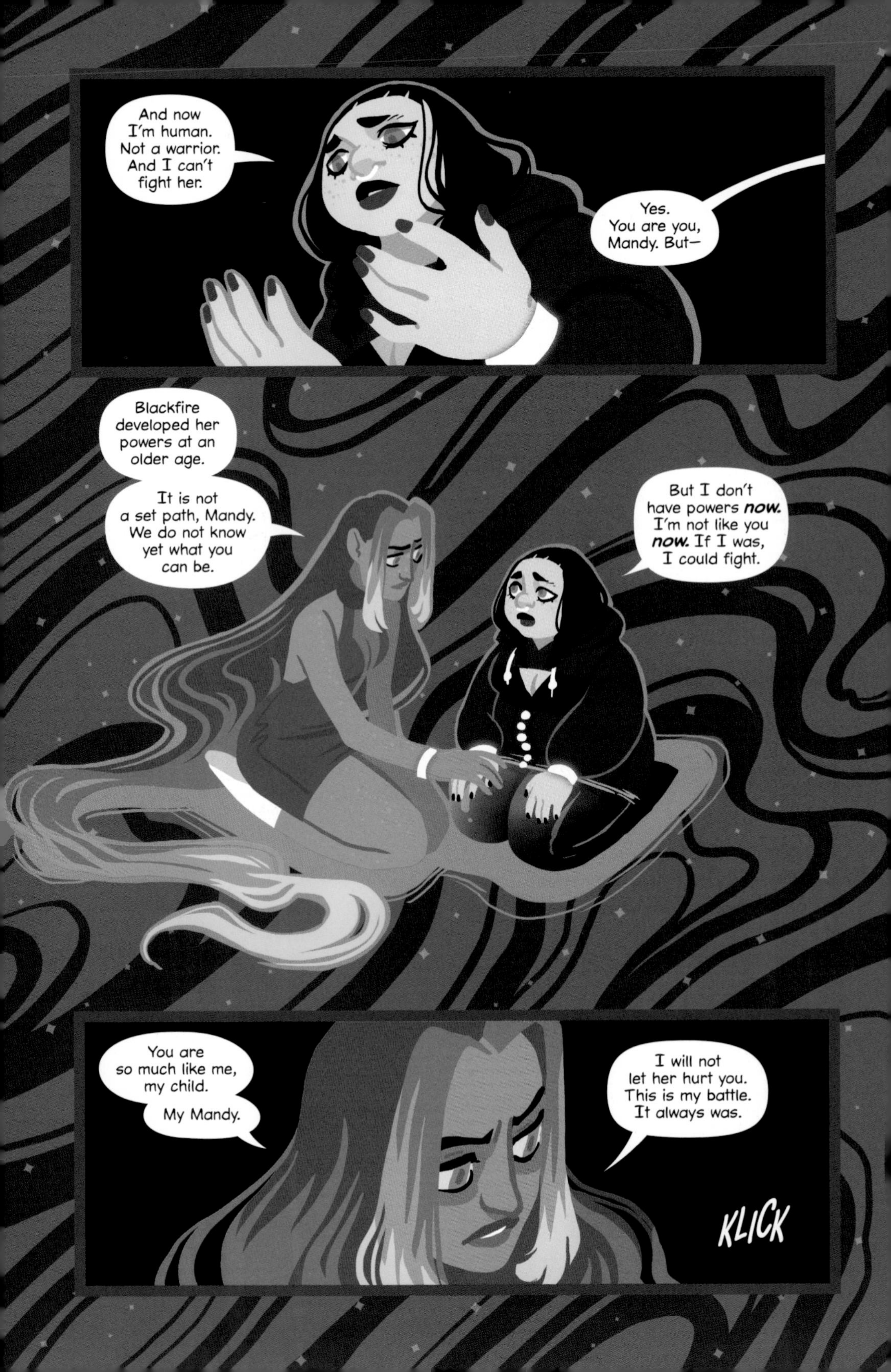
And now I'm human. Not a warrior. And I can't fight her.
Yes. You are you, Mandy. But—
Blackfire developed her powers at an older age.
It is not a set path, Mandy. We do not know yet what you can be.
But I don't have powers *now.* I'm not like you *now.* If I was, I could fight.
You are so much like me, my child.
My Mandy.
I will not let her hurt you. This is my battle. It always was.
KLICK

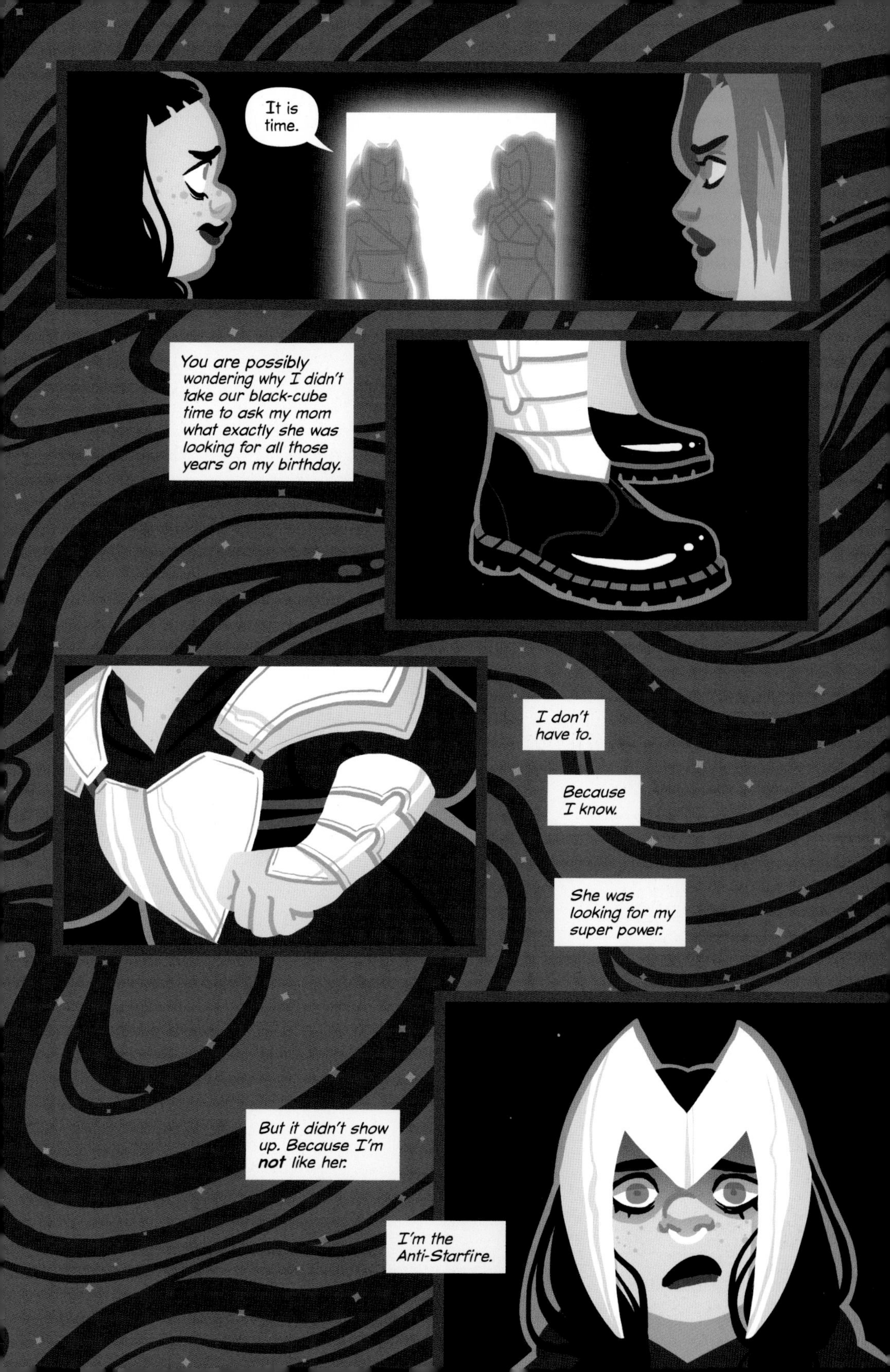
It is time.
You are possibly wondering why I didn't take our black-cube time to ask my mom what exactly she was looking for all those years on my birthday.
I don't have to.
Because I know.
She was looking for my super power.
But it didn't show up. Because I'm **not** like her.
I'm the Anti-Starfire.

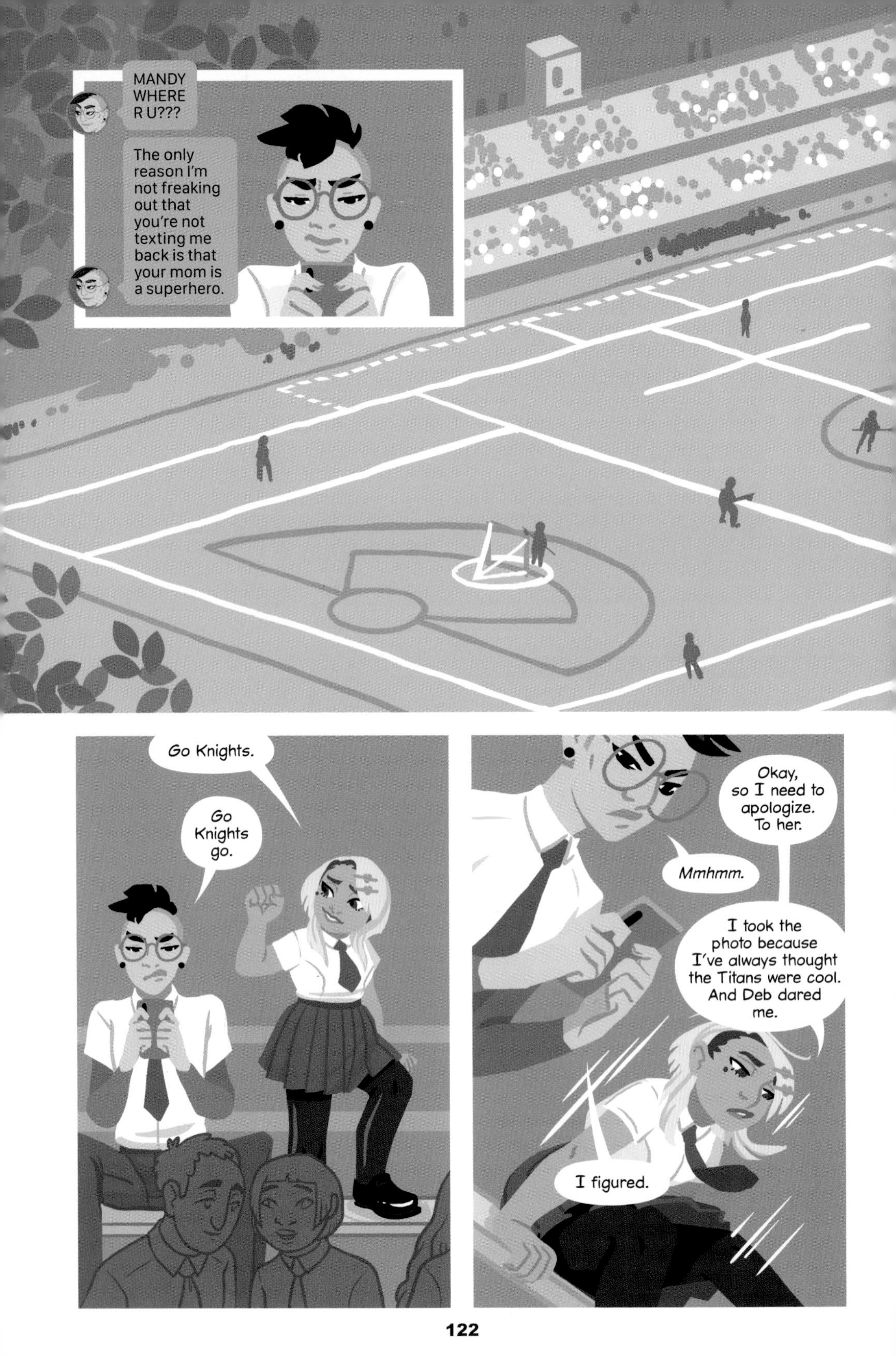

MANDY WHERE R U???
The only reason I'm not freaking out that you're not texting me back is that your mom is a superhero.
Go Knights.
Go Knights go.
Okay, so I need to apologize. To her.
Mmhmm.
I took the photo because I've always thought the Titans were cool. And Deb dared me.
I figured.

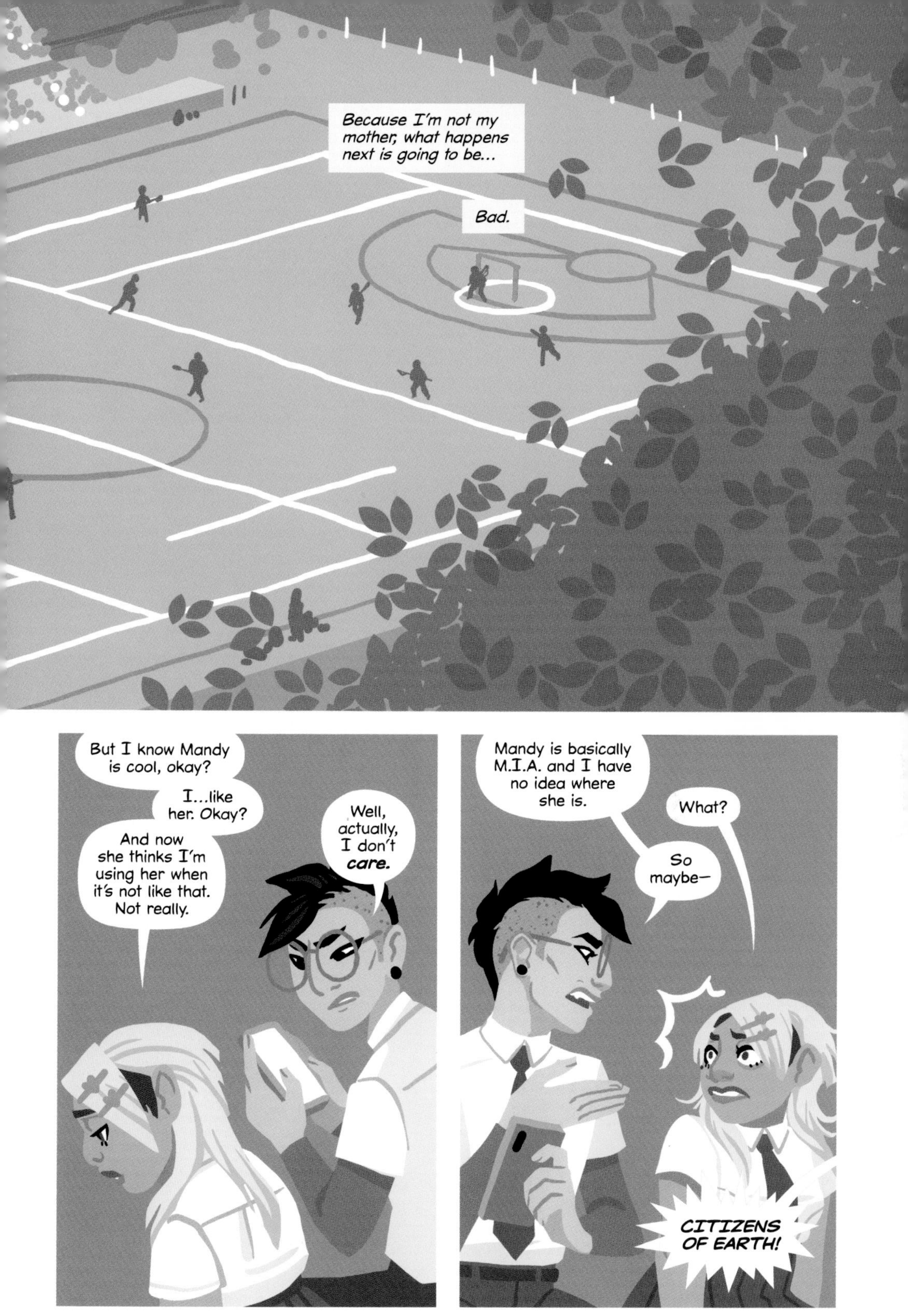
Because I'm not my mother, what happens next is going to be...
Bad.
But I know Mandy is cool, okay?
I...like her. Okay?
And now she thinks I'm using her when it's not like that. Not really.
Well, actually, I don't **care.**
Mandy is basically M.I.A. and I have no idea where she is.
So maybe—
What?
CITIZENS OF EARTH!

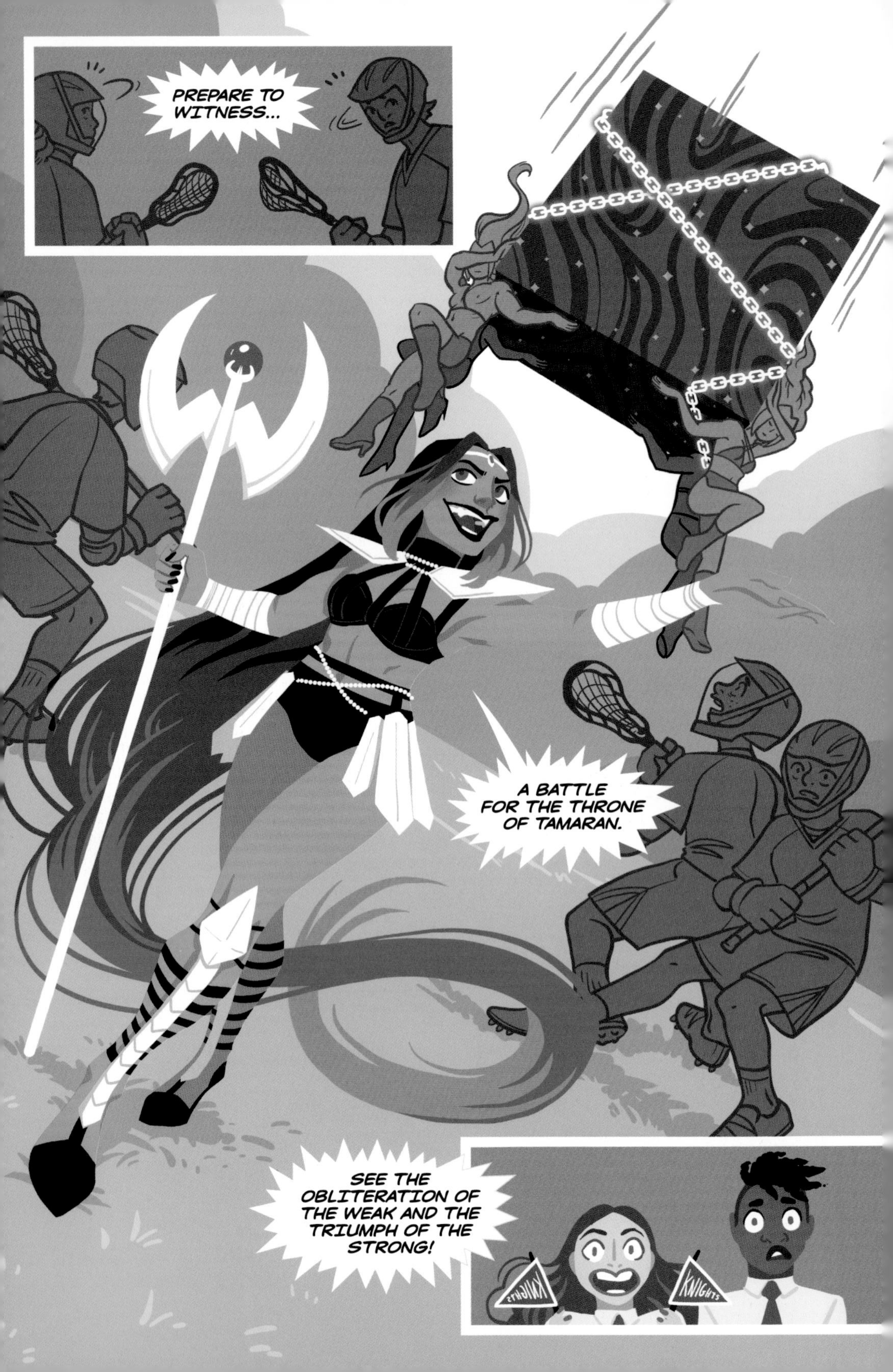
PREPARE TO WITNESS...
A BATTLE FOR THE THRONE OF TAMARAN.
SEE THE OBLITERATION OF THE WEAK AND THE TRIUMPH OF THE STRONG!
KNIGHTS
KNIGHTS

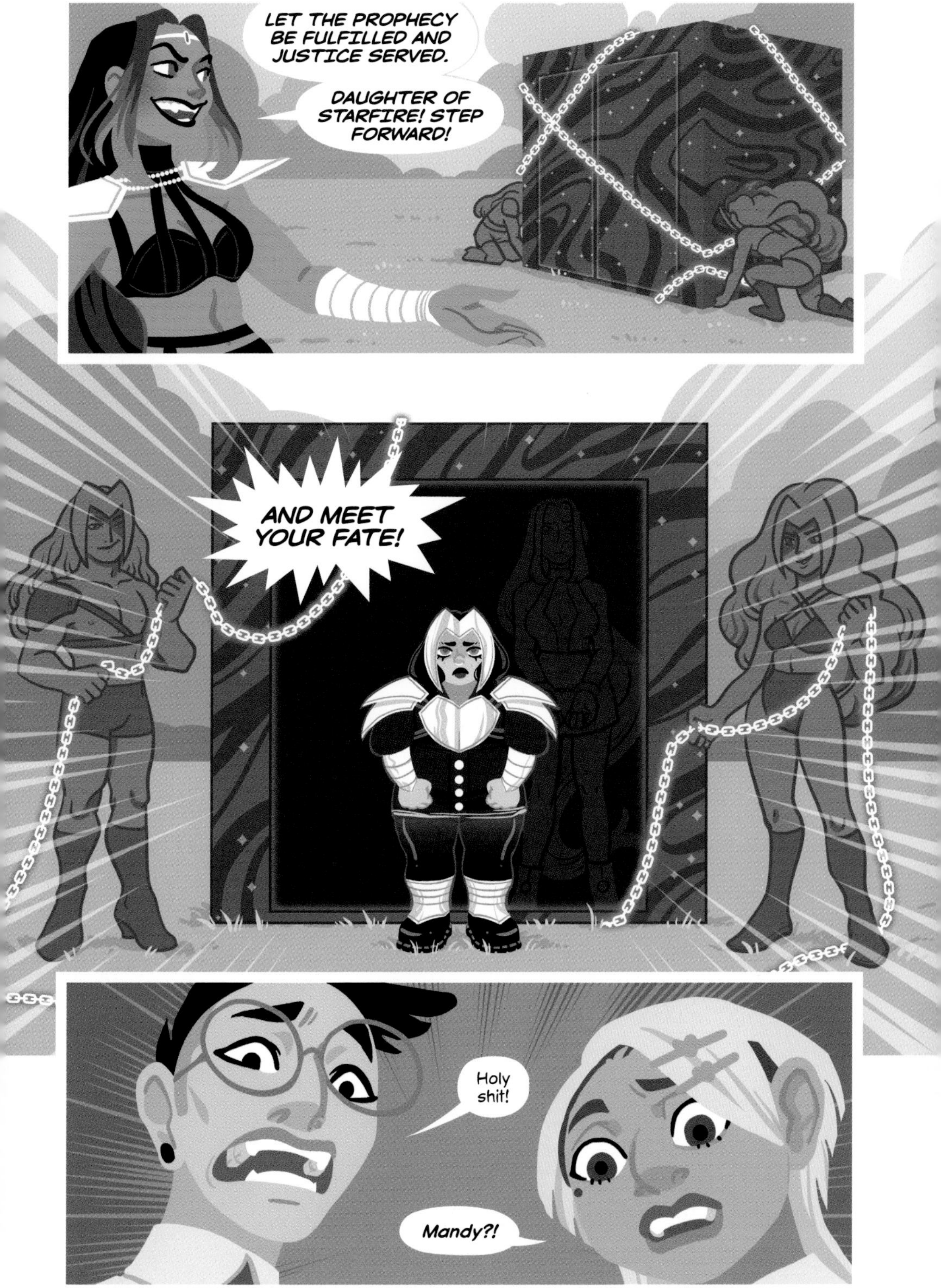
LET THE PROPHECY BE FULFILLED AND JUSTICE SERVED.
DAUGHTER OF STARFIRE! STEP FORWARD!
AND MEET YOUR FATE!
Holy shit!
Mandy?!

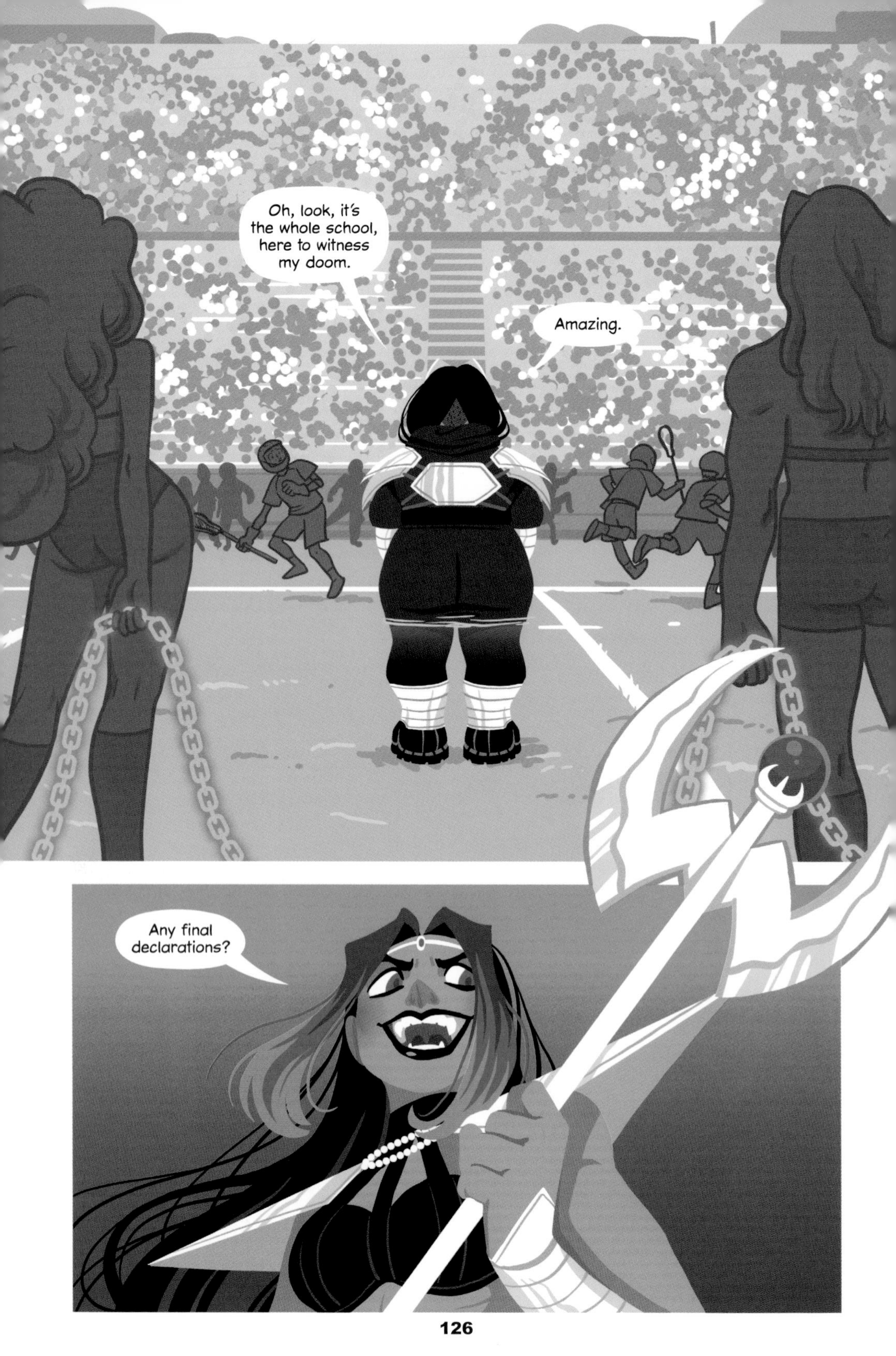
Oh, look, it's the whole school, here to witness my doom.
Amazing.
Any final declarations?

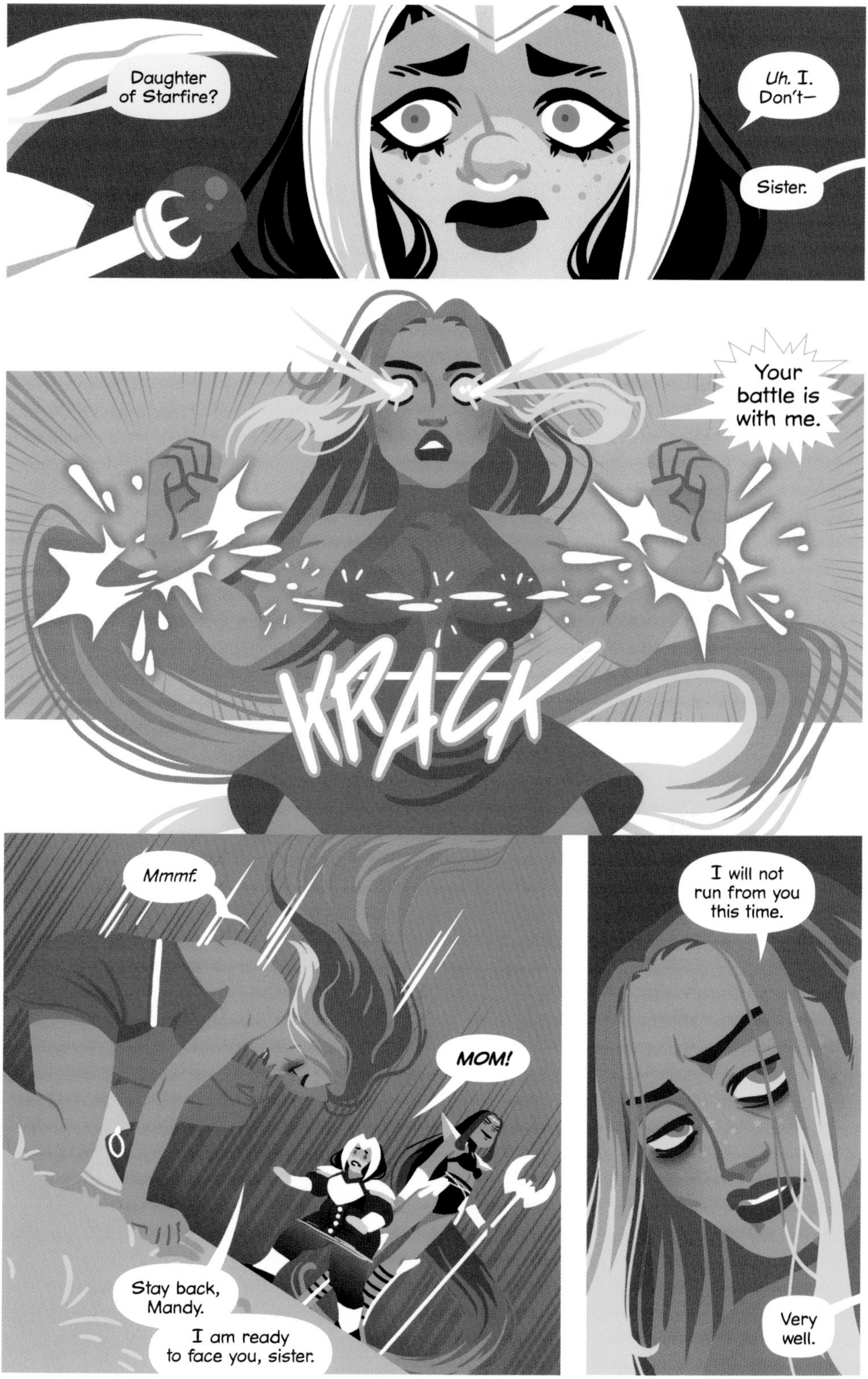
Daughter of Starfire?
Uh. I. Don't—
Sister.
Your battle is with me.
KRACK
Mmmf.
MOM!
Stay back, Mandy.
I am ready to face you, sister.
I will not run from you this time.
Very well.

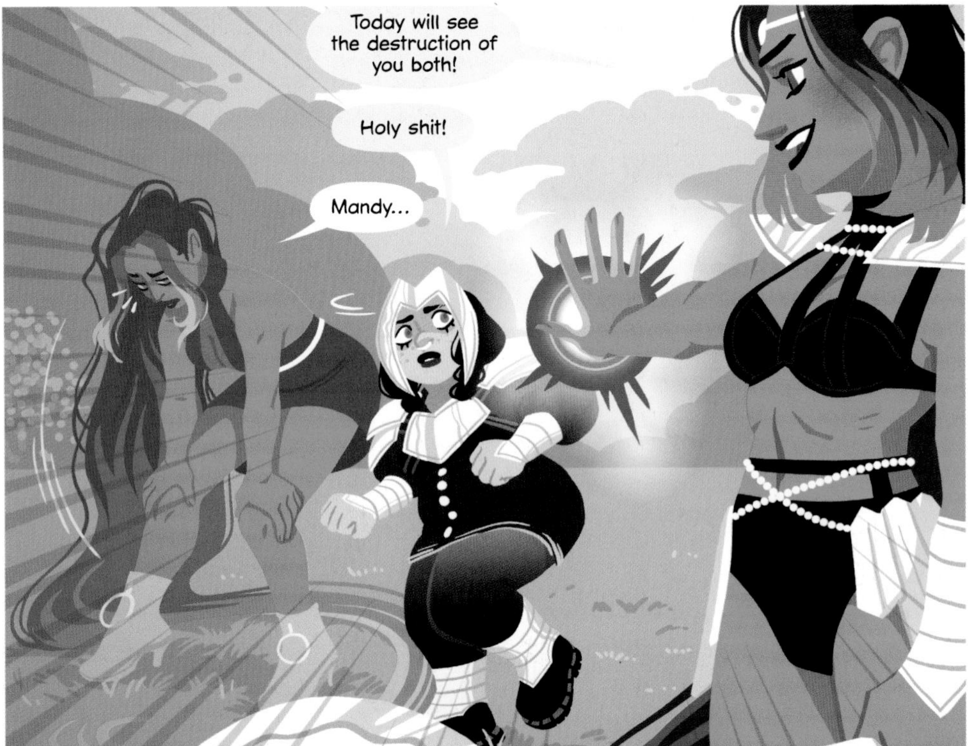
Today will see the destruction of you both!
Holy shit!
Mandy...

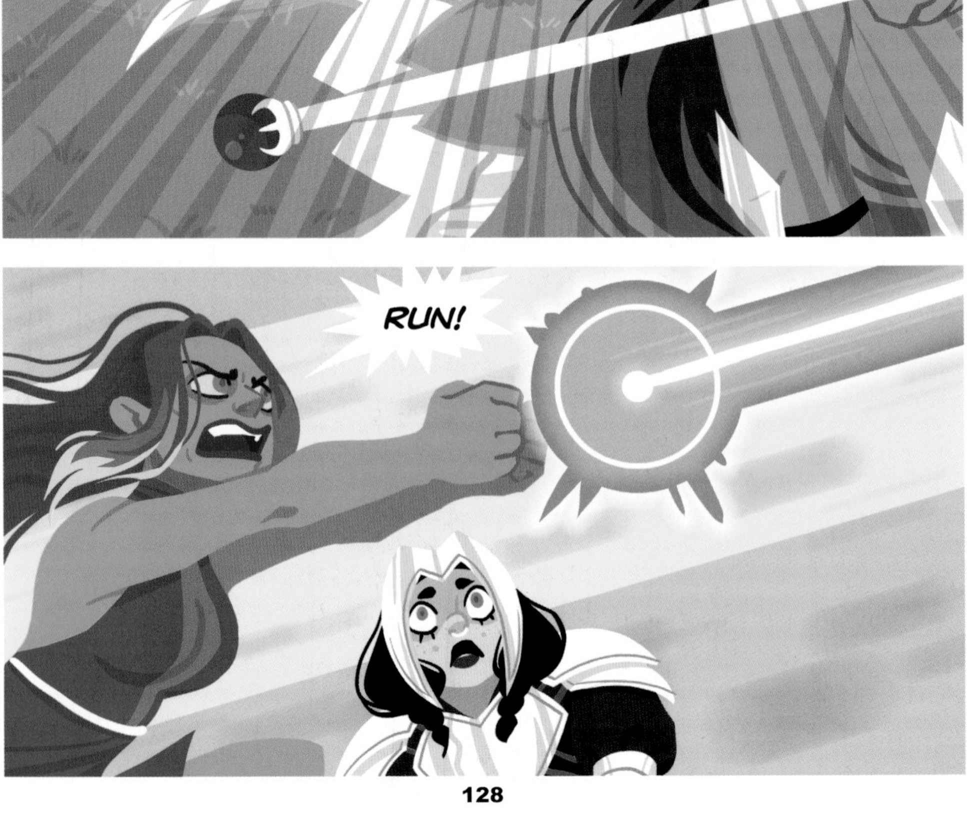
RUN!

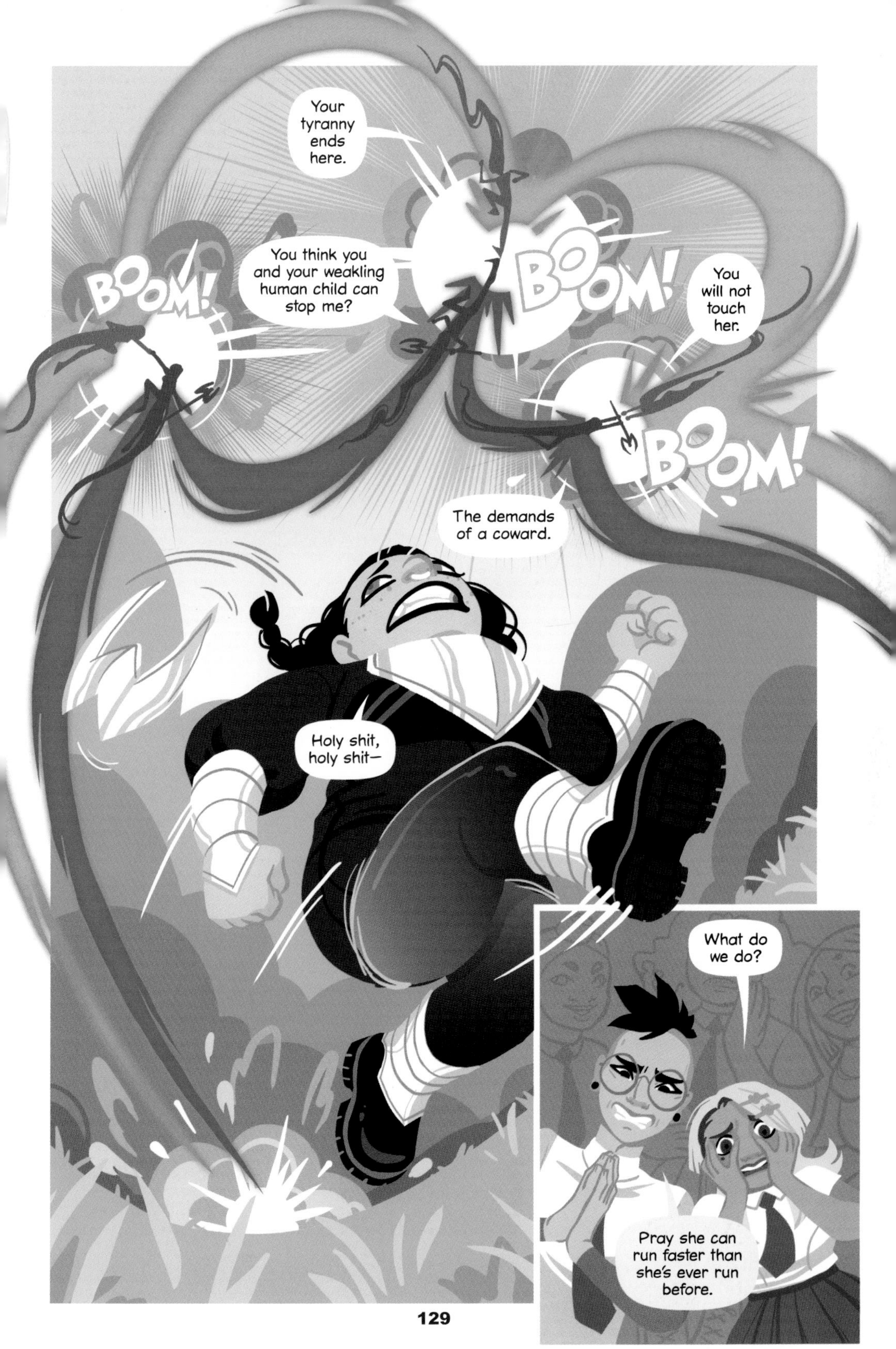
Your tyranny ends here.
BOOM!
You think you and your weakling human child can stop me?
BOOM!
You will not touch her.
BOOM!
The demands of a coward.
Holy shit, holy shit—
What do we do?
Pray she can run faster than she's ever run before.

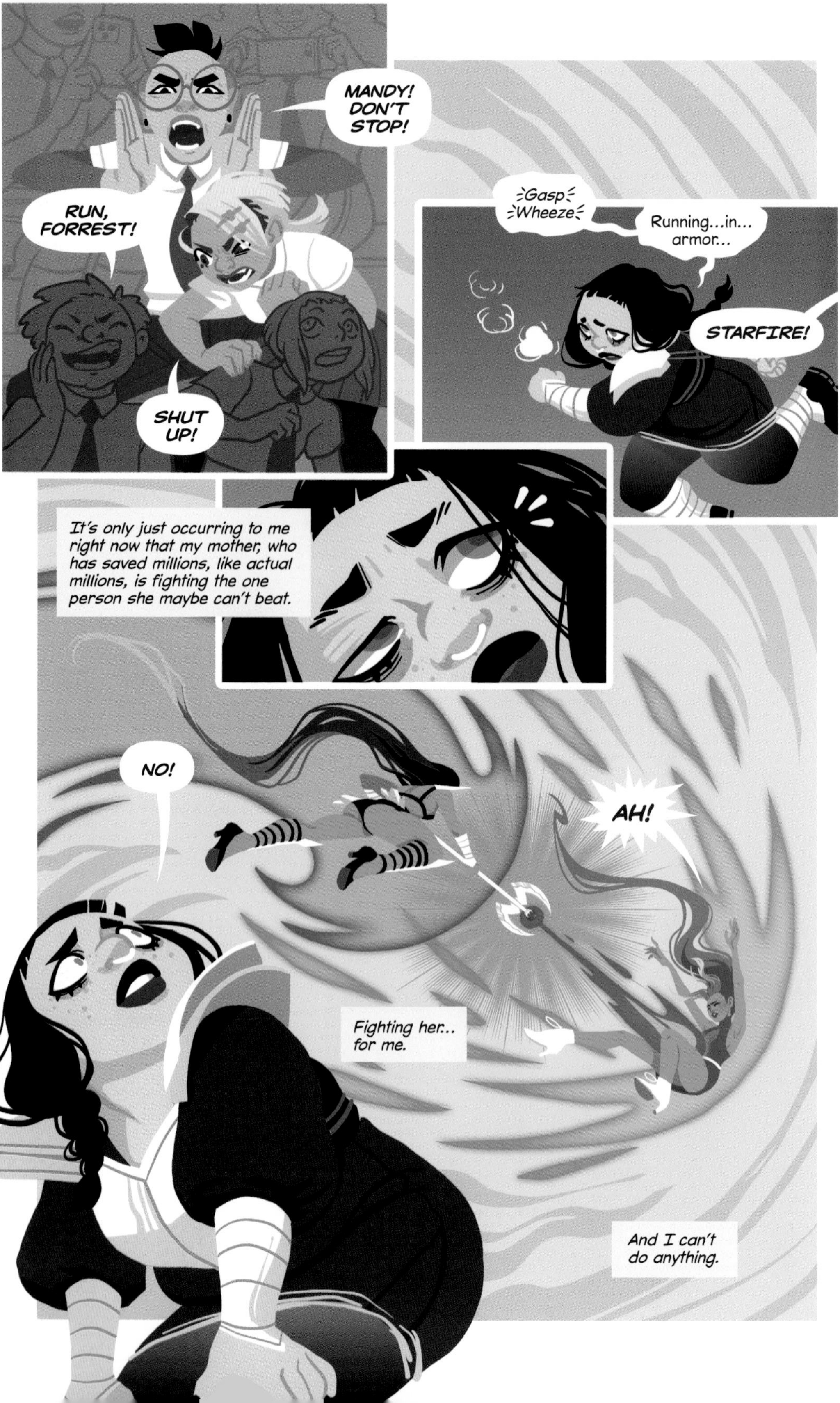
MANDY! DON'T STOP!
RUN, FORREST!
SHUT UP!
Gasp
Wheeze
Running...in... armor...
STARFIRE!
It's only just occurring to me right now that my mother, who has saved millions, like actual millions, is fighting the one person she maybe can't beat.
NO!
AH!
Fighting her... for me.
And I can't do anything.

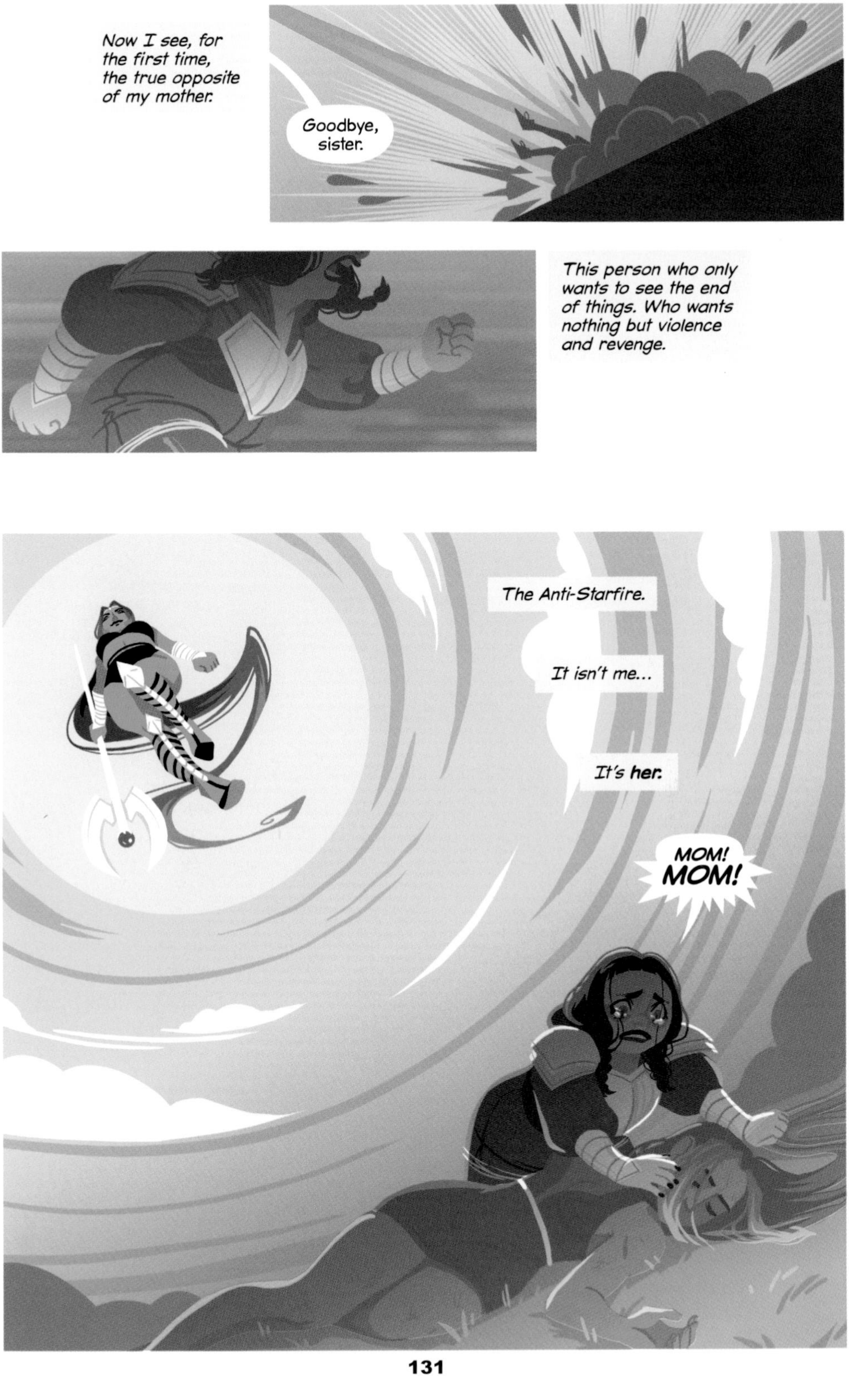
Now I see, for the first time, the true opposite of my mother.
Goodbye, sister.
This person who only wants to see the end of things. Who wants nothing but violence and revenge.
The Anti-Starfire.
It isn't me...
It's **her**.
MOM! MOM!

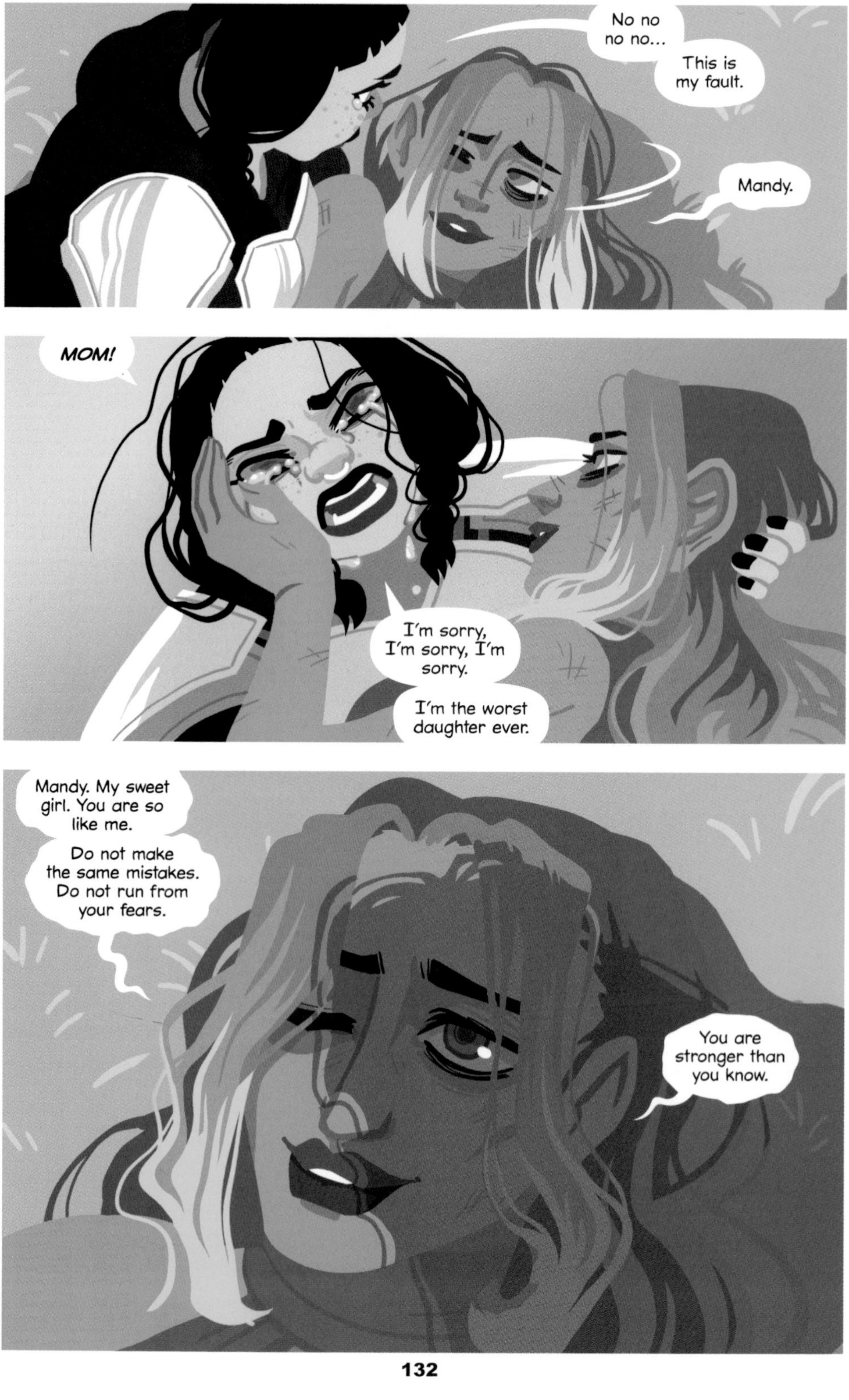
No no no no...
This is my fault.
Mandy.
MOM!
I'm sorry, I'm sorry, I'm sorry.
I'm the worst daughter ever.
Mandy. My sweet girl. You are so like me.
Do not make the same mistakes. Do not run from your fears.
You are stronger than you know.

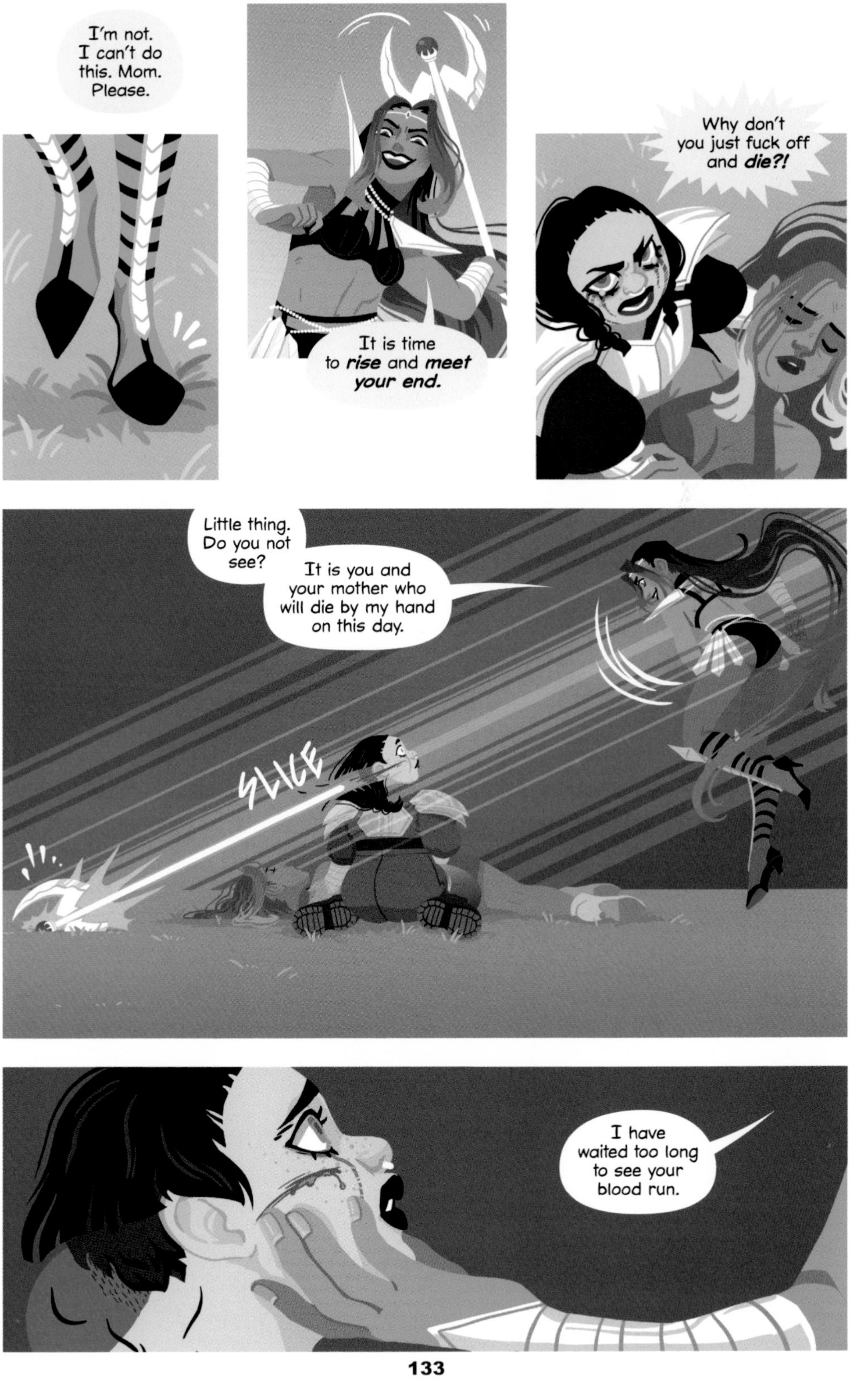
I'm not. I can't do this. Mom. Please.
It is time to *rise* and *meet your end.*
Why don't you just fuck off and *die?!*
Little thing. Do you not see?
It is you and your mother who will die by my hand on this day.
SLICE
I have waited too long to see your blood run.

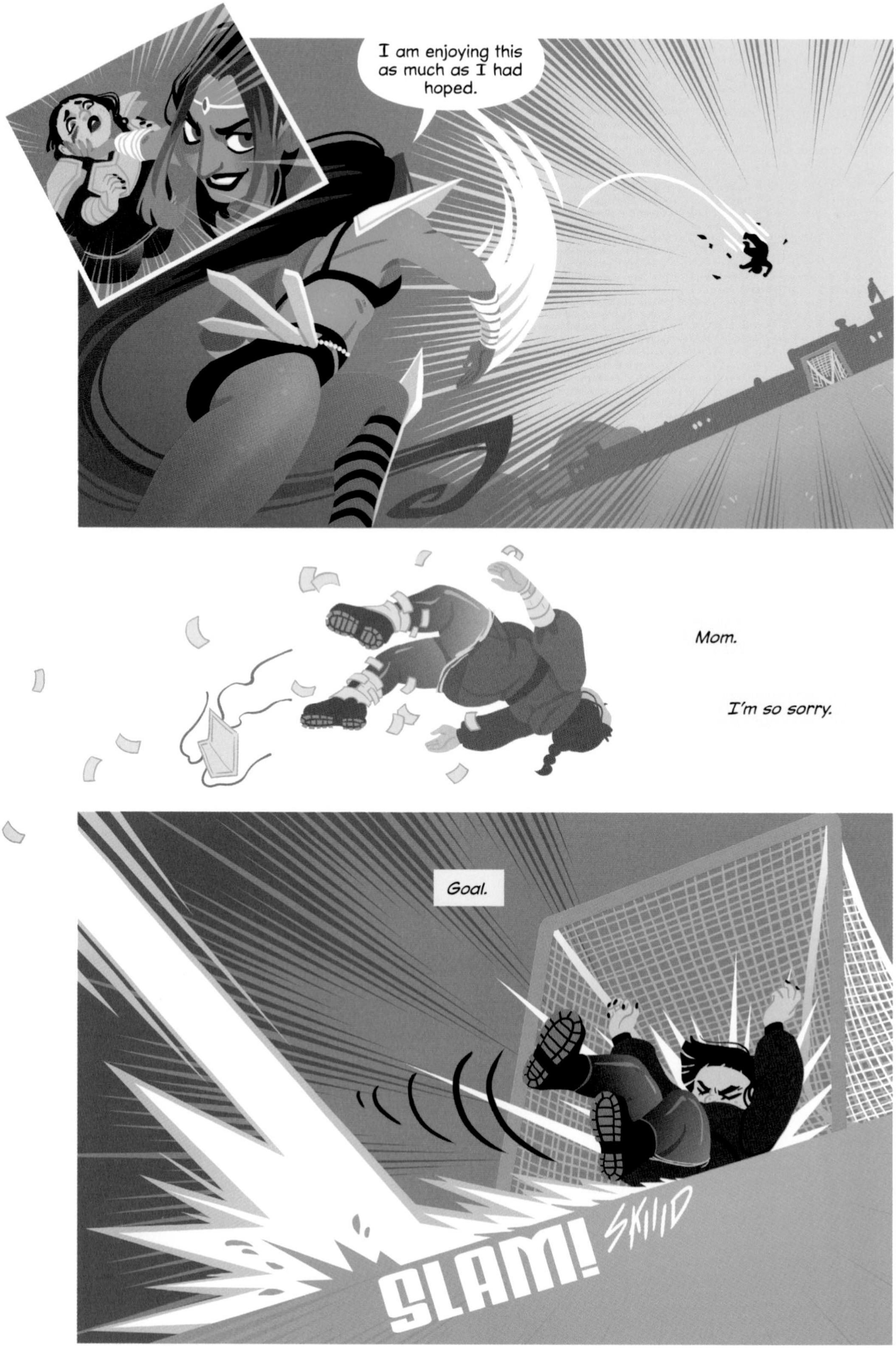
I am enjoying this as much as I had hoped.
Mom.
I'm so sorry.
Goal.
SLAM!
SKIIID

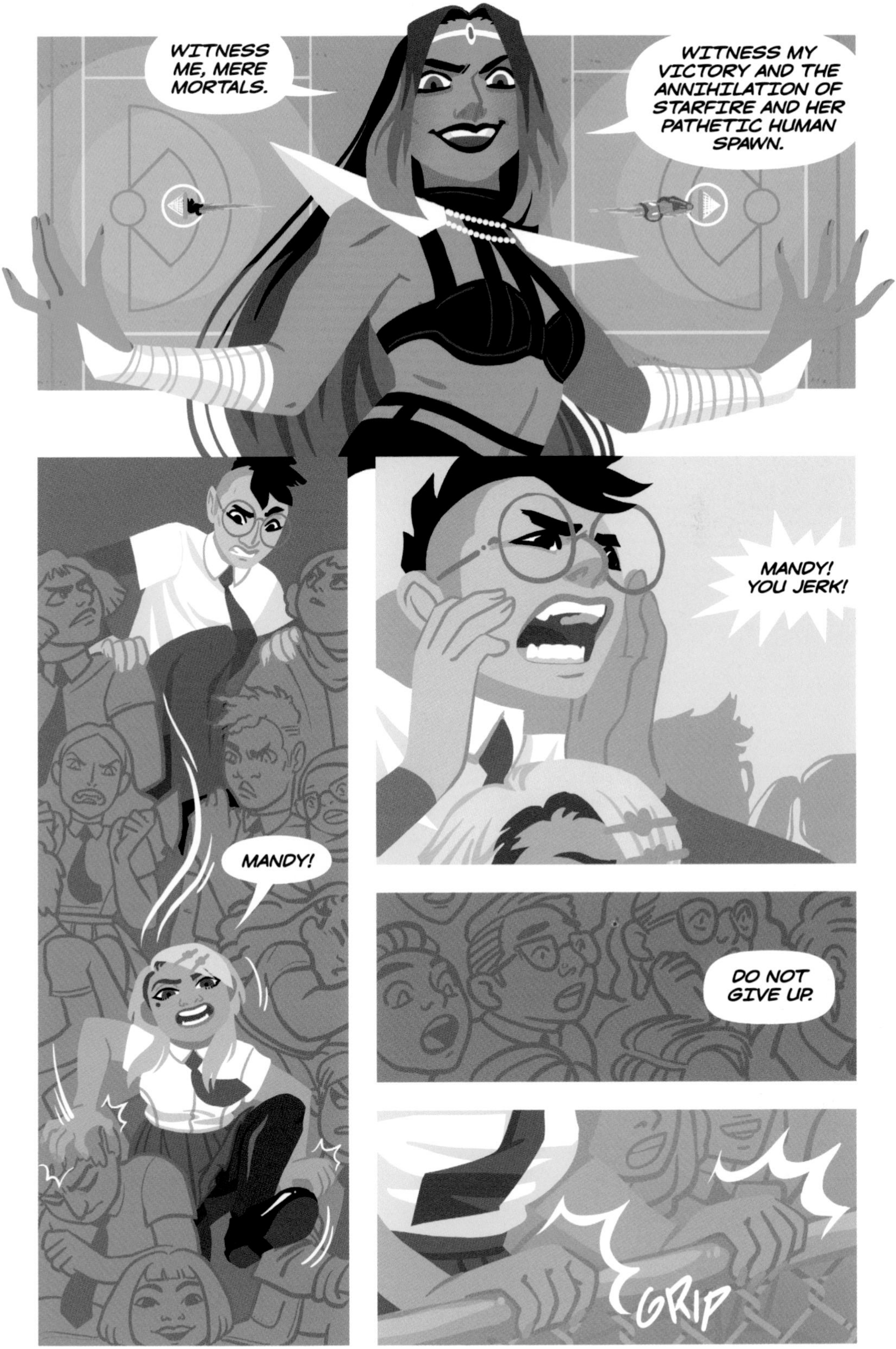
WITNESS ME, MERE MORTALS.
WITNESS MY VICTORY AND THE ANNIHILATION OF STARFIRE AND HER PATHETIC HUMAN SPAWN.
MANDY!
MANDY! YOU JERK!
DO NOT GIVE UP.
GRIP

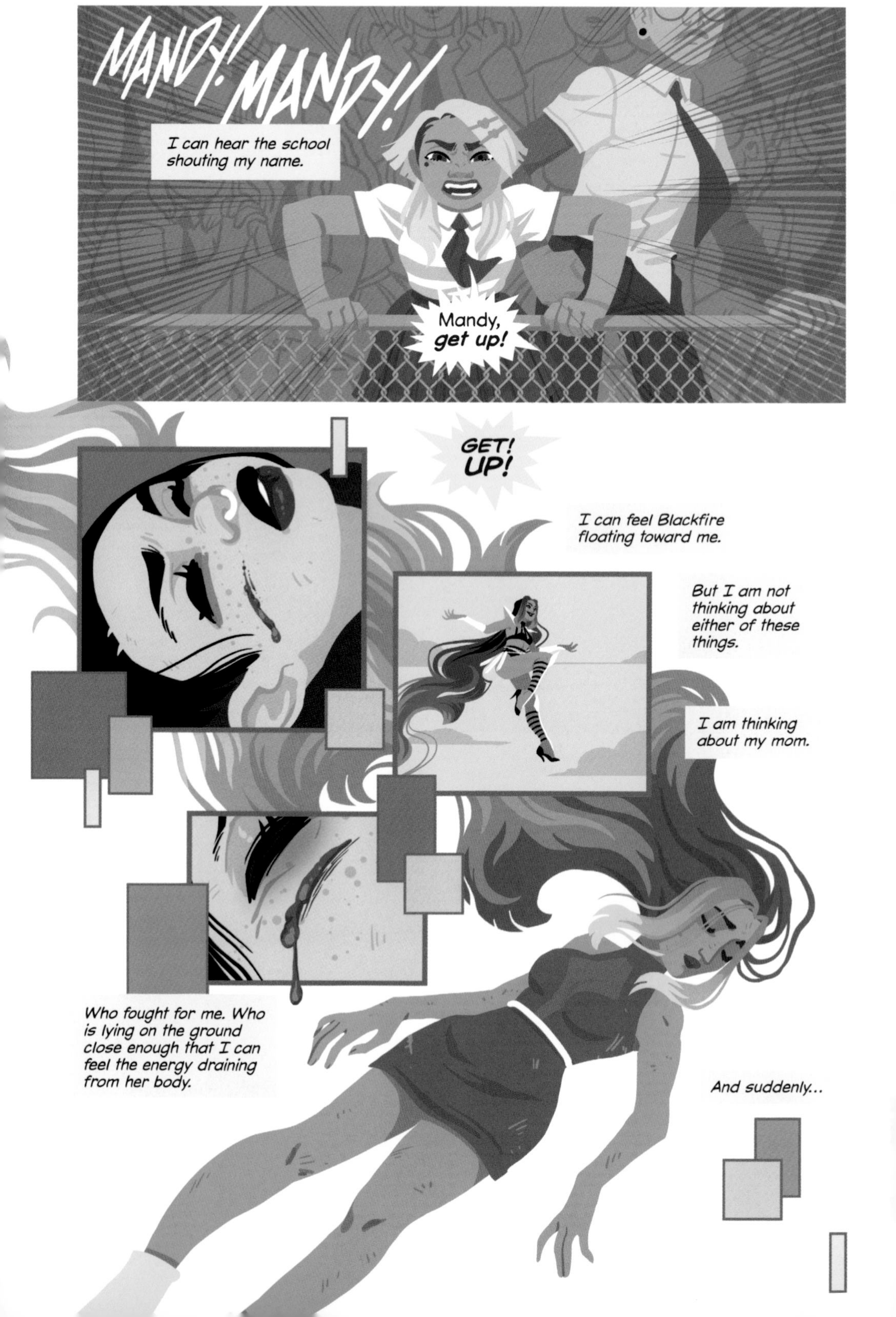
MANDY! MANDY!
I can hear the school shouting my name.
Mandy, get up!
GET! UP!
I can feel Blackfire floating toward me.
But I am not thinking about either of these things.
I am thinking about my mom.
Who fought for me. Who is lying on the ground close enough that I can feel the energy draining from her body.
And suddenly...

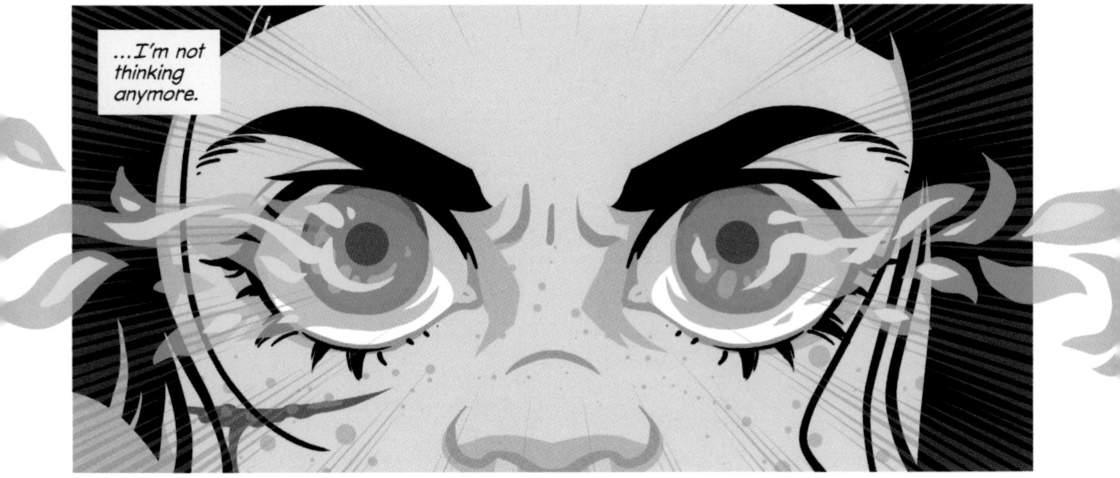
...I'm not thinking anymore.

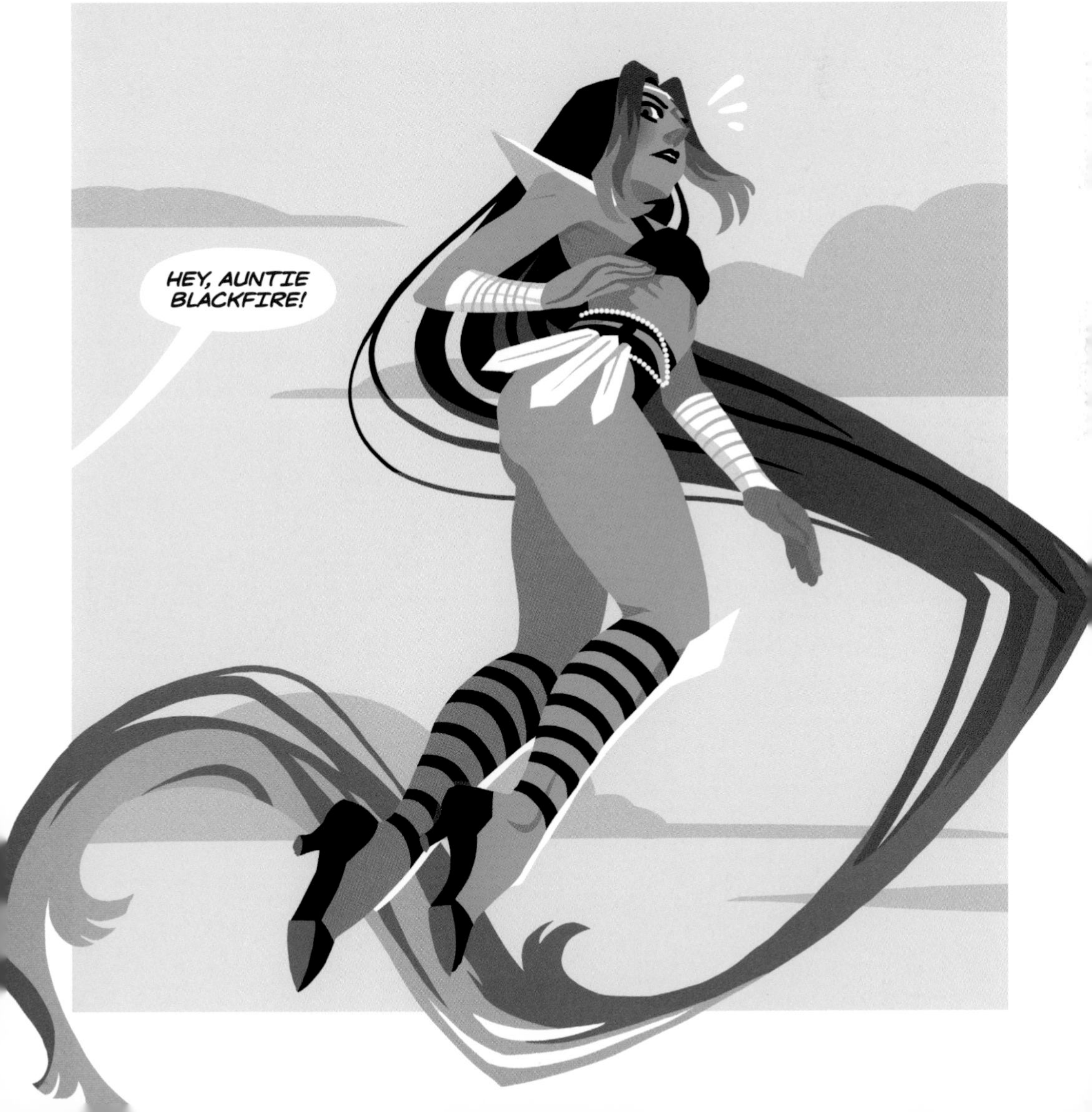
HEY, AUNTIE BLACKFIRE!

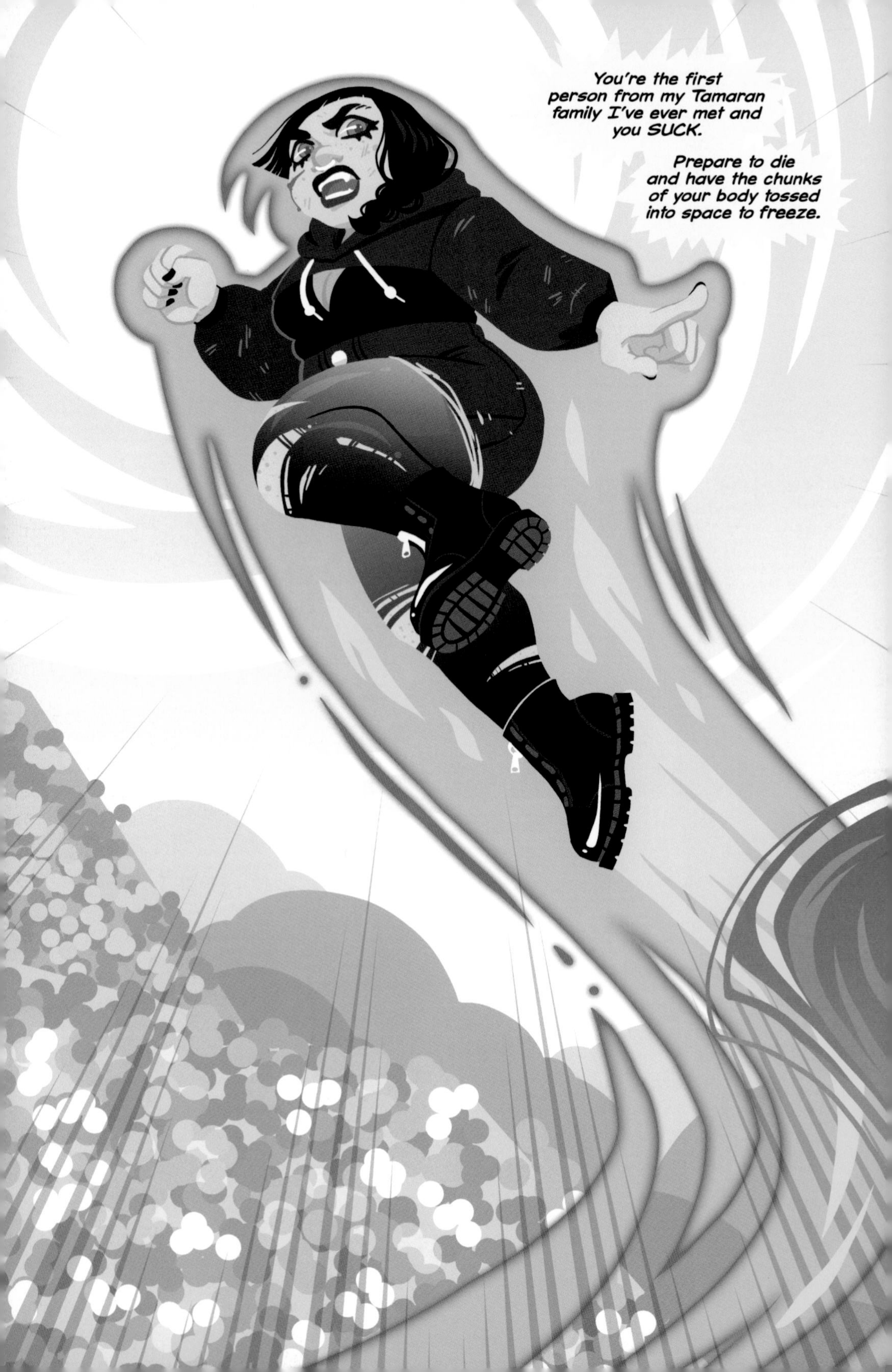
You're the first person from my Tamaran family I've ever met and you SUCK.
Prepare to die and have the chunks of your body tossed into space to freeze.

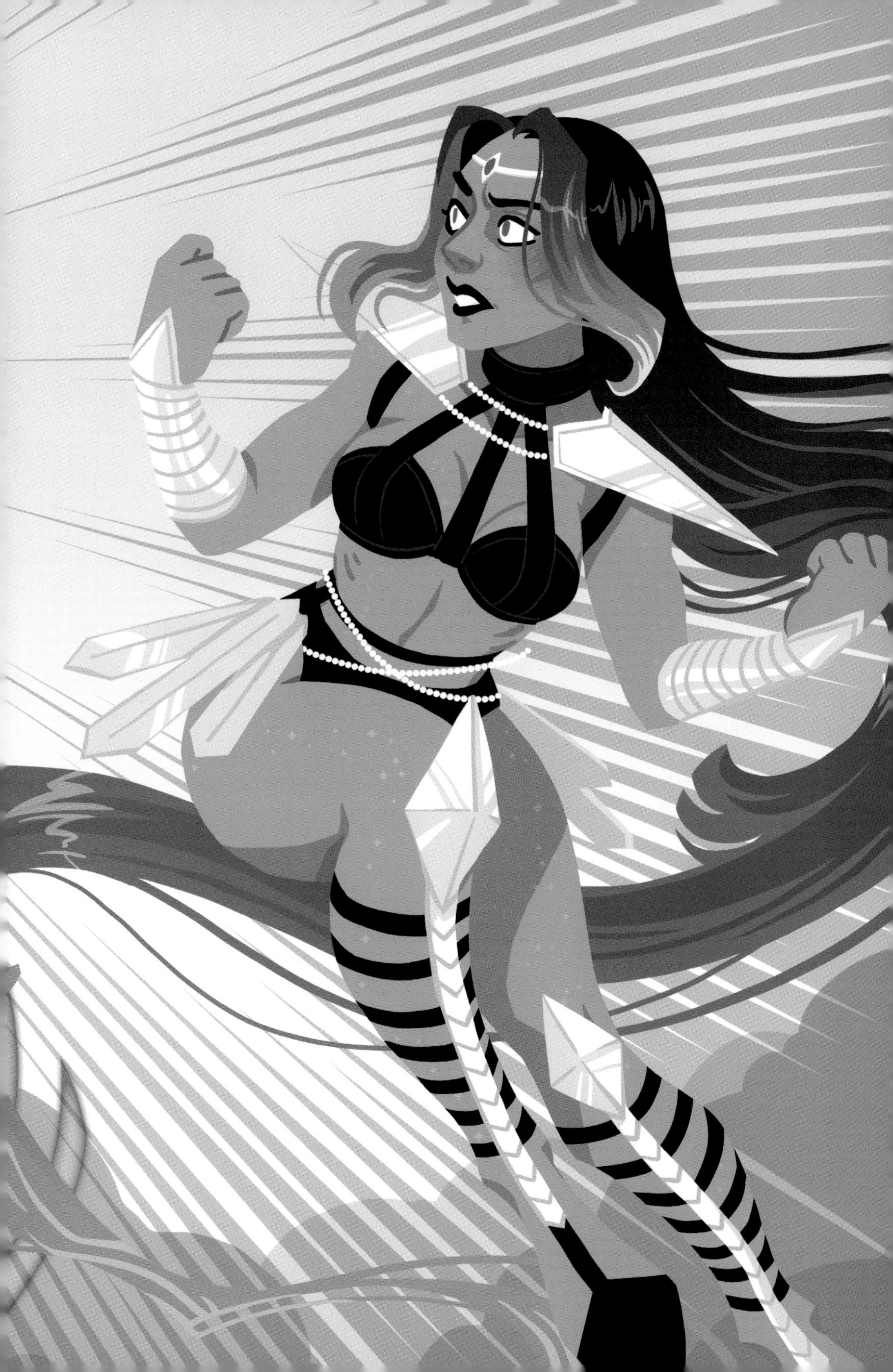

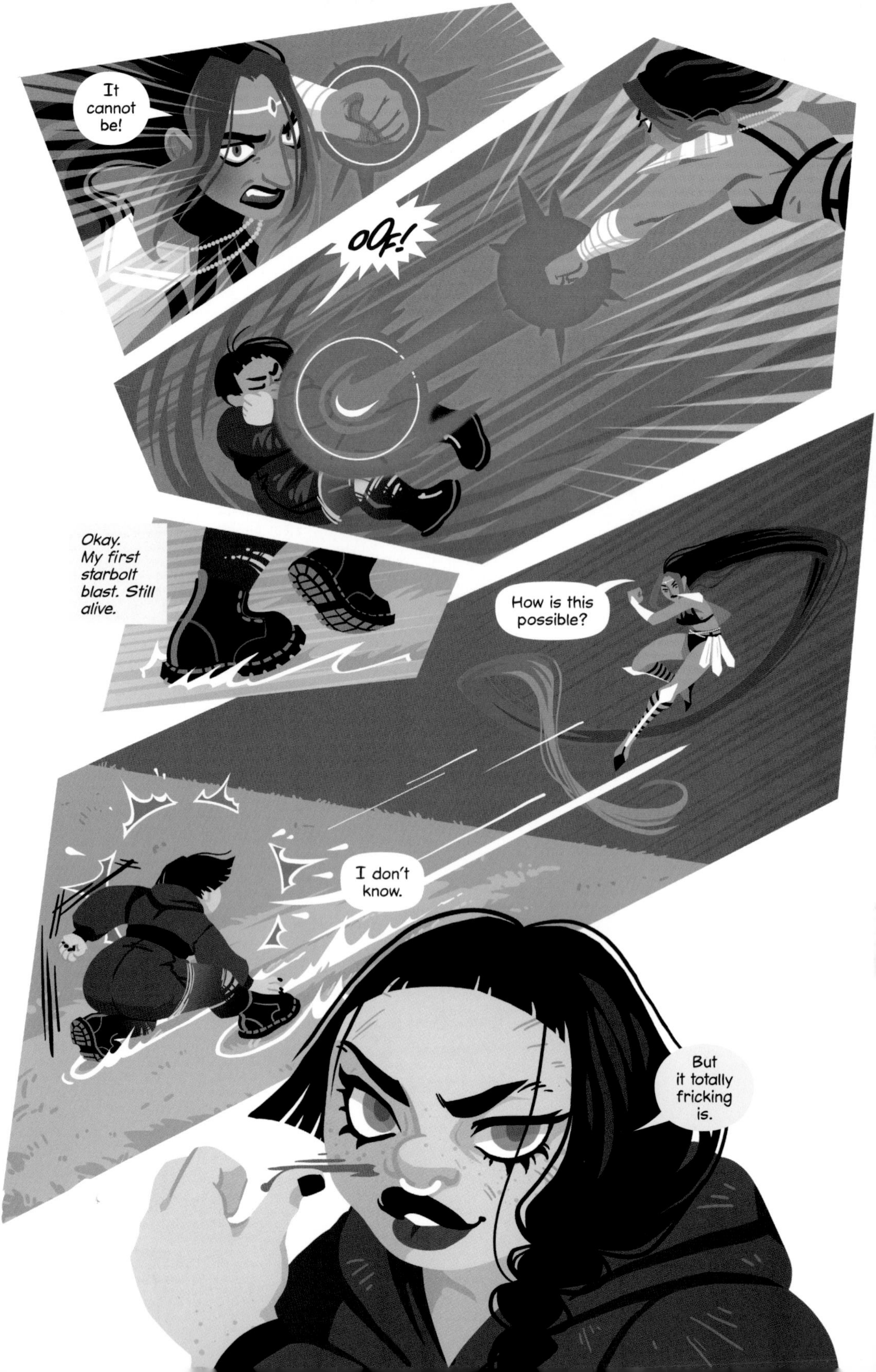
It cannot be!
OOF!
Okay. My first starbolt blast. Still alive.
How is this possible?
I don't know.
But it totally fricking is.

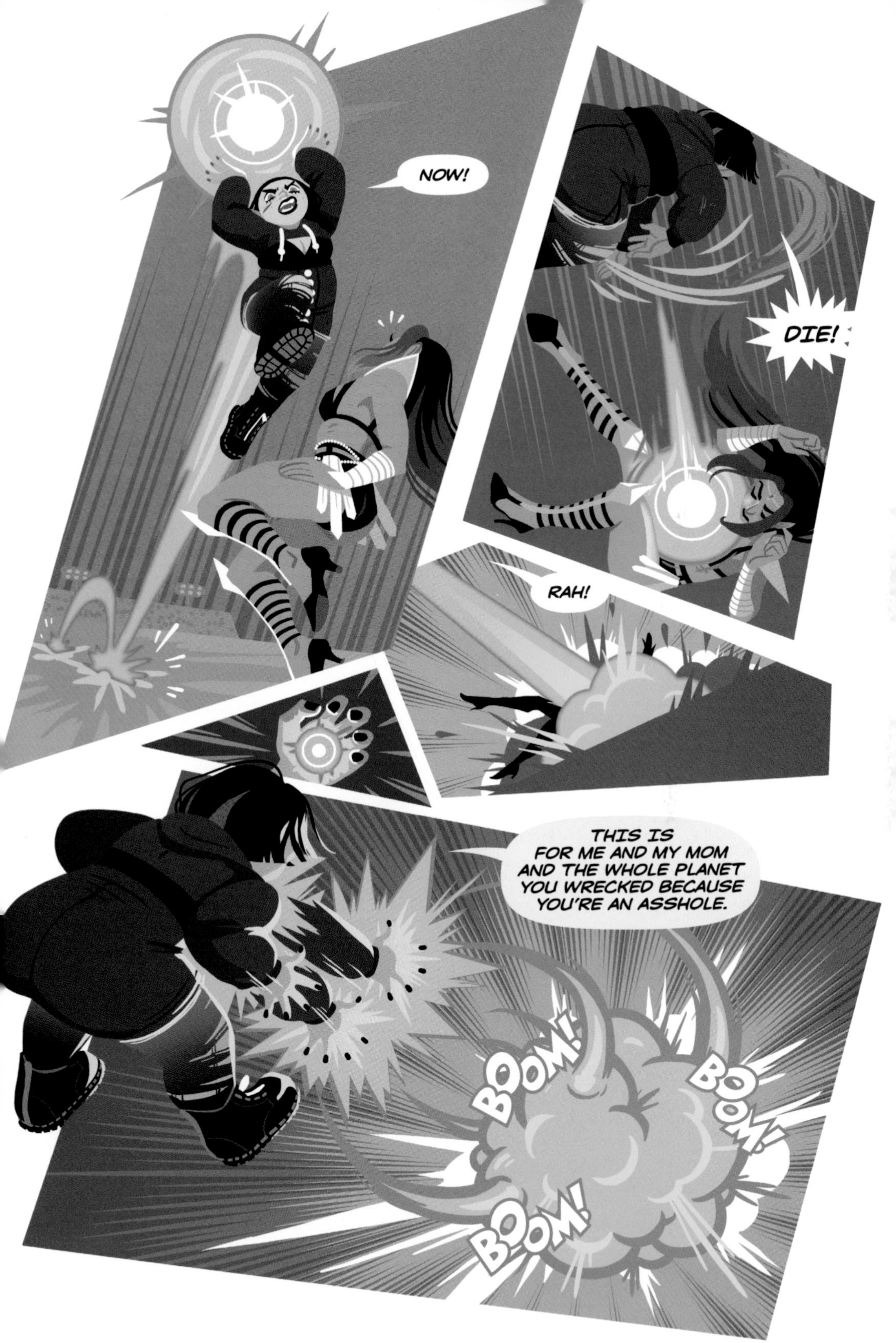
NOW!
DIE!
RAH!
THIS IS FOR ME AND MY MOM AND THE WHOLE PLANET YOU WRECKED BECAUSE YOU'RE AN ASSHOLE.
BOOM!
BOOM!
BOOM!

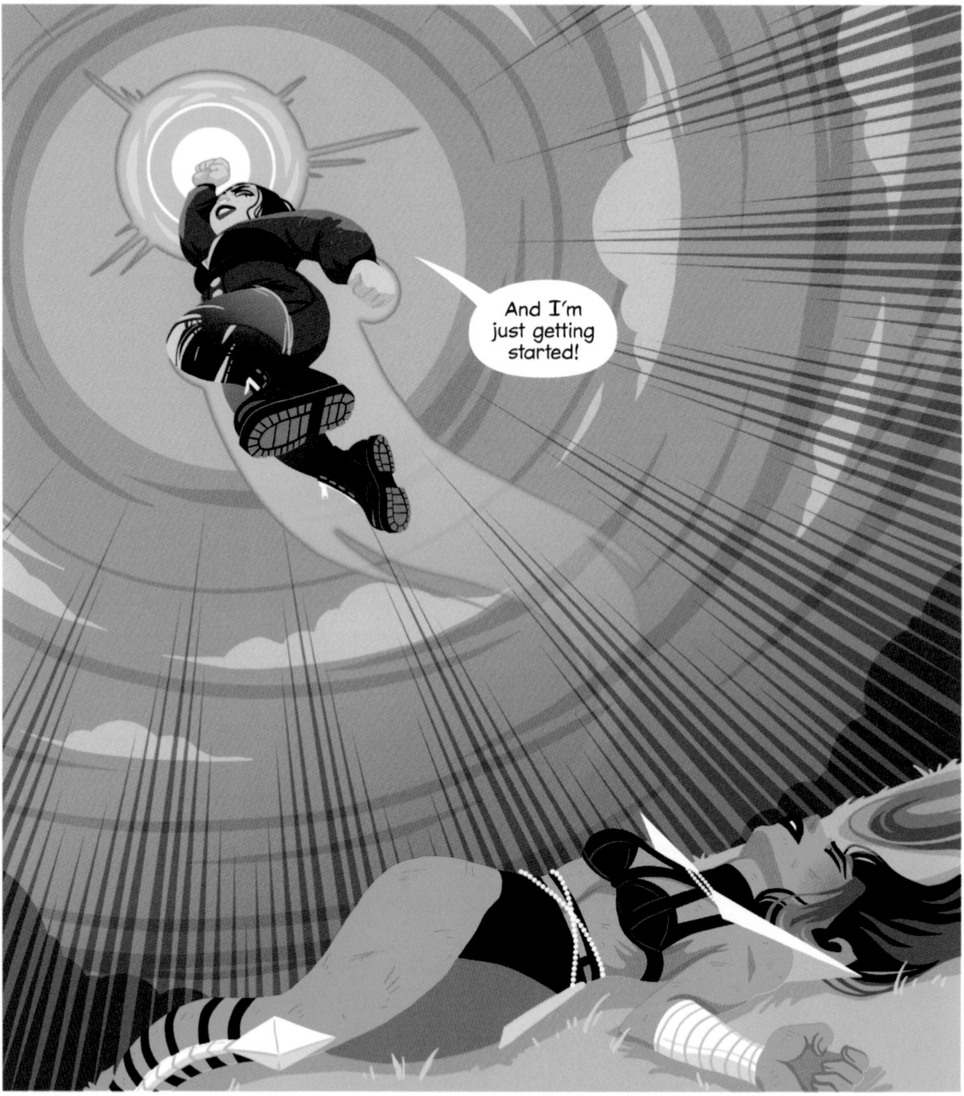
And I'm just getting started!

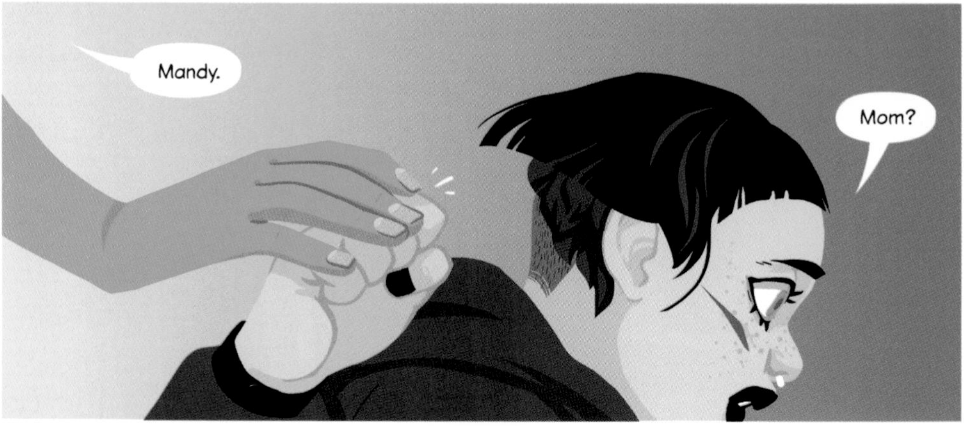
Mandy.
Mom?

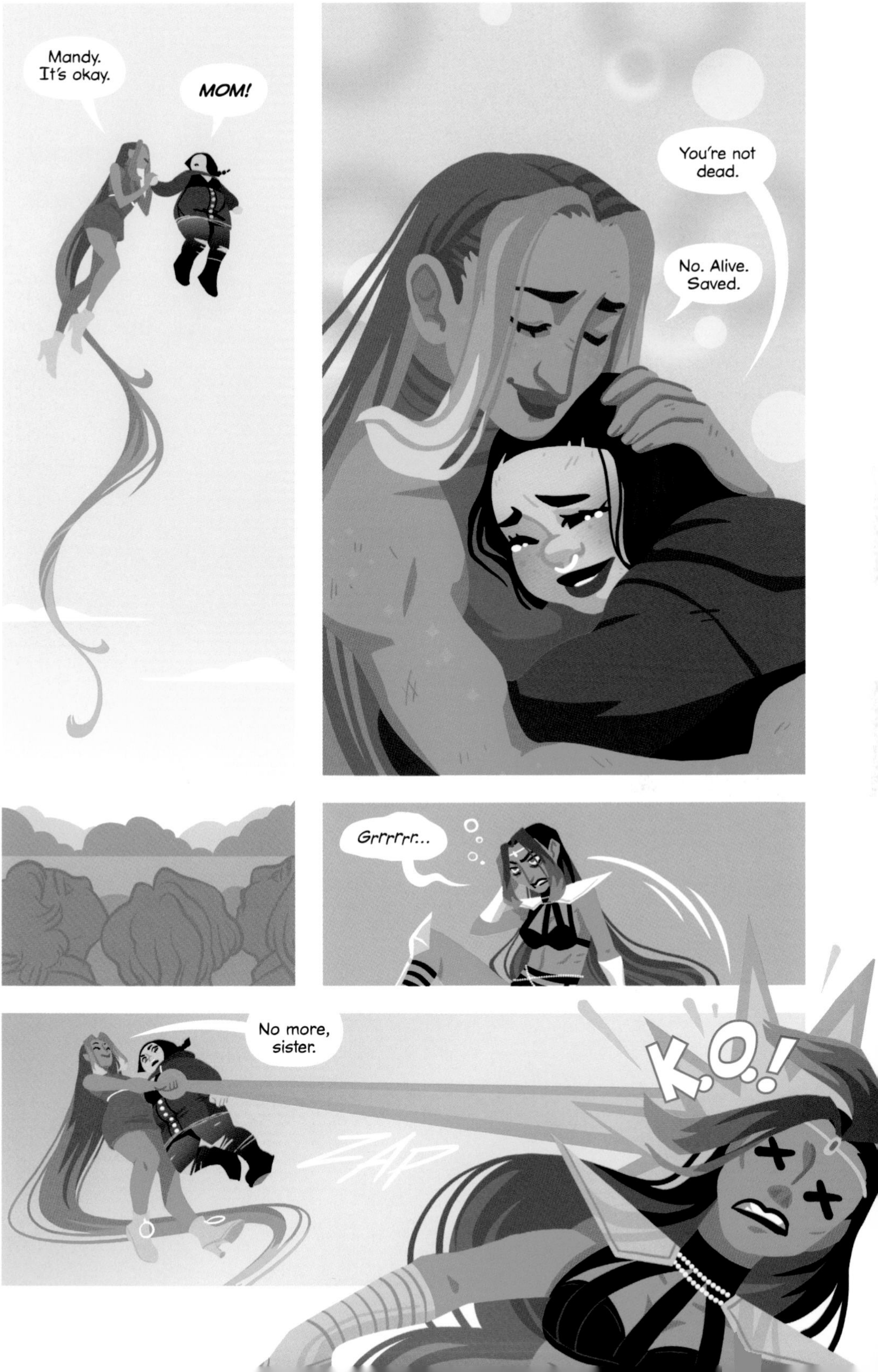
Mandy.
It's okay.
MOM!
You're not dead.
No. Alive.
Saved.
Grrrrrr...
No more,
sister.
K.O.!
ZAP

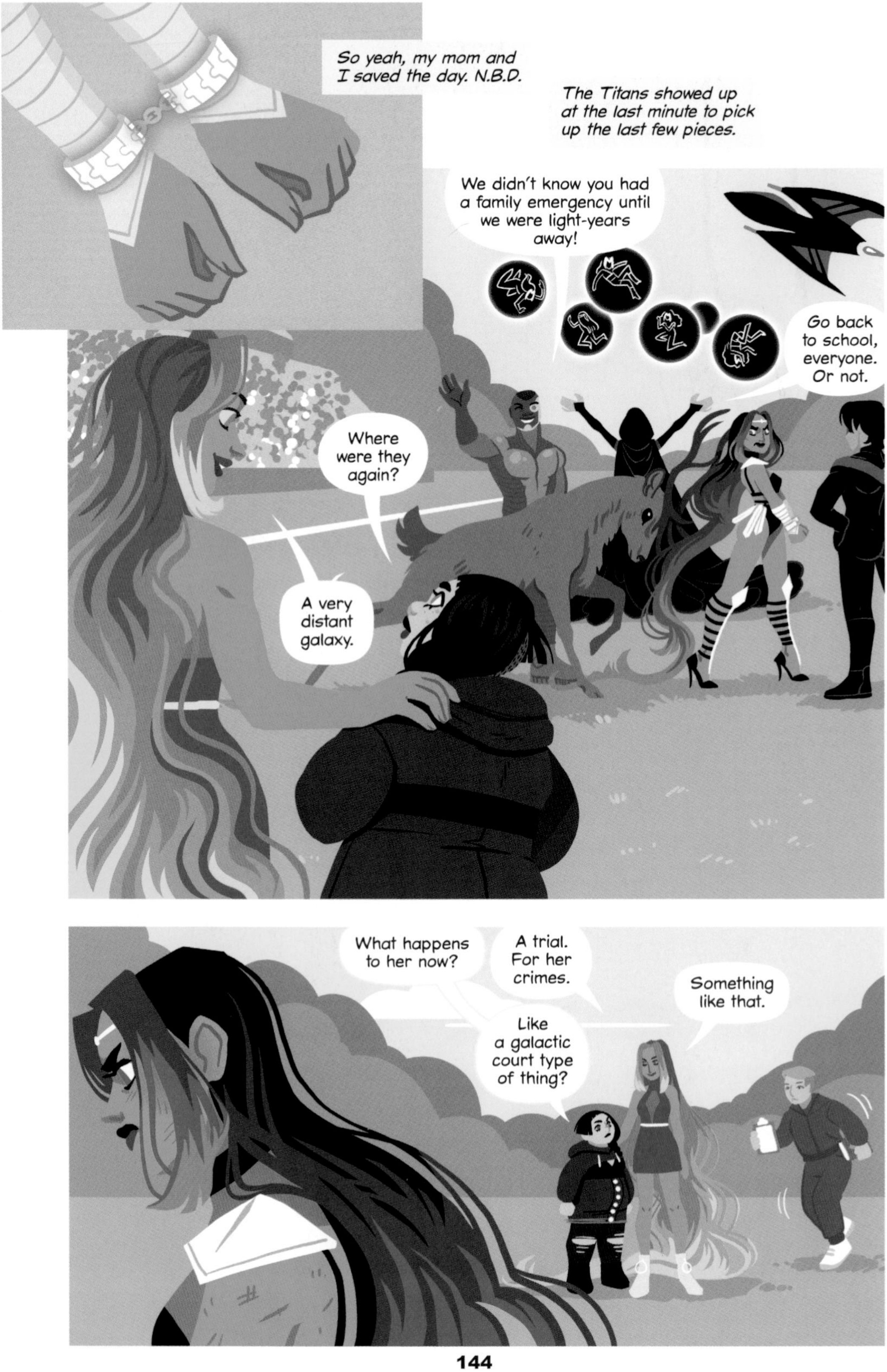
So yeah, my mom and I saved the day. N.B.D.
The Titans showed up at the last minute to pick up the last few pieces.
We didn't know you had a family emergency until we were light-years away!
Go back to school, everyone. Or not.
Where were they again?
A very distant galaxy.
What happens to her now?
A trial. For her crimes.
Like a galactic court type of thing?
Something like that.

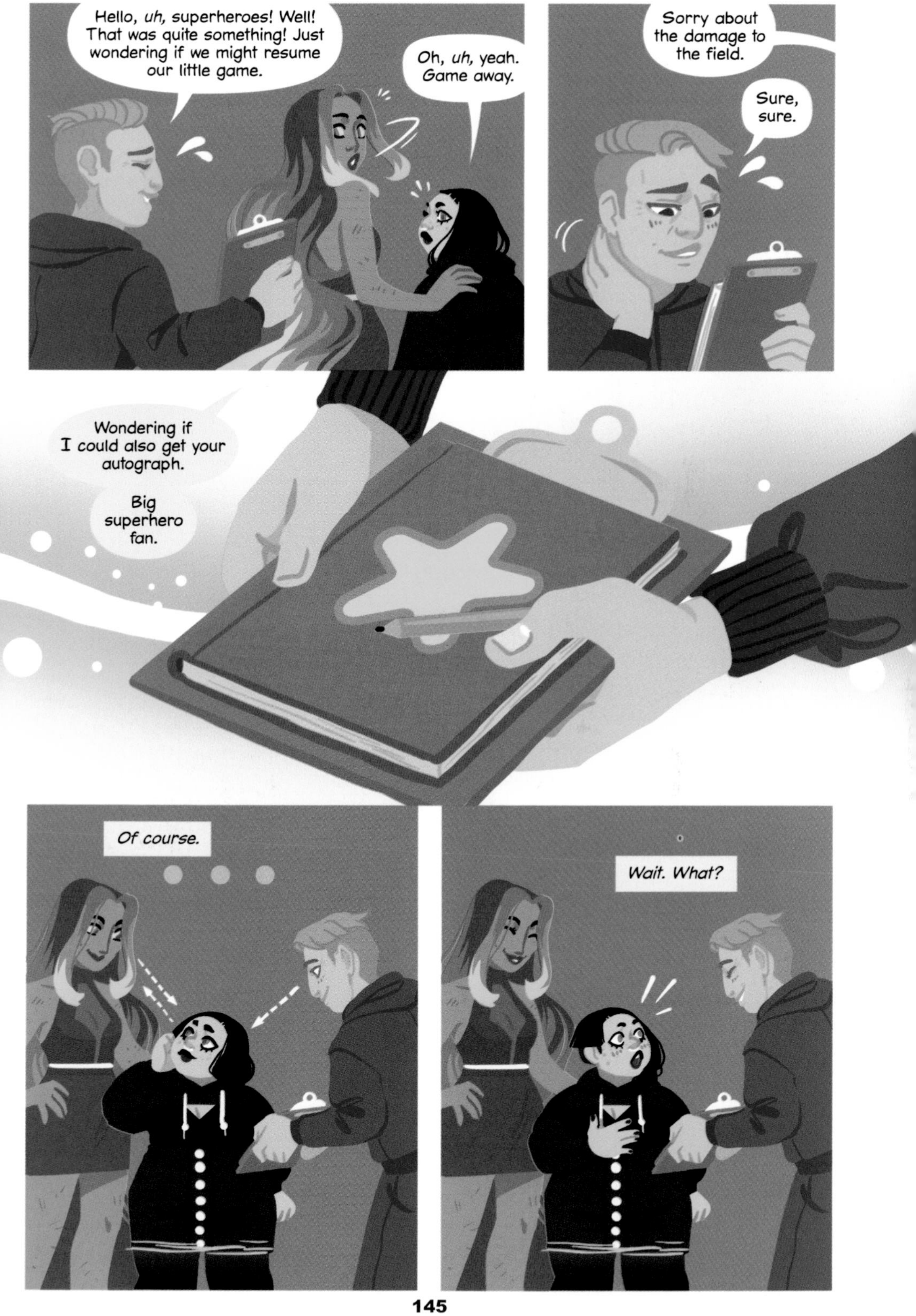
Hello, *uh,* superheroes! Well! That was quite something! Just wondering if we might resume our little game.
Oh, *uh,* yeah. Game away.
Sorry about the damage to the field.
Sure, sure.
Wondering if I could also get your autograph.
Big superhero fan.
Of course.
Wait. What?

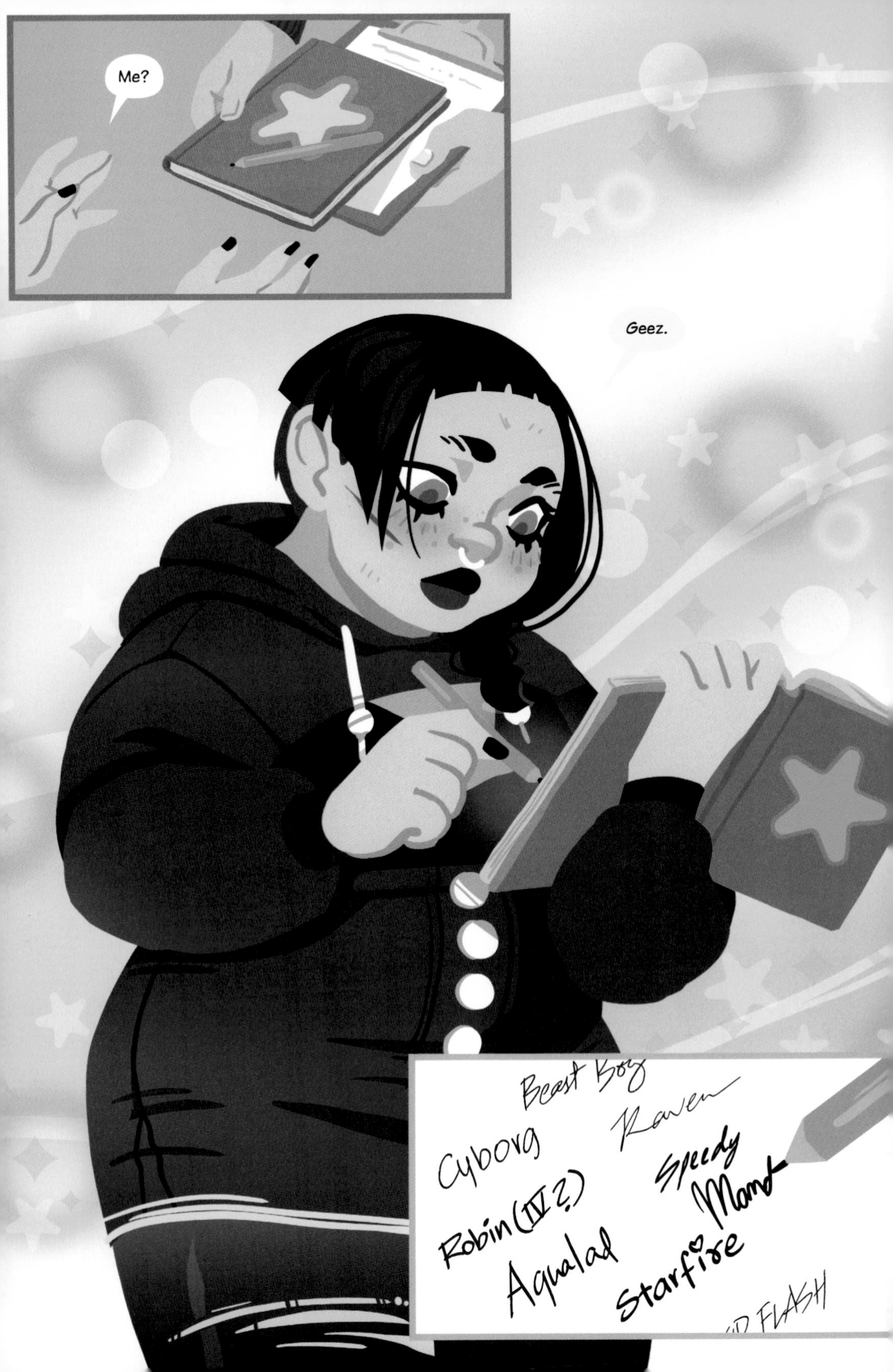
Me?
Geez.
Beast Boy
Raven
Cyborg
Speedy
Robin(IV?)
Mom
Aqualad
Starfire

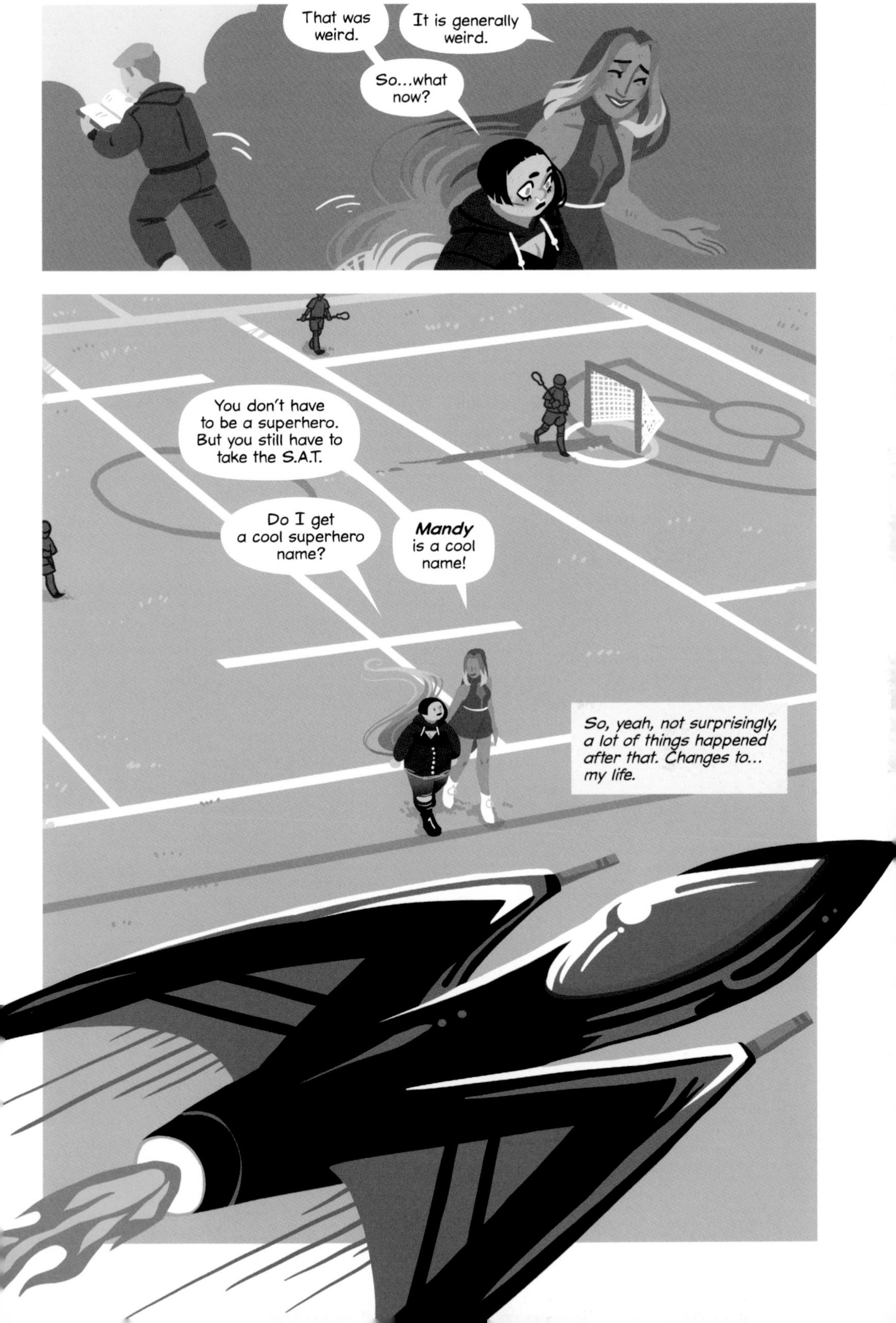
That was weird.
It is generally weird.
So...what now?
You don't have to be a superhero. But you still have to take the S.A.T.
Do I get a cool superhero name?
Mandy is a cool name!
So, yeah, not surprisingly, a lot of things happened after that. Changes to... my life.

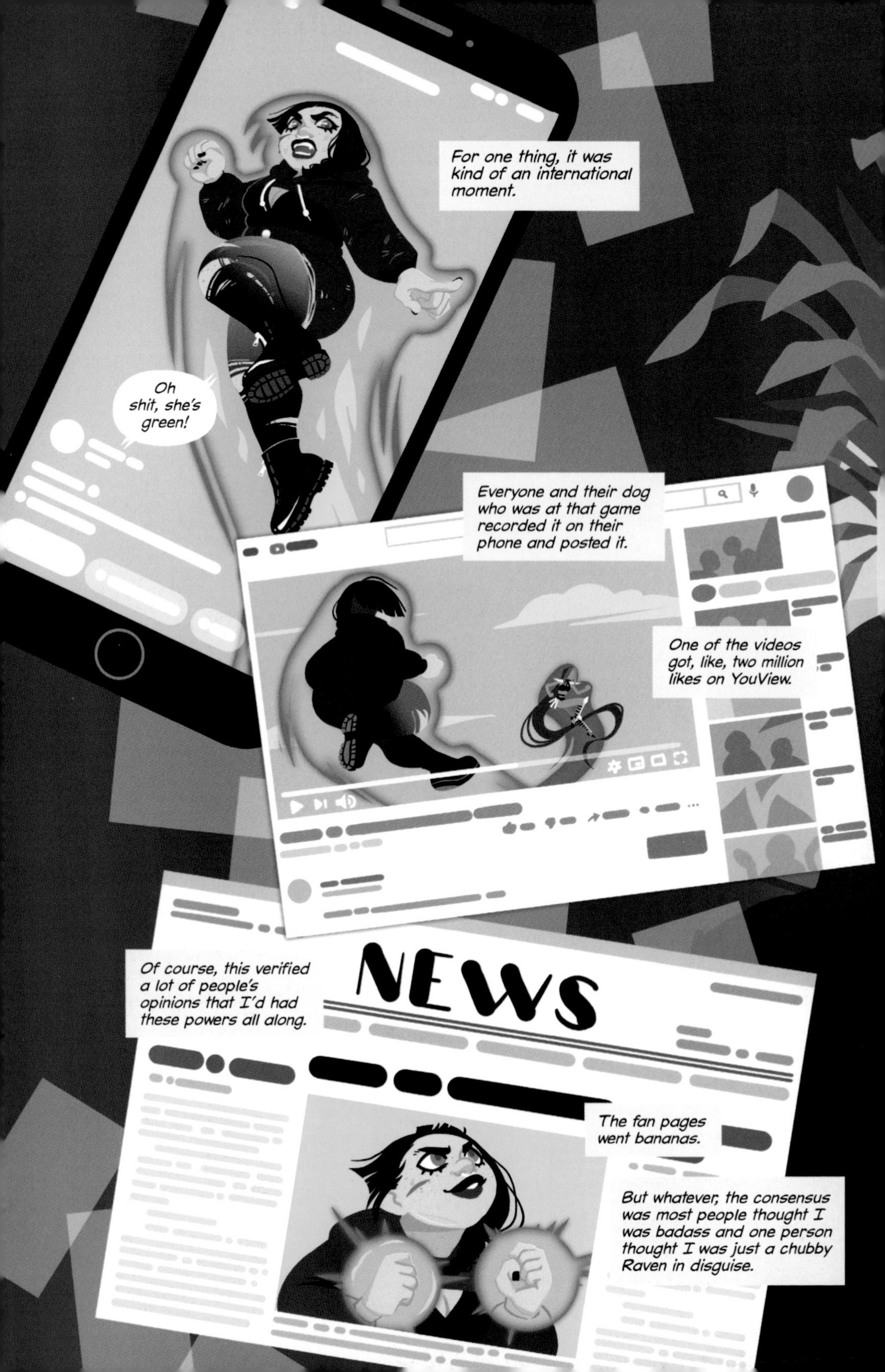

For one thing, it was kind of an international moment.
Oh shit, she's green!
Everyone and their dog who was at that game recorded it on their phone and posted it.
One of the videos got, like, two million likes on YouView.
Of course, this verified a lot of people's opinions that I'd had these powers all along.
NEWS
The fan pages went bananas.
But whatever, the consensus was most people thought I was badass and one person thought I was just a chubby Raven in disguise.

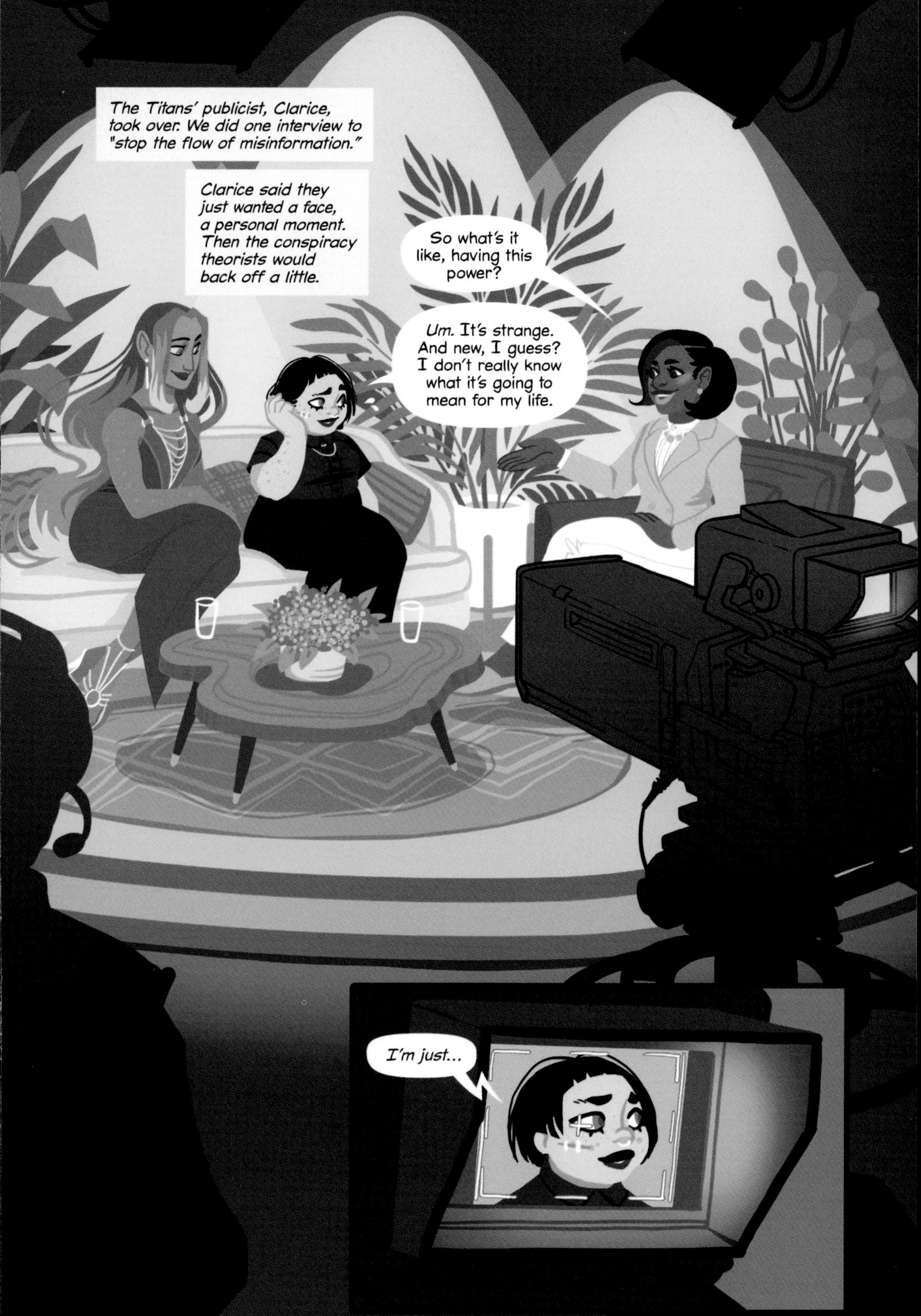
The Titans' publicist, Clarice, took over. We did one interview to "stop the flow of misinformation."
Clarice said they just wanted a face, a personal moment. Then the conspiracy theorists would back off a little.
So what's it like, having this power?
Um. It's strange. And new, I guess? I don't really know what it's going to mean for my life.
I'm just...

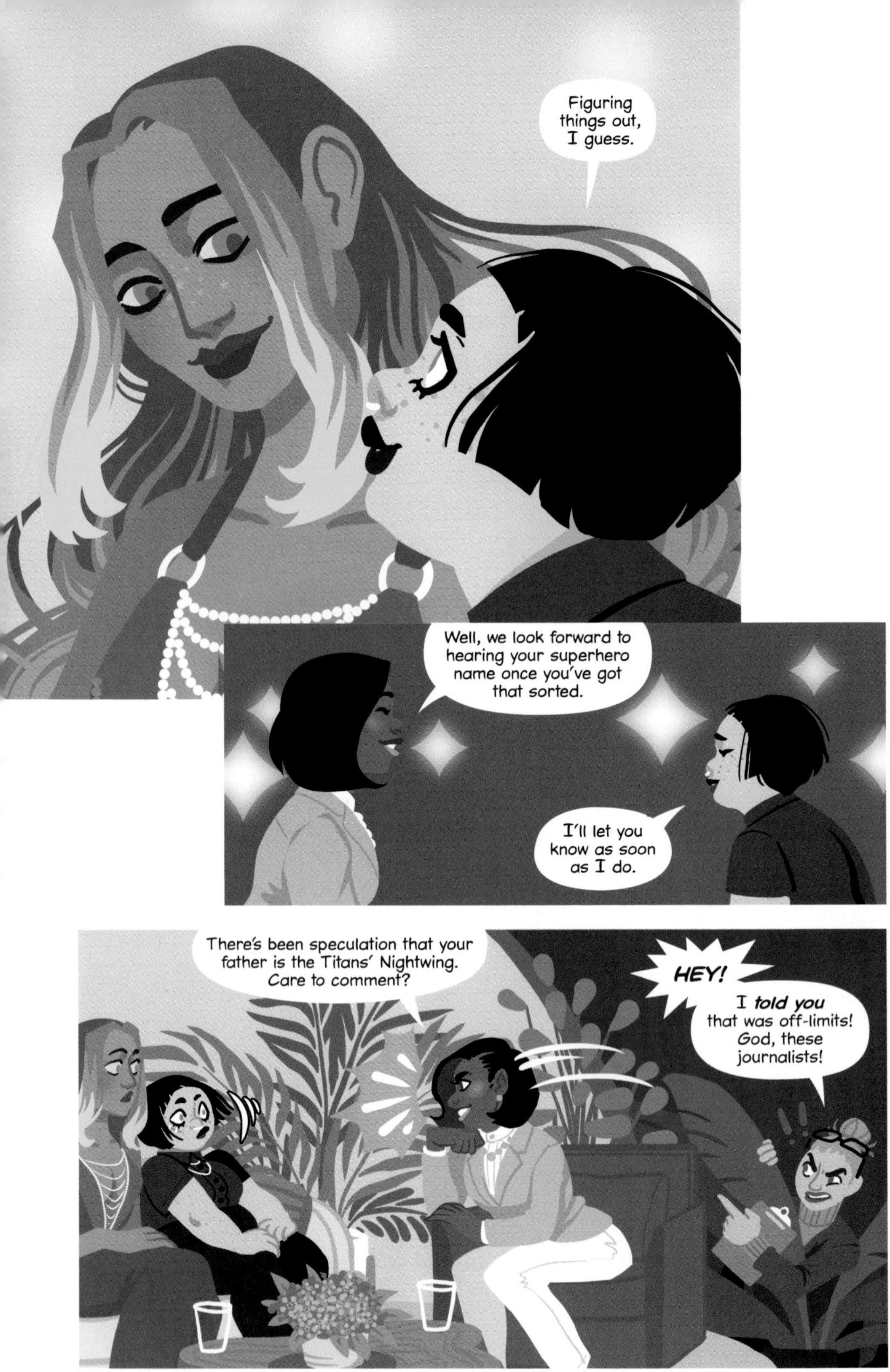
Figuring things out, I guess.
Well, we look forward to hearing your superhero name once you've got that sorted.
I'll let you know as soon as I do.
There's been speculation that your father is the Titans' Nightwing. Care to comment?
HEY!
I ***told you*** that was off-limits! God, these journalists!

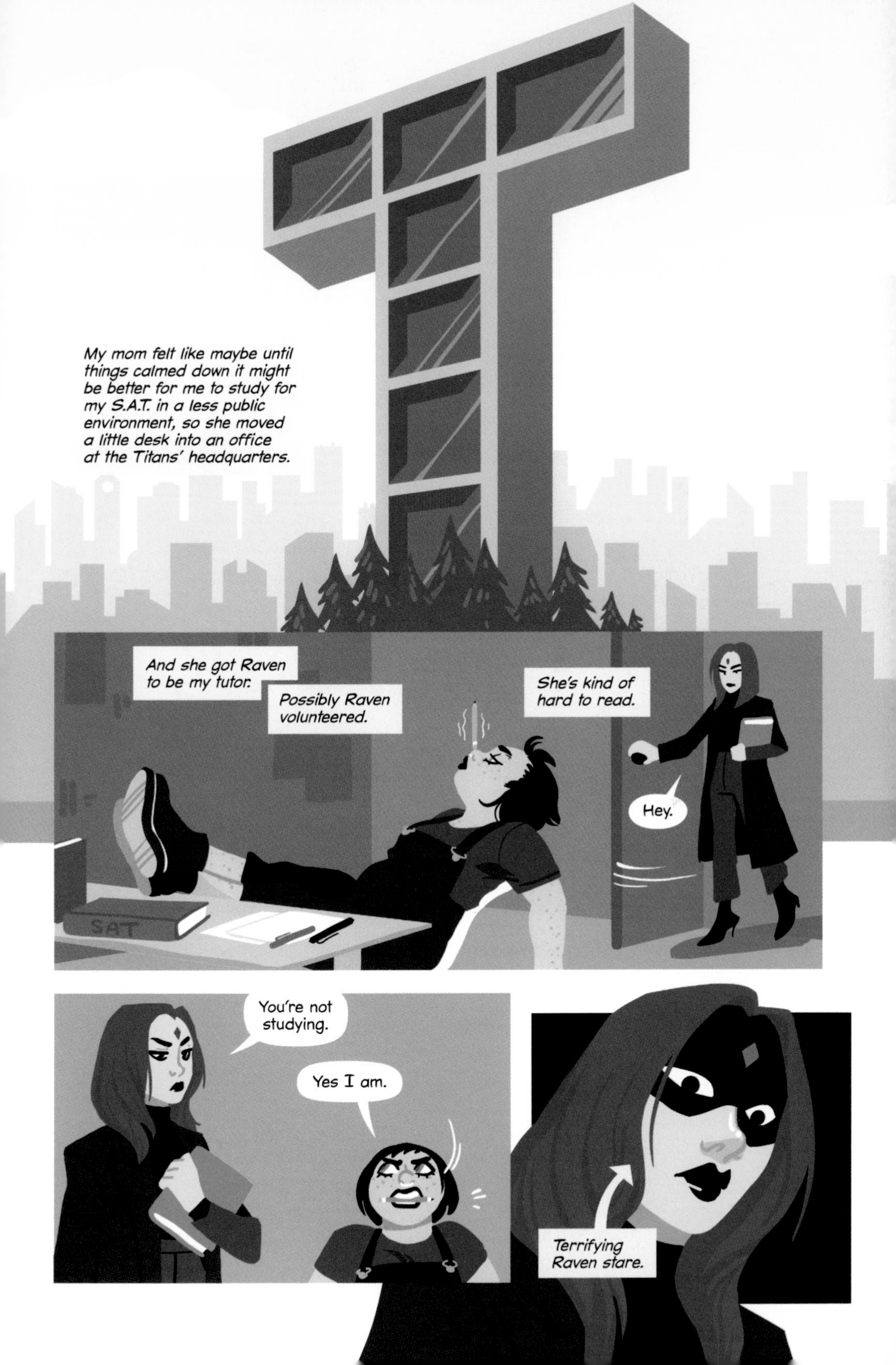

My mom felt like maybe until things calmed down it might be better for me to study for my S.A.T. in a less public environment, so she moved a little desk into an office at the Titans' headquarters.
And she got Raven to be my tutor.
Possibly Raven volunteered.
She's kind of hard to read.
Hey.
SAT
You're not studying.
Yes I am.
Terrifying Raven stare.

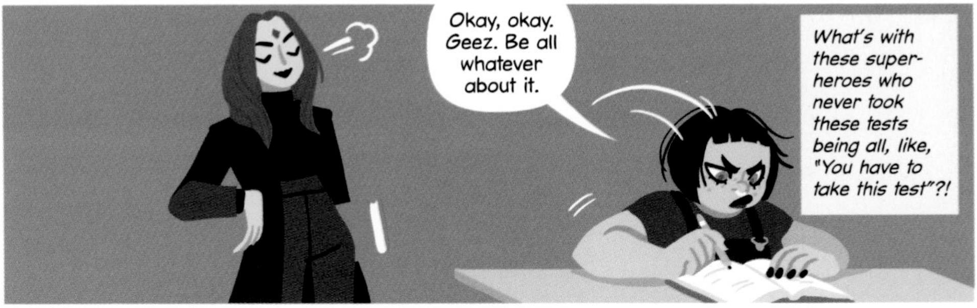
Okay, okay. Geez. Be all whatever about it.
What's with these superheroes who never took these tests being all, like, "You have to take this test"?!

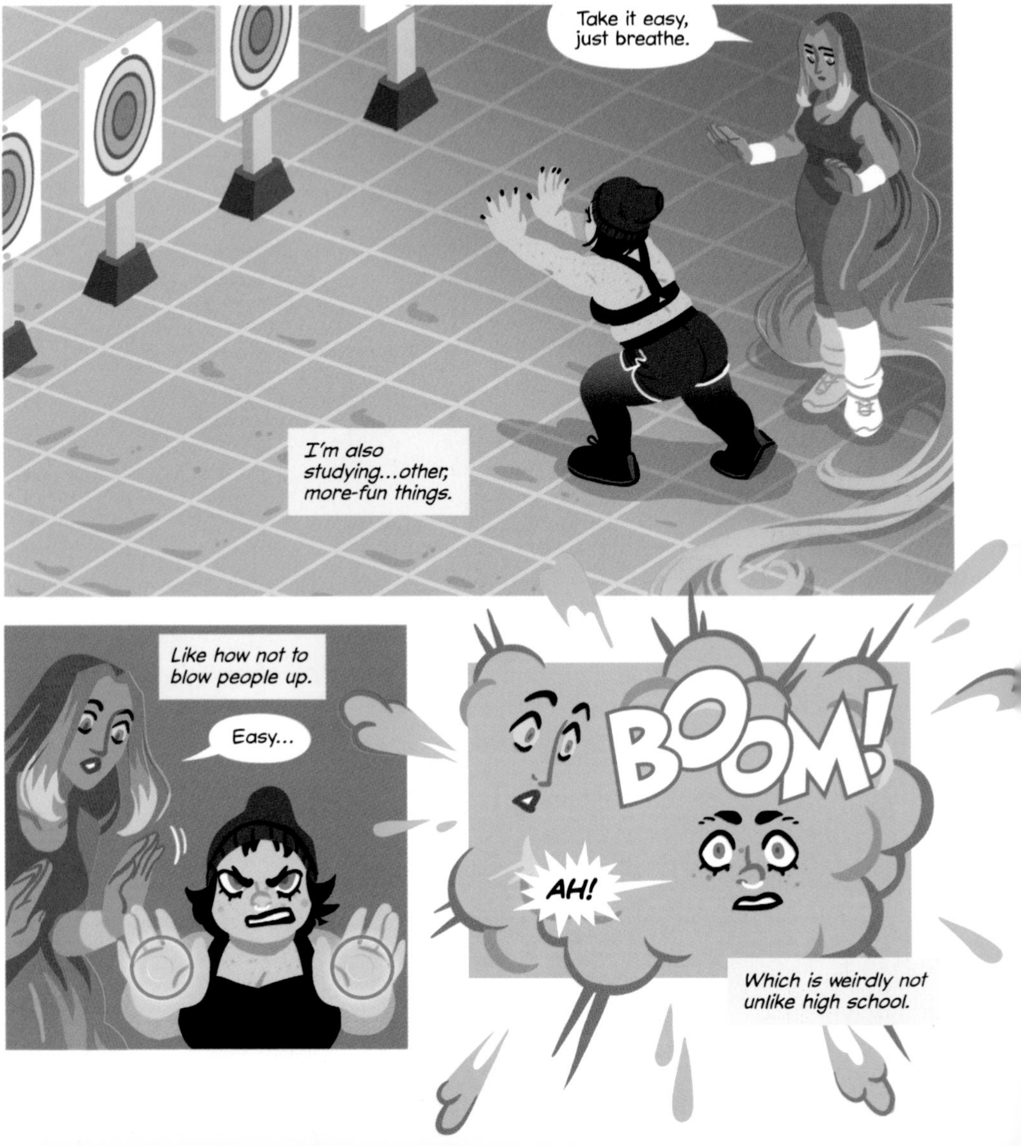
Take it easy, just breathe.
I'm also studying...other, more-fun things.
Like how not to blow people up.
Easy...
BOOM!
AH!
Which is weirdly not unlike high school.

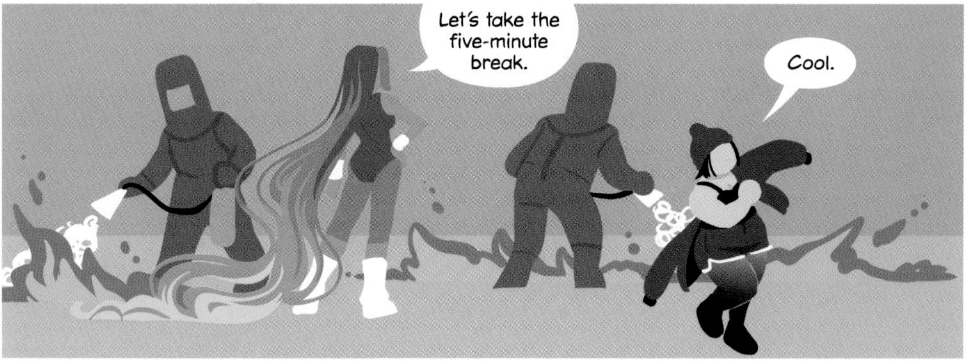
Let's take the five-minute break.
Cool.

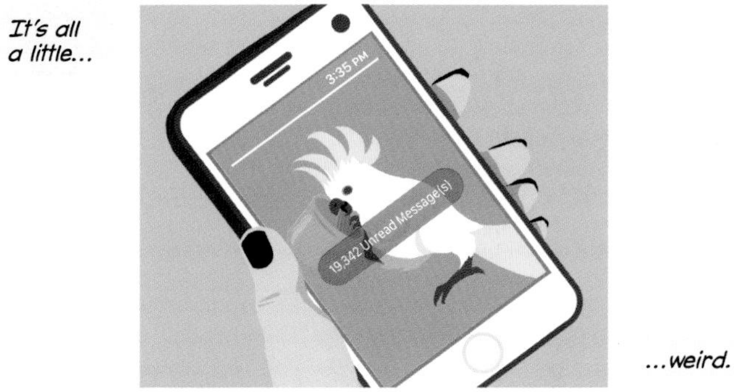
It's all a little...
3:35 PM
19,342 Unread Message(s)
...weird.

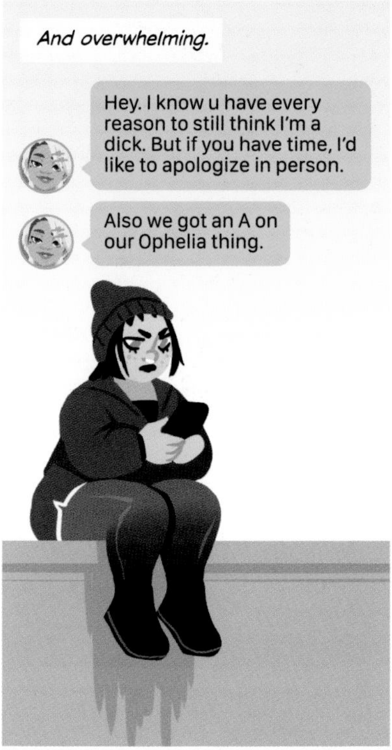
And overwhelming.
Hey. I know u have every reason to still think I'm a dick. But if you have time, I'd like to apologize in person.
Also we got an A on our Ophelia thing.

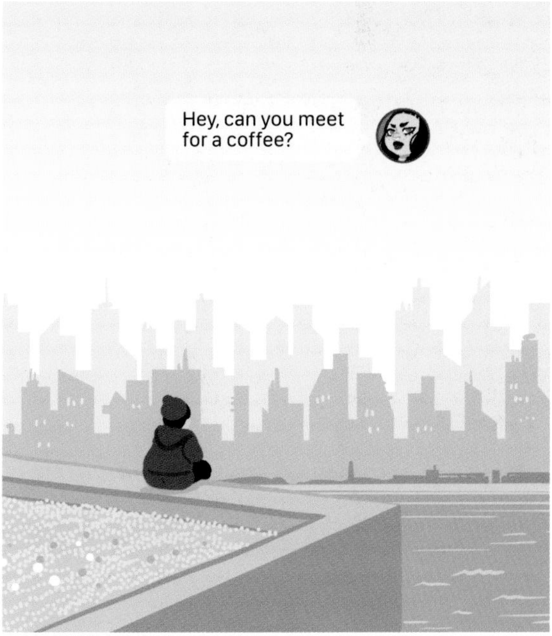
Hey, can you meet for a coffee?

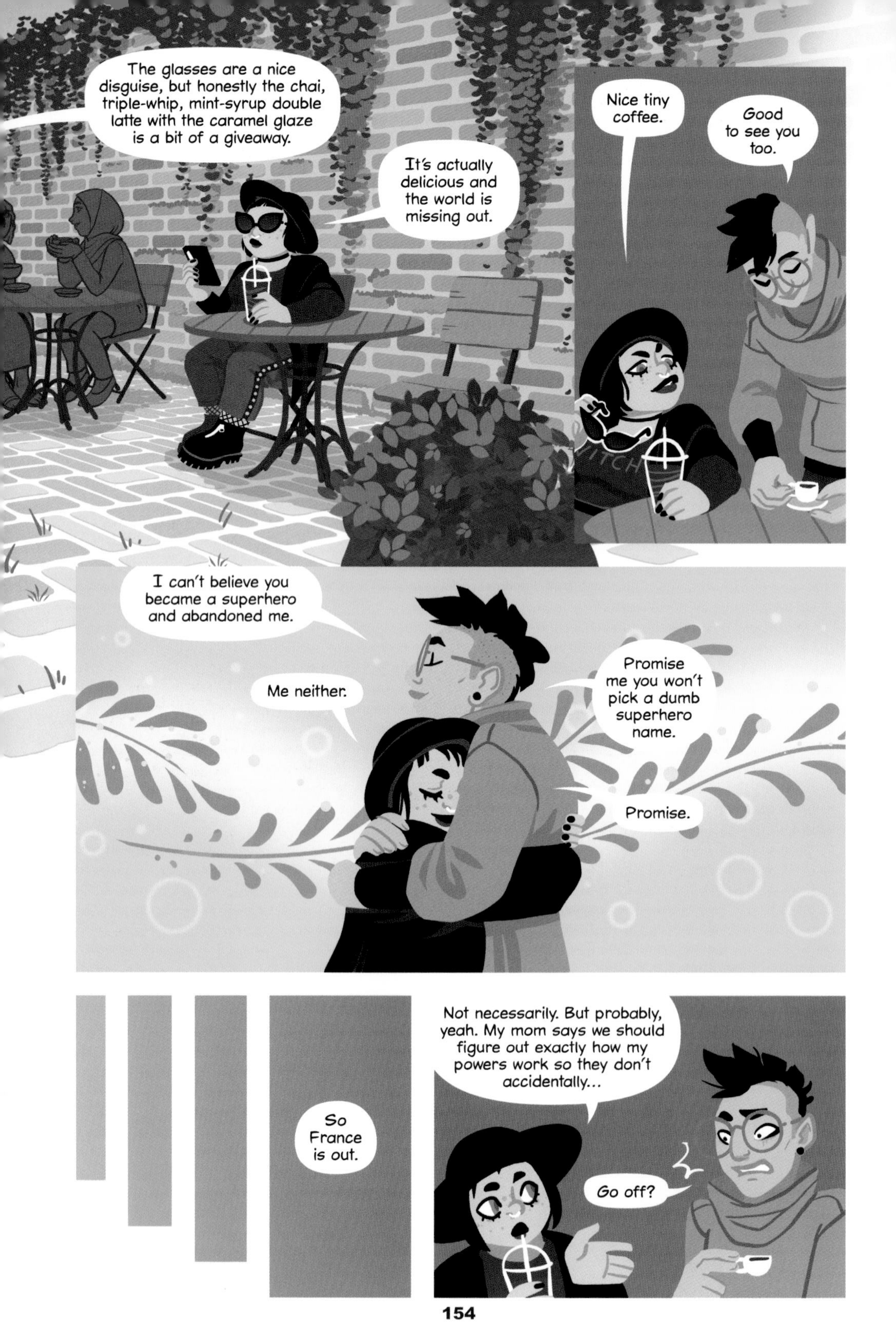
The glasses are a nice disguise, but honestly the chai, triple-whip, mint-syrup double latte with the caramel glaze is a bit of a giveaway.
It's actually delicious and the world is missing out.
Nice tiny coffee.
Good to see you too.
I can't believe you became a superhero and abandoned me.
Me neither.
Promise me you won't pick a dumb superhero name.
Promise.
So France is out.
Not necessarily. But probably, yeah. My mom says we should figure out exactly how my powers work so they don't accidentally...
Go off?

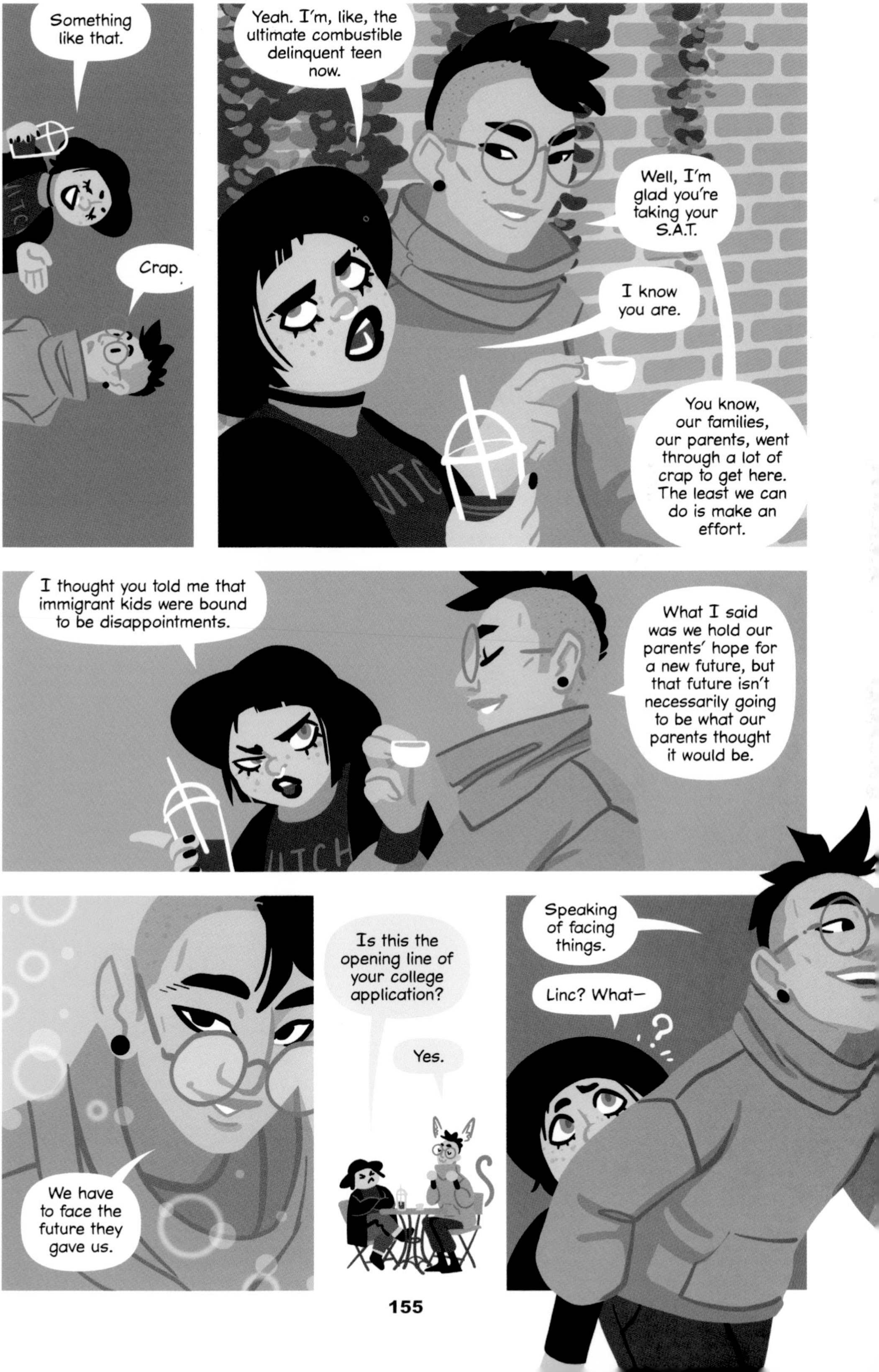

Something like that.
Crap.
Yeah. I'm, like, the ultimate combustible delinquent teen now.
Well, I'm glad you're taking your S.A.T.
I know you are.
You know, our families, our parents, went through a lot of crap to get here. The least we can do is make an effort.
I thought you told me that immigrant kids were bound to be disappointments.
What I said was we hold our parents' hope for a new future, but that future isn't necessarily going to be what our parents thought it would be.
We have to face the future they gave us.
Is this the opening line of your college application?
Yes.
Speaking of facing things.
Linc? What—
?

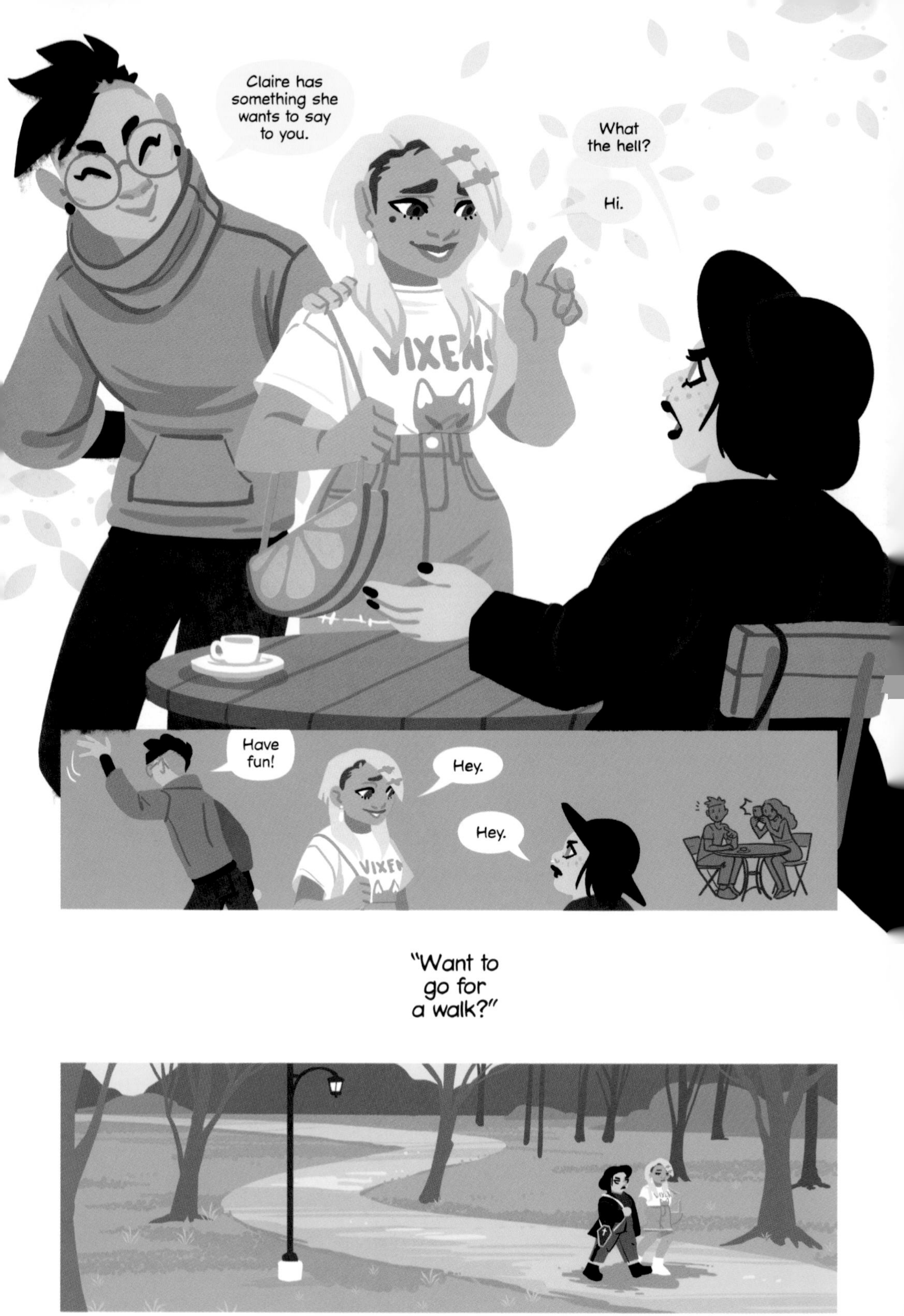
Claire has something she wants to say to you.
What the hell?
Hi.
Have fun!
Hey.
Hey.
"Want to go for a walk?"

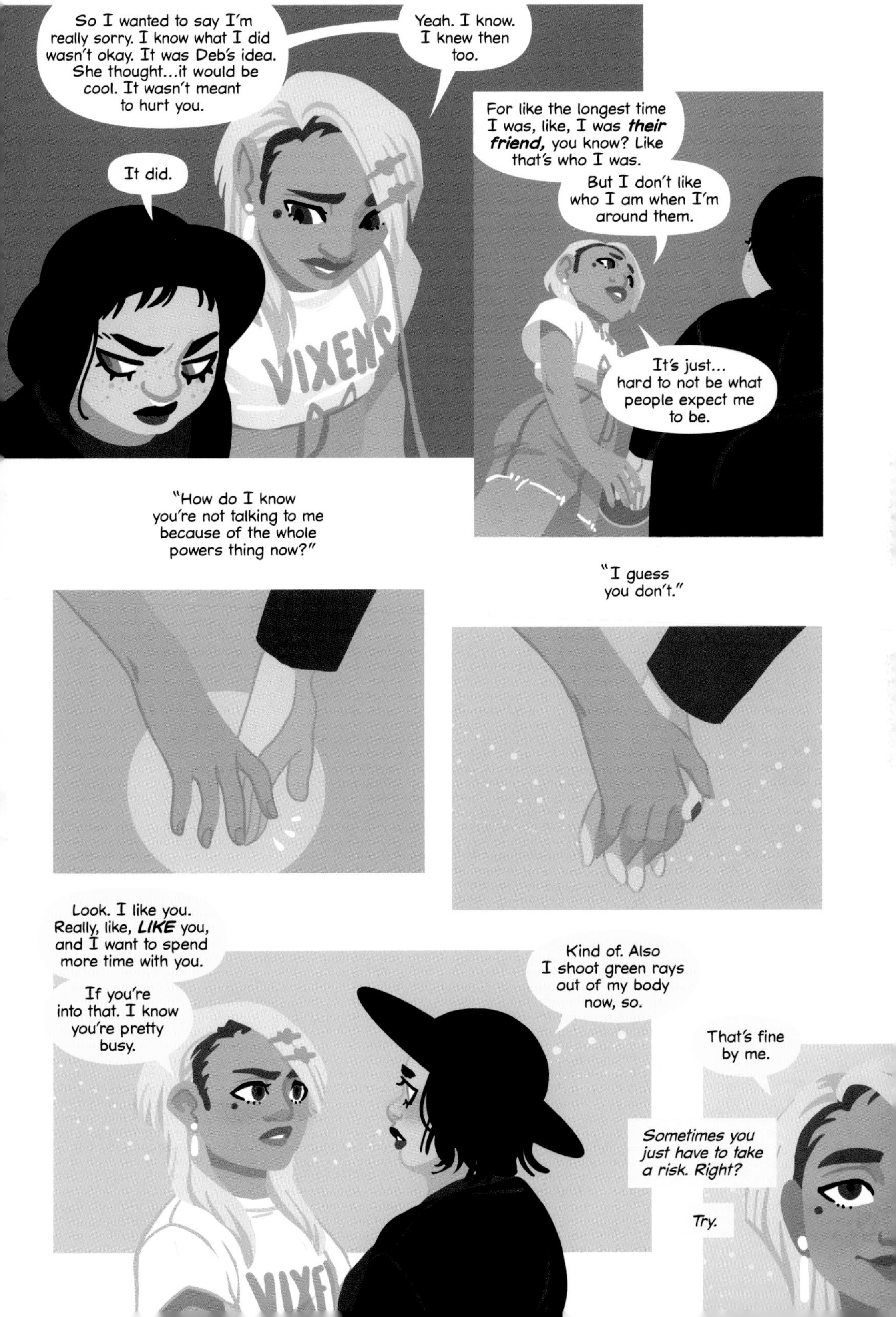
So I wanted to say I'm really sorry. I know what I did wasn't okay. It was Deb's idea. She thought...it would be cool. It wasn't meant to hurt you.
Yeah. I know. I knew then too.
It did.
VIXENS
For like the longest time I was, like, I was ***their friend,*** you know? Like that's who I was.
But I don't like who I am when I'm around them.
It's just... hard to not be what people expect me to be.
"How do I know you're not talking to me because of the whole powers thing now?"
"I guess you don't."
Look. I like you. Really, like, ***LIKE*** you, and I want to spend more time with you.
If you're into that. I know you're pretty busy.
Kind of. Also I shoot green rays out of my body now, so.
That's fine by me.
Sometimes you just have to take a risk. Right?
Try.

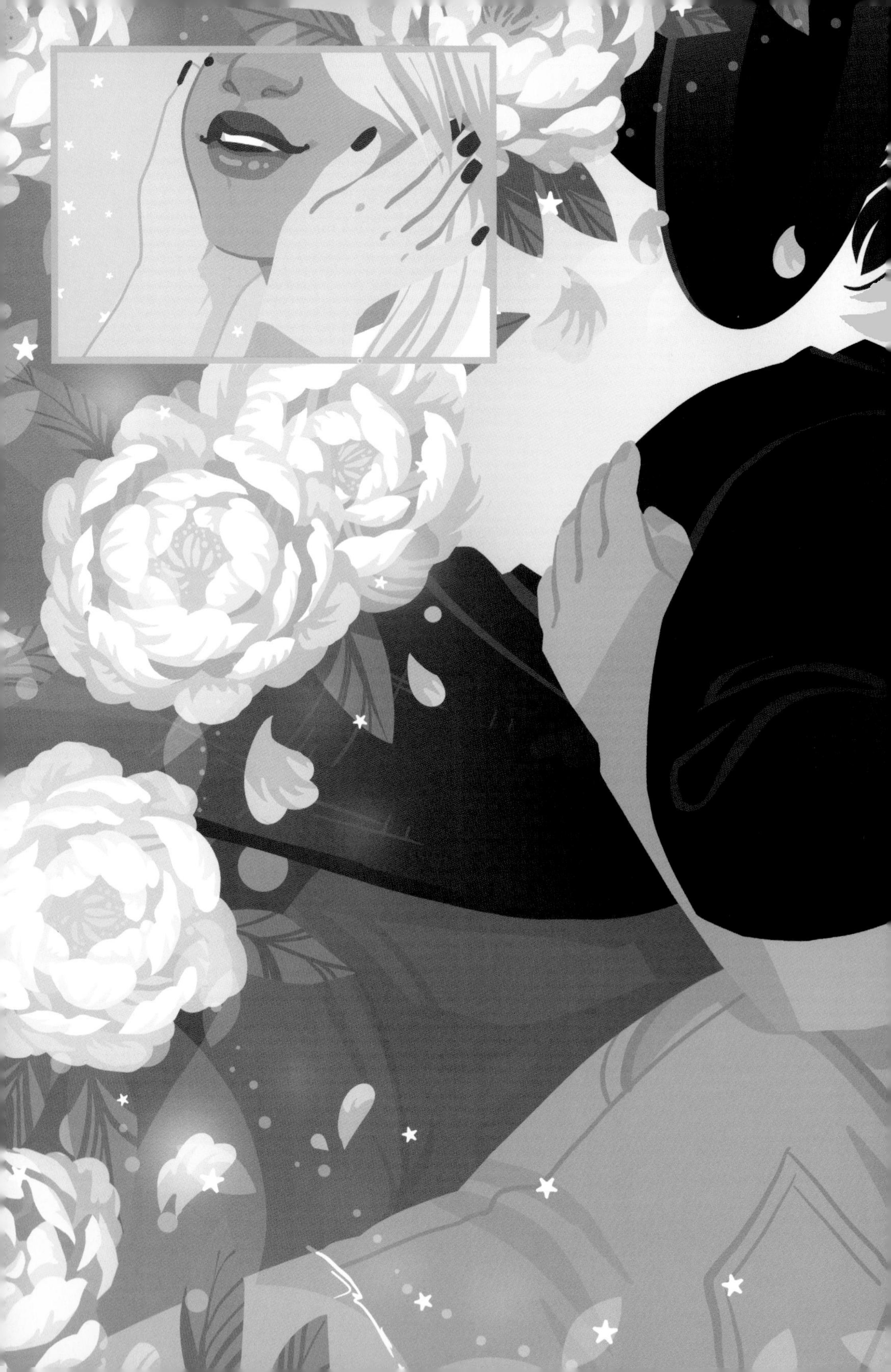

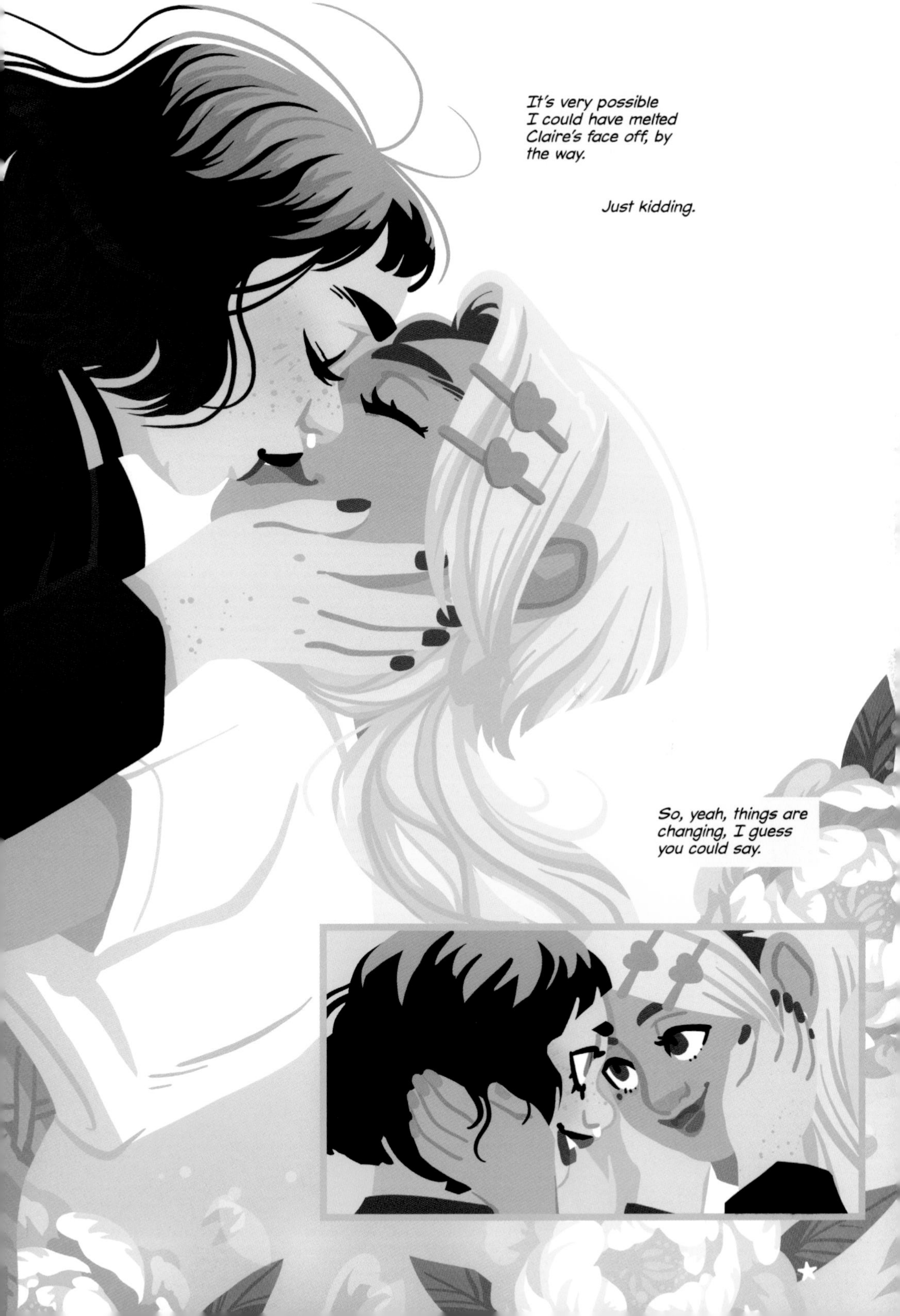
It's very possible I could have melted Claire's face off, by the way.
Just kidding.
So, yeah, things are changing, I guess you could say.

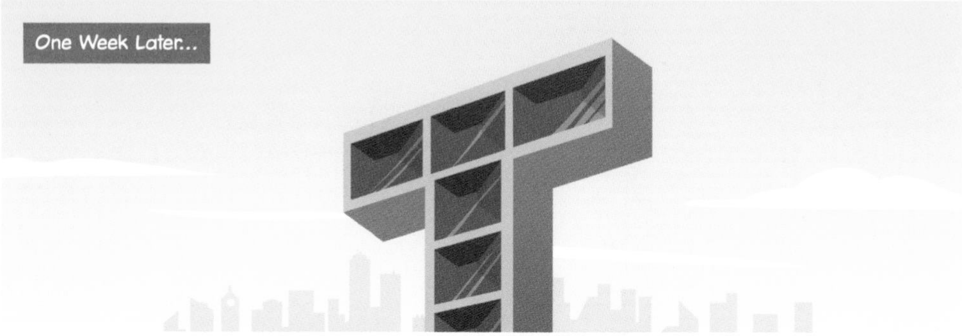
One Week Later...

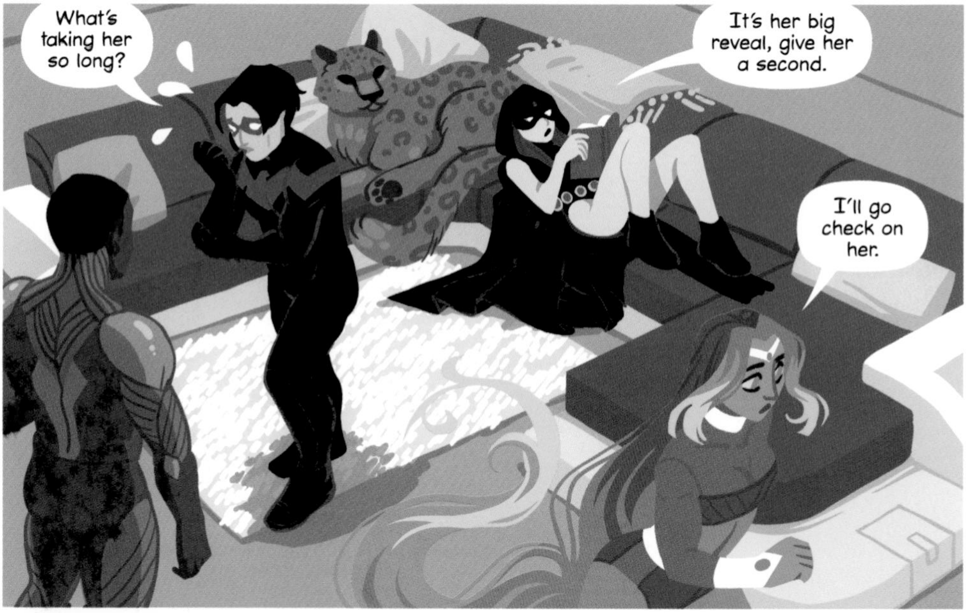
What's taking her so long?
It's her big reveal, give her a second.
I'll go check on her.

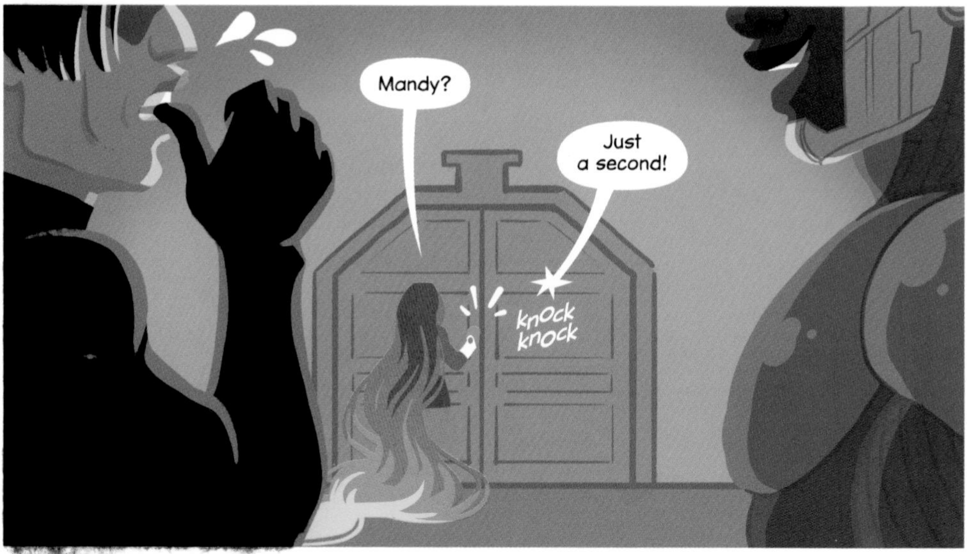
Mandy?
Just a second!
knock knock

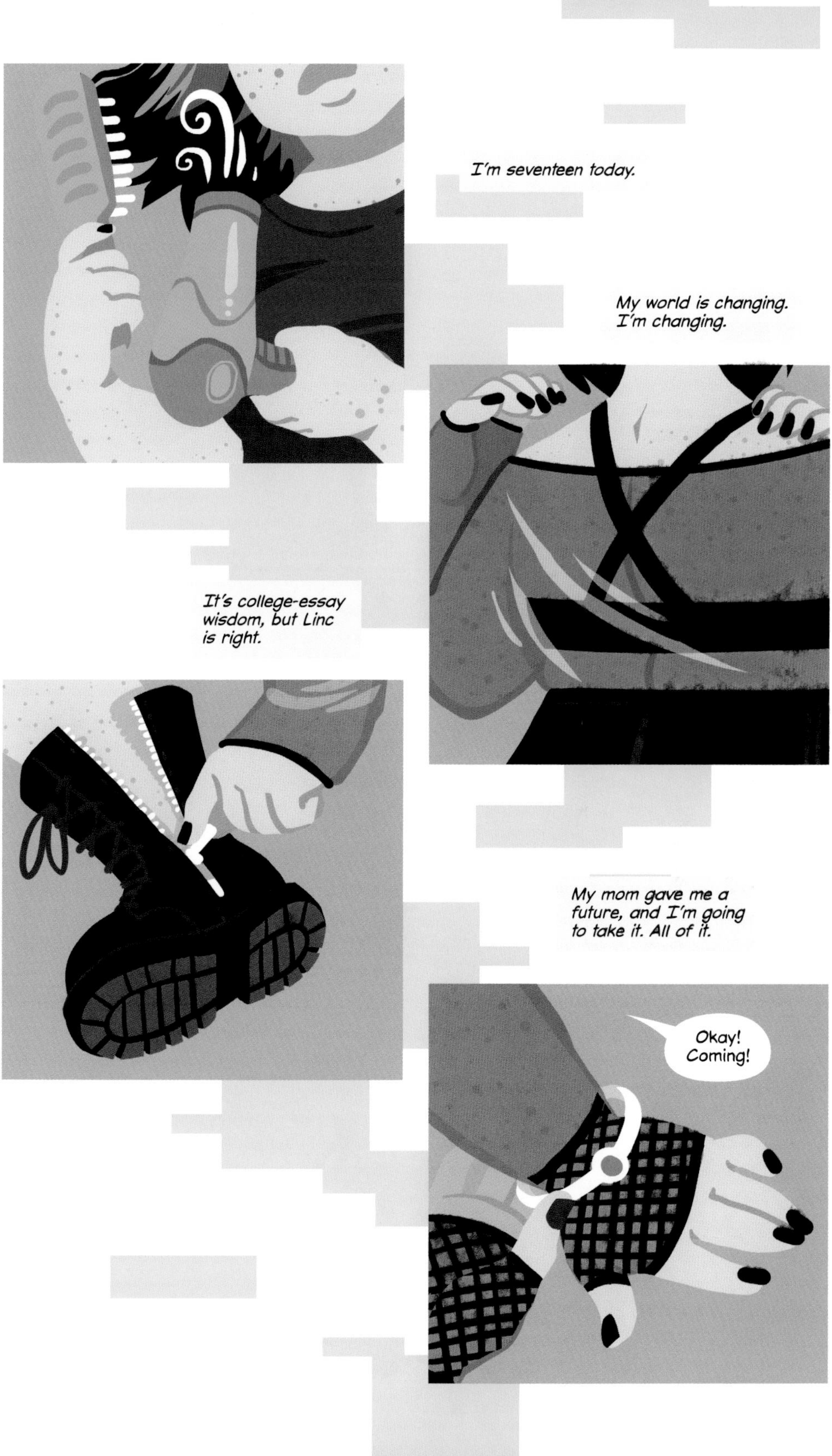
I'm seventeen today.
My world is changing. I'm changing.
It's college-essay wisdom, but Linc is right.
My mom gave me a future, and I'm going to take it. All of it.
Okay! Coming!

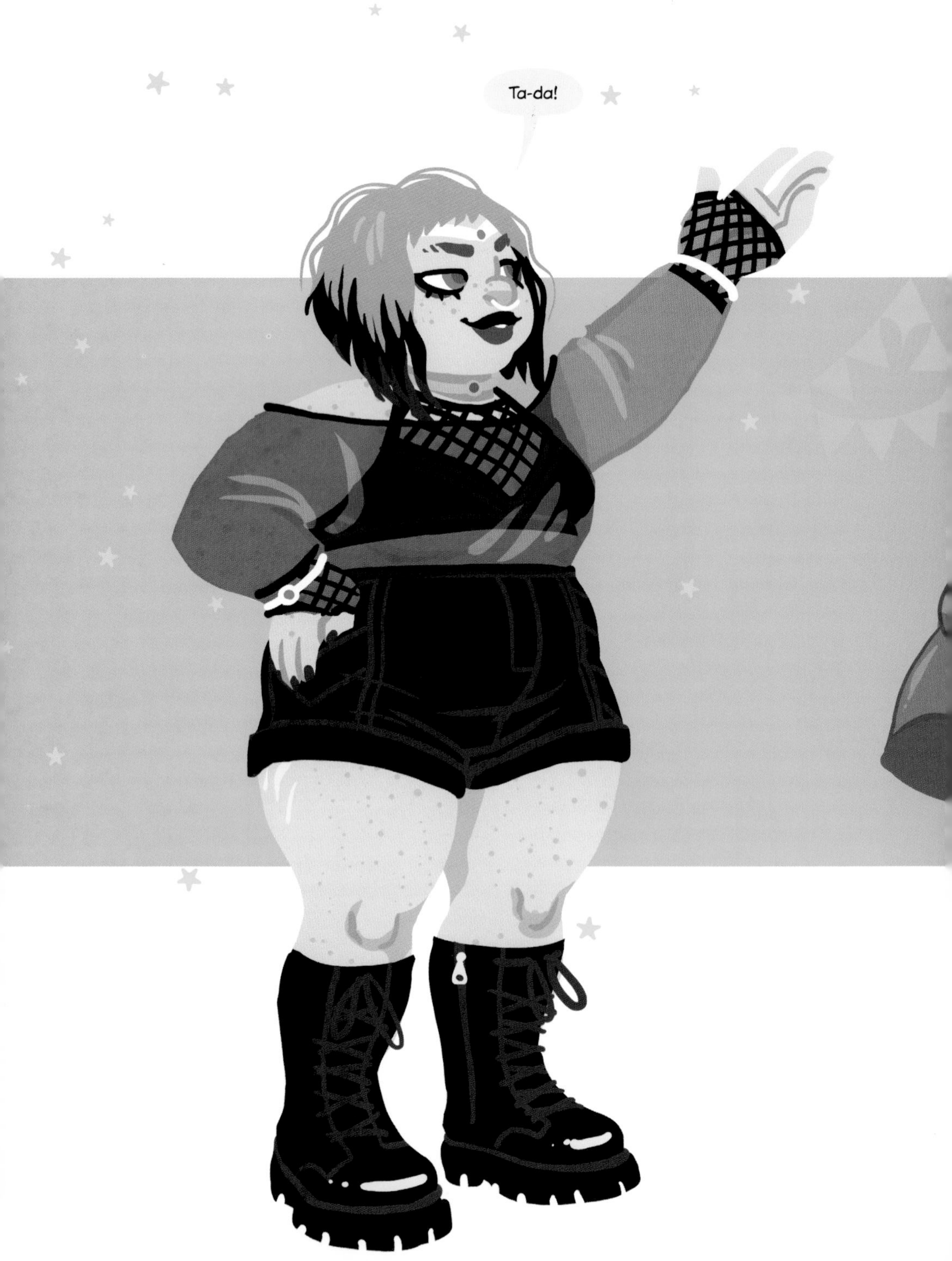
Ta-da!

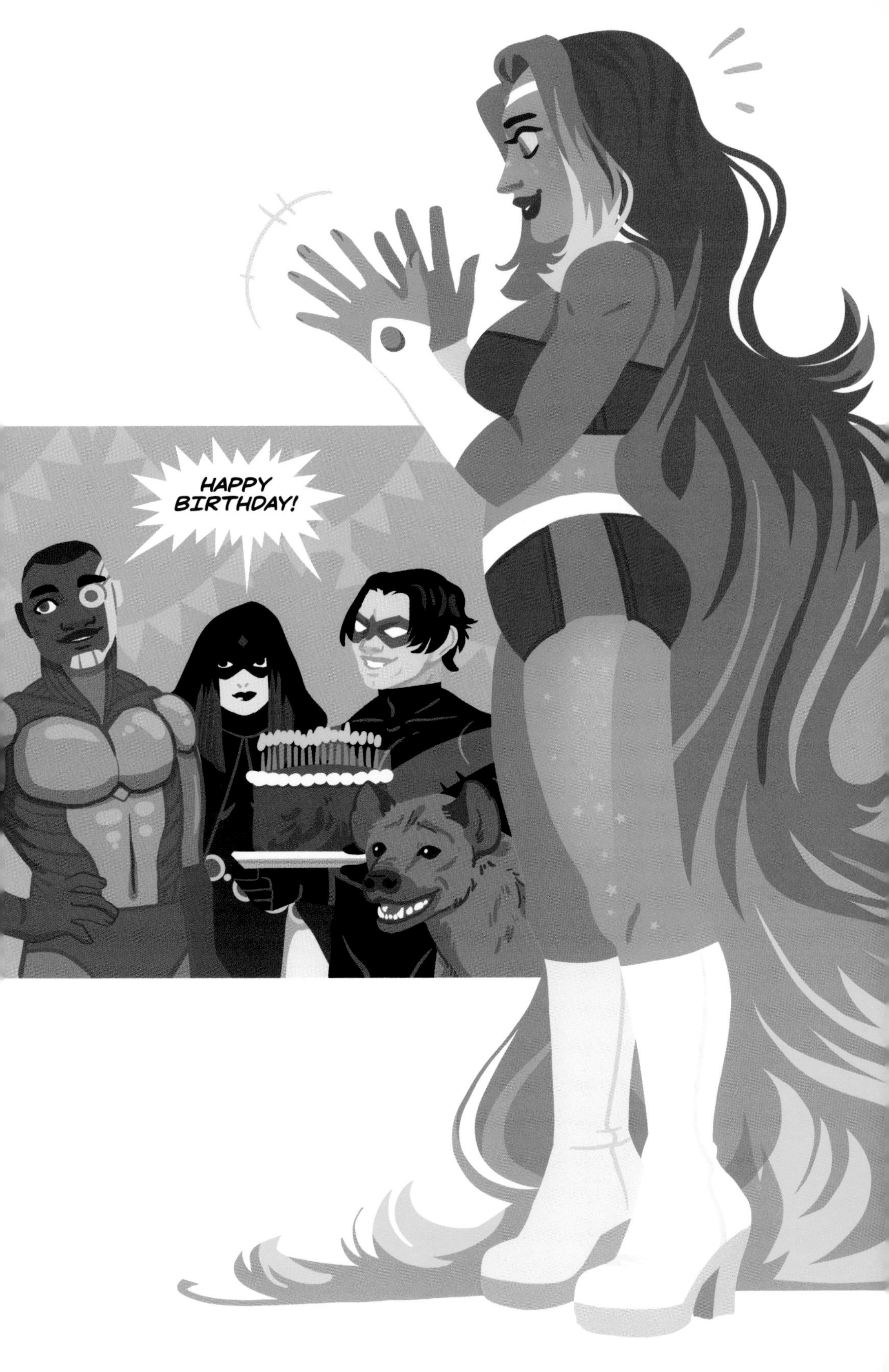
HAPPY BIRTHDAY!

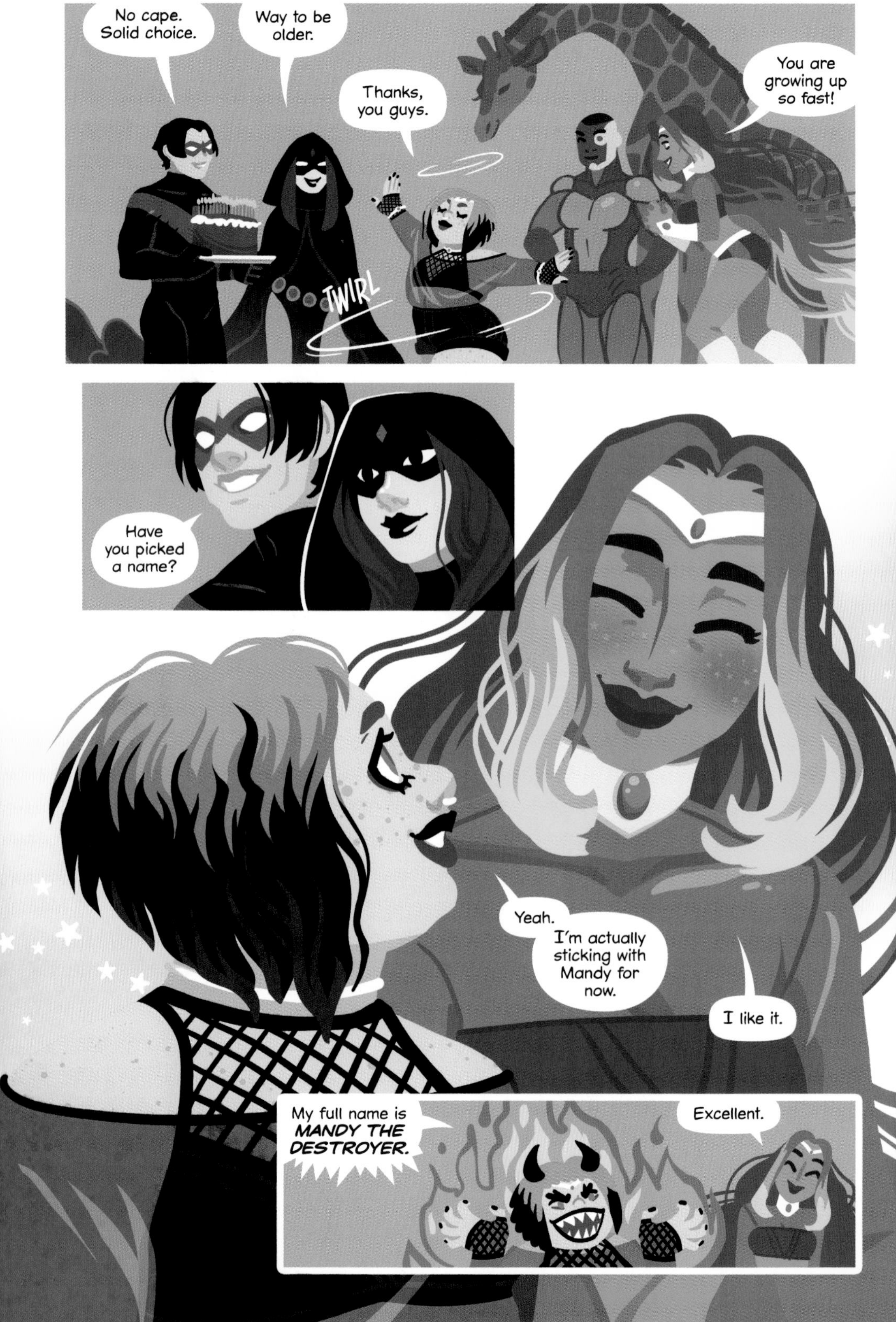
No cape.
Solid choice.
Way to be older.
Thanks, you guys.
You are growing up so fast!
TWIRL
Have you picked a name?
Yeah.
I'm actually sticking with Mandy for now.
I like it.
My full name is *MANDY THE DESTROYER.*
Excellent.

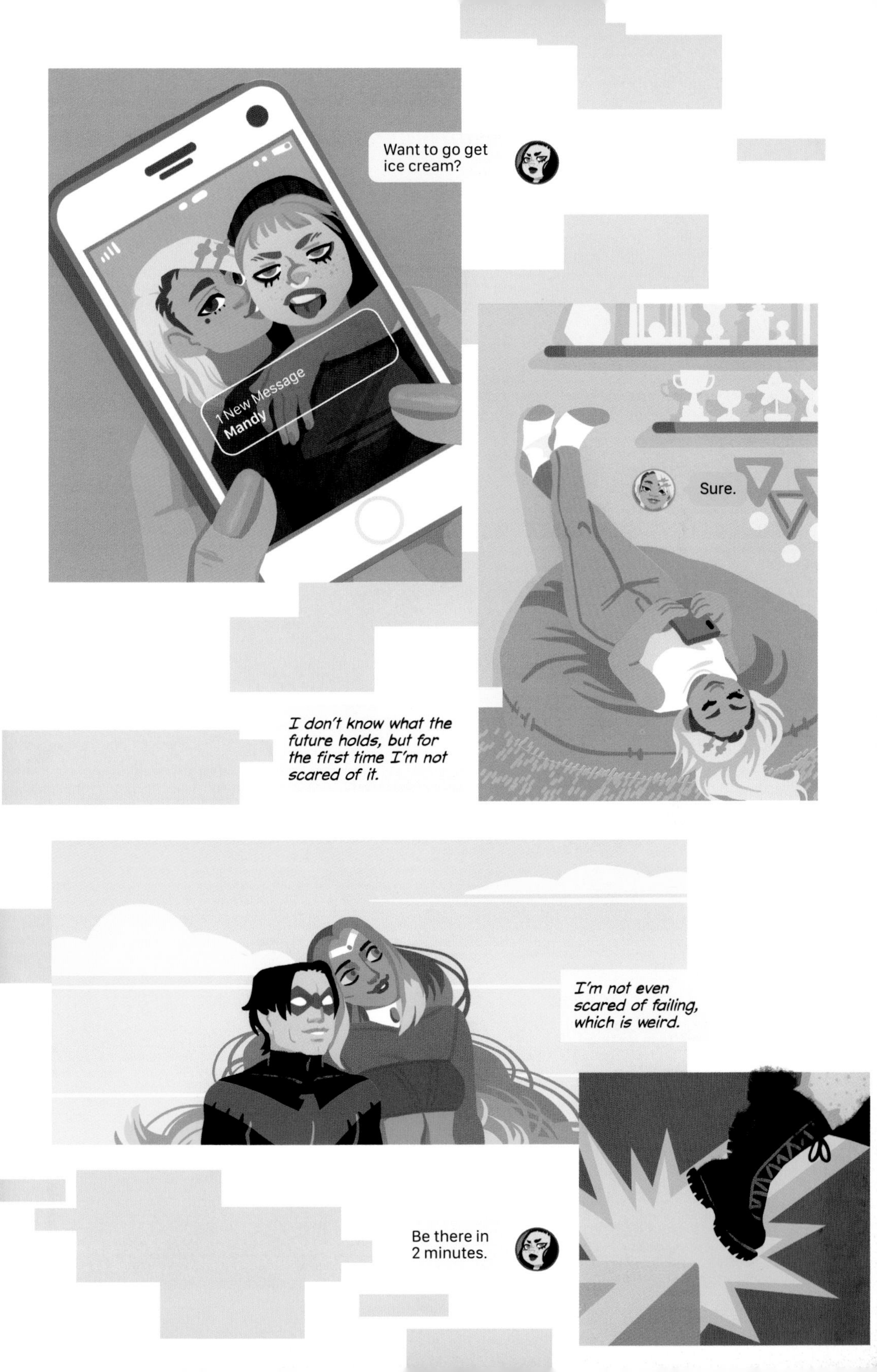
Want to go get ice cream?
1 New Message
Mandy
Sure.
I don't know what the future holds, but for the first time I'm not scared of it.
I'm not even scared of failing, which is weird.
Be there in 2 minutes.

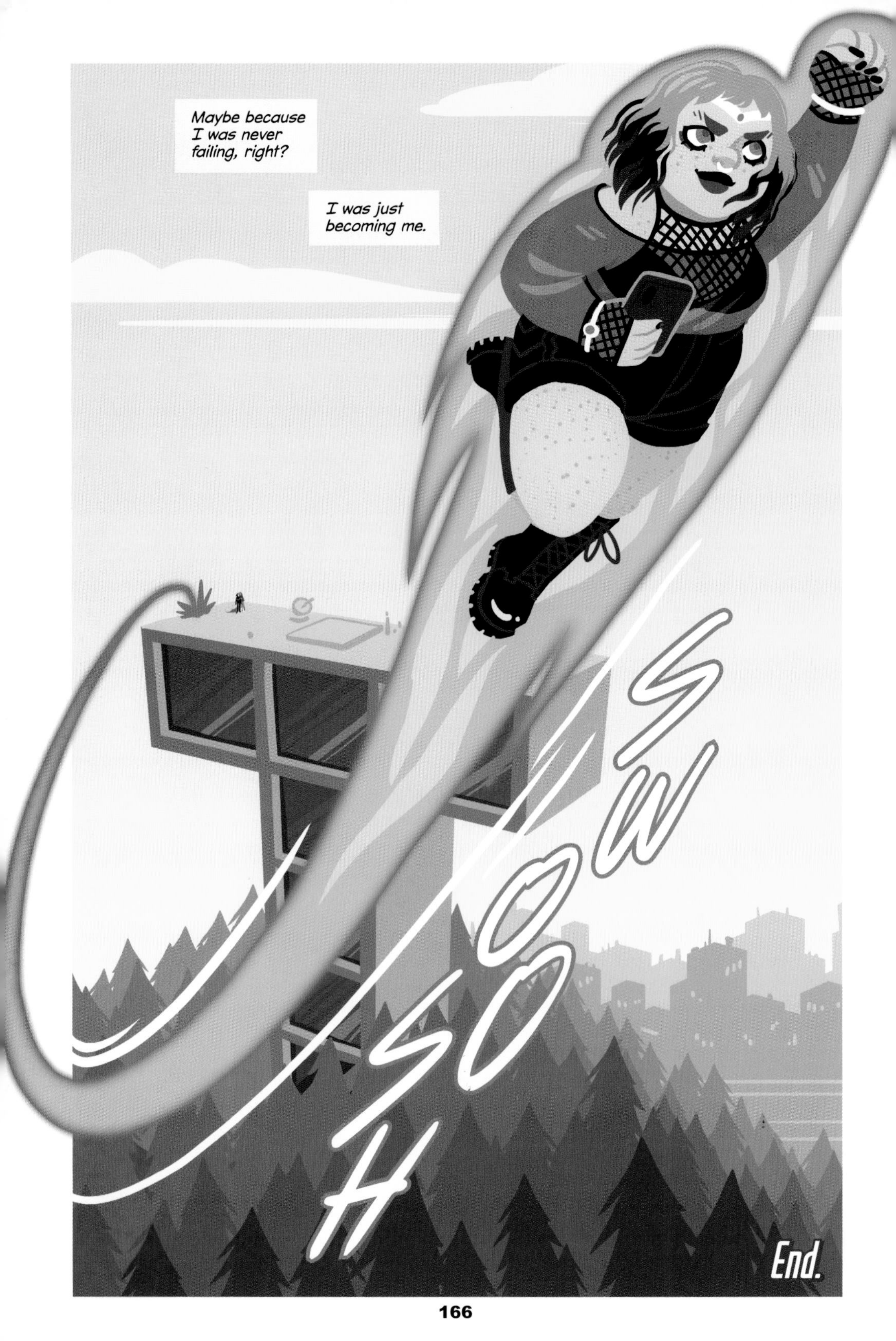
Maybe because I was never failing, right?
I was just becoming me.
SWOOSH
End.

Mariko Tamaki is an award-winning Canadian writer living in Oakland, California. The winner of the 2020 Eisner Award for Best Writer, Tamaki's graphic novels have received Ignatz, Eisner, Printz, and Caldecott honors. She is the co-creator, with Jillian Tamaki, of *This One Summer*, and of *Laura Dean Keeps Breaking Up with Me*, with Rosemary Valero-O'Connell. Her growing slate of critically acclaimed comics includes *Detective Comics*, *Adventure Time*, *She-Hulk*, *Lumberjanes*, *X-23*, *Supergirl: Being Super*, *Wonder Woman*, and *Harley Quinn: Breaking Glass* (with Steve Pugh).

Yoshi Yoshitani is a California-based artist whose vibrant illustrations draw on inspiration from across the globe, with a particular focus on multicultural identity. Past clients include Disney, DC Comics, Valiant, Image, DreamWorks, and Netflix. Yoshi spends time researching world mythologies, listening to audio-books, creating fashion inspiration boards, and attending comics conventions and art expos across the country.

Kami Garcia and **Gabriel Picolo** continue their *New York Times* bestselling Teen Titans series and give readers the romantic meet-up we have all been waiting for!

Turn the page for a preview of *Teen Titans: Beast Boy Loves Raven*!

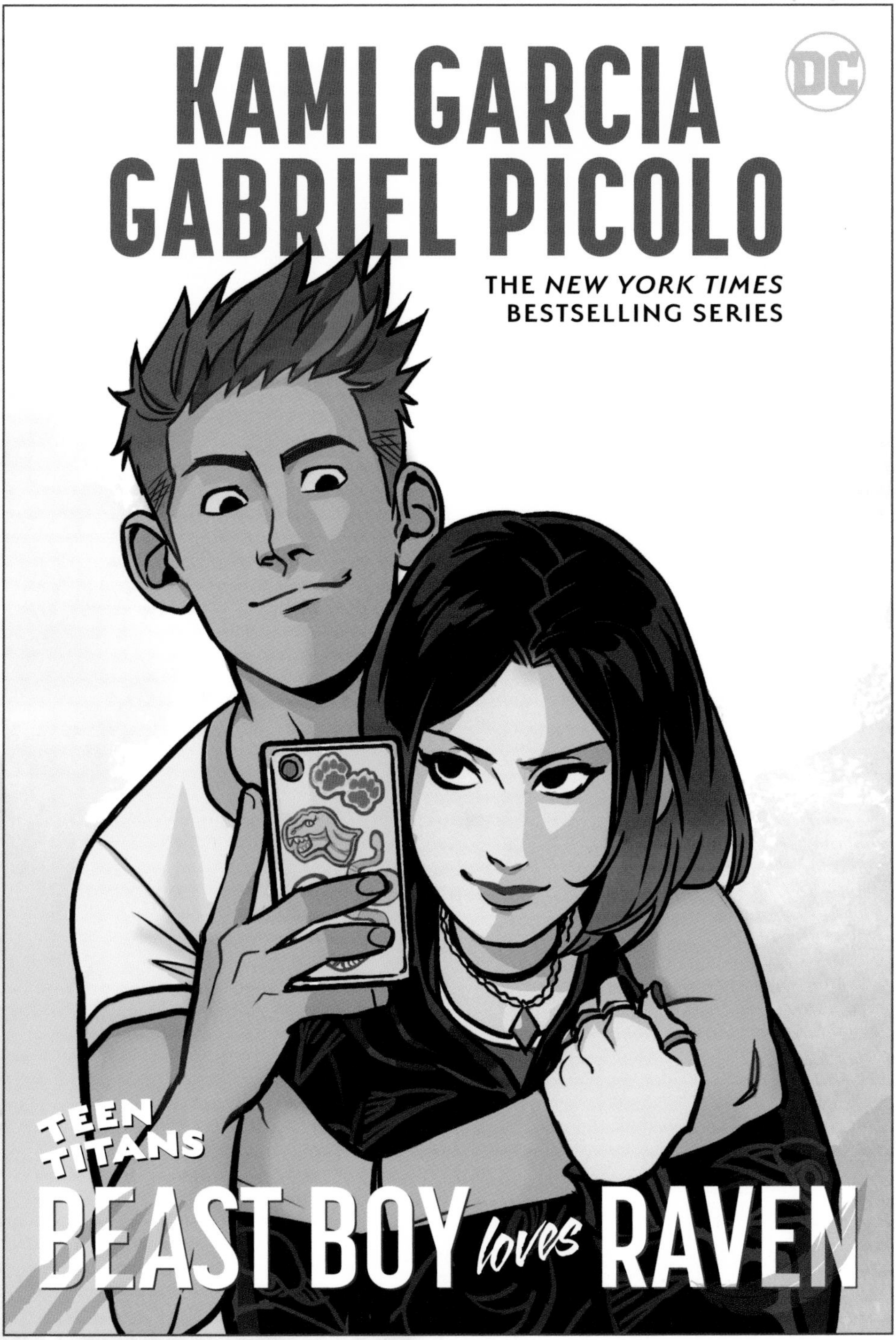
KAMI GARCIA
GABRIEL PICOLO
THE NEW YORK TIMES BESTSELLING SERIES
DC
TEEN TITANS
BEAST BOY loves RAVEN

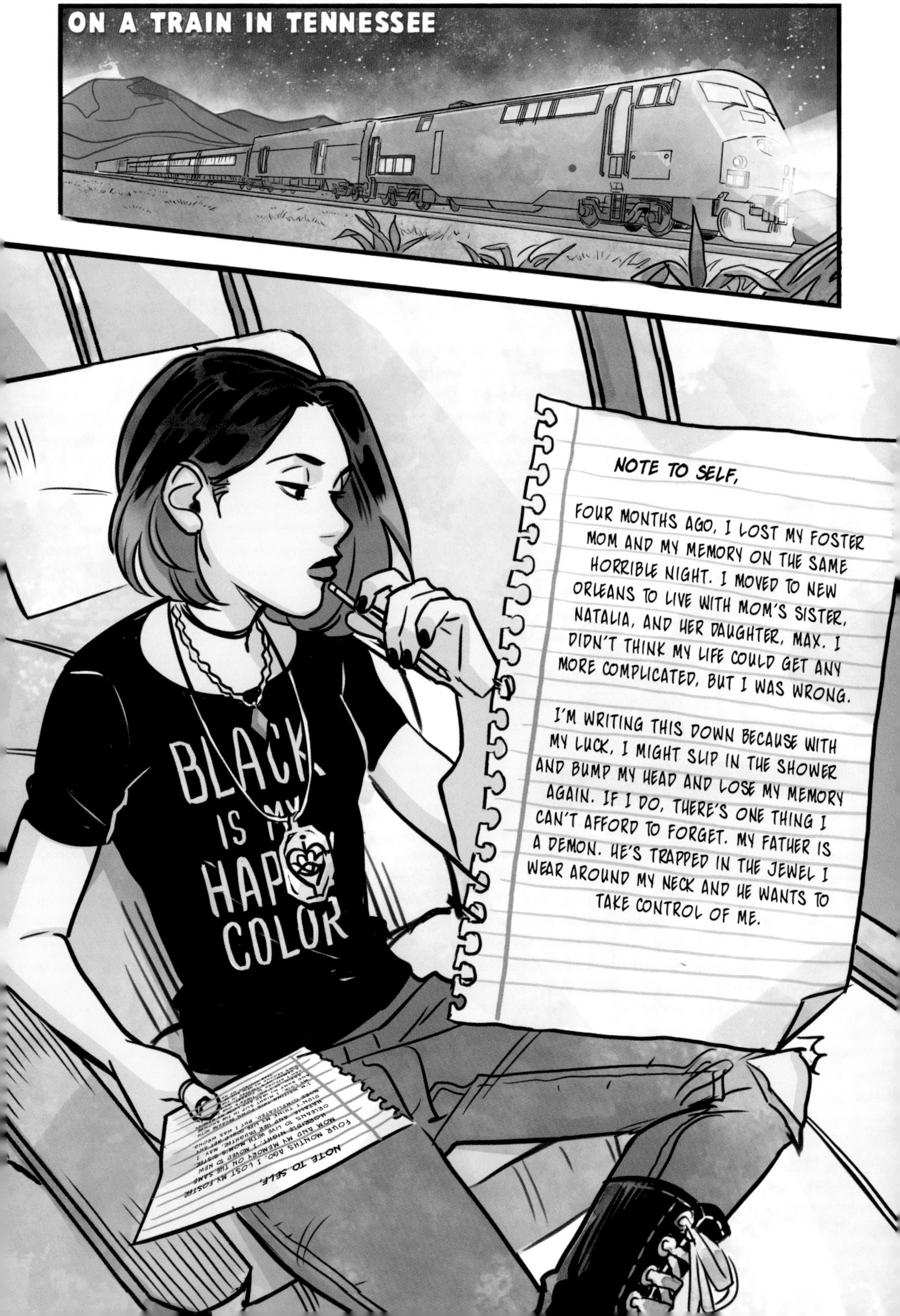
ON A TRAIN IN TENNESSEE
NOTE TO SELF,
FOUR MONTHS AGO, I LOST MY FOSTER MOM AND MY MEMORY ON THE SAME HORRIBLE NIGHT. I MOVED TO NEW ORLEANS TO LIVE WITH MOM'S SISTER, NATALIA, AND HER DAUGHTER, MAX. I DIDN'T THINK MY LIFE COULD GET ANY MORE COMPLICATED, BUT I WAS WRONG.
I'M WRITING THIS DOWN BECAUSE WITH MY LUCK, I MIGHT SLIP IN THE SHOWER AND BUMP MY HEAD AND LOSE MY MEMORY AGAIN. IF I DO, THERE'S ONE THING I CAN'T AFFORD TO FORGET. MY FATHER IS A DEMON. HE'S TRAPPED IN THE JEWEL I WEAR AROUND MY NECK AND HE WANTS TO TAKE CONTROL OF ME.

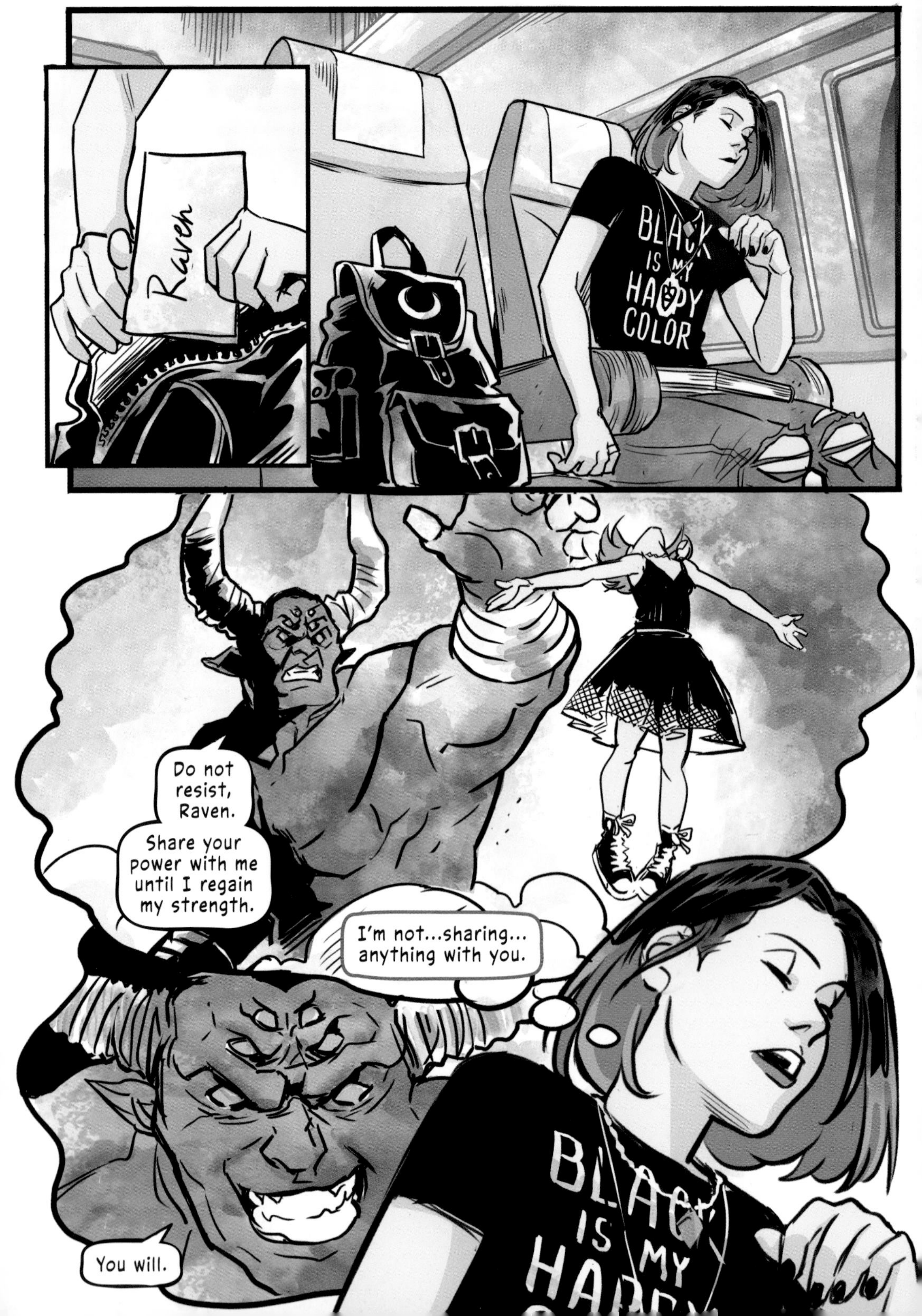
Raven
BLACK IS MY HAPPY COLOR
Do not resist, Raven.
Share your power with me until I regain my strength.
I'm not...sharing... anything with you.
You will.

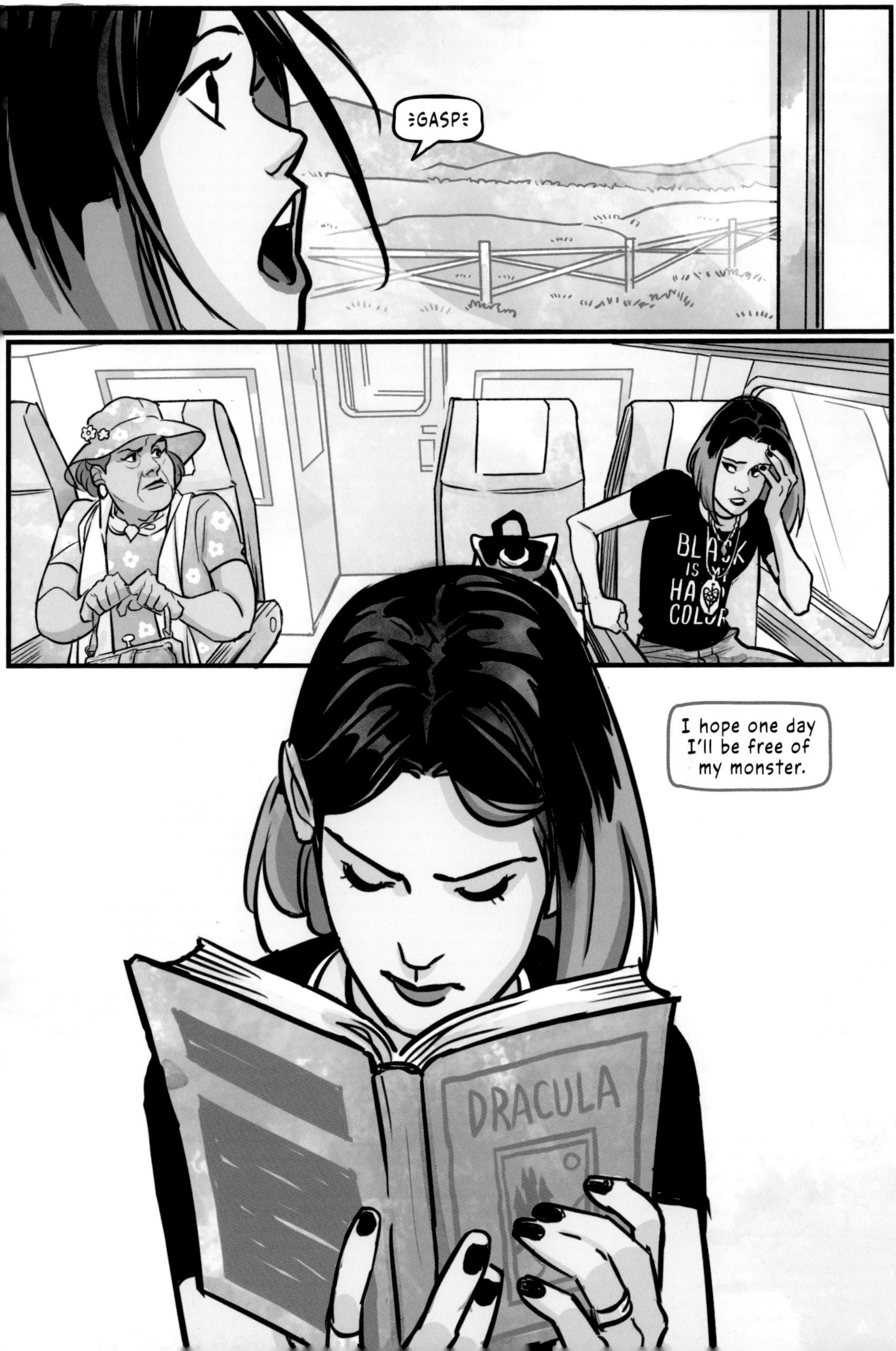
GASP
BLACK IS MY HAPPY COLOR
I hope one day I'll be free of my monster.
DRACULA

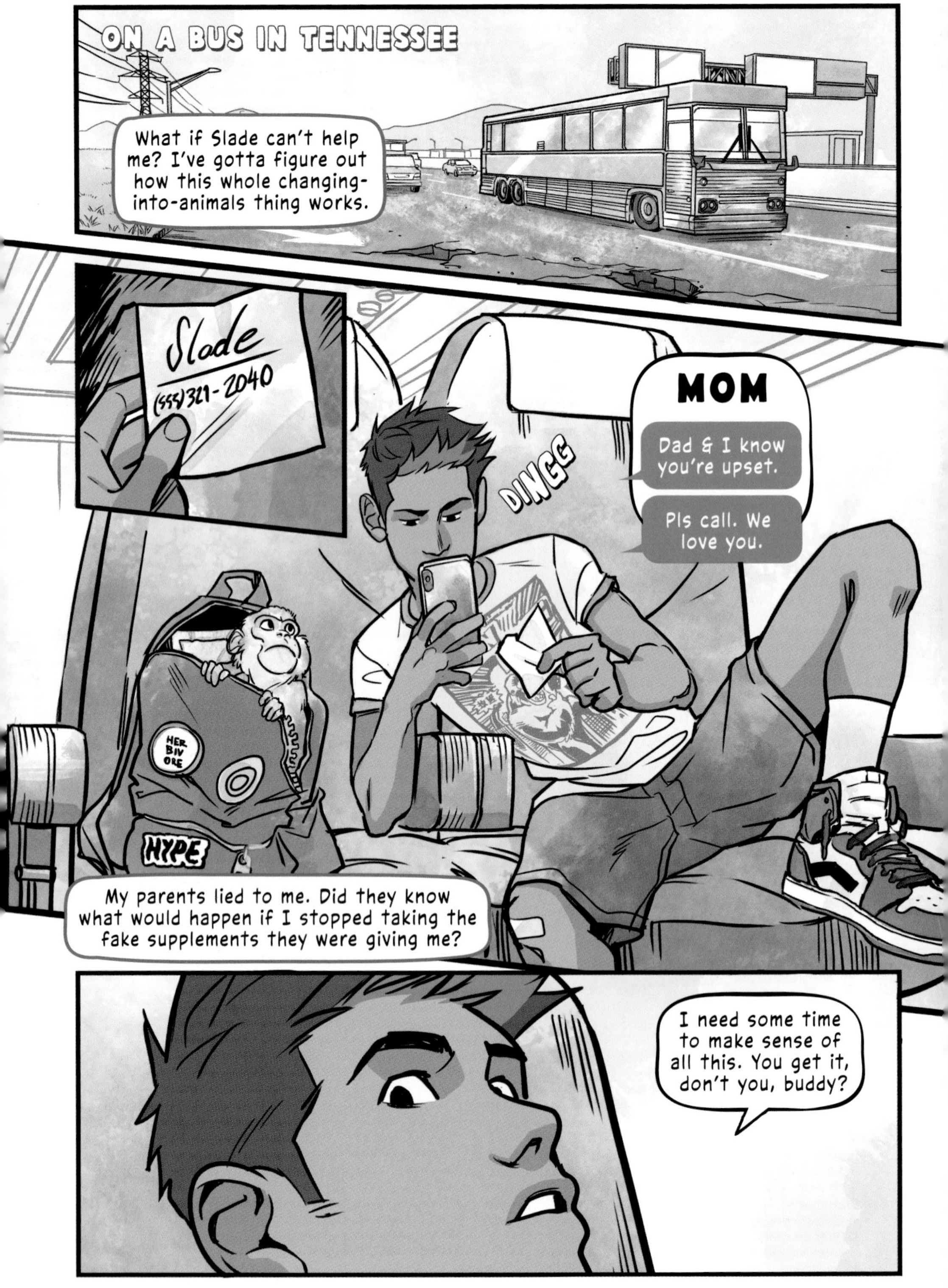
ON A BUS IN TENNESSEE
What if Slade can't help me? I've gotta figure out how this whole changing-into-animals thing works.
Slade
(555)321-2040
MOM
Dad & I know you're upset.
Pls call. We love you.
DINGG
HER BIV ORE
HYPE
My parents lied to me. Did they know what would happen if I stopped taking the fake supplements they were giving me?
I need some time to make sense of all this. You get it, don't you, buddy?

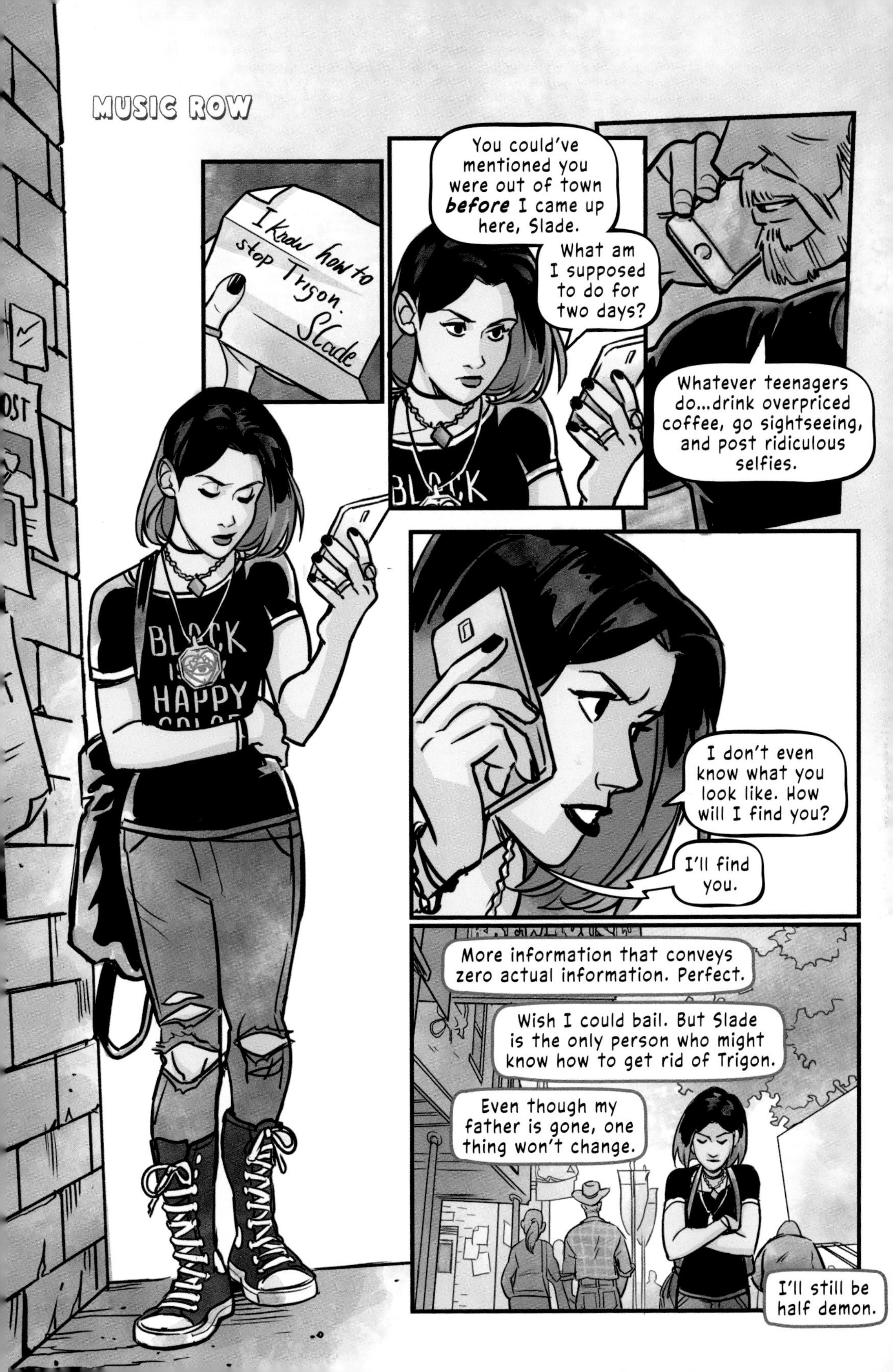
MUSIC ROW
I know how to stop Trigon. Slade
You could've mentioned you were out of town *before* I came up here, Slade.
What am I supposed to do for two days?
Whatever teenagers do...drink overpriced coffee, go sightseeing, and post ridiculous selfies.
I don't even know what you look like. How will I find you?
I'll find you.
More information that conveys zero actual information. Perfect.
Wish I could bail. But Slade is the only person who might know how to get rid of Trigon.
Even though my father is gone, one thing won't change.
I'll still be half demon.

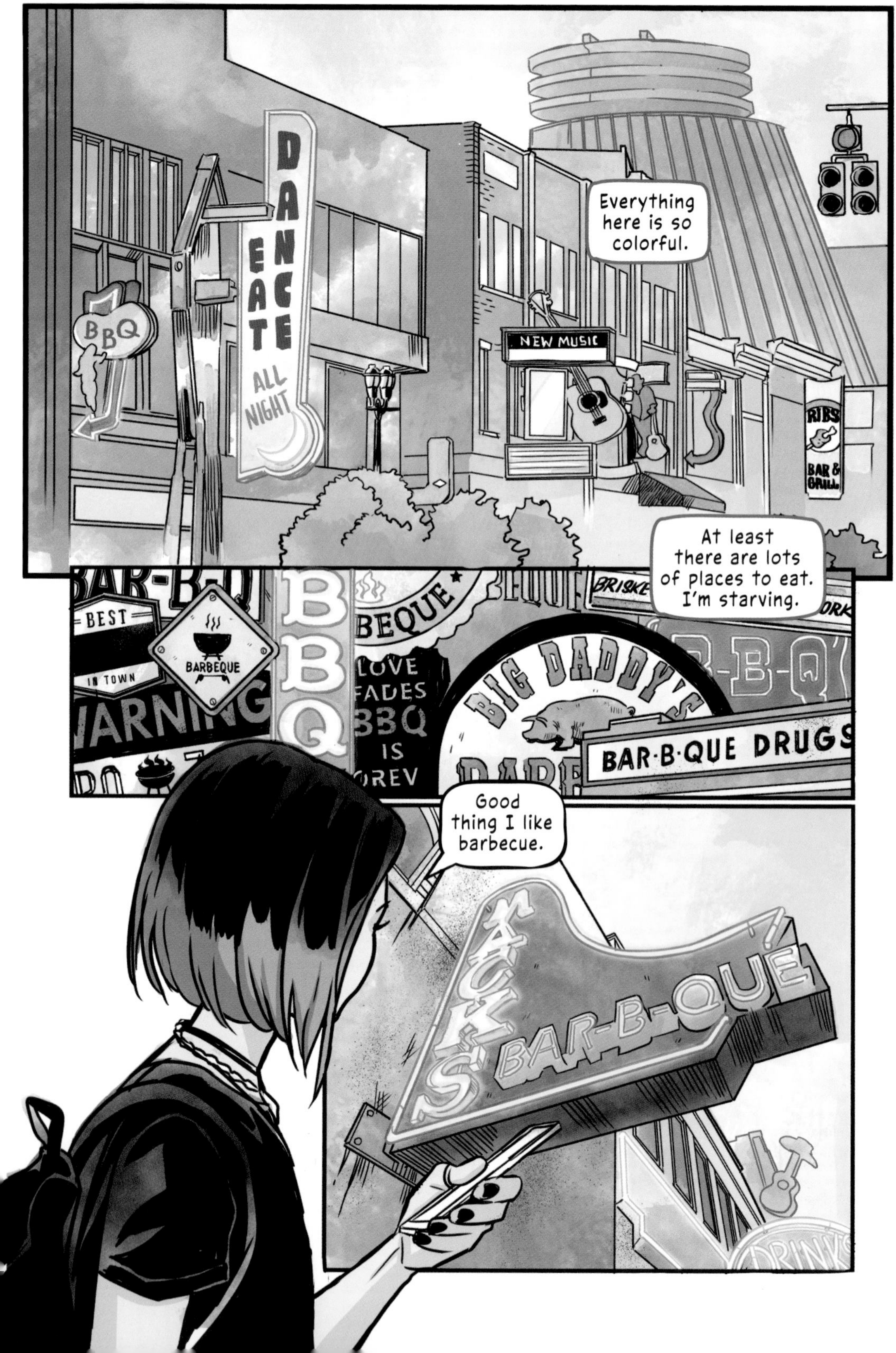
BBQ
DANCE
EAT
ALL NIGHT
NEW MUSIC
RIBS
BAR & GRILL
Everything here is so colorful.
At least there are lots of places to eat. I'm starving.
BAR-B-Q
BEST
IN TOWN
WARNING
BARBEQUE
BBQ
BEQUE
LOVE FADES
IS
BIG DADDY'S
BAR·B·QUE DRUGS
Good thing I like barbecue.
JACK'S
BAR-B-QUE

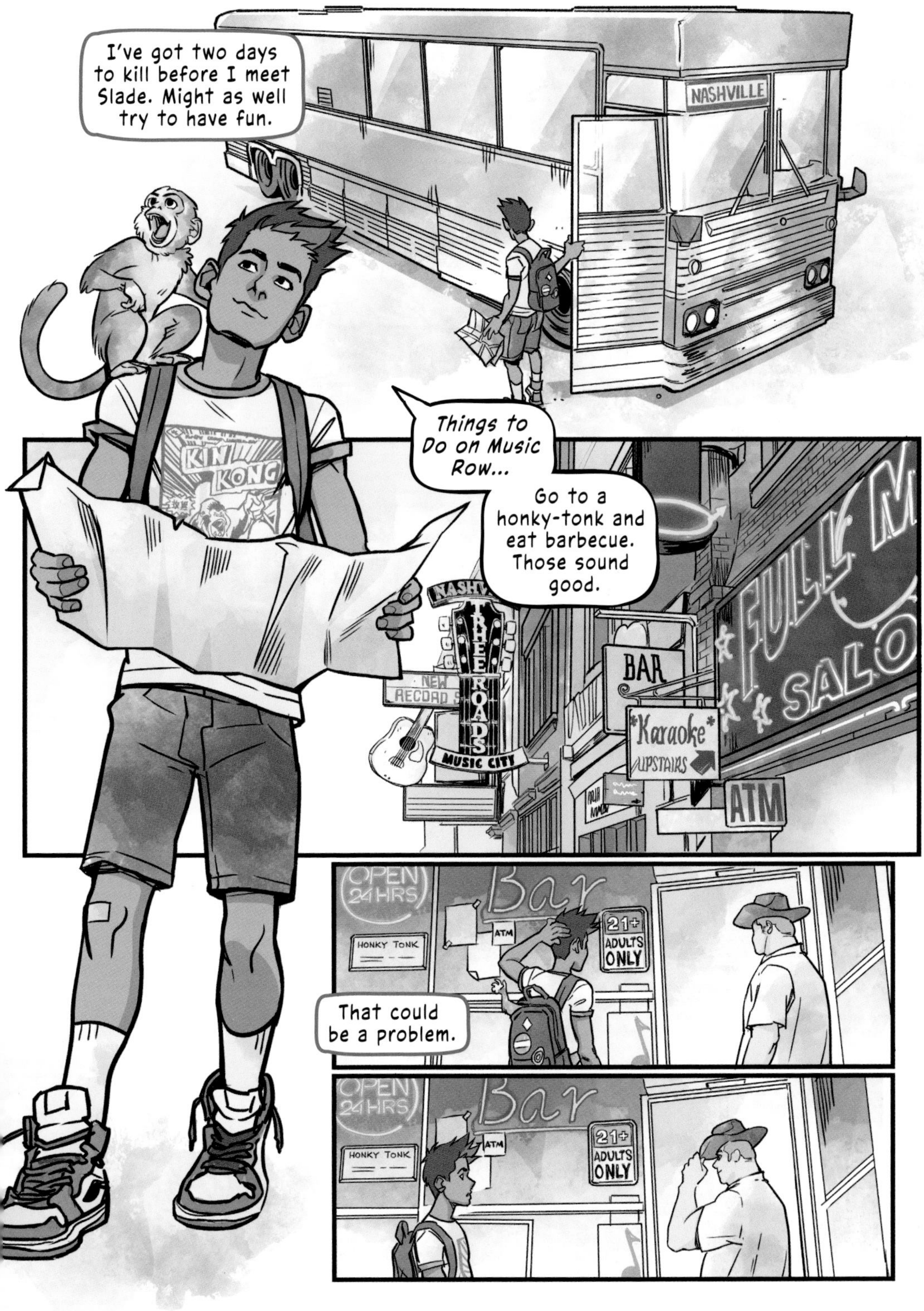
I've got two days to kill before I meet Slade. Might as well try to have fun.
NASHVILLE
KING KONG
Things to Do on Music Row...
Go to a honky-tonk and eat barbecue. Those sound good.
THREE ROADS
MUSIC CITY
NEW RECORD S
BAR
Karaoke UPSTAIRS
ATM
SALO
OPEN 24 HRS
Bar
HONKY TONK
ATM
21+ ADULTS ONLY
That could be a problem.
OPEN 24 HRS
Bar
HONKY TONK
ATM
21+ ADULTS ONLY

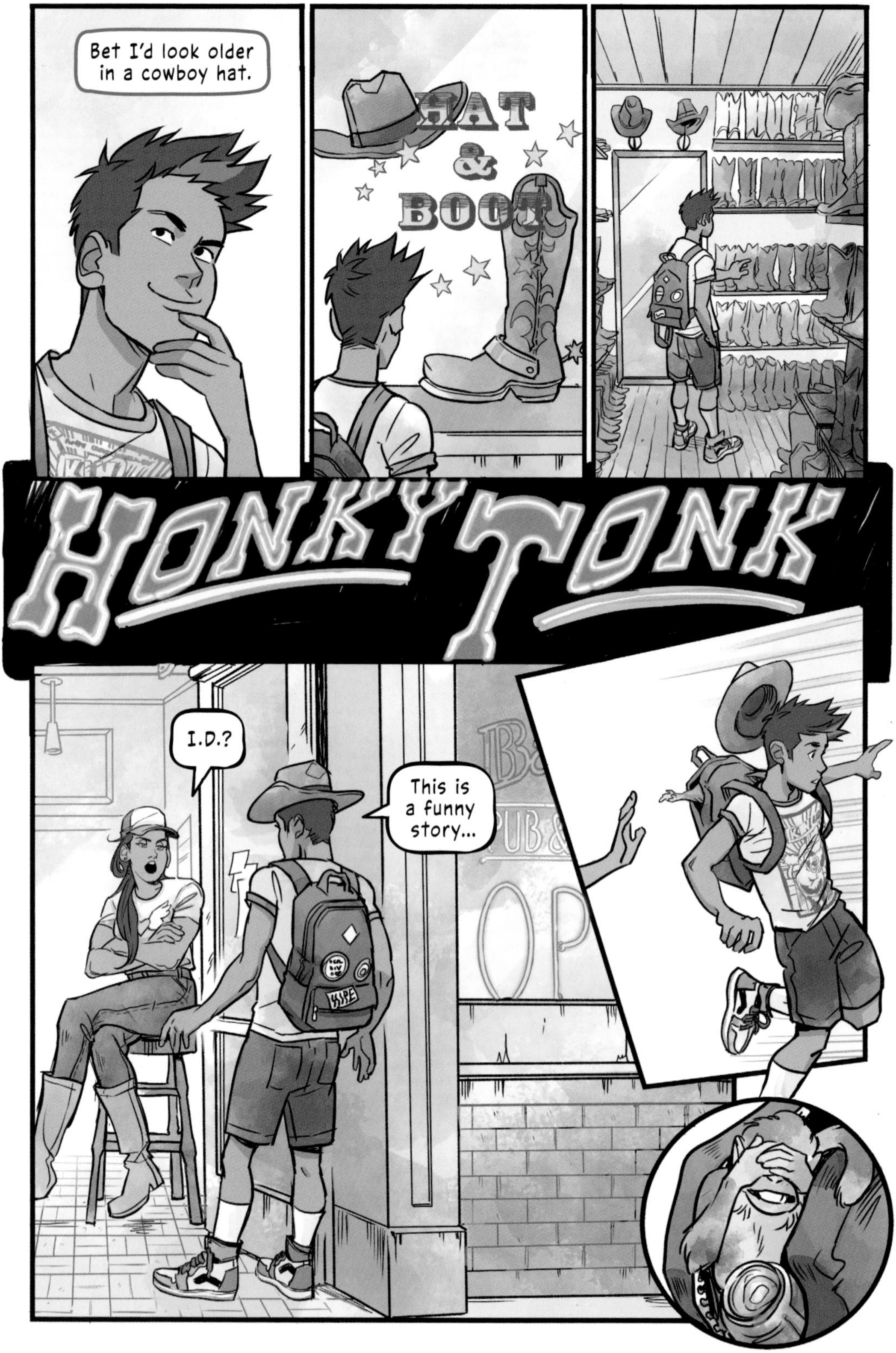

Bet I'd look older in a cowboy hat.
HAT & BOOT
HONKY TONK
I.D.?
This is a funny story...

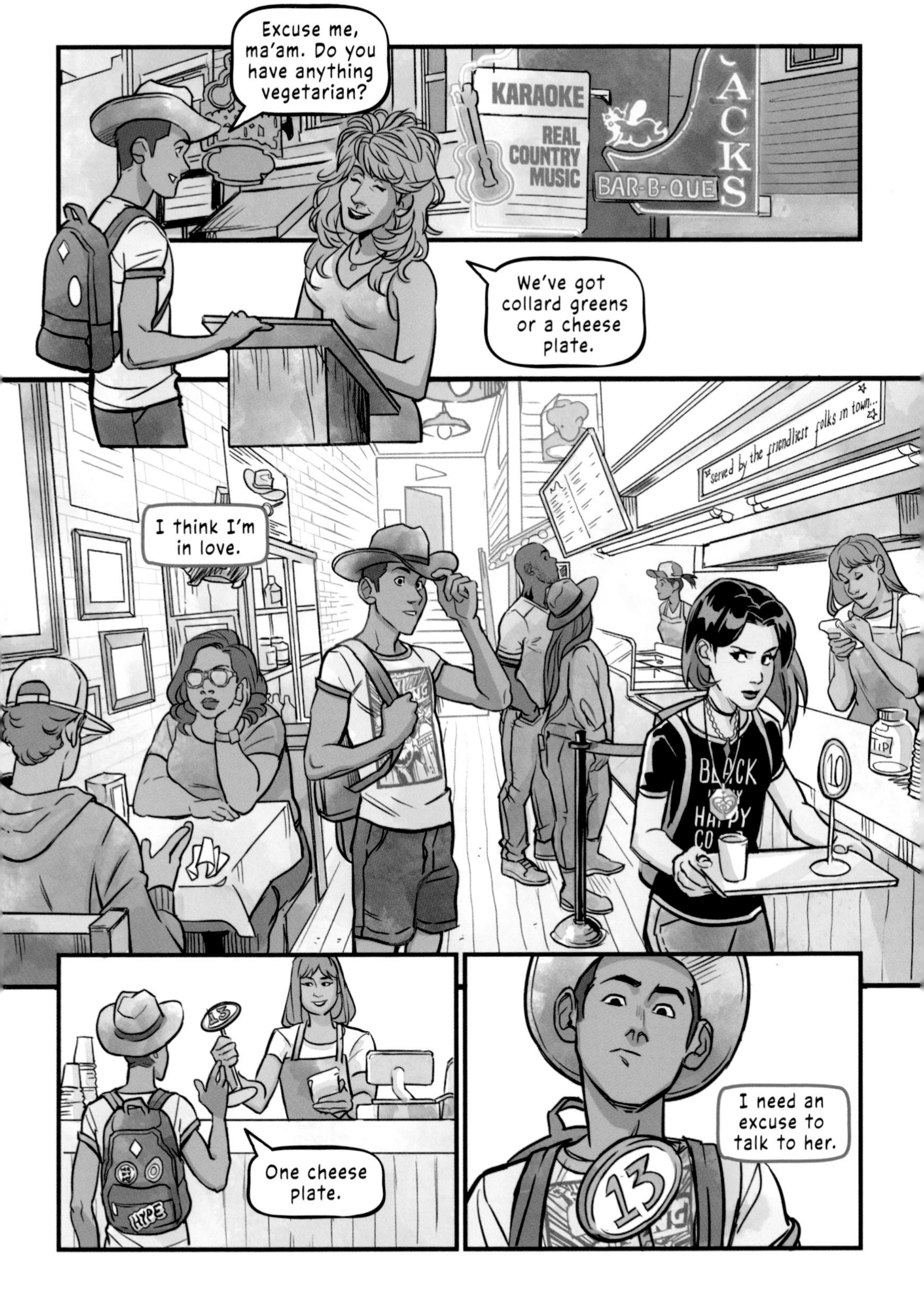
Excuse me, ma'am. Do you have anything vegetarian?
KARAOKE
REAL COUNTRY MUSIC
BAR-B-QUE
We've got collard greens or a cheese plate.
served by the friendliest folks in town...
I think I'm in love.
TIP
10
13
HYPE
One cheese plate.
I need an excuse to talk to her.
13

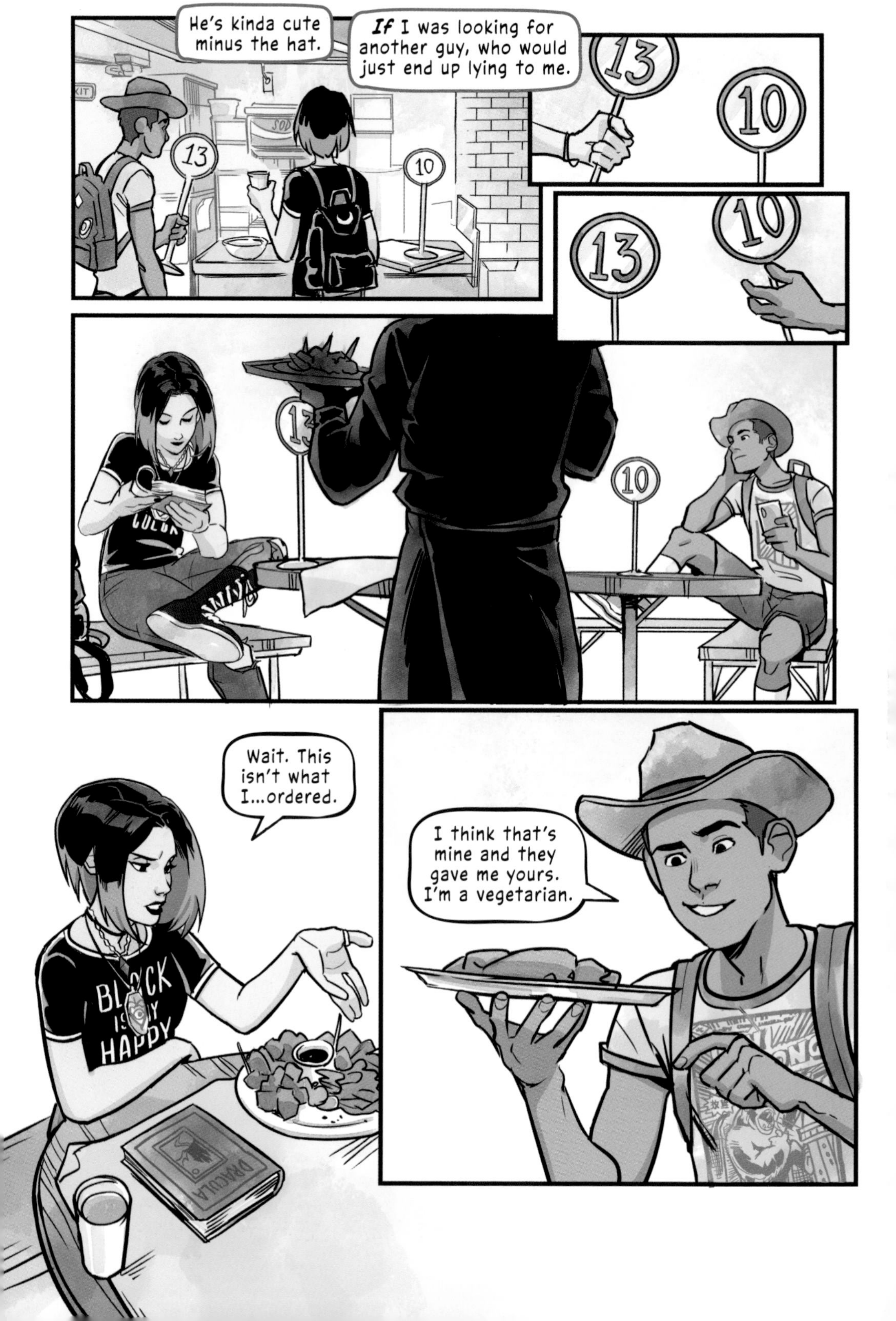
He's kinda cute minus the hat.
If I was looking for another guy, who would just end up lying to me.
13
10
13
10
13
10
Wait. This isn't what I...ordered.
I think that's mine and they gave me yours. I'm a vegetarian.

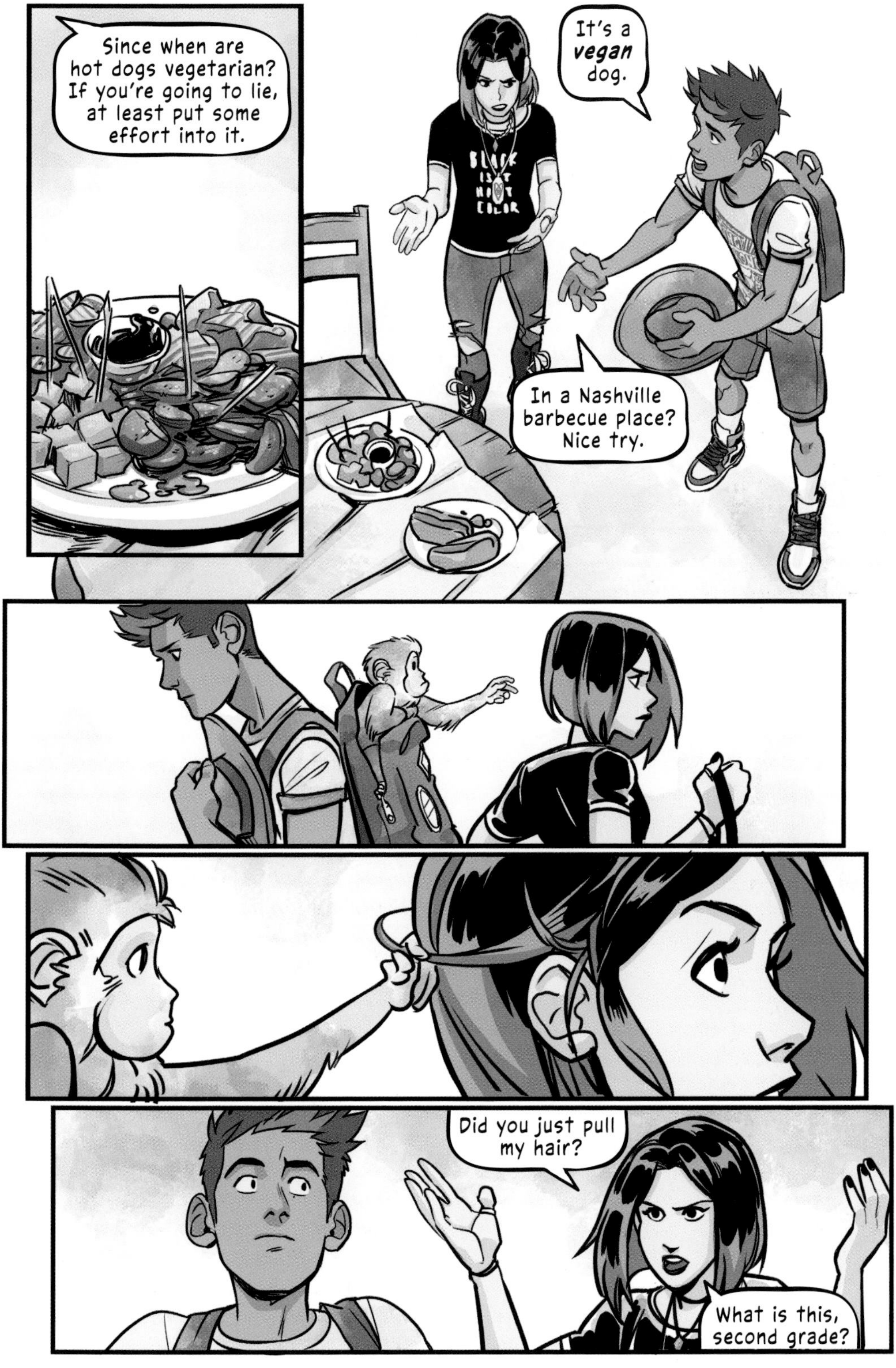
Since when are hot dogs vegetarian? If you're going to lie, at least put some effort into it.
It's a *vegan* dog.
In a Nashville barbecue place? Nice try.
Did you just pull my hair?
What is this, second grade?

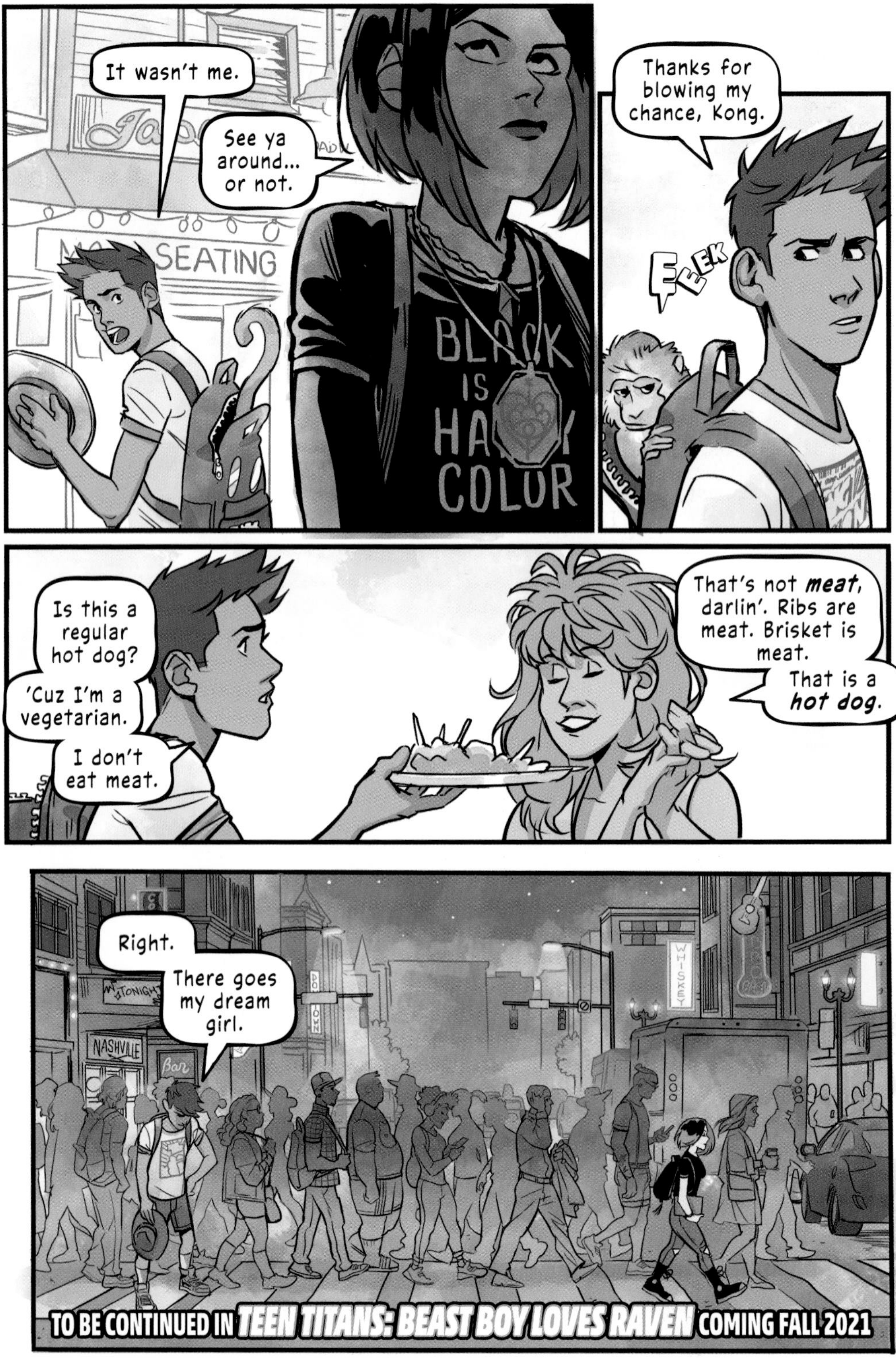

It wasn't me.
See ya around... or not.
SEATING
BLACK IS HA COLOR
Thanks for blowing my chance, Kong.
EEEK
Is this a regular hot dog?
'Cuz I'm a vegetarian.
I don't eat meat.
That's not *meat*, darlin'. Ribs are meat. Brisket is meat.
That is a *hot dog*.
Right.
There goes my dream girl.
TONIGHT
NASHVILLE
Bar
WHISKEY
TO BE CONTINUED IN TEEN TITANS: BEAST BOY LOVES RAVEN COMING FALL 2021